Oracle of Empires: The Seer's Rebirth

J. C. Leppard

Published by Magic Sphere Books
Website: jcleppard.com
ISBN: 978-1-7636321-1-0 - paperback
ISBN: 978-1-7636321-5-8 - ebook
Cover art by Peter Crocker
Typesetting by Rack and Rune Publishing
rackandrune.com

Oracle of Empires:
The Seer's Rebirth

Book II

J. C. Leppard

Also by J. C. Leppard

Perion: The Seer's Rebirth
Book I

PART I

Prologue

A sprightly fire fought against its confinement within the fireplace of an old stone cottage, casting its ragged glow upon an otherwise darkened room. It lit up the faces of two slaves huddled together in a corner and the bloody corpse of the reader of signs splayed upon the carpet. He stared at the ceiling as though frightened to death rather than killed by blows to his head. The murder weapon, his own crystal ball, lay inert at his side, covered in his blood and hair. Soiled clothing littered the floor and a pool of blood sank slowly into the floorboards near a stool where the mage's wounds had bled out before the healer had managed to stitch and bind them.

The shouting and violence had abated, the silence now pierced only by the fire that spat and raged, and the rhythmic crunch and creak of the rocking chair on which Mage Armin sought to ease his agitation. The healer watched, hidden within the shadow of a cupboard away from the accusing glare of firelight, waiting for a safe and appropriate time to offer a sleeping draught.

But the internal storm that had fuelled the mage's escape from Jasperen Palace and Aronaye's Almonos Guards, and the subsequent devastation of his cottage, still raged within him, as evidenced by the hand that gripped the arm of his chair and his eyes that moved back and forth. All those years of planning, all those years of waiting for his puppet prince to be in place and for the right moment to take what was his, ruined by the boy's father – the father from his previous life, of all people. His pathetic reader of the signs had not warned him of this possibility and left his move vulnerable.

Admittedly, Perian had been feistier than he had expected, but it did make his possession of the prince a little more interesting. Unfortunately, this meant that he'd have to keep Perian's idiot brother, Elian, to encourage good behaviour and obedience should Perian become too difficult.

But he had at least managed to frighten his puppet. His injury was worth it, just to see Perian cower and twitch upon the floorboards, to show them all how pathetically weak they were compared to himself, even the Royal Sorcerer, Grison. Mage Armin was a High Mage, after all. He knew the Council of High Mages kept his seat still. They watched his movements on the large table map they had created together. He wondered what it would take for them to expel him from their Council. Perhaps Council members weren't expellable due to their power.

Calmer now, his mind drifted back to when two little boys, Perian and Risenor, had stood before the Council of Mages and predicted the successful invasion of Rashinder by the Darna. In that moment his heart and mind had exploded with desire and a need to make these two great empires his very own. Gone in a flash had been his pathetic plan to take over the tribes and challenge Aronaye, Leader of the Felfar tribe. What had he been thinking? Such a paltry ambition. Instead, he would use Aronaye's sons, all three triplets, to seize and command the greatest power in the known world.

Gisela had been easily bought and tasked with the abduction of the triplets. She had failed him. Her excessive aggression had caught Risenor in the crossfire and she had secured only Perian and Elian. Armin had hoped for two seers: one to be reborn a Darna prince, the other to guide his way.

He sighed, looked up and shrugged at the shrivelled and petrified remains of the cottage's previous owner, suspended from the ceiling by his shoulders, his head lolling to one side.

'She redeemed herself,' he said to the body, 'by controlling the tribes through the abduction of two highly placed girls. And the look on the faces of the tribe leaders when she threatened to trap the souls of the dead in an eternal bubble to prevent their passage into the next life was a delight.' He smiled at the figure before him, tapped his finger on the wooden arm of the chair. 'The bubble was one of my masterpieces.'

He paused in his musing and stared unfocused into the farmer's eye sockets.

'And I suppose I must give her credit for the way she managed to keep the four children isolated and believing that she loved them. She hated them.' He smirked. 'Perian was easily persuaded to die and be reborn for the sake of the tribes, people he had never been allowed to meet.' He turned to the fire and stared at the flames. 'The Zamir's sorcerer, Shimester, poured magic into the boy, and the sacrificial wings of that ridiculous bird, a sygrilien, meant to wash off, became permanent.'

The fire's warm currents gathered around the old farmer and his corpse moved slightly. The mage looked up.

'I see you agree – a potential disaster, since he was sent away with his mother's slave to protect him from the fanatical priests. Gisela turned her back on our plans then and relieved me of the necessity of killing her. But fate has worked in my favour, my friend. Perian was always going to insert himself back into his designated place with the Darna royal family as Zameel and Royal Seer. Her actions merely alerted Perian to her deceit and have made the game a fraction more challenging.'

His rictus features briefly softened again at the thought.

'The timing was perfect,' he spat aloud, banging his fist on the arm of the chair, making the slaves and the healer jump. 'My shapeshifters had already removed all male heirs to the throne ahead of Perian. All but two – Zameel Saphrax, a great warrior but stupid, and Valamer, now Zamir after the death of his father.' He looked again at the farmer. 'It was the shapeshifting triplet, Elian. I had thought him useless, but he proved his worth when he mutilated the Voice, causing the priests to revolt and bringing about the grisly demise of Zamir Maltha.'

But there will be another chance, he told himself. His own destiny dictated it. At some point, Perian would step out from the protection of the castle. Would be alone and vulnerable.

Armin could feel his time ripening. He felt strong with the thought. He would not step into chaos the next time. His possession would be smooth and complete, with no opposition. He could feel it. He could smell it. The empires would be his at last – as long as the *other* didn't get to Perian first. The one who had no use for Perian other than revenge.

He sat up suddenly with the need to act, no longer morose, and turned to the slaves in the corner. 'Call the shapeshifters.'

1

Perian found himself sitting in a cell or tomb, one without bodies or a door. Admittedly, the light wasn't very bright and hardly reached into the corners, but it was enough to see by. The only illumination came from the tattoo on his chest: the wings of a vulture, a sygrilien, that symbolised the Sky God, Tarse. He hadn't realised that his tattoo lit up – it never had before, thankfully. It marked him for sacrifice, and he kept it hidden beneath his shirt. But this was not his main concern at the moment.

He had been sucked into the cell as a vacuum sucks upon loose things to fill its emptiness. In this case, he was the loose thing: a spirit seeking stillness for his trance.

At first he was too afraid to move. He scarcely dared to breathe. But nothing stirred. He was alone.

There was no movement or sound, other than his own thumping heartbeat, yet he felt vulnerable seated on the ground. He stood and placed his hand on the wall for support, but it slipped through the surface and vanished. Horrified, he snatched the hand back and studied it for a moment to check for any damage. He was dreaming! And yet … No, he wasn't.

He clutched the hand protectively to his chest and studied the tiny space with greater intensity: the walls, the barely visible corners, and the curve of the roof. It reminded him of the cell his Faran father had put him in so he could recall his own history. He had, and it had been shocking. He had no wish to relive this experience, but having touched on it with his mind, fragments of his previous life and the present one collided and fought for dominance. He tried to block the images without success until they surged forth, uncontrolled, into a trance within a trance and an ultimate point.

A white light exploded in his chest and pain raged through his body. Only a memory, yet the horror of that moment, when he had been killed by a streak of lethal magic, bore unexpected reality within his trance state. He fell back hard against the wall, and like his hand, he slipped through to the other side.

He now found himself in free-fall through empty space, his pain forgotten, overtaken by fright that momentarily froze his body and his breath. His logical mind told him it was not real, yet this did nothing to curb his terror, and he spluttered and gasped as though underwater. The experience was too visceral, overwhelming. He curled into a tight ball, his knees pressed against his chest, rolling slowly in space, his lungs heaving from the double shock. His mind struggled for control; demanded a semblance of calm in which to assess his situation.

With the room gone, only darkness and desolation surrounded him, as twilight on a cloudy evening but completely lacking the magical quality of that special time. *More like a curse,* he thought. One that stank in the way gangrenous flesh stank. Below spread a landscape of utter destruction, and above the stink, in the dark void that he thought must be the sky, a sound, growing in volume, rumbled like distant thunder. It created sharp waves in the firmament, causing him to roll and bounce. It grew into laughter and the waves into icy claws, grasping at his clothing. He knew that voice, and it made him shrink in terror and curl tighter into himself: Mage Armin.

'Tanais,' the mage said, using Perian's Darna name. 'There you are, my puppet. I'll have you for my own soon, and your brother's crown.'

Another voice suddenly pierced the mage's hold and his presence shattered like sheets of ice that scraped Perian's skin.

'Perian. Perian, forgive me, but you must return.'

The man's voice bounced like brightly coloured bubbles blown through a tube into the terrifying gloom. *Elian.* Perian stretched out his trembling hands to enclose the delicate spheres, but instead of bursting as they should, light exploded through his fingers and filled his suddenly open eyes.

His heart attempted to break the bounds of his ribcage, then settled into a chest-rattling drumbeat. He gasped for breath. Everything was too bright. He couldn't understand where he was until Elian's hands enclosed his face and stopped his mind from racing.

'Perian, I'm sorry. Breathe deeply and settle yourself. Valamer will be crowned Zamir in less than an hour. You must gather yourself and get ready.'

Reality slammed into Perian and assaulted every fibre of his being, sending streaks of fire through his body and muddling his mind even more. He was going to be late.

Perian peered through his window at the crispness of the morning and the cloudless sky. He needed some fresh air and a walk before he joined Elian in the map room to watch the arrival of the prisoners and the wounded from the Wellorn border, where they had defeated Queen Ishra of Wellorn's vast army. They were due to pass through Prisoner's Gate around midday.

'I'm going for a walk in the garden,' he announced to Hector and the startled guards casually standing about in the hallway outside. They gathered themselves and followed as he bounced down the stairs with a new spring in his step.

He took the back way into the garden by walking through the grand banqueting hall and into the festive hall on his way to the conservatory, recalling that fateful day of Jasperen's capture by the Darna. The battle had been quick, as battles went. He could still see the Darna warriors swarming through the garden, over the mosaic paving of the courtyard and into the festive hall, where he had, reportedly, burst into flames. He didn't remember this, but a large burn mark marred the polished floor near the entrance and confirmed what others had seen.

He looked away and continued through the conservatory and into the courtyard, where so many people he had recognised by sight had been slaughtered. Unarmed, defenceless people. He wondered whether he knew any of the offenders now. But that was a pointless train of thought and one he shouldn't pursue.

A slave sweeping near the doorway dropped his broom and knelt as Perian passed on his way to the steps that led down to the lawn. He reminded himself that he needed to speak with Hector about giving him his freedom; but not today. There was too much going on.

Holes either side of the steps were all that remained of the cages that he and numerous birds had been locked in on that fateful night. He nodded at the space where the tanga had died and wished him peace on his journey, before descending the steps to sit by the lake.

Resting his back against the trunk of a willow, he pulled his knees to his chest and gazed over the glassy surface of the lake through the willow's hanging stems that dangled in the water, creating little rings upon the surface with the slightest movement. He found it peaceful and quiet. The breeze ruffled his hair and kissed his cheek with its warmth and mingled perfumes, and water lapped rhythmically against the side of a small boat moored on the lake's small central island.

His thoughts drifted back to the ceremony that had crowned his half-brother, Valamer, Zamir over the empires of Darna and Rashinder, which he had nearly missed. The event had been incredibly tedious, truncated in the end by Valamer's loss of patience. He had enjoyed the feast, though. The new Zamir had left early, saying he had duties that could not wait. His officers had groaned and followed reluctantly. The dignitaries raised their glasses to Valamer once more, continued to partake of the fine food and wine, and had a very nice time.

Valamer had been Zamir for two weeks now. The radical priests had been executed, the new Voice of the Sky God had ensured that his predecessor disappeared, and a pigeon had arrived from Perian's other half-brother, Saphrax, on the battlefield to say that they had succeeded in pushing Queen Ishra back over the Silver River and across the border into Wellorn. Yet not once had Valamer called upon Perian's seer's skills. He didn't know why. This was a crucial time when some insight into the future might have been useful. Perhaps Valamer didn't trust such skills, or he assumed Perian would go to him if he had a vision of importance.

Elian thought the issue was due to Valamer's lack of confidence in his own abilities. He was probably right. Perian had watched Valamer on the few occasions he had been invited to dinner. Even relaxing amongst his friends, the burden of responsibility still lingered about him. They barely knew each other, yet Perian could feel how Valamer struggled with his role as Zamir.

When he had asked Grison about it, he said their father had criticised and bullied Valamer, stifling him and giving him no space to learn and make mistakes while they were still small ones. Valamer had fought to break loose, but now he was free of his father's dominating presence, he found himself thrown into the position of decision-maker, overseeing two empires, one newly conquered, with very little training to fall back on.

Perian plucked thoughtfully at the grass near his foot and his wary dislike of Valamer softened a little. He couldn't imagine how hard it would have been growing up under the scrutiny of his father, how differently his own life would have panned out had he not been sent away. The mere thought made his heart flutter with a slight panic. He thanked the gods, all of them, that he had grown up on the wetlands with his foster mother.

Sighing away thoughts of his youth and Valamer, he focused on the lake. 'What time of day is it, Hector?' he croaked. He was thirsty, his throat dry.

'Late morning, my Zameel. The sun is not yet at its zenith.'

Perian struggled to his feet and pushed through the willow curtain, stretching his back and yawning. He just had time for a quick walk about the lake before heading for the map room to watch for the arrival of the prisoners. He felt carefree and content beneath such a clear blue sky, surrounded by the songs of birds and the fresh greenness of both tree and bush. Ducks foraged about the edges of the lake, their flat beaks snuffling expertly amongst the reeds. He watched them for a while, briefly sharing their simple lives, then looked up at the movement of a lone swan floating beneath a leafy bower on the island opposite. It raised its head and looked him in the eye with its strangely shifting amber orb. Perian's easy gaze snapped tight. The amber eye squeezed into an oval and wrinkled in an unmistakable smirk as it sailed forward with grace and speed.

The bird had rounded the island before Perian could decide whether it was a shapeshifter. Although he was unsure, it frightened him, and he hurried back to the palace.

He found Elian already there, watching the gates open.

'They're early.'

Elian turned his head slightly and smiled. 'You're late.'

The map room was empty, since the only people normally allowed in there were all below the window. Perian and Elian had a good view through one of the bay windows. Slaves stood with stretchers to one side near a wall, while a group of healers waited impatiently close by, their eyes on the open gates.

Perian couldn't see Valamer, but two of his officers, Ben and Rolin Rothing, stood with a group of warriors. Rolin had taken Doran's place as Valamer's personal guard, as Doran had still not been seen since the battle with the priests, despite extensive searching. Perian knew the Rothing brothers quite well now, having sat with them in the daily discussions Valamer held in the Council Room and insisted Perian attend. Ben in particular was easily recognisable due to his unusual left eye. It moved about its socket of its own volition, or so it seemed, and was rarely where it should be.

Elian had his head pressed against the glass as the first of the wounded came in, some on horses, others walking. Most had head or arm injuries. The leg wounds followed, many in carts. Perian was about to ask Elian if he could see Valamer when Valamer's face suddenly appeared reflected in the glass.

Perian spun about. 'Shouldn't you be down there to meet them?'

'They will all go to the infirmary to be checked. I will visit them there. I wanted to see it all from a distance first. I don't shock easily, but it's better not to chance a first time now that I'm Zamir.'

Valamer moved closer beside Perian so he could see clearly. There weren't as many wounded as Perian had expected, and soon they had all been moved through to the infirmary, wherever that was. Perian was thinking he should get someone to give him a tour of the palace when the prisoners arrived.

Valamer leant closer to the glass. 'I am told there are about twelve,' he said. 'Not so many. Most Saphrax will sell on his way back.'

Of course he will. Having been regarded with general disapproval under the Shanahan's rule, slaves had quickly become one of Rashinder's highly sought after status acquisitions under Zamir Maltha. Perian wondered what the Rashinder slaves in Darna would think of this new trend.

Two warriors came through the gate first, followed by a group of men in dark blue uniforms, torn and blood-spattered. Radia, the Shanahan's sorcerer, came last, distinguishable by his lack of uniform and the glistening of his wristlets, which Ishra's priestesses had placed on him to prevent his use of magic. He sagged over his saddle and his head hung low, making it difficult for Perian to guess his condition, although it was obvious that he had been misused. He had no injury that Perian could see.

When he refocused on the glass, Valamer had gone.

Perian was summoned two days later to the library, where Valamer and Grison waited by the hearth. Their daily meetings having been cancelled, this was the first time he had seen them since the wounded and the prisoners had arrived, and it was clear by their demeanour that the interrogations weren't going well. Valamer slumped in his chair and the dark shadows beneath the men's eyes showed that both were sleep-deprived.

Perian greeted them with a slight bow and took the seat that had been placed for him opposite the two men. He glanced down at a worrying pile of hair samples tied with bits of string on the floor near Grison's foot.

'I see things are not going so well in the lower regions of the palace.'

Valamer looked up and appeared about to say something, but changed his mind.

'It has been a difficult time for all of us,' Grison replied in a voice that confirmed his lack of sleep.

Perian inclined his head toward the hair. 'You want me to do a little scrying for you?'

'If you would, Tanais,' said Grison. 'With your insight we may be able to avoid the messier methods of extraction.'

Perian didn't want to think of messy ways of extracting information. He was surprised that they hadn't already resorted to torture. But then, Valamer wasn't his father.

'They are a frightened bunch, as anyone would be, I suppose,' Valamer added. 'But they still withhold any information of interest despite our threats.'

'When you're ready, Tanais,' said Grison.

Perian took a deep, centring breath and settled himself in the chair, then nodded for the first small clump. Grison handed him a bunch of dirty blond hair, thickened with mud and the oils of the unwashed, yet beneath, it was dry and sunburnt. Perian's trance wasn't deep, but enough to see a healthy young man, lovingly stroking the long neck of a horse that was harnessed to a plough. He sang quietly to himself in the long shadows of early morning. The tranquil pastoral scene changed suddenly to riders appearing along the road, and Perian saw other workers scattering and running.

'The owner of this hair is a peasant rounded up by Ishra's men for her war. He has no value save to those who love him,' he said. 'His horse will miss him, unless they took him as well.'

When he opened his eyes again, Valamer and Grison were staring at him with surprise and disbelief. Perian described what he saw, but they still stared.

'The officers have exchanged uniforms,' he said, in answer to their unspoken question. 'Hopefully they were caught anyway and sold into slavery. I do not believe this man has any information to give you.'

Valamer leant forward and put his head in his hands briefly before looking up at Perian. 'Try another, Tanais.'

Perian did as he asked, slowly working his way through the pile. Six proved to be unwilling peasants, one was a volunteer and only four were minor nobles. They didn't bother with the last bundle of hair, which was probably Radia's.

'What does it mean?' Perian asked when he couldn't stand the silence that had fallen over the room any longer. 'Surely the officers would have preferred to give information and wait for someone to bail them out than slavery.'

Valamer inclined his head to one side before making eye contact with Perian. 'They probably knew that no one would bail them out and have paid someone for the exchange and release.'

'I doubt that the men in your cells had much say in the matter, unless they were promised something for their families. So, is this the work of a traitor or someone making a bit of money on the side?'

Valamer bit his lip and flushed red. 'Either way, it's treason. But as to their reasons, that is for Saphrax to find out.' He straightened his back and lifted his chin with sudden decision, shouting for the warrior at the door to fetch Rolin.

Raucous laughter from down the corridor slipped through the door with Rolin, who was rubbing his hand across his face to extinguish the vestiges of a smile. *At least someone is having a good time,* Perian thought as the closing door severed them from the sounds of normality and locked them in gloom again.

'Send a message to Saphrax by bird, Rolin. Ask him if he's lost seven prisoners, or possibly more, and if he has, he should see if any of his men have come into sudden wealth.'

Rolin's eyes widened, his eyebrows raising.

'Someone has been playing a game of *swap the clothes and see who I am,*' Valamer added.

Rolin glanced at Perian, then with a quick nod, strode from the room.

Perian brushed the crinkles from his tunic, going over in his mind some of the things he had seen during his scrying. 'I assume you'll change tactics and alter your questions now,' he said. 'These men might still have something of use to share.'

'Like what?' asked Grison. He looked even more depressed than Valamer.

'Oh, the predawn prayers to Ortus, when Ishra and her priestesses and priests stand beneath the stars, offering their crystal bowls of sacred water in little more than sheer gossamer. Everyone is expected to be awake for that. Where and what colour the sacred tent is, and that two Darna warriors of middling rank were brought in and executed without interrogation.' Perian's attention had drifted to the discarded tufts of hair about Grison's chair, and it was a moment or two before he became aware of the intensity with which the two men looked at him.

'Tanais, why did you not mention all this when you had the hair in your hands?' asked Grison. His voice was tight, as though excited or angry. Perian couldn't decide which.

'Because I was concentrating on who they were, but now I see that there were a lot of other things going on around some of them that may be useful when Ishra makes her next bid for the Empire.'

'I have been neglecting you, Tanais,' Valamer said, very softly.

At first, Perian thought it was a threat; he was uncertain what Valamer meant, but he could detect no animosity in his features.

Valamer shouted for Lono, his personal servant, adding, 'And tell him to bring paper and his quill.' He gave Perian a knowing smile. 'Lono told me that he took notes for you during Elian's absence when he was your slave. So perhaps, little brother, we can go through them all again, but with a different focus.'

2

Perian didn't see Valamer or Grison for the next few days after his summons to the library. According to Elian, who was his source of information on what was happening inside the palace and beyond, with the knowledge of who the prisoners were and enough details about their lives to make them all even more afraid than they were already, most of the prisoners had been compliant and forthcoming. Evidently, Saphrax, who had sent a pigeon from the border, had grudgingly admitted that they had 'lost a few' prisoners and referred to Valamer as having been lucky in his guess as to the number, insisting that he had full faith in all his men and that Valamer's mistrust of his own warriors should not be reflected onto Saphrax himself.

'He doesn't know about you,' Elian concluded. He sat on an armless chair he had discovered in one of the unoccupied rooms and brought into Perian's living room. Its covering of blue velvet had been a little dusty and the headrest shiny, suggesting that it had been the favourite chair of its previous owner, but Hector had wiped it down and brushed up the headrest to look almost new.

'But surely Valamer would have mentioned me in his communications to Saphrax.'

'No,' said Elian. 'I think he's been saving that one up, and I doubt that your father mentioned anyone had warned him when he sent that message not to parley. Perhaps he was afraid he'd ignore the order if he knew its source.'

'Don't look so smug, Elian. I doubt that he'll like you any more than he'll like me.'

Elian shrugged. 'How are your meditations going? Any more interference?'

Perian cocked his head, surprised by the sudden change of topic. 'Slowly, and thankfully, no.' He'd been sitting day after day, trying to improve the resilience of his mental barrier in the hope of protecting himself against interference and invasion during his trances. At this stage he was using his memory of Risenor – Elian's brother, and Perian's in his previous life – in mock attacks. But he knew that using his imagination to create an attack, or what really amounted to a mild infiltration, was no test at all of his ability to keep unwanted visitors out. He was still completely unprepared for a real event of any sort.

Elian studied Perian and rubbed his thumb over the palm of his right hand. 'Can I help?'

'No, not yet. But I will need you when I dig deeper.' If he ever had the courage to 'dig deeper'.

'Don't look so worried, Perian. I'll be here. You will be more than a match for Mage Armin. Just keep practising. You'll get there.'

Perian allowed a smile to creep over his face, but he could not release the tension or his worry about their future, despite Elian's confidence in his abilities. At some point Armin would come for him. The thought of just how flimsy his defences were made him feel sick. And then there was the 'other' Armin had mentioned before his failed attack. Grison would not be able to protect him, Armin had said. Perian's sense of failure was almost more than he could bear.

Perian sat cross-legged on the study couch. He ran his hand slowly over its soft surface to ease his tension and listened to the sounds of movement beyond the closed door. With a deep, jagged sigh, he gradually withdrew from his surroundings into a trance. Images flitted across his mind, gently pushing for attention, but this was an exercise in strengthening his boundaries rather than probing the future.

He sat quietly in his altered space. Previously, his attempts at protection had been more akin to defence, especially when he had invoked Risenor's image, but that meant that an attack was already in progress. He needed something more: a barrier that would prevent approach.

He was imagining a thin opaque wall and wondering how to thicken it up when the fragile mass began to quiver and distort. A slurred rumbling rippled through his projection and laughter tore holes into its fabric.

'What's this, my puppet? More games? Relax, Perian. I will come for you soon, then you won't need to worry and fuss about in your trances. I'll keep you too busy doing my bidding and running my empires.'

Perian tried to shout 'Never!', but no sound emerged from his constricted throat. Bitter cold deliberately traced the line of his shoulders and ran about his neck. Fear gripped his entire body in a tight embrace. His eyes automatically flew open, and even as he slipped back from his trance, he could still feel Armin's icy touch. His blood throbbed in his veins, his breathing shallow and quick. He felt cold and hot at the same time, and really, he just wanted to cry.

He slipped from the couch and walked to the window, where a glass of water sat upon a small table. He took a few sips and stared out into the soft predawn darkness, allowing himself a moment of self-pity. He had to be ready when Armin finally attacked. The battle would be hard when it came, and if he wasn't even a little more prepared, he would die of fright before Armin had a chance to raise his hand.

The question was: how to go about such a task? In truth, he didn't know, and he found it depressing to acknowledge his inadequacy.

He refocused his eyes and watched the golden light of dawn creep over the boulevard. He had no view of the back gate, but imagined Radia leaving for the harbour to begin his long journey toward Jolint, still babysitting what remained of the Shanahan's family east of Wellorn. There, he would try to dissuade the Shanahan's eldest son, Bardol, from attempting to reclaim Rashinder. That Valamer had chosen to release Radia was a huge relief. Perian quietly wished him joy in his life and was grateful that he wasn't mourning his loss instead.

Elian's planned visit to see Jolint was delayed due to the unexpected and imminent arrival of Saphrax. He must have travelled like the wind on the tail of the wounded to be here so soon and had barely given time for the relief troops to arrive. Valamer had been furious, which didn't bode well for the meeting of brothers. The palace had been in uproar, trying to prepare for the triumphal greeting of the Empire's heroes and a feast that was appropriate for the return of a Prince of the Blood. Perian needed no vision to tell him that the day was going to be fraught with fuss and tension, angry words and denials.

The palace burst into activity with the growing light. Messengers clattered back and forth along the boulevard and slaves ran in haphazard patterns across the courtyard. In other parts of the palace, carts would be arriving with produce for the evening feast.

Perian called for Hector. If he hurried, he might still be able to take a quiet, uninterrupted stroll in the gardens and sit for a while within the obscurity of his treasured willow bower. Soon the seasons would begin to change, the willow would lose its leaves, and he would have to find some other place for his contemplations. Not his visions, which he delayed for the safety of his chambers, but a place of peace.

Perhaps the small, abandoned cottage further around the lake would do until someone decided to demolish or resurrect it.

Once dressed, he threw his cloak about his shoulders against the early morning chill and swept into the corridor, where a confusion of guards were changing shift. All four stiffened to attention and near trampled each other making way for Perian to pass. Without slowing his pace, he greeted them with a nod, managing to ease through the bodies without touching anyone and accidentally scrying their private lives.

A brisk wind rushed at him as he strode through the conservatory and out into the fresh morning air, where the sweepers were collecting the odd stray leaf on the mosaic tiles and men were already erecting trellises to support banners and hanging lamps. Perian peered into the distance, where only the ducks and water birds – thankfully no swans – foraged about the glistening lake. He estimated that he would have an hour, maybe less, before the gardeners descended upon the lawn.

Dew soaked through his thin boots, and beads of moisture that crowned each willow leaf like bright diamonds burst upon his head, dripping down his neck and soaking his shoulders as he parted the spindly branches. He shivered and thrilled at their icy greeting, while his guards stamped their feet and snorted into the misty air, reminding him of bad-tempered bulls. He spread his blanket and sat, legs crossed, with a sigh of pleasure – pleasure that he would have to forfeit in the immediate future.

He floated happily in a world of light, his spirit drifting amongst the clouds; no boundaries, no demands, no future or past, only the glorious present. Muffled sounds swirled lazily about him: humming bees, busy ducks, distant voices, the whisper of leaves in the wind, water lapping gently on the shore and the little boat straining on its anchor. He inhaled the crisp perfumes of eager blossoms and the quality of a rare southern wind. He could smell the forest beyond the town, goats grazing on the common, and from the lake's small island, the occasional burst of honeysuckle and rambling roses and corruption —

His eyes shot open. He sniffed again. The fetid air was stronger with his awareness of its presence. His chest constricted with the knowledge of where it came from.

'Hector, please inform the guards that they will find Doran's remains in that boat near the island.'

Hector blinked, his great head protruding between the willow stems, scattering more diamond droplets. When he informed the guards, Perian could hear uncertainty in their voices before one of them rushed off to the palace.

Perian gave up on contemplation. The smell alone made it difficult to concentrate, and there would be a crowd at the water's edge soon. He didn't want to be here when they uncovered the corpse, which, in his opinion, should be left to sink with the boat or set alight where it was. The priests would probably want Doran's remains for their sacred vulture to peck at, although he wasn't so sure that even the sygrilien would want him now.

Warriors and a group of five slaves dashed past him as he ascended the steps to the mosaic courtyard. The guard who had taken his message waited for him near the conservatory. When he reached the landing on the first floor of the living quarters, he could hear Valamer shouting at someone further down the corridor, wanting to know why the island and boat hadn't been searched – and no, he didn't want to see the corpse, and yes, give it to the priests, that was their job.

Perian continued up the stairs a little faster in case Valamer left his room and saw him. What a miserable day it was going to be.

Elian was still asleep, oblivious to the chaos erupting in the palace. Perian strode across the room and pulled back the thick curtains around the bed. 'Get up, Elian, there will be a delegation in here any moment.'

Elian buried deeper into his sheets as a snail retreats into its shell when touched. 'Go away. They won't want to speak to me.'

'No, but I do. They've found Doran. Or more correctly, I found Doran.'

Elian sat up and rubbed his eyes. 'Is he all right?'

'Yes and no.'

'What do you mean?'

'He's dead. Now get up, I can hear them on the stairs.'

Elian groaned and slid his legs over the side of the bed. 'Poor Doran. Where did you find him?'

'In that little boat on the lake. No one thought to wonder why it was moored on the wrong shore. Valamer is furious. I could hear him shouting as I came up the stairs. By the smell, Doran has been dead a long time, and died of his injuries rather than starvation and exposure, as I think Valamer feared.'

After he had been questioned by an agitated Rolin, Perian spent the remainder of the morning refining his swordsmanship with Elian and exercising his mental skills by combating his remembered trace of Risenor. But he had gone as far as he could with just a trace; he needed an active will with which to joust, and he was beginning to play with the idea of actually engaging with Risenor directly. He wasn't sure how that would unfold, or whether his Faran father, Aronaye, would approve. He'd discuss it with Elian later.

He started when Elian entered the study and dropped into the seat opposite. 'The Zamir has sent for you. Saphrax is nearing the town gates.'

Perian uncrossed his legs and yawned. 'Did I hear Ben out there? Did he look calm or harassed?'

'He looked stressed and harassed. Valamer sent him to oversee the proper handling of Doran's corpse.'

Impatient shuffling came from the vestibule, so Perian made an effort to hurry. 'Where will you be while I am meeting my brother?'

'With the officers. I intend to stay out of everyone's way and avoid any introductions until I can't avoid them any longer. Hopefully, he'll ignore me.'

Perian laughed. 'I might join you.'

'Ah, there you are at last,' said Ben as Perian emerged. 'Valamer hasn't stopped since you found poor Doran, and now that Saphrax is almost upon us, he's speeding up. It's unfortunate that you found his body this morning of all mornings.'

'Blame the wind, Ben.'

Perian stopped abruptly on the first-floor landing, which led to his brother's chambers.

'Has Doran been put out for the sygrilien or torched yet?'

'No. Valamer wants him buried with the boat, which suits us all. The thought of getting the bits out was making everyone ill. We lost two of the wounded yesterday, so I doubt that the birds are hungry enough to eat a three- or four-week-old corpse.' He quickly touched his forehead and asked Doran to forgive him. 'The priests were beside themselves with joy at the prospect of having two sacrifices to celebrate Zameel Saphrax's great triumph without having to plead with Valamer for someone to kill.'

'Isn't it a requirement that they have a live victim?'

Ben laughed. 'No. A gift of something treasured is all that is required, and a human body is thought to be the most precious. Not that I've noticed the priests treasuring any life other than their own, but the principle is the same.'

'I'm not so sure of that, but we don't have time to discuss religion now. Are you a follower of the Sky God, Ben? You must find Valamer and myself very offensive if you are.'

'That's true, I would. But I come from the south-eastern border of Darna, not far from Lord Zeir's mind-bending ulla forest. We worship trees there.'

Perian burst into peals of laughter at Ben's unexpected answer. The guards at Valamer's door turned their heads and Valamer himself chose that moment to pop his head around the door to see where they were. Perian coughed his merriment down at the look on Valamer's face. 'Coming,' he shouted, rushing down the corridor.

The atmosphere in Valamer's living room doused all trace of Perian's remaining good humour. Valamer paced and Grison sat like a vertical pole, rubbing his hands together. Perian bowed his head in greeting and was about to take a seat when he remembered the purpose of his question to Ben. 'Ben, would you organise for someone to get a lock of Doran's hair for me?'

Ben stared at him for a moment, then turned to Valamer, who had suddenly stopped pacing to give Perian a worried look of surprise.

'I want to see who else might have been present when poor Doran was murdered,' Perian said quickly. 'I don't expect to find anyone else there apart from Mage Armin and the shapeshifter. It is not something I particularly want to do, but it would be foolish not to check.'

Valamer's shoulders relaxed a little and he nodded agreement to Ben. As Ben was walking through the door, Perian shouted after him, 'Make sure they wear gloves. I don't want any uncertainties.'

He finally took his seat and Grison patted his knee with a tentative smile. The mood in the room had lifted a little, and Valamer stopped his pacing to sit down.

'I can't think why no one checked the boat,' he said after a moment of silence. 'We could all see it there.'

Valamer's sadness filled the room and gathered about Perian like a thick blanket. He knew Valamer had been close to Doran and that the absence of his body had weighed heavily on him. 'He has been dead a long while,' he said. 'I have little doubt that he died that night when the shapeshifter took his form. I will confirm this as soon as I have finished my scrying.' Perian wondered whether he would lie to Valamer if this was not the case, if Doran had died because no one could find him. He thought not. Valamer would not wish to be lied to.

A guard came to the door to say that the returning troops were at the gates. Valamer sighed and rubbed his face before standing. 'Come, let's welcome our brother and praise him as he deserves.' As they approached the door, he grasped Perian's arm. 'Don't let Saphrax bully you, Tanais. I'm the only one permitted to do that.' He flashed a wicked smile at Perian and marched ahead.

3

The warm south wind nipped at Perian's hair and clothing. Its dryness chafed his cheeks and caused him to blink more often than usual. He could hear cheering in the distance as the troops rode through the township and thought it a strange welcome, considering this was a recently conquered empire.

Valamer stopped on the palace steps just as the horses, three abreast, came into view along the boulevard, red ribbons woven into their manes and their bridles shining gold and silver. Residents gathered behind their fences, and many had ventured out onto the street itself, waving at the men. Perian couldn't help but recall his own march along the boulevard, which had been quite a different event. The warriors surrounding him had been there to stop him changing his mind and turning back, and only the curious had come out to watch. Not a triumphant march, but still quite a spectacle, with Elian, his shapeshifting brother, walking at his side in wolf form.

Only Saphrax and his personal guards came through the palace gates, the remainder wheeled off to the right toward another gate that led to the barracks. Perian found the spectacle thrilling. Valamer took an audibly deep breath at his side, but exactly what kind of emotion this expressed, Perian couldn't be sure.

He squinted at the group of seven, in particular his half-brother riding proudly on a magnificent grey shirian, its long-haired hooves clipping sure-footed over the stone. Saphrax's long black hair, also threaded with red ribbons, blew in the wind about a strong-jawed face, ruddy from days exposed to the elements. He wore a short vest of long black fur. Valamer made a clucking sound and whispered, without changing his stance, that Saphrax's ridiculous vest was made from the skin of his favourite dog, which he had tearfully mourned for a week when it choked to death on a bone. Perian wasn't sure whether to laugh or sympathise with his half-brother. He'd never had a dog, only Elian when he was in the mood.

Those on the steps remained perfectly still, waiting for a signal from Valamer. Saphrax dismounted and approached them. He was of a height with Valamer, with a slender, sinewy body that moved easily. He stared up at Valamer, then swept his eyes over those with him, making Perian flinch slightly. Brown eyes, unlike his and Valamer's. His stern features broke into a smile, which Perian liked less than the former expression, and he dropped to one knee. Only then did Valamer move, taking the steps carefully to touch his brother's shoulders so he could rise and hugging him once he was standing. Valamer nodded a greeting to the others and urged his brother toward the entrance.

'Come, Saphrax,' he said as he took his arm. 'Let's celebrate your victory, and you can tell us all about your heroism and achievements.'

As Perian stepped aside for the two brothers to pass, Saphrax's eyes ran over him with a look of curiosity, and vague recognition briefly touched his face. Elian was right: Saphrax didn't know who he was.

Grison, who stood near the entrance, caught the look on Saphrax's face and came to Perian's side, taking his arm in an open display of acceptance. 'This is going to be interesting,' he whispered. His pale red hair blew over his face, obscuring his features and hiding in what way he thought the meeting was going to be 'interesting'.

When they had gathered in Valamer's vestibule, Valamer asked for a few minutes alone with his brother and the two disappeared behind closed doors, leaving Perian and Grison sitting on chairs set out against the wall. He could hear the brothers' muted voices in the next room. Very soon the voices became louder, quickly gaining momentum to shouting. Grison crossed his legs and hummed to himself, and Rolin remained stiff in his chair. Perian glanced about at the two personal guards that had come in with Saphrax, but they averted their eyes as soon as he caught them staring at him.

He felt as though he were waiting for an interview, which was probably the way it would turn out, and remembered waiting in a different vestibule within the palace, listening to other travelling minstrels playing for the overseer in the hope of work during the festival; a lifetime ago, almost.

His mind had drifted along a thin thread of thoughts and reminiscences when the shouting began again after a lull that Perian hadn't noticed. 'What are they shouting about?' he asked Grison.

Grison shrugged. 'Their father and the prisoners, I imagine, amongst an endless number of other possibilities.'

Suddenly the doors flew open and Valamer ordered them inside. He was flushed, but not angry, which Perian took as a good sign. Rolin and the other two remained in their seats but followed Perian and Grison with their eyes.

Slaves swept in at their heels like an incoming tide, bearing water, wine, fruits, cheese and sweetmeats. When the whirling tide left again, Perian found that he had somehow been cut off from the others already seated in a convivial semi-circle by the double window, and Grison was casually crossing his legs, having already welcomed Saphrax back.

Saphrax twisted his head to look past Valamer on his left and stare at Perian. 'Who's this?'

Valamer made an exasperated sound like a burst bellows. 'This is your brother, Tanais.'

Saphrax pointed an accusing finger at Perian, appearing oblivious to Valamer's announcement. 'I know who you are. You're the one who burst into flames and blew us all against the walls, and allowed the Shanahan to escape. You're the cause of all the fighting along the Wellorn border and the loss of countless warrior lives, not to mention Rashinder lives. You are the one responsible for the mutilation of the Voice and the rebellion of the priests, which led to our father's death. You killed our father.'

His voice grew progressively higher and louder, blasting Perian with every accusation that even Valamer's shouted protests could not rise above. Saphrax stood, his face near purple with rage and distress, as though he would leap over his brother's knees and pounce on Perian. Valamer grasped his hairy vest and pulled him back.

Perian froze, leaning slightly on the seat he had not yet taken, blinking in the glare of the bright light and the force of Saphrax's voice, his feeble defensive magic automatically pricking the tips of his fingers. Grison glanced at Perian and moved forward in his seat, preparing to intervene.

Valamer's voice finally exploded through the torrent of accusation. 'Saphrax, we've just been through all this.'

Saphrax remained standing, his hand shaking upon the armrest. 'No, *you* went through it, watering down his crimes with nonsense. He is no brother of mine.'

Well, Perian could live with that. He wasn't so keen on Saphrax.

'Ishra had already planned to make a play for Rashinder. The arrival of the Shanahan merely delayed her actions,' said Valamer. 'Without Tanais, we wouldn't have known she intended to invade until she was well into Rashinder and far more difficult to turn back. If that had happened, you would have something to complain about with regard to losses. As for our father's death, he could have prevented that himself by taking the priests in hand. He knew the Voice had brought his most radical priests with him. Their rebellion was planned well in advance of the taking of Jasperen, although I don't think that they had necessarily planned Father's demise. I have already dealt with that particular issue.'

Saphrax allowed Valamer to pull him back into his seat, where he sat poised, ready to pounce again. Grison relaxed back into his chair, clasping his hands upon his lap. Relief spread between them, allowing Perian to finally sit down, wishing he were back in the vestibule, or even better, his chambers.

'I don't hold with soothsayers, pretending to predict our future,' Saphrax spat through clenched teeth, moving forward as though to rise again. 'You're a fake, Tanais, like all fortune-tellers. It would be better if you went back to your former life of singing in taverns or separating the poor from their hard-earned money. Stay out of my way or I'll have you.'

'Saphrax!' Valamer elbowed his brother forcibly back into his seat.

Perian stood slowly and eased his chair back by straightening his legs. He was serving no real purpose here, save as an outlet for this man's frustration and ignorance, and he saw no reason why he should suffer Saphrax's insults any longer. He had begun to feel unwell. His head hurt and the room spun about him in a way that would once have made him panic. There was no common ground between himself and Saphrax; it was better that he left, since anything he said would be sneered at and seen as trying to seek his approval, and that Perian would never do. To remain in silence made him look weak, as would his leaving, of course. He inclined his head toward Valamer.

'Your permission to leave, my Zamir. My time would be better spent seeing if Ben has the item I asked for.'

Valamer glared at him. 'No, you do not have my permission. Sit down, Tanais. This is Saphrax's moment of glory, not Doran's.'

Of course it was – Doran was well past 'moments of glory', with the exception of the ultimate one. But Saphrax hadn't earnt Perian's admiration. He saw only the darkness around him; a darkness with tendrils that continually threatened to prod an unpleasant vision that lingered on his personal horizon. Saphrax had brought the horrors of the battlefield with him.

Perian did as Valamer bid, but remained silent, staring at the blue sky and sunlight through the window in an attempt to counteract the darkness in the room. Valamer was asking Saphrax about the battle and his journey – had the relief troops arrived before he started out? Grison added the odd question. For a moment their voices became distant, lost beneath the sound of bells building to an ear-shattering crescendo. Perian closed his eyes and turned his attention back to the three men.

'Father's bird only just reached me in time,' Saphrax was saying. His voice and mood completely changed with the concentrated light of admiration shining upon him. 'His initial instructions were to parley. I'm standing there, face to face with the enemy, wondering whether to go down myself and see what this queen looked like – she looked stunning, but so would our grandmother from that distance – or whether to send a messenger, and the bird near took my head off on its way to the birdman.'

The blood suddenly drained from Valamer's face and he stared at his brother, pale and startled. He glanced at Perian, but said nothing, nor did he tell Saphrax that it was due to Perian's vision that his father sent the bird. Saphrax wouldn't have believed it.

'How did it go?' Elian asked cheerily as Perian swept into his vestibule, nearly tripping over Hector, who was kneeling by the doorway.

Perian rolled his eyes and went straight into the study, calling for wine as he went.

'That well!' said Elian, following him in.

Perian flopped onto his couch and rubbed his head vigorously. 'He's an ignorant brute. He spent the first ten minutes verbally abusing me and accused me of killing our father. He thinks I'm a charlatan, a mere fortune-teller who should have stayed in the taverns.'

Elian laughed. 'I could have lived with that.'

Perian shot him a derisive look, then laughed with him. 'At least I would have only lovesick teenagers, weather predictions, and cuckolded merchants and sailors to deal with, and you could have tried your hand at love and fertility potions.'

Elian produced a small box and put it on the desk. 'Ben came by with a present for you.'

Perian stared at the small brown box tied with string, now sitting innocently amongst his books and papers. He shook his head. 'I need a moment to recover. Grison asked me to send for him the minute I had finished with the contents.'

Elian dragged a large chair closer to Perian and plumped up the cushions before sinking into their feathery mass. 'Saphrax is a good warrior. He is popular with the men, and they say his tactical skill is beyond fault.'

'That may be, but he is no diplomat – and, as Grison said, not suitable as a Zamir. Perhaps it is difficult to be both.'

'You don't have to like him to admire him for what he's good at.'

'Now you, my dear Elian, are the perfect diplomat.'

Elian kicked him softly on the shin.

'I'm still cross,' said Perian. 'I'll be over it by tomorrow's feast, unless he starts again. Hopefully he's not so lacking in sense as to do it in public.'

The feast was held in the Banquet Hall: a large hall with a decorative raked ceiling and leaded windows depicting scenes of battle and heroism. That the heroes and heroines were Rashinder, and in at least one window the skewered enemy was clearly Darna by the slant of his eye, appeared to go unnoticed by the new residents.

Perian sat on Valamer's left, looking down the great hall at the parallel tables either side that stretched to the far wall. The guests were mostly seated now, but the formalities of being announced and having to kneel before the Zamir had taken forever, during which Perian had sat stiffly calm. Saphrax, on Valamer's other side, fidgeted impatiently – eager to get on with the feasting and drinking, Perian thought, or more likely still uncomfortable with his brother's new role.

Lord Fimian with his sorcerer, Clementina, and a few officers had been one of the first groups presented. The startled look on Fimian's face and that of his sorcerer was the most amusing part of the event so far. His pleasure and self-importance had evaporated at the sight of Perian, who Clementina had tried to kill when he and Radia had sought refuge from the Darna warriors. But that was before he had returned to his royal family. Fimian faltered in his knee-bending, and for a moment Perian thought he would denounce him publicly as a traitor. Thankfully he held his peace and rushed through the formality to take his seat and glare at Perian, with the occasional whisper to Clementina.

Perian watched eagerly as the food and wine began to arrive. He was starving. His stomach had rumbled dangerously loud throughout the kneeling and presenting. Valamer proposed a toast to Saphrax and all those who had taken part in the valiant repelling of the enemy. Everyone fell upon their first goblet of wine enthusiastically, then cheered their new Zamir with another. Loud chatter and eating commenced almost immediately. Valamer sat back in his chair and watched his subjects with some satisfaction. Perian joined him in his surveying of the hall once he had seen to the needs of his belly.

'Did you enjoy Fimian's reaction?' Valamer asked him with a slight turn of his head.

'Enormously. Although I did think he was going to make a public announcement at one point.'

'Fimian is an odious little man with no manners, but even he wouldn't dare to openly question the presence of someone at my side. Who knows what rumours he is spreading now, though.'

Perian hadn't thought of that, but he could do nothing to remedy such accusations as may spill from Fimian's mouth along with the spray of food that accompanied his eager talk. Nor his eyes, which flickered toward Perian constantly. Perian made a point of not looking his way. The rumours would reach him soon enough, even if only through Elian, who sat on the opposite side and occasionally smiled at Perian if he glanced that way.

Eventually the chatter and laughter grew louder, the clatter of knives and spoons less. The sound of tolling bells came and went in Perian's head, always accompanied by a fluttering of his heart and a brief searing pain in his shoulder. The bells had disturbed his morning nap and sounded with his waking. He had ignored it, but now began to think that he should have taken a chance on arriving late and sought out their purpose that morning.

Valamer shifted in his chair. 'Time to mingle with the guests before I lose all feeling in my rear end and my legs refuse to support me,' he said to Perian. He stood, using the table to propel himself upward. 'Come, Tanais, I want you with me. We shall amuse ourselves by introducing you to Fimian. Stop him mouthing off about your presence and how you have fooled me with your silver tongue, and how you tried your tricks on him when you accompanied Radia. He is too stupid to realise that he is demeaning me as well as a Prince of the Blood. He was too busy gawking to notice the royal tattoo. Make sure it's on display as we approach.'

'I don't have a silver tongue, and even if I had, Clementina didn't give me time to use it.'

Valamer laughed loudly. 'Come. Let's make all that food and wine turn foul in his belly. I'm tired of watching and listening to his ranting.'

They made their way to the side table where Fimian and his officers sat. Fimian was too busy talking to notice Valamer's approach until his companion jabbed him in the side and nodded in their direction. Perian followed behind, his pace slowing with the insistent pounding of bells. He looked past Valamer at the windows, where he could see the fuzzy passing of people. They moved too quickly, too silently.

He saw rather than heard Valamer introduce him to a gaping Fimian, but his voice was lost in the crescendo of tolling bells that clearly only he could hear. A cold fear spread throughout his body.

When the sound in his head stopped suddenly, he heard a bell ring distantly somewhere in the palace. At that moment, a young man, his features tight and purposeful, broke away from a group of Saphrax's officers and strode toward them.

Suddenly Perian understood. Vision and reality became one and froze him to the spot. A dull glint of metal caught the sunlight from within the folds of the young man's uniform. When the blade caught the light again, it flashed so brightly into Perian's eyes that it released his rigidity.

His magic would not come to deflect the weapon that the officer released into the air, so he threw himself at Valamer, pushing him forward into Fimian's table. The table screeched across the floor at a slow, dreamlike pace and knocked Fimian backward in his chair.

Heat exploded in Perian's shoulder. The laughter and talking stopped, leaving a space of unbroken silence, which slowly shattered into chaos. Magic flew through the air, followed by the clatter of another knife, turned from its mark by Grison.

Perian reached out and grasped a wad of Valamer's shirt as Valamer moved to catch him. His body slid to the floor and his mind into semi-darkness with the sound of a loud crack. All other movement was lost, save the wet nose of a dog that pressed between the fingers he had fixed upon the cloth of Valamer's shirt, knowing that he must not let go. Then the darkness about him began to suck him in.

He called for Elian to help him, but Elian's frantic calls told him that he either couldn't hear, or could do nothing to stop Perian's descent into the hellish world of his visions.

4

The room was a little bigger than he remembered. Other than that small difference, his surroundings were the same as in his earlier vision, with the same dark grey stone; a mausoleum without bodies and no furniture or shelves for the eternal rest of the dead. The only light shone from the tattooed wings upon his chest.

He had no sense of time or how long he had lingered within this one room. The tunnel through which he had been sucked, clawing for purchase, had vanished without trace, cutting out the sound of Elian's terrified voice. He was alone, with no understanding of how to get out.

This time he had full awareness and knew he was in no dream or vision from which a gentle nudge or voice could awaken him, so he dropped to his haunches and waited. He felt heavy and numb and so afraid that he no longer shook, or was able to clearly identify the feeling as fear.

If he listened carefully, he could hear a low, continuous rumble, and occasionally the room briefly filled with light and he heard voices that faded quickly. Sometimes he felt something with five legs touching his body, at other times clawing at his right hand. The sensation made him shiver and gasp in terror. He wondered if they were enormous spiders that ran over him, testing the tastiness of his flesh. He twisted about frantically, searching for the culprits, but they were either invisible or hid in the crevices along the wall. Once, he had the sensation of being rocked from side to side, yet he saw no movement in his body.

Eventually, his fear gave way to boredom. He was restless to the point of screaming. When he could stand the monotony no more, he slid through the walls to see if the ghastly landscape of his previous vision remained the same.

Its features had changed, but not the desolation. Below him the tree ferns of the palace entrance stood in blackened rows of burnt stumps, and the gates hung open and lopsided on their hinges. Beyond, where the town should be, he saw nothing but darkness. He drifted swiftly over the land to where crops had failed and dead animals decomposed in the fields.

This was a future he had been hoping to avoid, once he had discovered its cause. But he hadn't had time, nor had he told those who needed to know. Elian knew. He would pass the information on, if he remembered before it was too late.

A distant pulse broke into his musing. It blew upon him in the way someone might have blown upon his arm or face: a soft exhalation through pursed lips. This exhalation was filled with terror. It screamed with a hundred silent voices. He swivelled his head about to find its source. The direction of Nor, he thought, although he couldn't see it.

When the air suddenly shimmered, his breath stopped. He wanted to go back to the room he had just left. He was too frightened to turn his back on whatever it was that lurked just out of sight, yet at the same time he was afraid he would see it. That it travelled his way, he was certain. He frantically spun about, searching for the wall with a growing awareness that he didn't know where it was or what the building looked like. Logic told him the palace, but how could that be?

The prickle and pull grew stronger as though the object had found its target. This was no time to debate about location with himself; he should just return the way he had come. When he turned again, to his amazement, the wall miraculously materialised in front of him. He had travelled some distance, he thought, yet there it was.

He looked over his shoulder and could just make out a slight movement coming from the direction of the terror. Without another thought, he slipped through the stone, hoping that whatever it was could not follow. The giant spiders felt quite friendly compared to what was out there.

'They're attracted by your connection to life,' said a lispy, grating voice. 'The bubble of souls. Farans, trapped by Gisela and your mage. Terrifying, aren't they? It's worse if you let them get close. They tried to get me in there, but I refused to die.'

Perian stared at the figure sitting on the floor with his back against the wall, unable to comprehend what he saw.

'Are you real? Or am I hallucinating on top of pursuit by some unknown horror and groping by invisible spiders?'

Risenor's laughter still sounded more like a hiss to Perian's ear, but he didn't show his teeth, which was an improvement. 'In deep trance, my intellect is not so different to yours or Elian's. It's only in normal life that I become confused and angry.' He grasped his stick-like left leg and moved it into a different position. 'You shouldn't be here. This is not a normal vision. It is a different reality, exhibiting features of the future, or possibly the present. I followed you here to see what you were doing.'

Perian could hardly believe what he was seeing and hearing. He found it incomprehensible that Risenor should wander these worlds sane. He had to be hallucinating, surely. He took a few steps toward the centre of the room and glanced away from Risenor to see if he would disappear when he looked back. The figure remained, unchanged.

'I'm a seer like yourself. A better one,' Risenor said. A sly smile of superiority spread across his face, showing his teeth this time. 'I've enjoyed our jousting, but you still can't best me. You would know that if you'd invited me into the game. You'll have to work harder if you intend to confront that mage.'

Perian felt himself blush with irritation and not a little anger. 'This is not a game. I am trying to protect myself and an empire – two empires – from manipulation and tyranny.'

'These things mean nothing to me,' Risenor said slowly, with a hint of anger himself. He moved again with a soft groan. Even in ethereal form, he was not free of his physical disability. Perian wondered if this was real, or if Risenor was unable to separate himself from the damage done to him.

He made an effort to soften a little and find some compassion in his exchange with his once-brother. It could so easily have been himself or Elian who had broken free of their kidnappers and clung to their mother when Gisela doused her in fire. The image of that moment flashed into Perian's mind and a knot of anger flared in his chest. Gisela was responsible for the way Risenor was today, and if Perian ever got the chance to take his revenge, it would be for Risenor and the ruination of his life, as well as for himself and Elian.

Perian turned his attention back to Risenor and his current problem. 'Assuming you are no illusion, why are you here, apart from having followed me for your own amusement?'

Risenor shrugged. 'As I said, you shouldn't be here. I listen to them talking, Aronaye and the others, at our evening meals and at meetings. Father is very worried about you and Elian. Not that I care. It was your lives he prayed for all those years ago when you were abducted, and I … Well! He prayed for my death in the same sentence, which is probably why I lived. My anger and disappointment are what kept me alive.' He ran his hand slowly over a shrivelled leg as though ironing out the creases. 'You need to go back to the real world, but you're too stupid to know how.' He snorted, his mouth distorting into another smile.

'I suppose you do,' Perian said, unable to keep the irritation from his voice.

'Yes.'

Of course he would. Risenor had obviously been travelling these other realities all his life. He let forth another triumphant chuckle, but this time, Perian pushed down his annoyance and pride.

'Show me.'

'I enjoyed our jousting,' Risenor said again. 'Invite me next time. You learn nothing in a one-sided game.'

He twisted his torso to more easily point at the wall to his left. The grit on the floor made a grinding sound with his movement, giving Risenor more substance than Perian thought possible. A gentle light emanated from his fingertips and danced upon the stones, causing them to glow brighter and brighter, until they illuminated the room.

The sudden flood of sensations made Perian gasp. The low rumbling burst into a loud cacophony of sounds. A searing pain in his shoulder and hand drew a husky groan from his lips and his eyelids flew open automatically. He found himself looking at a rough rock ceiling lit by a dull yellow light. His heart pumped faster and his stomach tightened. Risenor had been playing with him again. He felt foolish and angry; with himself and with Risenor.

He lay very still, trying to make sense of what was around him and exactly where Risenor's light had sent him. He could hear and smell the lapping sea. Voices and the crunch of boots on sand and gravel came from a short distance away. Water dripped close to him. The more he listened and sniffed the air, the more confused he became. Where was he?

He tried to move, to lift his head, but fire exploded in his shoulder, sending streaks of molten lava down his arm and across his chest. A shout of pain issued from his throat before he could stop himself and caused a wave of movement and scuffling feet beyond his line of sight. Then a face he didn't recognise peered down at him and shouted for someone to fetch Elian. His ears buzzed with its volume.

'Welcome back, my Zameel. Don't worry, you are safe. Elian will be here in a moment.' The face vanished, then reappeared. 'He's here now.'

Elian shouted Perian's name over and over until he was beside him. Pain rushed through Perian's body again when Elian knelt next to him and leant over to grasp his head between his palms and kiss his forehead.

'Where are we, Elian? What has happened to me?' he coughed through lips squashed tight by Elian's hands.

'Thank all the gods in existence that you're back, Perian. I thought you would never wake up.' Tears ran down Elian's face as he grasped Perian's left hand and held it to his lips.

How long had he been asleep? He studied the ceiling, the walls and Elian's face, which was cut and bruised. He listened again to the sounds around him and concentrated on the smells. He was in a coastal cave, and Elian had been fighting. He tried to move to sit up, but began coughing, his right hand cramping simultaneously – a pain almost worse than that in his shoulder. He was seized by panic; his body pulsed and his breathing quickened to a pant, his lungs unable to suck in enough air.

Elian called for someone to refill his glass of water and another to help his brother sit up. He placed a hand on Perian's forehead, and healing heat spread over Perian's head, calming his mind and body, settling his thoughts and releasing the tightness of his muscles and nerves. The water eased his throat, and sitting up made him feel alive. When the worst was over, he looked down at the cramping hand: a claw-like appendage, blue and stiff around a wad of white silk. He stared. His memory began to stir, but the images would not stay still long enough for him to make sense of them.

Elian followed Perian's gaze. 'Can you move it?' He took Perian's hand and rubbed it gently, but each stroke hurt and trailed a white line. Perian tried to pull the hand away, but his arm would not obey him.

He was tired and wanted to sleep. His head had begun to throb. This was probably just another dream, or vision, or one of those realities Risenor spoke of. But nothing had hurt in the place he had just come from. He dropped his head back on the rough pillow and closed his eyes, hoping that when they opened again he would be in his own bed in his chamber.

'Has he gone again?' asked the voice that had called Elian.

'No. I believe this is normal sleep. We must give him a little time. Ask someone to inform Grison that Zameel Tanais has woken up, but not to hurry to get here yet.' Elian turned his full attention back to Perian. 'Rest, Perian. I will stay here with you until you feel able to awaken fully.'

He enclosed Perian's hand between his palms and settled himself to wait. Perian could feel his warmth from the knee that rested against his side and the hands that covered his bent fingers, could feel Elian's innate healing energy travelling along his arm like the sun's summer rays warming and reviving a winter garden. He followed its drift about his body, listened to the sounds of life around him, and slept in the knowledge that he didn't need to think or make sense of anything yet.

After a length of nothingness, or at least, nothing he could recall, images that had danced before him in no meaningful order on first waking formed a sequential line that travelled across his mind's eye and were quite recognisable. Where was he? How many days had he slept, and what had happened in that time? He thought of Valamer and recalled the events at the feast. He saw the wolf's nose pressed into his hand and remembered the burnt tree ferns.

He managed to squeeze out Elian's name before his dry throat seized up again.

'I'm here. Open your eyes and drink.'

Elian held a cup to Perian's lips and dribbled water into his mouth. It felt like soft warm honey flowing over his parched tongue. He attempted to tip Elian's hand so he could gulp down the cup's entire contents at once, but Elian flicked him away, muttering something about choking to death, or even worse, vomiting it back up again. Perian relented, content that at least his arm was now doing what he wanted, even if Elian wasn't.

This time he was fully awake and knew that he was in no dream or vision. He took more careful note of his surroundings. The rough ceiling belonged to a cave, as he had surmised. A few lamps sat on little shelves along the walls, and the gentle light of day flickered from an entrance he couldn't see, where people walked back and forth, talking softly. He lay on a pallet at one end; folded blankets scattered about the bit of floor he could see told him that others slept there at night. A memory of shapes passing beyond the feast hall windows and his desperate grasping of Valamer's shirt came back to him from the depths of his mind and filled him with a prescient foreboding. He looked down at his right hand, still rigid and bluish.

'How long has it been like that?' he asked.

'About a week and a half. Since you fell into a deep sleep after hitting your head on the stone floor. You gripped Valamer's shirt so hard we had to cut him out of it, and we haven't been able to release the hand since. Now that you're awake, perhaps we can get some movement into it between us.'

Perian craned his head forward to see if his wing tattoo still glowed, but no light shone from beneath his shirt. He put his hand over the tattoo anyway.

'You are safe, Perian,' Elian said, mistaking the meaning of his actions. 'No one has tended you except Hector, Grison and myself. No one else knows.'

Perian touched Elian's face, the scabbed gash along his cheek. 'What has happened, Elian? Where is Valamer?'

'I'll tell you that once you have eaten and we've attended to that hand. As to Valamer, we don't know. I assumed that was why you clutched that piece of cloth so tightly. Sadly, I didn't understand the message until it was too late, although I'm assuming it may still be useful.'

Perian felt rather than saw the wet nose on the cloth – Elian's wolf nose.

A warrior he knew by sight appeared with a mug of thin soup, the drinking of which sent Perian spinning as though he were drunk. Once he had finished all that Elian would permit him to have and what he considered too little, he nodded. 'Now the hand.' He didn't want to know what had happened just yet; he wanted his hand back before it was beyond even Elian's healing abilities, if it wasn't already.

Elian smiled lopsidedly, filling Perian with warmth and love. He could bring the dead back to life with that smile. Elian called for a hot towel and wrapped Perian's hand in it. The heat from the steaming towel warmed his fingers at what seemed to be a distance. That he could feel something at all was a blessing.

It took three hot towels, Elian's gentle massage and a lot of concentration on Perian's part to loosen the digits enough for the cloth to be removed. Perian whined and groaned once the blood began to flow more readily. The pain was worse when Elian massaged his palm. Finally, when Perian announced that he could stand no more, Elian conceded that it was enough for the moment, wrapping it in a bandage and placing it in a sling. Even with his arm resting upon his chest, Perian could still feel the residue of Elian's thumb gliding across his palm, cajoling his muscles to relax.

He sank back into his pillows and wiped the sweat of his ordeal from his face with the sleeve of his good arm. 'Now, Elian, tell me what has happened – from the beginning, when the assassin threw his knife into my shoulder.' He was exhausted, but his need to know was greater than the pull of sleep, which probably wouldn't come anyway due to the throbbing of his appendage. Elian's narration would hopefully take his mind off his discomfort.

Elian sighed and shook his head. 'It is worse than you can imagine.'

5

Perian closed his eyes, preparing to listen to Elian without interruption and attempting to wipe from his mind all the ghastly scenarios his imagination had suddenly created.

'The assassin was one of Saphrax's men,' Elian began. 'Why he chose the feast for his attempt I cannot say; he must have known there was no escape. I can only think that he believed it to be his only chance at Valamer. What was left of him after most of the drunken horde had jumped on him was taken to the cells, and Valamer had you taken to our chambers, where Grison and I attended to your wound. I heard later that he managed to bring order to the event and the feast continued, although I imagine that the topic of conversation revolved around the assassination attempt.

'Saphrax went to the cells to interrogate the young man as soon as the guests left, rather earlier than had been expected. Grison said that Valamer went down to see how the questioning was going, but came away shaken and didn't go down again. Grison said that Saphrax is more of Maltha's cut than Valamer, so you can imagine what went on. Evidently the assassin was the same person who assisted the Wellorn nobles to escape. Saphrax was shocked and regretful, but not once did he concede that he had made a mistake.

'Hector and I sat by your side each day and night, but you didn't stir. Occasionally you opened your eyes, but I could see no spark in them, and we feared greatly for your life. Valamer visited each day to stroke the lump on your head and talk softly about something none of us were privy to. No amount of healing or cajoling by Grison or myself would bring you back.

'Then three days ago, the night after Fimian left, the Soldiers of the Sky God raided the feast hall where Saphrax was entertaining his elite warriors. The attack was quickly quelled without loss of life and the renegades called in by the Voice, who promised to keep them under control. Saphrax has demanded that they be handed back for punishment, but the Voice is adamant that he will undertake their punishment according to the rules of their Order. In my opinion, the Voice was on the scene too quickly.

'As soon as the fighting was all but over, Ben and I rushed up to Valamer's chambers to inform him of what had happened. We found Valamer's warriors dead in the corridor. When we ran through the door, we found Rolin lying in the vestibule with a mortal wound to his heart, and further in, we found Lono with his throat cut, left to bleed out onto the carpet, but no Valamer. There was blood everywhere. Only then did I understand why you had clung to that piece of cloth so desperately. I shifted into the wolf to see if there was anything else I could use to find Valamer, but he is fanatical about cleanliness, and all his clothes were clean save what he was wearing at the time. The bed linen was a confusion of both Valamer and Lono, and there was too much blood. We decided to wait and see if you woke before I tried again.'

'Valamer's blood?'

'Yes, and another's. Not Lono or Rolin.'

'Was there no blood trail or footfall you could follow?'

'None. I think he was unconscious and had to be carried. He didn't escape – I would have found his trace.'

Perian's energy drained away with Elian's report. He felt helpless with shock and struggled to fight his growing sense of defeat. This wasn't the worst of the scenarios his imagination had spewed forth, but it was close. He didn't know his half-brother, but found he cared for him, and feared for his life. He feared for himself and for Rashinder. This was just the opening Mage Armin needed.

He turned his mind to his vision and was about to ask about the tree ferns when Grison appeared at the entrance. Strands of hair had broken loose from a plait at his nape, flying loose about his pale, taut face, adding a wildness to his features.

'Tanais, thank the gods you're awake and alive. I assume you're sane?'

'What are you blathering about, Grison? Of course I'm sane.'

Grison sat on the edge of Perian's pallet opposite Elian and automatically took his hand. 'Have you told him?' he asked Elian.

'Yes, but we haven't had a chance to discuss it yet.'

'How are the tree ferns?' Perian blurted, desperate to know whether what he had seen was the past or the future. He noticed that Grison had developed a tic above his left eye, causing his eyebrow to move like a hairy insect and his lid to twitch. Perian looked away before he developed a tic of his own.

'They're fine,' said Elian. 'Or they were when I last saw them.' He glanced at Grison for confirmation.

'Why?' asked Grison. His face drooped slightly, as though the effort of keeping the muscles rigid with constant tension had suddenly become too great with the possibility of more bad news.

'While I was away, asleep as you say, I saw them burned to stumps and the gates hanging loose. Jasperen was in darkness. In the south, crop fields were laid waste, and dead animals littered the pastures as far south as Darna, including the ulla forest. Blood and death clung heavily to the winds from the east.'

When Perian refocused his eyes and turned his attention back to his audience, he noticed that Grison had stopped massaging his hand and even his wriggling brow had frozen in a raised position above sagging cheeks. Elian had lost his tan.

'I can't tell you why yet,' Perian continued. 'Let us be thankful it is a future I saw rather than the past or present.'

Elian raised his eyebrows and looked Perian in the eye. 'That is the vision you had the day of Valamer's crowning!'

'Yes, but it never came again, even when I'd plucked up the courage to seek it out. I was too afraid that I'd never get out of that tomb. I didn't imagine that it would be a vision within a vision. In fact, I would never have got out this time if it hadn't been for Risenor.'

'Risenor!'

'He's quite sane, or perhaps I should say, rational, in the places we go to in deep trance. His has been a lonely life, I think.'

Grison finally stirred and twisted about to look more intently at Perian, making the bed squeak and rock. 'Tanais, this is a truly awful picture of the future. You have described the end of Rashinder, not just our occupation here. Will you be able to seek out the cause of what you saw? Do you think it is connected to Valamer?'

Perian felt suddenly heavy with the burden of foresight – with the fear of failing those he loved and all those whose future relied on his ability not just to have visions, but to interpret them and find ways of deflecting fate from its dreadful, rectilinear path.

'Perhaps. If it is, it is the loss of him that is the cause. Something important is missed and allowed through when it should have been seen and stopped.' Perian pulled his hand back from Grison. 'Help me up, Elian, I'm beginning to feel sluggish lying here. I need to get my strength back, and while I'm doing that, you or Grison can tell me why I'm here.'

'For your safety,' said Grison. He stood so Perian could free himself of the sheet. 'The Voice kept asking about you. The questions started before Valamer disappeared and intensified after.'

With Elian's help, Perian had manoeuvred himself into a sitting position on the side of the bed and was in the process of testing his legs. He would have slipped to the floor if Elian hadn't been holding him.

Grison studied his hands for a moment. 'I don't think they know about your tattoo, Tanais. There is something else going on. My spies in the priesthood have gone quiet and my other contacts know less than I. The new Voice outwitted us and continues to. Beneath his obsequious manner is a sharp, intelligent, scheming mind as hungry for power as his predecessor. No wonder he agreed to the previous Voice's demise so readily.' He dropped back onto the side of the bed.

Elian heaved Perian to his feet again, where he swayed despite Elian's strong grip. The ground felt strange beneath the soles of his feet and his knees wobbled. He moved them about a bit for the sake of his circulation and took two or three steps before sitting back on his pallet. He'd try again in an hour or so.

'Is Saphrax in charge?' he asked.

Elian coughed.

'Yes, he is,' Grison said, rather too quickly. 'More or less. He is weak before the priests. Their demands grow and they push for power in Valamer's absence. He has conceded the Wellorn prisoners for sacrifice, which is a mistake, I believe.'

A debilitating helplessness crept over Perian; sadness and anger mingled together. His mind filled with the image and sense of the young blond-haired conscript who had stood in a field somewhere in Wellorn, caressing his horse with such love, joyful in the simple pleasure of being alive. The thought of this young man stretched upon a stone nearly choked him. *I will destroy the Priests of Tarse,* he swore to the image, *for you and all the other innocents they have tortured for their pleasure.*

His attention returned to Grison, who had pushed himself up from the pallet as though his strength had left him. 'I must go. Saphrax becomes impatient if I am out of his sight for too long.' He turned his hollow eyes toward Perian. 'It is my strong belief that the priests have Valamer, assuming he lives. That they are wheedling their way into power, and will, at the slightest opportunity, take over by force or guile. Perhaps they won't wait for an opportunity and will just take it anyway.'

Grison's gait perked up as he walked toward the entrance, the gravelly ground crunching beneath his boots.

'I'll drop back later. Do you think you will up for a bit of scrying by then?'

'I believe I must be.' Erely came to mind. She was Valamer's aunt and a truthseer of great skill who could detect lies and deception from any speaker. 'Is Erely present when Saphrax meets with the Voice?'

'No. Another concession.'

Perian shook his head slowly. 'Bring me something of the Voice's, or at least something he has touched,' he asked Grison. 'Do we still get messages from the Wellorn border?'

'Every other day.'

'Bring me any that you still have and any that come, once Saphrax has read them.'

Grison hesitated as though to ask a question, but changed his mind and turned back to the entrance, his tunic swinging about him as he left.

Perian remained propped up on his pallet and moved his slung arm up and down and sideways, then massaged it through the cloth. His mind raced with all that had happened in his absence and he struggled with all the possibilities in his attempt to put it all into order. Clarity evaded him. It was too soon.

He turned his attention to Elian. 'Where is Hector?'

'In our chambers, pretending you are still there,' said Elian.

'And my guards?'

'All is as it was on the surface. Who knows what will happen if the priests decide to force their way in?'

Perian took a deep breath and inclined his head. 'We must act before that happens.'

Perian stopped trying to rearrange his thoughts and emptied his mind to watch as though the observer, allowing all the pieces to gradually form themselves into some sort of order. Only when he sensed Grison's return did he slowly emerge from his contemplations. Tiny ripples ran through his heart and his stomach tightened. The time had come for him to separate the truth from the lies.

Despite his trepidation, a smile crept over his face at the two familiar faces that looked down at him. He felt stronger now, although still shaky due his forced recovery. One and a half weeks trapped in his vision – that was a long time for both body and mind.

'You look pleased with yourself, Grison. Do you have what I asked for?'

'I do.' Grison reached into the pocket of his coat, withdrawing a bundle of crinkled papers with gloved hands. 'Saphrax had screwed them up and thrown them into a desk drawer in the Council Room.

We have had three communications from the border since Valamer vanished three days ago.'

'And the Voice?'

Grison's face transformed in a glow of satisfaction. 'He had a document supposedly written by Maltha before the uprising, giving the priests permission to restrict religious diversity by closing the temples of Aramo, the god of harvest and fighting men, Relani, the goddess of fertility, Selani, the sun god, and an assortment of nature spirits, as well as ousting the leaders, priests and priestesses, and removing shrines to all deities within the city – a recipe for civil unrest. It is thankfully a false document, although, I confess, the signature is a masterpiece. Maltha would never have agreed to such a thing.

'Fortunately, Saphrax hesitated and said he would consider the request and let the Voice know his decision. When the Voice complained and pushed for an instant decision, saying it was a legal document and that the Zameel should abide by his late father's wishes, Saphrax coolly told him that anything his father may have agreed to was now invalid, and if the Voice spoke to him like that again, he'd find that sygrilien who took out the other Voice's tongue and get it to do the same to the current one. Saphrax is difficult and out of his depth as Zamir, but in that moment, I was very proud of him.'

Perian pushed himself up to a sitting position with his left elbow and asked Elian to remove the bandage from his right hand. The sight of it made his breath catch – bright red with a purple tinge. No wonder it hurt so much.

'That's good,' said Elian quickly at the look on Perian's face. 'The colour will subside with time and use. It's meant to look like a lobster.'

A lobster! Perian shook the image free and looked away from the throbbing claw, hoping that Elian was telling him the truth. He absently noticed that evening had come by the dull light at the entrance as he took the deep breaths required to find his central point and concentrate on his scrying, then held out his hand for the first item.

'The earliest of the messages, if you please, Grison.'

Grison handed him the message, which Perian held in his left hand and moved about as best he could with his right. He found it held little of concern: a strong imprint of the writer, whom he assumed was the noble in charge of the relief troops. He dropped the paper into Grison's lap and indicated for the next one. He found the same imprint there, with the addition of handlers, including Saphrax. All seemed calm, although he was sending a few men over the line to investigate movement spotted against the evening sky. Perian sensed no agitation or concern from the man.

The next prickled with feelings, though, and made Perian sit forward. 'What does it say, Grison?'

Grison took the paper and read it out. '*Nothing to report. All is as it should be. I sent some men over the line to check on movement, but it was merely a cattle herder. I will report again in two days.* It is signed by Captain Nuffield, as were the others.'

'This is not by the same hand. It lies,' said Perian. His blood raced now and his hand throbbed. 'This person is highly emotional, triumphant and nervous. He is one of Ishra's men. They have come again, and march into Rashinder.'

Perian glanced briefly at the stiffened figure of Grison, whose eyes were so large they could have bounced from their sockets.

'Are you sure, Tanais? Look again.' His voice was hushed and strained.

Perian looked again, but saw the same images. There had been too few men, only watchers to report back on any activity, not a fighting force. Saphrax had been too confident and returned too soon. He didn't say this, though, merely reported what he saw. His personal opinion was of little use now. 'The border troops have been vanquished. The writer of the other notes is dead. They march on Jasperen.'

Grison stood as though to rush back to Saphrax, but Perian stopped him.

'The other, if you please, Grison. It won't take long.' He could feel the Voice's document from where he sat. It burned with treason in Grison's trembling hands as he gave it to Perian, who sucked in his breath at the hatred and avidity that flowed from it. 'This is a false document, as you surmised, Grison. This new Voice is vile in every way.' He stopped suddenly and moved his hand over the document again. 'They have sold Valamer to Ishra!'

His own shock was matched by that of Grison and Elian. 'Sold him! But why?' Grison gasped. His tremor had ceased, replaced by a deep red stain upon his cheeks and neck.

'Who can tell?' Perian glanced from one to the other. 'Perhaps Ishra thinks he is more useful as a hostage than dead. Whatever the reason, the priests would have been overjoyed to get rid of him.'

He needed to move and dispel the hint of hopelessness that had begun to settle about his shoulders, so scooted forward to drop his legs over the side of the pallet. He screwed up his face in concentration as he searched the document for more information.

'The priests have been collaborating with Wellorn, but I cannot see their purpose. I doubt they know that Ishra is in the process of invading Rashinder for the glorification of their god, Ortus, the Empty Eye.' He turned a glazed eye on Grison, who had shrunk within his clothing. 'That is not all. Valamer's abduction is only one part of the agreement. I am also part of this bargain. Why, I am not sure. I can only surmise that somehow she has learnt that I am a seer and fears that she will be unable to take Rashinder successfully if I am here to foresee her every move. The Voice doesn't know why I have been included and appears hesitant. He is thinking of keeping me for himself until he understands Ishra's use for me.'

Elian whistled through his teeth. 'Mage Armin won't like that.'

Perian shot him an irritated look of disapproval. He had almost managed to forget Armin for a while, but now he wondered whether the mage was in this mix somewhere, manipulating the players. The eyes of the Magi would be on Armin, not on the priests, which meant they might miss the larger play of events. But their eyes were also on him, and he hoped that this would alert them to Armin's machinations, if it were his doing.

'She has her own seer – Ortus's Oracle,' said Grison.

Perian twisted his head to look at Grison over his shoulder. Of course she would. It suddenly felt as though everyone was juggling with fate. 'In that case, she will kill me to leave the way open for her Oracle.'

Grison closed his eyes and rubbed his face, leaving it mottled and sickly. 'Is there any more, Tanais?'

'Elian and I must leave. We must find Valamer and bring him back before Rashinder crumbles from within and Ishra pounces from without. Soon the priest's soldiers will break down my door, as they did before. Then they will begin to search, if they haven't already, and we will find it difficult to get away.'

'Leave when?'

'Tonight,' Elian said. 'Before Valamer is too far away for me to pick up his scent.'

6

G rison stood slowly and placed a hand on the edge of Perian's pallet. 'I agree that we must get Valamer back. But are you the person to do it, Tanais, especially if Ishra intends to kill you?'

'Between myself and Elian's nose, we will find him if he lives. A battalion won't get near him, and we must leave anyway. At some point I will be discovered if I stay. Could you get us something suitable to wear so we don't stand out from the people?' Perian added.

Grison nodded. 'We sorely missed your insight while you slept, Tanais, and now we will miss it all over again.' He patted Perian's arm and walked toward the cave entrance.

'It is imperative that Saphrax gain control of the Voice and the priests,' Perian called after him. 'I have been thinking about my vision, and I can see no reason for the horror I witnessed in the south, despite the drought and all that follows in its wake. While not an easy task, Rashinder's lush north can easily support the south and Darna if the flow of resources is not interrupted by cheating and hoarding. My father was wise to set this flow in motion; Rashinder merchants profit and Darna survives until the rains come. But, of course, I could be seeing the result of a Wellorn victory. In the meantime, Saphrax might look to the priests if he suspects hoarding. And don't forget the clothes, Grison.'

Grison turned and looked back at Perian. Disconsolate, his shoulders bent forward as though to protect himself from what was to come. When Perian stopped talking, he left without a word, the swirl of his robes ushering in the chill evening air.

'Doesn't that mind of yours ever stop?' Elian spluttered. 'I'm exhausted just listening to you. I think if you had said one more word, poor Grison would have burst into tears or fainted.'

'I did notice him flinch with every new sentence, as though I were hammering him into the ground. But we aren't going to save Rashinder or Darna by feeding out what I see in small doses. There is so little time. My senses tell me that the priests gather as we speak. If they find me and see my tattoo, I am lost.'

'Have you foreseen this?'

'No. But that doesn't stop my imagination creating its own visions, nor my fear, and at the moment that is very great indeed.'

Elian stood and grasped Perian's face in his hands again. 'Fear will not help you. It will distract you into making mistakes. We will step into our unknown future together and do the best we can.'

Now Perian wanted to cry. He sniffed loudly and hit himself in the face with his enlarged right hand, trying to catch a small droplet that had slipped over his lower lid.

'Help me to walk, Elian. We need to be ready to leave once Grison returns with our clothing.'

Leaning heavily on Elian, he walked the length of the cave and back, which wasn't very far. His legs were thin, the muscles already wasted, and his joints felt stiff and unstable, his coordination wobbly. The whole exercise was quite painful. Thankfully, one of his guards arrived with their evening meal.

'Eat, Perian, then we will try again,' said Elian.

The entrance was now dark, the tick of night insects and the hearty thrust of waves echoing softly through the cave, carried on a cold night wind. Perian felt better and stronger with food in his belly, but this didn't stop him from wondering where Grison was. He was impatient to begin their journey, knowing that he could not go far for the next few days until he had regained at least a semblance of his original strength.

He swung his legs over the side of the pallet and placed his feet on the ground. They still tingled on contact, but not so much. Elian had just pulled him to his feet when a cloaked figure appeared in the entrance and stopped to watch the proceedings. Both Elian and Perian stared at the figure for a moment, their bodies tensing for action.

'Well, this doesn't look very hopeful,' came a woman's voice; a voice out of place, yet unmistakable.

'Jolint!' Elian shouted in surprise. He released his hold on Perian, letting him drop back on his pallet with a groan, rushing at Jolint and disappearing into the folds of her cloak.

Jolint's smile was all Perian needed to feel himself again. His head spun with pleasure and astonishment. He could scarcely believe that the sun had finally shone on this awful evening of doom and escape. 'Leave that man alone and let me see you!' he shouted from his bed.

She threw back her hood and, arm in arm with Elian, crossed the cave to where Perian stood wavering on the pallet's edge. He grasped her in his arms as soon as she was within reach and held her tightly to him with a controlled grunt of pain. Her arms about his chest made him feel safe and whole. They were together again. He had missed her dreadfully, and now, with her in his arms, he realised just how much – and how much he still missed Cerister. He'd caught a fleeting glimpse of Cerister, and others, in a bubble of sorts, in a vision he'd had prior to returning to his Darna family. The image began to connect with something Risenor had said. He cut it off; this wasn't the right time to trance. He had to leave.

'Look at your hand,' Jolint said as she released him back onto the bed's edge. 'It looks like …'

'A lobster, I know.'

She laughed and stroked his cheek. 'I got bored babysitting ex-royalty, so I came looking for you two. I thought Radia dead until I miraculously bumped into him along the harbourfront, waiting to board a boat. He caught another a week later.' She stretched out her arms for Perian to see. 'And he removed the ghastly wristlets the priestesses put on me.' She smiled happily and ran her hand over the fine silk shirt Perian wore. 'Prince after all, eh?' she clucked in her teasing way.

'And on the run again,' added Elian.

'I know. I asked to see Zameel Tanais and was met by Maltha's sorcerer, Grison. He will be here shortly with someone called Ben, who will be joining us on this adventure of yours.'

'Adventure! It's hardly that.' But a certain heaviness had lifted with Jolint's arrival; why shouldn't it be an adventure of sorts?

Because someone's life depends on it, said a little voice in his head.

He cast the voice aside and tried to recapture his moment of joy. 'Who said that Ben was coming with us?'

'I did,' said Grison, from beneath a bundle of clothing. 'Saphrax has insisted, and I agree with him.'

'He's too memorable,' Perian pointed out.

'Yes, but with that roving eye, no one will think him lethal,' said Elian. 'It will be a split-second judgement that will cost the enemy their life. I think it's a good idea.'

'Are we going to kill anyone?' Perian had been thinking along the lines of swooping into Ishra's encampment and whisking Valamer away without being noticed, which was unlikely when he gave it a little more thought.

Elian shrugged. 'Probably not, but we should take him just in case.'

Grison had spread the clothing over Perian's bed, separating it into two piles. Ordinary clothing; travel wear of good, yet inexpensive materials – rough cotton and wools, mostly, and hooded cloaks. He had probably borrowed Perian's from one of the taller warriors. Perian sniffed the shirt and was relieved to find it clean.

'You never used to be so fussy,' Jolint said. Perian ignored the comment and allowed her to help him change his clothes.

Ben struggled in with four satchels and blankets. Perian hardly recognised him out of uniform and dressed as a traveller, with trimmed and tousled hair and a rough-cut beard.

'One each,' he said, dropping them on the floor. 'And enough food and wine for several days. Longer if we miss breakfast.'

'Hopefully we'll find an inn before then. I like my breakfasts,' said Perian.

He slipped his arm into the sling. They were ready to go.

'Follow the coastal pathway to Pearl Beach, where you'll find a boat waiting to take you across the harbour to the White Cliffs. From there you will have to find your own way,' said Grison. 'I believe this is the route that would have been used to transport Valamer, but if not and they have gone overland, you will catch up with them sooner. Daniel here will go with you as far as Pearl Beach and report back to me that you have left safely.' Grison pointed to a stocky warrior with a sparse beard, a barrel chest and strong limbs, then grasped Perian's left hand and held it tightly between his palms. 'I would go with you, Tanais, but Saphrax needs me. Stay safe and come home, all of you, with or without Valamer.'

Perian smiled broadly at Grison's warm farewell. 'I'm far too used to the comforts of being a prince to stay away.' His mind drifted toward

Hector and he cursed himself for not having already acted upon his decision to set him free. He fixed Grison with his gaze. 'Free Hector for me, Grison, and ask Saphrax to release enough of my inheritance to him so he can return home or set himself up in a small business, or just drink himself into poverty. Whatever his heart's healing requires.'

'Of course.' Grison retrieved a bag from near his feet and handed it to Jolint. 'I believe there is enough of everything in here.'

Elian looked at her askance. 'Strips of leather, beads and ribbons,' she said, 'and strips of cloth for each of us to make our own headwear, desert Faran style, just in case we don't catch up with them before they re-enter Wellorn. With those eyes, Ben would probably be speared even before we crossed over the border, and Perian – well, they may err on the side of uncertainty and torture it out of him.'

Perian shook his head at her and walked to the cave entrance. He stopped for a moment to breathe in the fresh night air, where a star-encrusted net covered the sky and a sliver of moon hovered on the horizon. The warriors at the entrance stood to attention and placed their fists on their chests. Perian placed his left hand upon his heart and nodded as he passed by onto sand dotted with tussocks toward the chalk path that clung to the rocky cliffs this side of Zanig Harbour. He stared over the dark, heaving mass of ocean, welcoming the droplets of salty spray that splashed upon his face. Thoughts of travelling the open road once again had his spirit soaring to embrace the universe.

'Come, Perian,' Elian's voice broke in. 'You can commune with the stars another time. We must hurry.'

That was all very well for Elian to say, but he hadn't been lying on his back for a week and a half, nor trapped within the palace for who knew how long. Perian slogged on until they reached the pathway, then pulled out the stick that Grison had thought to provide so that he could take the gentle slope without appearing to be too much of an invalid or liability. Even with the aid of his stick, his lungs ached and his legs felt like jelly. He was gasping for breath before the path levelled out. The others had sprinted ahead, leaving Daniel to assist him.

A little way along, when the path followed a bend in the coastline that formed the Pearl Beach inlet, those ahead stopped suddenly and dropped to the ground, crawling backward until they had reached Perian and Daniel.

'Soldiers of the Sky God hiding in the rocks,' Jolint whispered. 'Is there an alternative plan?'

'Is there, Ben? I don't have one,' said Perian.

Ben turned a worried face toward the group, his eye moving about disconcertingly of its own volition. 'No, not really. Your departure was all too rushed.'

'How could they have known?' said Elian.

'Radia said the palace is riddled with secret passages for escape,' said Perian. 'I believe the priests have found them.'

Daniel stepped forward. 'My Zameel, if that is the case and they have been listening to Zameel Saphrax's conversations and plans, then all their eyes will be on the boat anchored in Pearl Beach. If we go back a little and down a narrow goat path to the beach, there will be a boat there that will take you to Andonin along the great curve of Zanig Harbour. You will have to pay well for the journey, and you will need to keep your face covered, as these are people who make it their business to recognise those they should avoid.'

Daniel stiffened at a look from Ben. 'It is of no matter,' Ben said after a moment. 'As long as they get us there safely and don't inform the priests, I think we can ignore their trade this once. You will do the negotiating for us, since you are clearly more familiar with them than we are, and you don't look like a tramp.'

They skidded and slid down the path, and Perian arrived in the sand on his bottom. Elian pulled him up and tugged his hood forward over his face.

'Daniel's right – everyone has seen you and knows what you look like. You sat on the royal platform at the solstice sacrifice for half an hour or so, in full view of the entire city and those further afield. The beardless Zameel, they call you, or the Prince of Flames.'

'You didn't tell me that!' Perian was shocked that the people talked about him at all.

'I just did. You didn't need to know before. You were the talk of the taverns after the aborted ceremony, evidently. Ask Ben, or Daniel.'

Perian didn't think he'd bother. People always talked about royalty and anyone else who had a scrap of power, which he didn't, as it turned out.

'I'd hide that hand as well,' said Jolint, rather louder than necessary. 'They might want to cook it.'

Ben, who walked beside to her, clicked and coughed, looking the other way to hide his mirth.

'They'll be just around this spread of rocks,' said Daniel. 'I'll go ahead, if you would follow slowly. Someone will come out to stop me and ask my business, and I will beckon when I am sure of those I speak to.'

Daniel disappeared over a low point where the cliff stretched out a rocky arm toward the sea. They waited as close as they dared, but still heard no voice or sound from the other side. Elian shifted into a wolf, pricked up his ears and sniffed the air.

He's found them, he said into Perian's mind. *They're talking about his request and haggling over the fee. They've agreed on two gold coins for each passenger.*

'Two! That's eight gold coins!' Perian exclaimed.

Ben looked up, startled.

'Shh,' said Elian, already back in human form.

Daniel popped his head over the rock and waved at them. 'They will take you.'

'We know,' said Ben. 'Two golds each.'

Four men in their later years stood waiting for them around a pit fire in the sand, while in the background, at least twenty other men of different ages, dark-tanned with threadbare clothing, busied themselves with fishing lines or openly stared at the visitors. Further back, amongst the rocks, were the women. They were scratching at fish on a table, sewing or preparing food. Perian could see children gawking at them through hanging curtains spread across small cliff cavities. Glancing further along, he saw rocks like buttress roots of varying sizes creeping across the beach toward the sea, providing privacy for the makeshift homes built in between.

Perian had met people like these, who lived in penury, their children begging on the streets and often pickpockets too. He surmised that their trade was delivering goods, mostly illegal, back and forth across the harbour to the various towns and villages. They were also fisherfolk who probably didn't have licences, but fished anyway because they had to.

While the older men stared at them, three younger men pushed a clinker fishing vessel out into the waves. Another stood upon the shore, waiting to release the rope. A chill wind whipped suddenly about the inlet, pulling on their cloaks and stirring the fire to pirouettes that cast flickering light and shade across their faces like the final dramatic act of a play. Perian pulled his hood closer.

''Arf now an 'arf when ye get there, as agreed,' said one of the men, whose lack of teeth gave his speech a nasal quality, muffled by the wind.

Ben laid four gold coins in the proffered gnarly hand.

'Don't remove yer hoods. We don't want to know who ye be should someone come askin'.'

As the others walked toward the boat, Perian grasped Daniel's arm and pulled him close. 'When you report to Grison, don't forget to remind him of the secret passages.'

A dribble of exhausted waves ran over Perian's feet as he watched the others clamber into the boat; Elian lagged behind to help him in. They sat on wooden benches on either side, the rear being taken up by a large box that stank of fish and brine. Boards covered part of the bow for the storage of goods to be transported, keeping it dry and hidden from any glancing eye.

Once the toothless negotiator was aboard, they pushed the boat out and the younger men, six in all, scrambled on board and began rowing them out to sea. Despite the gusts of cool wind that teased the gentle rips, it was a calm night, the ocean as gentle as it was ever likely to be. Perian stared up at the stars again, trying to pick out the constellations and allowing the whoosh and plop of the oars to settle his thoughts, the rhythmic pull and ease of the boat releasing his body's tension. No one spoke. Jolint, who sat next to him, placed her hand in his and gave it a squeeze; a private and intimate greeting. It was so good to have her close again.

Sooner than Perian expected, he could see the harbour lights of Andonin wriggling across the horizon. Fishing boats of different sizes with brightly coloured hanging lanterns began to dot the waters like a gathering of glowworms. Jolint released his hand to turn and gaze at the spectacle just as the boat lurched in the backwash of another vessel. She grasped the side rail to support herself, and Perian automatically put his freed hand upon the bench.

Recognition shot through his arm. He snatched his hand back, leaving himself vulnerable to the eccentric movement of the vessel. He touched the spot again and, although it was weak, he knew without reservation that Valamer had sat upon the bench within the last five days. That he lived was all Perian could tell.

'Another group used your services,' Perian said to the older man, when the boat's movement had settled again. 'How many days since?'

'That's no business of yers,' he replied.

All eyes turned to Perian. Ben acted quickly and spread five silver coins across his palm, which drew a derisive sniff and slight turn of the head from the old man. Ben got out two more silver coins, and again the amount was shunned.

'It is of no importance,' Perian said, looking out to sea again. Ben put the money back in his pocket, producing the desired effect.

'Two golds,' the man said.

'One gold, final,' Perian said, more to test the man's trustworthiness than a need for the information. He could tell the trace had been laid down recently.

The man flicked his head back to indicate acceptance and waited for Ben to produce the correct amount.

'Three days gone,' he said.

The harbour town had drawn inexorably closer during this brief bargaining. Already Perian could see the white strip of sand that led to a natural wall of rock, above which sat the dock where people promenaded before the little harbour coffee houses and tea merchants. He would be very glad now to be within the safety of that crowd beyond the sea, beyond the beach and just beyond the wall. The smuggler had been too easily bought, assuming he had told the truth. It wouldn't be long before the priests' men wandered down to that inlet and asked questions, which meant they would be on their trail in a day, or two at the most – unless, of course, they had already asked for notification of any cloaked and hooded individuals requiring quick passage. If that were the case, who knew whether they even had a day's grace?

7

Ben had spent two weeks in Andonin soon after the Darna conquest, so he was familiar with the layout of the streets, where the inns and taverns were. More importantly, he had made friends with a man who kept horses on the edge of town. Once they had scrambled up the beach and joined the flow of traffic along the concourse, he led them down the town's winding back streets to where the horse trader lived. They raised him from his bed and secured four sturdy horses, riding several miles along the coast before turning off onto the trade route that led to the Silver River in the direction of Sun Mountain. They didn't stop until dawn began to blossom ahead of them.

'We should stop for a bit, before I get blisters,' said Perian.

'I agree,' said Elian. 'It's time for the prince's breakfast, and I'm famished.'

Perian lifted himself in his saddle to peer along the road where knotted brambles guarded the fields either side with no break that he could see. Beyond the hedgerow on his right, the dry pink stubble of harvested crops awaited the plough, and to his left sheep stirred to begin their busy day's grazing in a field of lush grass. There would be a gate further along the road, and if they hurried, they could nip in out of sight for a short rest before the farmhands arrived to begin work.

The dewy grass dampened their feet, but a fallen tree kept them mostly dry while they ate and rested in silence, listening for any riders that may be following. When no one appeared and they had eaten their allowance, Elian shifted into a dark grey wolf. He pressed his nose into the piece of Valamer's shirt that Perian kept in his satchel and loped onto the roadway to sniff the air and snuffle about the dirt.

'There were rumours that Elian led the Almonos Guards the night of the uprising,' said Ben, drawing Perian's attention back from the activity on the road. 'But I took little notice, it seeming so impossible, until the day we found Valamer gone and poor Rolin and Lono dead in his chambers. Only then, when he changed into the wolf, did I believe it. One minute he stood next to me, as shocked as all of us, and the next he was a wolf, sniffing about the floor and over the bed linen. I had to shout at the warriors to stop them from running him through with their swords.'

Perian thought it just like Elian not to warn anyone. He thought about how it must have been for those present and for Ben to see his brother dead in the vestibule.

'I was sorry to hear about Rolin, Ben. It must have been dreadful for you. I think my heart would break if I lost Elian.'

'It was, and it did,' said Ben. He looked away from Perian and pretended to concentrate on those along the road.

Elian returned, shaking his head, rescuing Perian from having to think of something appropriate to say.

'Nothing.' Elian put his hand on his horse's neck and gathered the reins. 'We should go now if we are going to close the distance. It would be better if we found him before he gets to Carios, if that's where they are taking him.'

'I think the soldiers still have him. They will exchange near or on the border,' said Ben.

'Then we must get him back first,' said Perian. 'But exchange for what?'

Ben shrugged and shook his head. 'Who knows? They must be getting something. Why risk transporting him otherwise, when it would be easier to kill him and dispose of the body, or lock him up until they have control, then stretch him out on the stones?'

The thought of Valamer laid out across the sacrificial stones made Perian shiver. He wished Ben hadn't mentioned it.

He heaved himself onto his horse with a gentle shove from Jolint. He would have to stop again soon, to rest and sleep. His joints ached and he was lightheaded from lack of proper nourishment. He allowed his horse to follow the others from the field and clung to his saddle in a daze as they galloped toward the next village.

It was Jolint who suggested they stop when they came to a cluster of cottages with an inn for tired travellers. 'We must stop at the inn for a decent meal, perhaps hire a room for Perian to sleep for a while.'

Ben and Elian looked from Jolint to Perian, who was slumped over his saddle. Elian nodded his agreement and they rode into the small stables behind the inn.

'Food first, Perian, or sleep?' he asked as he pulled him from his horse.

'Food, then sleep.'

Yesterday's stew arrived piping hot, and Perian consumed most of his bowl in no time at all once it had cooled a little. The speed with which he ate left him nauseous, and he'd burned his tongue in his rush, but overall he felt better.

They were seated outside, and six or so locals sat drinking ale on the benches either side of a long table opposite. They glared at the visitors suspiciously until Ben removed his hood and waggled his eyes at them with a flashing smile, bidding them a good morning with the lifting of his mug. The women roared with laughter until Jolint dropped her hood and shook out her long, red hair. Elian, like Perian, just raised his glass.

Ben fixed one of his eyes on the women and asked them what news they had from the glorious banks of the Silver River.

'War,' said one of the men before the women had a chance to reply. He had sunken cheeks and bushy eyebrows.

'Me cousin from the next village visited two day ago now,' said one of the women. 'Said that Kellerton, a day's ride from her brother in the next village to her, was inundated with them's escaping the fighting.'

'Burning, killing, raping and a-looting, she said,' put in the other.

'You'd best turn back if the Silver River be your destination,' said the man. 'None too many travellers come this way, but yer's the second in three day. The others will have heard the news by now, but they not come back this way yet.'

'Where you four from?' asked a round woman with a green ribbon about her hat. 'Not seen many Darna round these parts, nor Faran these past years. Faran used to come by regular with their physiques, dancing and singing.'

Jolint turned to look at Elian and Perian. Elian stared from within his hood. Perian couldn't remember the tribes singing and dancing, definitely no physiques, and this was obviously a surprise to Jolint and Elian. Gisela was poison.

'We're from Andonin,' said Jolint in answer to the woman's question.

The group nodded and went back to talking amongst themselves. Ben, Elian and Jolint started arguing about how long it would be before they encountered the first refugees. Perian began thinking of the group before them, of there not being many Darna along this road. It would have been surprising if there had been, since most of the Darna in Rashinder were in Jasperen or on the border with Wellorn.

He tugged at Elian's shirt. 'Ask them if the other group were Darna.'

Elian pushed his hood back a little and asked as Perian had requested.

'Nah,' said the man. 'Rashinder like us. Why, you lost someone?'

'Yes,' intervened Ben. 'I'm looking for my brother, who left to find a bit of work as a farrier. He found Andonin too crowded.'

'Landed in a heap of trouble if he got as far as the Silver River,' said the woman with the green ribbon.

'We heard that one of the other group to pass through was very ill,' said Perian.

The locals stared at him with narrowing eyes. Perian pushed his hood back a little; it was unlikely that any of these people had attended the aborted sacrifice.

'Aye,' said a woman who hadn't spoken so far. 'Could hardly stand. Supported by two woman, he was.'

Jolint gasped. 'Ishra's priestesses,' she whispered.

Of course the priests had relinquished their prize earlier, possibly in Jasperen. Ishra wouldn't want the Voice to know too soon about her push into Rashinder, and had they got this far, they would have discovered her deceit and turned back.

Perian stood and pulled his hood forward again; he needed to lie down and sleep for a short while. He wondered what the priests thought now, with Saphrax's troops rushing to the border. It occurred to him that he had left too soon, but he would always have gone in search of Valamer regardless of what the priests intended. This was the path he was meant to take. He hadn't seen it in a vision; he felt it deep within his heart.

Elian woke him from a deep sleep two hours later. 'There are Soldiers of the Sky God downstairs asking questions.'

Perian shot upright, shaking a little from the suddenness of his movement. Jolint was peering through the window, hidden by the curtain, and Ben was listening at the door he held slightly ajar.

'The innkeeper is refusing to let the soldiers inspect the rooms and disturb his clientele,' said Ben.

'They're going,' said Jolint, relaxing her stance. 'Two came in and two have left. There are five altogether.'

Elian joined her at the window. Perian slid from the bed to stand between them and peer down at the two leaving the inn. One of them looked up at the window as they approached the others waiting on the other side of the street.

'Shapeshifter,' hissed Elian. He turned to Perian. *A shifter,* he repeated, into Perian's head this time. *Does this mean what I think it means?*

Perian suddenly felt sick. A shapeshifter meant only one thing, they both knew that: Armin was getting ready to make his move. There would be a dead soldier hidden along the road somewhere.

Perian closed his eyes and put his left hand to his forehead. Just how much worse could it all get? He thought briefly of the swan. Perhaps he hadn't been imagining things after all.

A knock on the door made them all jump. When Ben opened the door, the innkeeper's son, a tall, muscled youth, announced that the soldiers had gone and one of the kitchen hands was watching to make sure they left the village.

'If you're heading for the Silver River, there is another, smaller road that the locals use, which will take you to the same place,' said the youth. 'The soldiers have continued along the road, but they may decide to come back, so you must leave now.'

They gathered up their satchels and followed him down the stairs. Ben offered the innkeeper a few gold coins to repay his kindness, but he refused, saying that it was his pleasure to 'put the buggers off their scent'.

Ben asked him about the previous group.

'Aye. A group of six running from the soldiers stopped here for a bite to eat three or four days ago. One of them could hardly stand and left blood all over the bench.'

Ben shook his head. 'Let's hope they don't stop along the way and are far beyond those you have just turned away. The soldiers are cruel to those who cross their path.'

'Aye,' said the innkeeper. He flicked his head toward his son. 'Young'un here showed them the local road, as he will you, so's they could take their time and the sick one heal a bit.'

Any benefit Perian might have experienced from food and rest had been diminished by the appearance of the shapeshifter, and although he felt physically stronger, his spirits plummeted. His sense of defeat increased with the knowledge that Armin must be watching him. That the mage had not made his move yet suggested he was not close enough, but he couldn't be far away. Perian was easier prey now that he had left the palace, and he found himself studying everyone they passed with breathless suspicion.

We have Jolint now, Elian said into his head.

Perian glanced at him. Armin's attack in Jasperen played out in his mind. Even with Jolint, their chances against the mage were slim.

They passed the first of the refugees two days later at Kellerton: glassy-eyed villagers from further east travelling along the roadway with carts of possessions and children. Some had minor injuries; others lay groaning in the carts amongst household goods. Perian found it a miserable and disheartening sight. As soon as there was a break in the flow of dispossessed families, he pulled down his hood to let the wind blow through his hair and clear the murk. He looked over the lush fields of contented cows and sheep still untouched by the devastation and listened to the birds singing sweetly from their branches.

After another day's relentless ride, they could smell smoke blowing in from the east.

'I must stop,' said Perian. His body hurt more than the pressure that was building in his head. The road wound about woodland on their right and there was another break in the stream of people. 'It's time you had another sniff at the road, Elian.'

Elian changed quickly and inhaled deeply of the scrap of cloth Perian held in his hand. He sniffed the road, snorting from the dust, then ran along the grass verge, where he began to circle excitedly at a bend in the road further up. He followed the scent for a short distance and sniffed the air before bounding back.

'Got him,' he shouted. 'They have slowed their pace and rested up there on the side of the road.'

'If it's Perian they want as well, they might just wait somewhere and jump us, knowing that he will follow,' said Jolint.

'How would they know that?' put in Elian.

Perian couldn't follow the conversation, and their speculations were driving him mad, like bees buzzing about looking for something to settle on. He was angry and hot, although he didn't know why, and he just wanted to sit on the grass and close his eyes. He stretched his neck to loosen his jaw and noticed that his hands shook upon the saddle. The constant stress of waiting for Armin to strike was wearing him down.

He swung his leg over the horse's back and slid down the animal's side until his feet touched the ground. He pressed his hand against its side and dropped his forehead onto the saddle until he felt Elian's hand on his back.

'What is it, Perian?'

'I need to sit on the grass, feel the earth beneath me, inhale what is left of the fresh, uncontaminated air.'

Elian raised his eyebrows at the others. 'To the field.'

He found Perian a patch of healthy grass near a young elm, where he sat with his legs stretched out and his back against the trunk. With a deep sigh of relief, Perian grasped Elian's hand, held it to his chest and closed his eyes. He wanted to sleep forever. He had never been so tired. He could vaguely hear Elian telling him not to trance, that it was the wrong time and place, but the desire to give in to his needs and drift was too great.

Then a woman's voice broke sharply into his reverie. 'Perian Tanais, wake up. We must talk.'

His eyes shot open. At first he was confused, then, with the dark squeeze of despair, he realised he was back in the cell of his nightmarish vision; he had fallen into trance. He shouted out his frustration and fell to his knees. Would he never have a different vision and forever end up here, in this worst of all places?

'I hope not, Tanais, but it is possible if you don't hurry,' came the voice again.

He looked up sharply and glanced about, but he could see no one else in the room and wondered if he had imagined the voice.

'Hurry where?' he said, just in case. 'There is nowhere to hurry to.'

'Wake up, Tanais. You're still asleep. Wake up and open your mind. You of all people are never trapped. It is for you to shed light on this room. For you to create your own safe place in which to view your visions. Aronaye should have taught you this. No matter now.'

'Shine a light! How do I do that?' Perian nearly choked on his great desire to know and, at the same time, his need to get away and back to Elian. As before, the only feeble light came from his tattoo, and he had no control over that.

'What a tiny light,' she scoffed. 'Come to me, Tanais. We need to talk.'

He felt her leave, although he wasn't aware of her *being* there. He resented her insult concerning his glowing tattoo – that he had light at all was a blessing, no matter where it came from or its intensity. He put his head to the floor, closed his eyes and released himself to the slow rhythmic swaying he distantly perceived in the space about him.

Elian's arm tightened about his waist, pulling him closer, as Perian gasped his way back to his senses. He didn't stir immediately. He watched the movement of the horse's neck and the strands of its mane flaring in the wind, letting his eyes slide slowly to stare at the ground as it sped past with the animal's cantering. The day was still bright and he felt the sun high on the back of his head. A few birds sang in the heat of the early afternoon. He flexed his shoulders before lifting his head and turning to Elian.

'Have I missed lunch?'

'No, you're in luck, we haven't stopped yet.'

'Perhaps we could stop at the next village. I feel in need of something sturdy to eat. Was I gone long?'

'No, not so long. We needed to keep moving. Can you ride? We'll get there the quicker and I'll be able to see where I'm going.'

They stopped briefly for Perian to change mounts, arriving in the next village within the hour. They had zigzagged around people and carts much of the way. Families of dazed men, women and children gathered briefly in the village before moving on to find relatives or shelter further along. From what people said and the thickness of the smoke haze, Ben judged that the Wellorn army was probably less than a day away.

They took seats away from the crowded tavern frontage and ordered bread, cheese and ale.

'What happened?' Elian asked Perian after swallowing the last of his bread, whispering into Perian's hood, which he kept a little forward. 'I haven't lost you like that for ages. And who were you talking to?'

'Did I speak? I wasn't aware.'

'Not exactly. You made little noises. The cadence of your grunting was like that of speech.'

'I am afraid, Elian. I feel that I no longer have control of anything anymore. I thought I had for a while, yet still my visions are invaded by others, even those I don't know.' Elian made no comment, so Perian continued. 'I found myself in that awful vault. I'd hardly had time to realise where I was when a woman's voice addressed me. She knew my name – both of my names – and she said that Aronaye should have taught me how to create my own vision cell. She wants to talk to me.'

Perian's voice had been rising with his frustration, and Jolint turned to give him a warning look.

'Who is she?' Elian asked. 'Friend or enemy?'

'Friend, I think, or at least neutral. But I cannot be sure. She sounded cross with Aronaye, rather than amused as an enemy might if they were triumphant that you were left vulnerable by improper training.'

'Do you think she is one of the Magi, or a teacher?'

'Perhaps.' Perian drank down the remainder of his ale. 'Stay close to me, Elian. I feel safer knowing you are within reach, even if I am whisked away again, which I think I will be sooner rather than later.'

'And I will feel safer once we are all back in Jasperen Palace, especially with Armin's shifters searching for you. Let's go.'

Jolint took Perian's arm as they walked toward their horses. He squeezed it with his right hand and, with a burst of happiness, realised that at some point during their journey his hand had returned to normal. 'What will you do when this is all over, Jolint?'

'We had a wonderful week together, Radia and I, talking and walking along the harbour, but in the end we decided to go our separate ways. So, I have decided to hang about with you two again; the three of us, as it should be.'

She smiled at him and he squeezed her arm again.

They mounted and sped along the road. Fearful of coming across another of Armin's shapeshifters, Perian continued to study everyone they passed, a debilitating exercise.

A turn-off to the north, away from the fighting, came up unexpectedly. Elian confirmed that Valamer and his kidnappers had followed the north road. It skirted a thick forest in a wide arc before turning east again toward Sun Mountain, shrouded in heavy cloud. When they crested the hill, the Silver River glistened before them in a cradle of grassland outlined and protected by water-loving trees and shrubs.

They stopped for a moment to survey the road ahead and enjoy the beauty of the river as it slithered rapidly toward the sea, before riding down to the wooden bridge, where they slowed to walking pace to listen to the roar of rushing water and feel the fresh, cool air that wafted up either side as they crossed. Perian found it exhilarating and refreshing after the dusty, hurried journey they had taken.

That feels better, said Elian into his head.

Perian threw back his hood and smiled happily at his brother. He would try to remember this moment in the days to come, during their days of separation and difficulty that he knew in his bones lay ahead.

They stopped on the other side of the bridge to let the horses drink, to stretch their legs and, in some ways, to delay what was to come; they were close now to their destination, wherever that was. Elian knelt by the water's edge and splashed his face like an overexcited child. When he had shaken his hair free of excess water, he shifted into the wolf and began sniffing along the road. Perian could see that he'd caught a strong scent even before Elian bellowed it into his mind and took off up the rise toward the hilltop. Perian's heart jumped, and he could not quell the panic that suddenly took hold of him. Why was the scent suddenly so strong when the object of their search should still be a day or so ahead – unless they had laid a trap?

He called after Elian, but the wolf had taken over and Elian vanished over the hill. Perian felt the strike within him even more than the wave of dissipating magic that wafted down the hill. Jolint looked up, startled. Perian grabbed his horse, threw Valamer's rag to Jolint and raced after Elian, leaving Ben and Jolint behind. He turned and called back to them as his horse strained up the slope. 'Get Valamer and come for me when I call.'

Over the hill, Perian found a very different scene to the tranquillity he had just left. Elian lay on the verge and at least fifteen men and two women spread across the road. One of the men was approaching

Elian. Perian drove his horse between them, forcing the man to step back. He glanced at Elian. He was not bleeding, and his chest still moved rhythmically with breath; he was alive.

'Leave him,' Perian shouted, trying to control his overstimulated horse. 'I am Zameel Tanais, and it is me you want. Leave him and I will go with you freely.'

One of the women shouted at the man to stop, and he took the reins of Perian's horse instead and led it toward the middle of the road.

'Get down and show me your arms,' said the same woman.

He did as he was told. Moving away from his horse, he removed the leather about his forearms and lifted them to display his tattoos: one showing him to be a Darna prince, the other showing him to be a sorcerer of some power, although not in the way the priestess probably thought.

The man who had approached Elian stepped behind him, so close that Perian could feel his breath on his neck – they were going to kill him after all. Perhaps Valamer was already dead. Anticipation of sudden death tightened his throat and gripped his lungs, so it was hard to breathe or speak. He waited, tense and terrified, for the knife to slide across his throat and his lifeblood to gush out upon the roadway.

He jumped when the man gripped his shoulder, feeling faint with the misery of life lost in the dust. As he averted his eyes so as not to be staring at the woman in his last moments, he caught a glimpse of silver wristlets beneath her cloak. Sudden hope lit the dark spots of his despair. Why bring such an item if they didn't mean to preserve him, for a while at least?

She stepped closer to him, confirming in his mind that he was currently safe. The woman was slender, with a rounded face and harsh grey eyes that Perian could not imagine ever softening. He recognised her as an Ortus Priestess by the power that danced about her. Jolint was probably a good match for one, but not two of them.

He nodded toward her cloak. 'You won't need those,' he squeezed through a throat still tight from the expectation of death. 'I have said I will go with you freely. I am a seer and have little power that could assist me in escape or injury to yourself or the others.'

She stared at him as though he had said something shocking.

'An Oracle!' burst out the other priestess.

'Be quiet,' snapped the first woman. She turned back to Perian. 'Very well, but if you cause any trouble, I will not listen to you again. Put the leathers back on and your hood up, and come with us. My Mistress is waiting for you.'

8

The day hovered on twilight when they stopped at what remained of an abandoned single-room cottage. Perian was guided to a windowless corner, where someone had gathered old and decaying hay. The central fire had been previously prepared and one of the men struck a flint to catch the kindling while another pulled their stores from a cupboard. The partial collapse of the roof, which included the smoke hole, gave Perian a view of the still-bright sky.

He had thought Ishra would kill him to remove a potential heir and Rashinder's advantage of a seer, but perhaps she wanted him as extra leverage in negotiations for her takeover. If this were the case, she would be disappointed – Saphrax had no love for him. So, what was it that Ishra might want of him? It couldn't be his seer's skill that she required; she already had a seer. After all, how many did you need to contradict each other and demonstrate the contrariness of fate? If she just wanted to question him, then she would again be disappointed. He knew nothing – and why, when she had Valamer in her cells? If she hurt him enough, even Valamer would talk, he imagined.

The fire had died down, most of his captors were asleep and the moon had passed overhead when Elian finally spoke to him.

I'm sorry, Perian. I'm all right, just a little sore. We are behind you, following at a suitable distance. Be safe, my brother.

Elian was alive and safe! Perian closed his eyes and savoured a wave of emotional and physical release, then fell asleep.

Their journey the next day was much the same as the day before: silent and hurried. They passed fields and woodland, squeezed through rocky passages and crossed streams with little bridges over which they rode single file, only to ride even faster on the other side, as though time had been wasted. Birds sang merrily amidst the trees and bushes, belying Perian's apprehensive mood and the vague trembling fear that sat within his chest.

Around early afternoon, they crested a hill and stopped to look over a small town, the first they had come to that day. At its centre stood a tall, rounded building of white marble surround by a skirt of formal gardens, fruit trees and topiary bushes in the shape of the Empty Eye – a temple dedicated to Ortus. Somewhere along the way they had passed into Wellorn and travelled upward on the slopes of Sun Mountain, where the frigid air carried the smells of high altitude. By the looks of pleasure on the faces of his captors, Perian assumed that this was their destination, or at the least the first stop.

People in the street stopped what they were doing and averted their eyes as the troop passed by; the sounds of everyday life were brought to a sudden halt, leaving only the wind and animals to intrude on the thud of eighteen horses pounding toward the temple gates. Perian found it an eerie and strange experience, especially the conflicting emotions that accompanied their passage: the haughty demeanour of the troops, the priestesses in particular, and the nervous energy that emanated from the people.

He remembered Elian saying that everyone in Carios was overly religious. He hadn't taken much notice of his comment at the time, but now he began to understand: Ishra controlled her people through fear. No wonder the Magi were keen to stop the spread of the Empty Eye. The Shanahan of Rashinder had been a sloppy ruler and his brothers had diced with rebellion through their dealings with the lords, but the people never had cause to be afraid, as far as he knew.

The sudden clatter of horse hooves on stone slabs brought Perian back from his speculations as they passed through the gates into the temple grounds. A hint of frankincense and sandalwood wafted through the temple entrance with the opening of its doors. Young men and boys in white robes came from nowhere to take their horses as the troop dismounted. One of the soldiers tapped Perian's leg for him to get down and told him to remove his leather guards. With his feet on the ground and his horse whisked away, he was overcome by a sense of helplessness, as though his last chance of escape had been taken from him.

They entered a large round hall that mirrored the curve of the outer walls. The sounds of their entry bounced strangely off the interior marble, overlapping at its centre and causing a slight vibration in the air. Perian viewed the vestibule with only a vague interest, the major part of his concentration being on the door ahead and the ordering of his breath to calm himself and keep his wits sharp for his encounter with the woman who ruled over a vast kingdom and now controlled his life and future. Above all, he wanted to keep his dignity. Whatever happened in the next few minutes or hours may determine whether he and Valamer lived, and possibly the future of Rashinder and Darna, since these two empires were now entwined.

A guard opened the great wooden doors and Round Face prodded his shoulder to urge him forward into a large square hall. Queen Ishra sat near the far wall on a white marble throne bathed in fractured sunlight from a large oval window in the roof. The sight of her shocked him, although he didn't know why, since he'd known they were taking him to the queen. Perhaps it was the light used to illuminate their sovereign rather than blind the populace, as it did in Jasperen Palace.

Queen Ishra wore a simple white robe and had pulled her dark hair back to hang loose beneath a single band of diamonds that glistened about her head. At the front of the band sat a large, clear crystal carved into the shape of the Empty Eye.

Despite his calming techniques, Perian's body vibrated, his trepidation nearly overwhelming him. He forced his lungs to expand and take breath. He clenched his hands at his sides in case they began to shake.

As the trio came to a stop about thirty paces from the throne, a smile broke across the queen's thin, slightly pointy features. 'Welcome, Zameel Tanais.'

Her eyes glistened with predatory pleasure, which took Perian by surprise. He bowed his head by way of reply, but the impatient priestess by his side pushed for proper protocol and shouted at him to kneel before their queen.

'Leave him, Timary.'

Queen Ishra stood and walked slowly toward him. A hem of stiff braid kept her feet hidden and gave the impression that she glided. The drumbeat in his chest echoed in his ears. He braced himself for an assault, but instead she stopped in front of him, her dark eyes slowly studying him from head to foot, then she walked around him as though appraising the quality of a purchase. To his disgust, he blushed with her slight nod and smile of approval; why did he care whether she liked the look of him or not? Her eyes drifted toward his forearms and he lifted them for her to see his tattoos before Timary could shout at him again.

'Take him to the Oracle,' the queen said, as though she had made a sudden decision, and turned away before he could make eye contact.

The Oracle! Why the Oracle? Was she going to scry him for information instead of torture it from him? Preferable, of course, but his nerves jangled, nearly suffocating him. They would find that he had no information to give, with the exception that Darna warriors were heading toward her army, and she didn't need him to tell her that.

The guard stood in front of him, blocking Ishra's back from his sight, so he put his head around the man's large frame and called to her, 'Does Valamer live?' Afraid as he was of the answer, he needed to know.

'Yes, and will continue to do so unless you refuse to comply,' she said without turning.

The guard nodded toward the door and Timary produced a silver rod – from where, Perian could not say. He decided to 'comply', as she put it, and followed the guard from the room. He was still alive and wasn't going to the cells, yet; he should probably be thankful. And Valamer still lived. He had enjoyed the look of surprise on Timary's face. Or was it disappointment?

Their march took them through another door off the vestibule and into a large courtyard filled with trees showing their first flush of autumnal colouring. A cold wind swept down from the peak of Sun Mountain and whistled about the confined space, scattering leaves and forming tiny dust whirls along the path. At the centre of the courtyard a fountain sprayed them with water, diverted from its natural downward plunge in the fast-moving air. Perian pulled his cloak tightly about him and hoped that the Oracle had a fire going; he hated the cold. If they wanted him to submit, they should keep him warm and his tendency toward stubbornness at bay, although they'd probably find a way around that kind of thing; threats to Valamer's life, for instance, or his.

They passed beneath an arbour of woody stems, the wisteria having already answered the call to hibernate, and out into a cloistered courtyard. At its centre stood a round, one-storey tower of whitewashed wattle and daub, capped by a pointy thatched roof. The windows were circular and glassless, spiralling around the building to the top, the first being just above head height. Perian found it strange, yet beautiful in its natural simplicity and not at all at odds with the fine marble walls that surrounded it. The smell of sage and rosemary escaped the spaces around the plain wooden door.

'Remove your boots,' ordered Timary. 'You must not wear boots inside.'

Perian placed his boots on the flat stone she pointed to on the right of the door, leaning them carefully against the wall so she couldn't see the knives he hid in special pockets in the lining. He was amazed that they hadn't checked him for weapons when he was first taken.

Before he could straighten, the door opened and a young woman of eighteen or so stood within the doorframe. She was a novice, by her grey attire. She gave him a quick nod and beckoned for him to follow.

The door closed behind them, shutting out the guard and priestess and plunging them into darkness relieved only by a dim, jagged light that ran across the top of a curtain. The latch clicked into place, finally severing the priestess's malevolent grip on him. Perian shivered with relief at his release. He pulled himself upright to counter the sag of his shoulders and his sudden desire to lie down and scream.

The young woman pulled the curtain aside, and he found he was standing in a small foyer that followed the curve of the building, as did the benches along the walls. She urged him into a round inner room lit by the spiralling windows that now reminded him of the passage of moon and sun. A single lit candle stood on a small table.

The Oracle sat cross-legged at the room's centre on a large, padded mat the colour of saffron. She patted it for him to join her as the curtain closed behind him, leaving them alone.

Perian glanced about, but there were no corners or hidden places for someone to crouch awaiting who knew what, with the exception of a curtain behind the Oracle, which presumably led to another room. Behind him, near the entrance, he noticed a rolled mattress and blankets. The hard-packed earthen floor was covered by a woven carpet of dyed grasses typically used by desert Farans, and the crisscross weave of this one formed dizzying squares of red and indigo, which had fortunately faded with use.

He accepted the Oracle's invitation and sat similarly cross-legged on the edge of the mat in front of her. Her white hair hung loose about her shoulders and her face was creased with age, but her violet eyes shone wide with a never-fading youth. Her pallor, though, told him something different. He needed no seer's skills to tell him that she was dying. She smiled at his surprise that she was Faran, and tinkling laughter issued from her small frame.

The room was thankfully warm and comfortable. Perian was astonished to find that he felt safe, as though the outside world had been shut out and could not get to him. It occurred to him that he had almost forgotten what that felt like. He had been afraid for so long.

The Oracle nodded as though she understood his sense of peace and stretched out the long fingers of her thin hand to touch his knee. The physical contact sent a spark through his body, but he didn't flinch, nor did he find it disturbing.

'Welcome,' she said in a soft, melodic voice – the voice that had invaded his vision.

'Why am I here and not dead or in a cell like Zamir Valamer?' Perian's deep masculine voice sounded coarse and out of place in the calm envelope of the Oracle's towering room.

'Because your role in this great game is different to Valamer's.'

'What great game?' He had interrupted and wished he hadn't, his voice overly sharp. He was becoming impatient and, deep down, was still uncertain of Ishra's intention, despite his current sense of ease.

The young woman suddenly reappeared with a jug and two glasses balanced on a tray. His eyes bulged slightly at a plate of small delicacies, the whole of which he thought he could devour in one mouthful had he not been restricted by good manners. She placed the tray beside them and left without a word.

'She is small for her age, but she will make a good Oracle when needed. Not a brilliant one, but quite good enough for her time.' The Oracle leant forward and poured water from the jug for them both. 'The water is pure and brought straight from the spring. The vine puffs are for you. They are a Wellorn specialty, crunchy on the outside and soft and sweet on the inside. We warm them in the cooler weather.'

Perian picked one up and studied it for a moment, trying to decide how to eat such a delicacy without the insides escaping. In the end he tossed the whole into his mouth and clenched his lips tightly, as one does with small tomatoes that have a tendency to squirt. The little vine puff was delicious and he took another. Once he had washed the second puff down with water, he turned his mind back to why he was here in audience with the Oracle.

'Do you intend to scry me for information?' he asked.

Her smile was delightful, and its appearance upon her face warmed him, although he could not tell why; perhaps because she was Faran and familiar for that reason.

'No, Tanais, there is little you can tell me of yourself or anything of political significance to me. Ishra would be very interested in what you could tell her, but that is not why you are here. She will not ask, and she will not demand it of you.'

His thoughts swung about for a moment, trying to sort themselves into order. It made him cross that everyone had a foot in his life and his trances. Were his boundaries so transparent? And what happened to privacy? Did no one have any morals? Beyond his indignation, there was the more worrying aspect to what she had said. Why wouldn't Ishra ask?

'The novice,' he said. 'Does she know you are dying?'

'No. She mustn't, not yet, nor should anyone else. Only Ishra knows, and you, now.'

'So, she *is* your apprentice. Is she capable of taking over once you have gone?'

'You already know this, Tanais, but I will tell you so it is clear in your head. I have taught Lili all I can. As I said, her seer's abilities are limited, and I can teach her no more. She is not my apprentice. You are. You will be the Wellorn Oracle when I pass from this life.'

Perian stared at her, unable to comprehend what she had said. His mind whirled and his stomach clenched tight; his whole being shouted for him to run, to escape this place and the life of servitude they planned for him.

He shot to his feet and took a step backward, pressing his fists against his chest in an attempt to fight down the need to scream and bolt like a frightened animal. 'No,' he shouted. 'She cannot expect this of me. How can I submit to such a life, enslaved to Ishra and Ortus? Does she intend to keep Valamer locked up until he dies of old age, watching his empire and life dissipate in damp darkness?'

He thought of Elian, where his hopes of rescue had dwelt. Impossible now. Everyone wanted to possess him. His blood pounded through his veins with anger and his inability to escape. Helplessness and horror left him weak and breathless. He fell to his knees and put his head in his hands.

'Please stay calm, Tanais,' she said. 'I know how you must feel —'

'You do not,' he interrupted. He looked up at her face, which was serene despite his outburst.

'How repulsive the idea is to you,' she continued. 'But there is more to your presence here than you can see. You will need the skills I can teach you. Most importantly, how to build your own trance room and how to protect yourself against invasion. For High Oracles such as you and I, there are greater dangers than the ones who watch you – dangers that you have not yet encountered, but that you will in the expanse of your life, as I have. I have lived a very long life and encountered horrors you cannot conceive. My Mistress passed to me the knowledge that kept me alive and sane. I have built on that knowledge over the years and waited for someone worthy with whom to share it. I mean you no harm, and more importantly in the present, nor does Ishra.'

His panic subsided a little with her words, and despite his inner turmoil, Perian noticed for the first time that her lips had not moved – that she spoke into his mind as Elian did. He forced himself to calm down a fraction so he could hear what it was that she could not say aloud.

The Oracle sat perfectly still, watching him. She stirred a little now, her silent voice softer. *Without what I can teach you, Tanais, you will die.*

Her words hit him like a whip that left him trembling inside. She had seen an alternative. She had seen his death.

Who is it that watches you? she asked.

'Apart from you?' he said, suddenly finding his voice. He looked down at his hands, which remained surprisingly still. 'A renegade mage called Armin. He is intent on controlling me in order to rule over the Greater Empire of Rashinder and Darna. Then there are the Magi, who reportedly follow my every move upon some magical map. No doubt Risenor has a peek every now and then.'

And the trapped souls, she said with a sigh.

Perian's head shot up in surprise. 'What trapped souls?'

The ones you encountered in a trance, that later chased you back to your tomb. The bubble that contained those you know, including your friend Cerister.

Was there nothing about him that she did not know? He suppressed another surge of anger and thought of the lost souls she claimed he had seen. The pieces came together suddenly when he joined the two visions. How could he not have understood this?

We can do nothing for them now, she said into his mind. *This may be your task in the future if it proves more independent than I believe it is.*

'Who has done this?' His voice came out louder than he had intended, echoing softly about the circular walls.

The mage who watches. This is how Gisela was able to control the tribes, by threatening to imprison their souls after death. The power that binds it comes from the mage. Gisela was meant to oversee his creation, but this she has not done, having turned her thoughts to her new victim and her potential future of power. It is better this way, for the moment. You have other things to worry about.

'What could be more important than to release them?'

You. Staying alive and placing yourself in a position where you can *do something if necessary. But that is, as I say, all in the future.* Her voice carried a hint of impatience. *That you are here with me now comes of a choice you have already made and cannot be undone. What you do next is yours to choose freely: learn what I offer or refuse. Decide with your heart and inner knowing; I will see the truth. I will not take you as my apprentice or share my knowledge if you are unsure or unwilling on any level.*

She sat silent and motionless for some time, studying him, waiting for a response. The sudden absence of her voice left an emptiness inside him. Even as her silence continued, he could think of nothing to say – he needed to sort out all she had said, but quietly and alone.

She finally took a deep breath and leant forward to stretch her back. 'The day outside is fading quickly.' Her physical voice jarred as it filled the room. 'Before we eat our evening meal, you will cleanse yourself and put on the clothing appropriate for an apprentice, or not. Lili will show you.'

Lili had slid into the room without him noticing, and her sudden presence made him jump. He stood obediently on legs stiff from inactivity and, dragging his eyes away from the Oracle, followed Lili to a hole in the ground he had not noticed, through which a gentle puff of steam occasionally emerged. Without looking back, he followed her down a wooden ladder that dropped into an underground cave lit by lamps. To one side of the cave, a hot spring bubbled and gurgled; on the other stood a table, two chairs and a cupboard. A large jug and bowl sat on the table, a small plate with lightly perfumed soap beside the bowl.

'You wash with the water, then rest for a while in the spring. It is very refreshing and will help you relax after your journey. Your new clothing is in the cupboard. Call me if you need anything. When you have finished you should rejoin my Mistress, and you will eat together.'

Lili's lips were tight with resentment, confirming the reason for the Oracle's silent communication. Perian felt sorry for her. She had probably expected to be the apprentice and to receive the knowledge now being offered to him. She ascended the ladder and disappeared through the hole.

He washed quickly with the cold water and stepped into the hot spring. The mineral water bubbled and tickled about his body deliciously, and his muscles responded, releasing their tightness within the warmth.

After a while his mind began to relax, and he was able to think clearly about all that the Oracle had said. What could be worse than Mage Armin trying to take over his mind or the horror that awaited Rashinder? Yet some part of him suspected that she told the truth. Who knew what lurked in the higher realms of trance?

And how could he pass up the opportunity to gain greater skills in the one area he knew he was weak: his protection? If Wellorn's Oracle could teach him to create his own room, his own safe space in which to trance, he must take it. He had been afraid for too long; constantly nervous and jumping at shadows. He wanted it to stop. What was the point of being a seer if he was too scared to trance? To enlist the help of Risenor was not only inadequate, but very chancy and no solution to his dilemma. There would be opportunity enough to ease Risenor's loneliness.

This Oracle was the mentor he had been unconsciously seeking, and since he could see no way of escaping at present, he would embrace what she had to teach him with pleasure and without guilt. And she hadn't mentioned what would happen to himself and Valamer should he refuse.

He had not foreseen this outcome, but there had been little time to look clearly into the near future when every trance took him into that ghastly vault, with the horrors of destruction and lost souls waiting for him on the outside and the expectation of Armin's taunts, his icy claws, his threats of taking over Perian's mind. More likely, though, the Oracle had blocked this scenario, since she appeared to have such easy access to him.

So, from Zamir's seer, he was now to be apprentice to the Oracle of Ortus, the Empty Eye! Yet again, fate had twirled him about like so much flotsam and dropped him, helpless, into the heart of the enemy.

9

Perian dried himself as best he could with the small, thin towel Lili had provided, shaking his head vigorously to expel as much water from his hair as possible. He laughed out loud when he looked around and found his choices limited. Although he had not heard her creep in, Lili had taken his old clothing left in a pile on the floor; the only choice he had been given was to wear the clothing neatly folded in the cupboard and take up the Oracle's offer of apprenticeship, or to go naked.

He dressed leisurely, picking each item from the pile and shaking it out: pale grey, loose cotton trousers cut above his ankles and tied with a string at the waist; a sleeveless tunic finished with a brocade hem just below the knee. A wide belt of plaited grey silk that sat neatly on his hips completed his attire. Despite his efforts, his wet hair left a mantle of dampness about his shoulders.

The Oracle greeted him with a smile as he emerged from the hole. She sat at a small table with two chairs and pointed to the one opposite. Lili appeared with soup before he had time to take his place.

'You look pink-faced and clean,' said the Oracle. 'Do you feel better?'

'I will once the soup has cooled.'

She picked up her spoon and stirred her soup slowly and thoughtfully, creating waves of curling steam about her face. 'My name is Neesa,' she said, 'but you will address me as Mistress until your apprenticeship is complete, at which point you will be my friend, I hope, and peer.' She paused her stirring, then continued. 'I was young when my father sold me to King Lennos, Ishra's father.'

Perian looked up suddenly from his own soup. He had never imagined that Farans would do such a thing as sell their children, but then he wondered why he thought they were better than any other race when he had Gisela as an example. He continued his stirring to encourage her to continue.

'I was a difficult child, and my parents didn't understand my gift,' she said, as though to excuse them of their crime. 'Lennos gave me to my Mistress, who trained me to replace her when she passed into the other world.'

She placed an elbow on the table, her chin upon her bent wrist, and looked at him with a hint of amusement in her eyes.

'I remember clearly the day that you three boys caught her attention. You were being displayed at the gathering of the tribes. We were as amazed as the Magi that triplets had survived and that all three demonstrated such abilities. Risenor was the firstborn. He shone with an unruly power, and his clarity of foresight, even at that age, was to be envied, my Mistress said.

'We watched in confusion as the High Magi retreated into the Deserts of Albys, and then with horror when Gisela committed her heinous crime. That Risenor survived was a miracle, and perhaps not the best outcome for him. He is a lonely soul, wandering dark places in his trancing.' She stopped to sip soup from her spoon, looking at him over its rim.

Perian wondered again whether any part of his existence was sacred. 'Have you watched me all this time? Both lives?'

The corners of her mouth twitched mischievously. 'No, Tanais, you're not *that* interesting. You caught my attention briefly when you were reborn into Darna royalty, but it wasn't until you sent shockwaves through the seeing eye of every Oracle of worth in the known kingdoms, and probably beyond, with the blasting open of your own seer's eye that I looked more carefully. Even though you nearly sent us all mad – although I can really only speak for myself – with your uncontrolled waves of powerful inner sight, I knew that you were the apprentice I waited for.

'Each Oracle, once they can master their gift with skill and ease, waits for an apprentice to find them – someone worthy in ability, and morality, one hopes, to keep the knowledge alive. I had begun to wonder whether fate had no student for me. Whether the unbroken stream of knowledge passed down from Oracle to Oracle over many, many lifetimes, and given to me, would perish with my body. I cannot express the joy I felt watching you cower in that ancient vault where Elian and your friend Jolint waited for you to release them from their hibernation. And later, when you lay beneath the stars, suffering the consequences of having blocked your trances for so long. When Aronaye locked you away and then began to teach you how to use your gift, I stopped watching. By then I had seen that you would make your way safely to me, and that you would recognise the importance of what I so willingly offer you.'

She made it sound as though he had made his way here by choice, but he hadn't. Or had he?

Although it was still a little hot, Perian spooned in his soup to quieten his stomach so he could think more clearly about what the Oracle had said. He glanced at her, eating with great delicacy, her mouth still curved upward in amusement, and put his spoon down; he suddenly felt like a great bear attacking its prey. He found he had squeezed the soft bread he held in his other hand into a hard lump and popped it into his mouth to chew quietly.

Her words spun about his head chaotically, and he tried to slow his thinking to put them into sequence. What she offered was very enticing, and it was hard to believe she had chosen him for this honour. From the jumble of thoughts, two questions dominated: why hadn't he seen this, and why had she chosen a man when the lineage was clearly female? He put these questions to her.

'I blocked myself from your view,' she replied. 'It served no purpose for you to see this too soon. As to your second question, I believe I have already answered this. Fate will have its way. That you were a man was unfortunate and has caused considerable difficulty with Ishra and Lili, but that will be sorted out with time. Oracles are outside the politics of the moment. We must be, so we can see the truth and not be swayed by those who think they control us. None may control us.'

Perian thought of Mage Armin and wondered whether her teachings would make him strong enough to resist Armin's controlling magic before the mage came for him again.

Neesa teased her soup with a little bread. 'There are precedents. Our lineage is dotted with one or two, perhaps more, men in the past – before our predictions were said to be the voice of Ortus, that is.' She sat back in her chair, her soup unfinished, and looked toward the curtain behind Perian. Lili appeared soundlessly and startled him by placing a plate of meat and a few vegetables at the side of his bowl. She vanished again just as silently. 'I eat little these days, but you are still young and have the appetite of an active male. Eat and enjoy.'

She sat in silence as he finished his soup and attacked the plate of meat. When all was consumed, he dabbed his mouth with the small cloth provided. The spiral of windows had turned to large black dots through which he could see stars twinkling in a cloudless sky.

He yawned, surprised at how tired and contented he felt, and Neesa stirred from her contemplations.

'I must retire, and so should you. You will sleep over there.' She pointed over his shoulder at the mattress and blankets. 'Tomorrow, we begin your training. Lili will wake you with breakfast as she does me. Do not mistake her for a servant. She serves me as my apprentice and will serve you until you are more familiar with your surroundings.' She stood with a soft scrape of her chair. 'Sleep well, Tanais. The day will be hard and merciless, since you must learn quickly. Events move at a pace that is inconvenient for us, and you must be ready.'

She disappeared behind the curtain, presumably into her bedchamber. Perian wondered what he needed to be ready for. The Oracle was dying, but he didn't think her death was imminent.

Lili appeared and snatched up his empty plates with ill-concealed animosity, and he made a note to be wary of her while trying to feel some compassion for the disappointment his presence must be causing her.

He remained seated at the table, even after Lili had gone, running his eyes appreciatively over the curve of Neesa's Oracle Tower. He found its smooth symmetry pleasing, and the room peaceful, safe. If he ever got back to Jasperen Palace, he would ask Valamer for a house of his own. Just a little house, like this. *If* he ever got back; if Valamer ever got back.

His eyes drifted toward Neesa's mat, where a string of roughly cut amethyst beads sat beside a small bowl of clear crystals. He left his seat with as little noise as possible and picked the beads up, running them through his fingers. They held the imprint of the Oracle, but no power other than their own. He replaced it quickly so as not to accidentally see into Neesa herself.

There was little else to do but sleep, and he was extremely tired. He unrolled his mattress and slipped beneath the blankets, not bothering to undress or extinguish the lamp.

A gentle breeze puffed through the windows, bringing with it the smells and muted sounds of night: moon flowers and cactus, chittering bats, crickets and the occasional distant howl. Otherwise, all was quiet. Perian could hear no music, no screams of laughter or anger emanating from the taverns or alehouses, no night market or domestic upheaval. Ishra's strict rule had taken the life and joy from this town. Elian and Ben would be disappointed.

His eyes drifted to the highest window, where a cluster of stars, both large and small, winked at him, reminding him of the bubble of souls – and Cerister. He remembered how she had tried to tell him something through the wall of the bubble. Jolint had said that if it were important, she would reach him again in some way, so he had stopped worrying – or at least put the worrying off until he saw her again. He realised now that she had been warning him about Gisela and Armin, but probably also asking for help. They had all asked for help in their way, now he came to think about it.

Perian finally understood the true nature of their plight, although how their prison had been created and how to release them, he did not know. But this was for him to find out when he was able, and if they had not been released in the meantime.

He dreamt of Cerister that night. They were once more in their Faran wagon, Cerister, Jolint, himself and Elian, huddled together to keep warm. Entwined as though one person, breathing together and dreaming together. He could feel Cerister close to him, smell her hair, feel her skin against his, hear her laughter and teasing, the tartness of her words and harsh opinions. He watched Cerister and Jolint train with Garin in the use of the sword and felt Cerister's arms enclose him seductively when she secretly taught him to use a bow.

He wept even as he slept and, in his dream, a caressing hand ran gently over his cheek and brought back a thrill he had almost forgotten: the tingle of Cerister's spirit hand when he was still an exiled prince and she was in hibernation along with Elian and Jolint.

Perian didn't need Lili to wake him. A cockerel stood beneath the windows and sang a welcome to the dawn, if such a call could be said to be singing. He stared into darkness, the lamp having gone out, and waited for the first visible signs of day, listening to the cockerel and a competing call further away.

When the rim of the lowest window showed a hint of colour, he slipped outside to relieve himself and nearly collided with Lili and her tray on the way back. She curled her lip in disgust and stomped on to disappear into Neesa's room once she had put her load on the table. She passed close to him on the way out and trod purposely on his bare foot. The childish gesture made him smile. They would get on in a roundabout way, although he would need to check his food carefully to avoid any nasty surprises.

Neesa emerged from behind her curtain and they ate in silence. Perian was completing his meal with a great gulp of water when Elian's voice entered his head.

Good morning, brother, was all he said.

Perian's throat closed involuntarily, sending water down into his lungs and resulting in a paroxysm of coughing and spluttering until tears streamed down his cheeks. Neesa looked up briefly, then continued to pick at her food. Eventually, when he had recovered, she pushed her plate aside.

'Come, Tanais, we will begin,' she said after a while. 'It is a little soon after eating, but the meal was light and its digestion shouldn't interfere with our training too much.'

They sat opposite each other on the saffron mat as they had the day before. She beckoned him forward as though to whisper in his ear and placed a long finger in the centre of his forehead, at the place of his seeing eye. A bright light exploded in his mind and, for a brief moment, he thought his head had bounced from his body. When she withdrew her hand, Perian felt himself swaying where he sat. A wind blew through his head as though a door had opened onto the outside world, with such clarity that his physical eyes blinked automatically. He thought he had fallen sideways, but in fact he remained upright, and once his spiralling thoughts and emotions had settled, all around him seemed brighter and more alive. The Oracle watched him with what he thought was satisfaction before speaking into his mind.

Now speak to Elian and tell him not to call again until you say he can.

Her words floated like music on the wind, and only then did he realise that she had removed the block that stopped him from talking to Elian, or herself, and that their previous communication had been jagged and difficult. He thrilled with the feel of it and immediately spoke to Elian to pass on her message and boast of his new skill. Elian's shock bubbled through him until he wanted to laugh and clap his hands with joy.

We are in town, staying at the Temple Inn, Elian said. *Are you safe?*

Perian quickly assured him that he was safe and well, but could not be disturbed, and that they would talk later.

'Good,' was all Neesa said when he had broken his contact with Elian. He wasn't sure whether she had listened in or could see the separation by the look on his face. She held out her hands, palms up. 'Now, place your hands on mine and invite me into that ghastly tomb of yours.'

He wasn't sure how he was meant to 'invite her in', but did as she bid and settled his mind in a way that always ended in the 'tomb', as she called it. All was dark as usual, save the soft glow of Neesa's ethereal body and the dull light that shone from his wing tattoo through his tunic.

Neesa clicked her tongue as she looked about. 'How did you manage to create such a place?' she said at last. It wasn't a question, more a statement. 'Is this your attempt at security – stone and mortar?' Another statement.

He looked about at the large dull stones that formed his vault and shrugged. It hadn't occurred to him that this was his own doing, his way of keeping himself safe from intrusion, but once she had pointed it out, he knew it was true. Not a very elegant solution. It had worked, with the exception of Risenor. Most likely he had invited Risenor in without realising it, since he had been thinking of trying to enlist his help. Now that he understood it was his own creation, he looked at it differently.

He was still looking about at the walls with a mixture of satisfaction and disgust when Neesa asked him to open his tunic.

'Let your wings speak for themselves,' she said.

He instinctively put his hand to his chest and clutched the material of his tunic tightly in his fist, as though afraid she might rip the fabric apart.

'You have associated your tattoo with capture and death for too long, Tanais. Think beyond the symbol of sacrifice. What do wings represent to those who are not influenced by the infernal Sky God?'

Initially, he couldn't comprehend what she'd said, it being so antithetical to his current viewpoint. The wings had shaped his life: exile as a child, and later, constant fear of exposure. Her request made every part of him shriek in terror and warning.

Neesa smiled and tipped her head slightly to one side, urging him to relax and look at the symbol in a different light. He dropped his hand, already damp and clammy, and tried to shed the usual emotions that surrounded the exposure of his tattoo, nudging aside his rigid, narrow belief about the symbol's nature. Slowly, slowly, he began to understand, then in a rush: freedom, of course. Seen in any other context, wings represented freedom – carefree flight, escape into the upper world, the air, the true Sky God.

The Oracle's laughter tinkled and echoed about the walls. 'Well done,' she said. 'Now release the knots on your tunic and let them shine as they should.'

Even though not in physical form, Perian's body felt moist and his hand shook a little. He fumbled with the ties, wishing he had not pulled them so tight, until his tunic fell open at the chest. The tattoo's dull light flickered brighter, then darker, like a candle in the wind, as he struggled to let go of his ingrained emotions and remain calm. Only when he began to hyperventilate and nature took over did he start to relax through sheer exhaustion.

Light gradually filled the room. The tattoo was not large – approximately seven inches across from wing tip to wing tip, enough to cover his heart – yet as it grew even brighter, it bled out into the shadows until even Neesa was lost within its glow. The extent of it frightened him, and threw them both back into darkness.

'H-How does it do that?' he stammered.

'The light comes from your heart and your desire, Tanais. Wings of freedom. They will light your path wherever you go.'

At present there was little chance of him going anywhere, but she referred to a use other than just illuminating his vault. What that was, Perian didn't know, and something told him that it was for him to find out.

Neesa clicked her tongue and glanced about again. 'I think that is enough for the moment. We can start in earnest later.'

Perian found himself seated in the Tower with a speed that took his breath away. Neesa removed her hands and placed them on her lap.

'You must sleep for a few hours, then you may accompany me on my walk.'

He watched her as she stood and disappeared behind her curtain. The sun was just visible on the edge of the second window facing east, indicating that it was mid-morning. He felt drained, so he did as she suggested and staggered to his mattress, falling instantly into a profound sleep.

Perian woke with Neesa's shadow passing before the midday sun that beat through the third window onto his face. She poked him in the shoulder with her stick and urged him up with its quick motion toward a cloak hanging above his bed. When he was ready, she took his arm and they strode out into the courtyard. She gave him a parcel wrapped in cloth, which he carried in his other hand. A brisk, icy wind blew out his cloak as they stepped into the sunlight. He looked for his boots, but someone had removed them, along with his favourite knife.

The pathway had been swept clear of leaves and grit, and the stone's weathered smoothness and ambient heat felt pleasant upon his feet as he spread his pale, sun-deprived toes with a sense of wellbeing. He looked down at Neesa and saw that she was also barefooted. She was small, like most Farans, but more so with age, and her leaning weighed nothing at all. They were a mismatched pair, yet perfectly at ease, he thought, as though they had walked together for many years.

She led him around the cloister, passing an exit at each corner, before turning into the last, a spacious tunnel that ran the full length of the building and came out into the mottled shade of a rose arbour. Their pace was slow, so Perian had time to glance through the windows as they went. All were in darkness, save one, where the priestesses were taking their lunch in apparent silence.

The arbour opened onto a formal garden of flowerbeds and small shrubs. Neesa turned onto a gravel path that meandered toward a wooden bench beneath a drooping willow, where she stopped and sat with a contented sigh. Perian picked out the little stones that had rubbed between his toes as soon as he was seated.

When you have finished picking at your feet, you can open the bag, she said into his mind.

He pulled at the knot and found, to his relief, bread and cheese for their lunch. He shuffled along the bench a little and put the cloth between them so they could help themselves. He munched quietly on the sparse fare, listening to the birds, busy amongst the foliage. Late blossoms filled the air with a subtle perfume that attracted honeybees and wavered in intensity depending on the breeze.

He thought of Valamer and then Elian, spoiling the moment. *Does Valamer live, as Ishra said?* he asked, with a certain satisfaction at his new skill. He had already understood, without being told, that communication with Neesa should be conducted in this way.

Yes. He is well fed and cared for, although not comfortable. His spirit diminishes in that darkened hole of a cell, but he is strong-minded and his confinement is unlikely to overcome him completely.

To know he was alive was enough; Perian was unable to help him. Valamer's return to Jasperen was for Elian, Jolint and Ben to accomplish. His task had turned out to be something else.

When they had finished their meal, he shook crumbs from the cloth and a flock of little birds swooped down instantly, having been waiting patiently on surrounding branches. Perian watched them peck about their feet until disturbed by the approach of several priestesses returning to their duties from the refectory. One of the priestesses was Timary, and like the others, she stopped to bow low before the Oracle, her eyes wide with surprise as they travelled over the length of Perian and noted his apprentice apparel.

She is very bright, that one, said Neesa, *and as fanatical as Ishra. She doesn't like you.* Perian felt her laugh, although there was no evidence of this in her outward demeanour.

Are you suggesting I should be careful of her? he asked. It was bad enough having to watch where Lili put her feet or look for surprises in his soup, but Timary would be a far greater threat should she put her mind to it.

You won't need to be. She is devoted to Ishra. While you please Ishra, Timary will be your ally. Should Ishra consult you, always tell her the truth of what you see, no matter what that is. It will make no difference to the outcome and will keep you alive.

But what if she didn't like what he saw? What if *he* didn't like what he saw?

Don't juggle with it, Tanais. The path is strong and will come out where it will.

He wondered what she had seen, but again, he did not ask the question. If one saw only snippets, as was often the case – for him at least – how could one decide which way the future might twist and turn toward what one desired and what one did not? He could see her point – who were they, Neesa and himself, to decide what was right? He would do as she suggested and hope this path she referred to moved in a direction that kept his friends safe and Rashinder from the autocracy of the Empty Eye.

The little birds returned to their feast, chirping and hopping about in their alert way, and Perian let his attention stray to enjoy their simple happiness. Neesa disturbed them again by pointing to the mountain behind, into which the town nestled. A thick patch of forest covered the mountain's base like a green lake, before the rock rose vertically, jagged and deeply creviced.

The forest is beautiful. Thick and vibrant in a magical hollow protected from the icy wind off the peaks and warm with hot springs, she said. *The trees never lose their leaves, and strange plants wind about their trunks, producing exotic flowers with pungent odours that are not always pleasant. The toadstools are the size of a plate. I have often walked there. It is left alone by the people due to its strange feel, and they feed their children with tales of horror that pass from generation to generation. They say that huge, malformed creatures live there, but I have never seen one. You should take the time to go as far as the cliff. Many of the crevices lead to beautiful caves filled with different precious stones and formations to please the eye. I have never travelled far into the caves for fear of being missed, but local legend says that they go through to a strange and mysterious kingdom on the edge of the ocean, where giant fish swim in a little harbour for the pleasure of their king.*

Perian wondered what had brought about her sharing, since this was a secret escape for her, if she was afraid of being missed. But he allowed himself to be transported through the forest and caves and imagined a marvellous magical kingdom by the ocean, a brief but pleasant distraction.

10

Perian took Neesa to his vault as before. 'Perian's Tomb', she called it, which he thought in very bad taste, since she only ever referred to him as Tanais. He was not insensitive to her meaning: the name Perian referred to his past, his previous life as a Faran and Elian's identical twin. That part of him existed only in his memory now, yet he continued to stubbornly drag it around like a heavy chain, which no doubt held him back and restricted his view ahead. But he wasn't ready to release that particular shackle yet, and would cling to his Faran name for as long as it suited him.

They sat on the floor facing each other, Neesa's hands flat on the knees of her crossed legs.

What is it you require of your Oracle space?

He stared at her, unable to think beyond his need to keep Mage Armin at bay. He closed his eyes and turned his concentration to his breathing until his worries had been pushed far enough aside so as not to distract him and to allow other thoughts to emerge. Peace and solitude came to mind – a safe place to allow his visions to run free undisturbed. He put this to Neesa.

A start. This is what all seers hope for. She indicated the walls with a wave of her arm. *This is your first attempt, but now you must transform it and create a space you enjoy, one that has the qualities you require. When you are satisfied with your creation, I will teach you to strengthen your defences and increase the clarity of your visions.*

He stared blankly at the large blocks of rectangular stone that made up his tomb: the rough surface and jagged edges that fitted so perfectly together. How did he do this? Without knowing, how could he change it?

Express that which is in your heart, Tanais. Express it through your mind and give your greatest desire life.

Perian ground his teeth and cursed under his breath. He would if he knew what that was, and exactly how he had achieved this monstrous room.

He tried to imagine circular stones as a test, to get an idea of how it worked, but nothing changed. He tried again with a different shape; still nothing moved.

A terrible sense of defeat washed over him and he dropped his face into his hands. He wanted to weep with frustration. He could feel Neesa's calm presence as she patiently watched him, yet she remained still and quiet, adding nothing to what she had already said.

He closed his eyes to aid his thinking, letting her words run through his mind and silently travel across his tongue. In that moment, with the release of all expectation, his chest filled with a need for his tomb to change. His desire infused his heart and body, and his mind automatically unfolded like a flower to express that desire in a physical way.

The experience was exhilarating. He dropped his hands to his sides and stood a little too quickly. The room rolled and spun, mimicking his slight dizziness, and Neesa spread her hands in an attempt to remain upright amidst the turmoil.

She laughed at the look of bewilderment on his face. *Now change it to what you want, or at least something that doesn't move.*

His walls creaked and groaned, formed blobs, then stretched so thinly that he had to crouch and Neesa bend her head. At one point his vault vanished altogether, leaving them both in a dark void with blackened tree ferns beneath their feet.

Neesa placed her hand on his heart to stop his rising panic so he could recreate his tomb. He fell to his knees, shaking with the shock. Neesa laughed so loudly she also took to her knees. As soon as she had control of her mirth, she held out her hands to him.

Come, Tanais, I invite you into my space. It may provide you with inspiration, or not. I for one need a change of scenery and some respite from your highly amusing antics.

Perian grunted. He shook and sweated, his heart near seizure, and she called it 'highly amusing'!

Come, Tanais. I haven't had so much fun for many years, but even I can stand only so much joy. Lili was never so interesting.

He allowed himself to be teased from his tension and placed his hands on hers. He was asking her what Lili's protection looked like when they entered Neesa's space and his words caught in his mouth.

He found himself in a near-perfect sphere; inside a smoky crystal ball. Only where they stood, on a saffron mat, was there a flat surface. The small bowl of crystals and the amethyst beads were also there.

Sit, Tanais. Apart from my Mistress, you are the only other person to ever have shared this with me. I was privileged to see my Mistress's space when I was half your age, which she shared to give me inspiration for my own as I do with you.

She swept her arm about to encompass the small globe under which Perian stooped slightly. Images shifted in the walls, dull grey shapes that he could make no sense of.

So, this is where you spy on everyone. He laughed, but in fact he was astonished. She really had meant that his space could be anything he liked. He could expand his creativity and it would still work. It occurred to him that he had been restricting his creation with what he thought it should be rather than what he truly desired.

Despite all that Aronaye had taught him, he had never felt in full control of the space in which he received his visions; he was the tool rather than the craftsman. This was different. Neesa was the creator through which her visions could be expressed. This revelation changed everything. He felt dizzy with the thought that he could indeed take control, and his tattoo shone in the knowledge that he was free. Free to create as he pleased.

He stared at Neesa. He wanted to hug her and dance about the sphere with her. He did neither of these things, but he would devote himself to her teachings. Already her gift was greater than he could have imagined.

He felt safe within the walls of the Oracle Tower, but here, in Neesa's sphere, he knew no one could touch him, not even Mage Armin. This was his greatest desire. He expanded in mind and emotion, breathing freely, he thought, for the first time.

Look away from the images. This is meant for your inspiration, not for your use. And no, I don't spy on everyone, only you.

She startled him by winking. He noticed then how young she looked: a young woman, beautiful, in fact. Only the hollowness of her eyes spoke of a terminal sickness, which he surmised was the vestige of extreme old age that she was unable to deny.

Her laughter tinkled like a small bell and dimples formed in her cheeks. *This is my space. You don't think I see myself as an old lady, do you? Here I am always as I feel: young, but now ailing. We will come again, but for now, look around and let the ideas grow within you, and in the meantime, we should return, eat and sleep, and start again.*

The creation of Perian's personal space took several days. His mind spun with the endless possibilities and he spent his nights and spare moments sorting out those with potential. But in practice, many possibilities flowed from just a few of his painstaking selection with greater or lesser success.

During one session he tried a cube of different polished stones, but it felt like a prison no matter how large he made it, and his visions bounced from surface to surface, nearly sending them both mad. Another time he tried both a hexagon and octagon and experimented on each with different common surfaces: glass, gold and silver, including one with a delicate network similar to the web of a spider, which he was particularly proud of. None were satisfactory.

And then there was the day of the rainbow pyramid. The swirling colours made them both feel dizzy and nauseous and they had to take a long break to recover. Neesa was mopping her face with a damp cloth and Perian stood by the small table, pouring them both water from a jug, when Lili stepped through the entrance and bowed to Neesa with a quick glance at Perian. Ishra came in behind her. Neesa ushered Perian and Lili out with a wave of her hand. Perian glanced back as he left to see Ishra carrying the water he had just poured to Neesa.

Outside, he stood in the chill air and soaked in the glory of the sun hovering in a cloudless sky. Lili stood beside him, stroking her white tunic with a sense of pride and a smirk upon her lips. Only her grey sash indicated that she was a novice. Timary stood nearby, erect and haughty as usual. Eventually he asked Lili if Ishra was consulting her Oracle.

'She doesn't need to,' she snapped back. 'She has me.'

Perian wondered what he was doing there if Lili was all she needed, but said nothing. He moved his feet about to stop them cramping on the cold surface of the stone and hoped the interview wouldn't take too long. Ishra was probably checking on his progress. He pondered what would happen if Neesa gave him a bad report. Would his and Valamer's lives be forfeit? Probably. But he had no misgivings about Neesa or her report, despite their recent experience with the rainbow pyramid. He shivered again at the thought of it.

To pass the time, he ran through all the creative spaces he had tried out so far. He was anxious to begin the real work, the difficult process of strengthening his chosen space – *making it a part of himself, like breathing*, Neesa had said. He wasn't exactly sure what she meant by this, or how it worked, but clearly this was the basis of a secure protection. That he was still stuck fumbling around with the very first stage left him frustrated, and he felt that he was wasting precious time.

He was still trying to quell his growing anxiety when a sense of something unpleasant began to creep over him. He glanced at Lili, but she appeared not to notice. The feeling grew and the sun diminished around him like a shadow separating him from the surrounding brightness. Still, neither Lili nor Timary showed any sign that something was amiss.

This lack of confirmation made him slow to react. Armin had already sent a gripping trickle of magic to wind about his ankles by the time he was alert enough to surround himself in a basic shield as Neesa had taught him.

He pushed his panic down, but his sudden fright left his shield weak and inadequate, yet enough to temporarily interfere with Armin's little game. A chuckle of delight buzzed in Perian's ear. The shadow faded, and he sighed with relief and the returned warmth of the sun, but the sense of Armin close by did not fade. That Armin was on him as soon as he set foot outside the Oracle Tower without Neesa meant that the mage was watching his every move, yet Perian doubted that he was physically within the temple grounds. His confidence at being ready when Armin made his move began to diminish again.

He was still inwardly trembling from his encounter and the effort of concentrating on his protection when Neesa called into his head to stay calm, and soon after, Ishra appeared in the entrance. She swept past him without a glance and Lili followed with a look of triumph on her face.

The relief of being back inside was immense. He threw himself onto the mat and rubbed his face in his hands.

Did you feel him? he gasped. He knew she had, but asked anyway. *He's out there waiting for me. He'll strike before I'm ready.*

If that's what you think, then that's what will happen. Neesa patted his knee. *You did well out there, but no, you aren't ready yet.*

Perian completed his creation the following day. He and Neesa had enjoyed experimenting with his various inventions; they had laughed and played and got to know each other, but his encounter with Armin had taken the shine off their innocent endeavours and brought back the urgency of Perian's training.

In the end he settled on a construction that was not dissimilar to Neesa's. In fact, it was the same, except that he used faultless clear crystal through which he could see between the worlds into endless space. Only when they both lay exhausted on the saffron mat of the Oracle Tower did she confess that her crystal ball, as Perian called it, was the same as her Mistress's, and her Mistress before her. The only change Neesa had made was to use smoky crystal, whereas her Mistress had used amethyst, as had *her* Mistress.

That evening, after Neesa had retired, Perian slipped down through the hole that led to the cave below and soaked in the hot spring. He found that he was happy. Happier than he could remember ever being. Under Neesa's guidance and the protection of her Oracle Tower, his gift no longer felt like an unwieldy burden, and although he had not reached the point of seeing his visions play out upon the walls of his own sphere, he knew that he was becoming a more powerful seer. The creation of his own sphere and protection had enabled him to expand his awareness.

More than this, he felt himself expanding as an individual. As he loosened his grip on the fear that had accompanied him through life, he found the confidence to blossom, to share and look to the future, even if that did seem a little hopeless in his current situation. This was what he had always needed: a mentor. Someone who could answer his questions; who understood him through a common gift, and more, had fun with it. He would never have guessed that creating spheres and protection could bring so much pleasure. He sensed that Neesa was also happy, and that pleased him a great deal.

Jolint and Elian popped into his mind, and he felt a twinge of guilt that he should be having a nice time when they were no doubt bored and worried. He called to Elian and asked what he was doing.

Freezing to death on a branch and watching the activity around the building where we believe they are holding Valamer. Or perhaps I should say, the lack of activity. There is no pattern to the comings and goings of the guards, or at least no pattern that I can discern.

Do you think they are worried about a rescue attempt?

We think so, yet the inns and taverns haven't been searched.

Perian thought of Lili and wondered whether she had foreseen Valamer's rescue. A lack of routine he thought uncharacteristic of Ishra, and would account for what Elian was seeing.

Have to go, said Elian. *The priestesses have arrived to check for anything unusual, like me.*

Yes, Perian thought to himself. *Definitely Lili.*

Your vision chamber is near complete, Neesa said the following day. *The next stage is to strengthen it, and that comes from within.*

They sat on the bench beneath the willow, munching happily on bread and cheese as they had each day. The sky was overcast, and the covering cloud pressed down on them. Faded shadows indicated that it was mid-afternoon; no wonder Perian was so hungry. He crushed a piece of apple between his teeth, and the juice was sliding deliciously down his throat when a sinewy thread of magic wound about his neck and forced the juice into his windpipe.

He froze in shock, unable to cough or breathe. Armin's laughter blew into his ear like a putrid wind. The little birds flew off as a group even before Perian's apple fell from his hand and rolled across the path. He felt rather than saw Neesa turn toward him. Armin swore and quickly withdrew his phantasmic projection.

Perian coughed and choked for a while, unable to get down a full lungful of air. Neesa stood.

Come, Tanais. The sooner you begin to build your protection, the better. This kind of intimidation cannot be allowed to go on.

She didn't wait for him to recover, but strode ahead so he had to run to catch up.

Armin's blatant intrusion was a turning point in Perian's training. With a deep sigh of sadness, Neesa announced that they would no longer go for walks in the gardens and that midday meals would be taken within the safety of the Tower. Perian knew that

Armin's attack had shocked and frightened her, although she had said nothing and he hadn't asked.

Over the next few days, Neesa set out a rigid training programme. She demonstrated a series of elegant movements designed to enliven the mind and stretch and strengthen the limbs. He was to complete two rounds of these movements each morning before breakfast under Neesa's sharp eye, and once before he retired at night to release the tensions and worries of the day.

After a light breakfast, he spent a period of time concentrating on his breathing, followed by the creation and projection of a personal shield.

Your personal shield must be as natural to you as wearing clothes, enclosing you at all times, whether inside or out. When out, you should expand it and strengthen it, and if you sense danger, strengthen it some more.

Perian rolled his eyes, a sense of defeat slithering through his mind, but after a few days of intense practice, he found this simple exercise came naturally to him. The sudden intensity of Neesa's training, with the added incentive of Armin's recent attack, inspired him to learn quickly. Each morning upon waking, he would form the image of his shield around him with his mind and give it life through his desire, until one morning he realised that it hovered about him in a gentle way all the time, even in sleep.

He was overjoyed by this small success and dropped onto Neesa's mat with a great sense of achievement. Neesa snorted, a mischievous sparkle lighting up her eyes; a look that Perian now recognised. The prospect of a challenge sent a thrill through his body and he willed his shield to strengthen with the enthusiasm of playing a game.

The shapeless blob that appeared beside him with Neesa's squinting concentration was unexpected and nearly threw him off guard. He hadn't realised she could do such things. It rubbed a protuberance that resembled a hand over his shield, and Perian burst into laughter and repelled it with a greater firming of his barrier. The shapeless blob disappeared, and a slender version took its place and attempted to poke a finger through. One minute it was colourless, the next bright red with rage, at which point it punched his shield hard.

To his delight, Neesa created many odd creatures to thrust themselves against his shield, testing for strength and Perian's ability to respond, and each time he repelled them and laughed; he was actually quite good at this, he thought.

Neesa smiled at him and, with a deep breath, closed her eyes. Without warning, a great dragon with three horns protruding from a whiskered purple face suddenly appeared behind her and threw itself at Perian's shield. So great was the shock that he forgot Neesa's instructions about keeping his shield flexible, and instinctively did the opposite by creating a solid barrier. It was a bone-shattering mistake, and the impact of the creature's horns knocked him over with the ensuing weakening of his protection.

Dead! shouted Neesa, as though she had just won a prize. *Your shield must absorb the impact. Keep it fluid, yet thick enough to dull the impact of a magical strike. A hard shell will shatter or set you off balance, as you have just experienced.*

Perian stood, dusted himself down and rubbed his knee and elbow joints. He felt quite put out, as though she had cheated. *Will it protect me from Armin?* he said, louder than he had intended.

Yes. Once you have mastered your fear.

Perian shook his head. There it was: she asked the impossible. He didn't want to die, but it had occurred to him more than once that death might be a better option than what Armin had in store for him.

Neesa cocked her head, a challenge twinkling in her eye again, and he cursed himself for his attitude of defeat. That alone would be his downfall and the demise of all he loved. Elian and Jolint, and Valamer, on whose fate two empires rested, appeared in his mind's eye, and Neesa, who stood before him. He understood that his greatest challenge, his greatest hope, was the defeat of Mage Armin. There was no place for fear in his life, nor for the role of the victim; they were all victims, or would be if he failed. He had manipulated fate with his visions before, and he would do so again. This was no different, except that his current training prevented visions. He needed to learn faster.

His demeanour changed with the shifting of his thoughts. Neesa smiled and he was certain he saw her sigh with approval. Or was it relief?

She had referred to 'dulling the impact of a magical strike', and Perian thought about Armin's shield when he had rebuffed his attackers in the Council Room at Jasperen Palace. He told her about it and asked if his would also do this.

That's magic, and draws on the strength of those who wield it. The shields that you and I create are not, and are in no way draining. Your shield will not protect you from a physical attack nor hold against a powerful magical strike, but it will dull the impact and protect you from non-physical attacks such as the ones you have been experiencing. He will not be able to influence your mind with mental projections, whether present or distant, as long as your fear does not make you weak. Come, Tanais. Time for a break before you take me to your sphere.

They sat at Neesa's small table and picked at some fruit that had been laid out earlier for their occasional breaks. They never went straight from shield training to sphere training. Neesa said the separation of events was good for digesting what was learnt in one session before the other. Their breaks were always a pleasant interlude between the two that they both enjoyed, but Perian also suspected that she needed the rest.

What was it like, living in that wagon Gisela imprisoned the four of you in?

He hadn't expected such a question and was surprised at her use of the term 'imprisoned'. But that was what Gisela had done – incarcerated them.

He sat back in his chair and looked at Neesa. She had pinned her hair back from her face with two small silver clips, the rest hanging long and thick down her back, shining whitely in the light. Although she wasn't smiling, her mouth lifted naturally at the corners with a look of serenity and contentment that came from within.

Ghastly, he said, unable to keep the disgust from his inner voice. *Now that I have another life to compare it with. We grew up in that one tiny space and were only allowed out when she chose. We were kept from the rest of the tribes, although we could see them moving about the camps. The only people we had contact with were Gisela and her personal guard, Garin, who was charged with training Jolint and Cerister in combat. Elian was sent to spy on the rest of the tribe, but I was left to sit on the steps of the wagon, swimming about in visions I could not control.*

We were occasionally taken for supervised walks in the forest, but I never knew when I would be overtaken by a vision and clung to Elian. It was Aronaye who taught me control and gave me my independence. Garin tried to include Elian and me when Gisela wasn't there. He taught us both to use a sword and knife. He was very nice to us, but Gisela was our focus.

Neesa shook her head, a frown destroying the smoothness of her features. *No wonder you believed all her lies. She is a daemon of the worst kind, weak but with an overwhelming ambition for greatness that she could not possibly achieve on her own merit. You were lucky to have a chance at another life when you did, although I doubt you thought so at the time.*

Perian barked out a laugh. *No, I didn't. But you are right. I cannot imagine what life would have been like had we remained. Perhaps we would have seen her lies and broken free. Then, perhaps not, and we would have become as ghastly as she is.*

Neesa stretched out her hand and placed it on Perian's. *No, Tanais, you would not have. You all have great hearts and would have eventually seen her for what she is.*

Did you see this?

She made a clucking noise. *No, I just know it's true.*

Images of Perian's past danced through his mind. Armin had given him this chance at a new life, but it was also Armin who controlled Gisela, and through her he had taken their original life from them. Through him Gisela had killed his Faran mother and ruined Risenor's life, leaving him to wander in empty spaces alone. Perian shook his thoughts free before they settled too heavily on Cerister's fate.

And what of you, Neesa? How did you find the restrictions of your new life as an apprentice Oracle?

A relief, to be honest. Like you, I swam in a world of visions that separated me from everyone else. My parents couldn't wait to get rid of me — my presence made things awkward in the tribe. Our tribe leader wasn't as wise as Aronaye. Like my parents, he didn't recognise the gift I had to offer. My Mistress became everything to me and gave me the love and freedom I could not have found elsewhere.

Love and freedom — that was what Neesa gave to him, as she had been given it by her Mistress. Perian looked down at his hands so she would not see the glow of gratitude and love that had infused him. He could scarcely believe that he had been blessed with such a special relationship, one that sometimes existed between mentor and apprentice.

She patted his hand again and stood. *Let's see what you can do with your sphere today.*

They sat in his sphere, staring out at the darkness beyond. No images danced upon its walls; Neesa prevented it. Yet beyond the walls, in the darkness itself, Perian thought he caught a glimpse of movement, and for the briefest of moments, a vague outline appeared, which he felt sure was Risenor. He remembered what Neesa had said about Risenor being 'a lonely soul, wandering dark places in his trancing', and he was seized by a wave of unexpected sadness and compassion for Risenor and the lifelong misery he experienced. It made him shudder to think of what it must be like to live in constant pain and be so physically damaged. When he had completed his training, he would perhaps make contact with Risenor and speak with him occasionally from within his sphere to ease the loneliness of his wandering.

Perian angled his head toward Neesa as she broke the silence. *This was a good choice, Tanais. There is such peace in the void, and it will provide a needed respite between your visions. I almost wish I had thought of it myself.*

Peaceful, yes, unless one of your phantasms appears.

She chuckled and turned to look at him. *You are safe from my phantasms. I cannot create such things to attack your sphere. We must judge its quality by feeling it with our senses. This is truly all your creation and more receptive to your needs.*

In what way does my sphere differ from the shield I create? Surely my shield is also my creation.

Yes, but your sphere is in the non-physical realm, whereas your shield is in the physical, and you draw upon the natural elements to assist with its making.

Did he?

Think about it later. For the moment we are working with your sphere. Now, make it thicker. Make it thinner. Make it bigger. Make it smaller. Do it again.

On the third repetition, Perian nearly exploded. *Enough, Neesa. I will injure myself if I have to do another repetition at that speed.*

She laughed and very quietly told him he had done reasonably well, but still needed to practise. *Make it thicker and stronger at your own pathetic pace and follow its increased strength with your senses. Feel its texture and look for any distortion in its clarity. It doesn't have to be very thick to achieve what you want and need. If it loses clarity, you are at a visual disadvantage.*

But your sphere is smoky and has no real visual clarity.

That's not quite true — it has a degree of transparency, and there is a point at which it loses its crispness. But you may as well make use of all your senses since you had the foresight to make yours clear.

Well, it hadn't exactly been foresight — he had just wanted to be able to see into the void. And yes, to see with his physical eyes if anything was out there, such as the unfathomable things Neesa had hinted at.

She let her eyes travel around the walls of his sphere and leant forward a little to stretch her back, her hands flat upon her thighs. *More importantly, any loss of clarity in the sphere indicates a weakness in that you have pushed its structure beyond its point of greatest strength. Now, build your walls gradually and feel its formation with your senses, taking it to its loss of clarity so you can tell the difference and see for yourself what I am suggesting.*

He rolled his shoulders and stretched his neck, turning his attention inward to connect with his mental projection. He noticed that Neesa had closed her eyes to follow his progress. He took a deep breath and willed his sphere to strengthen through his mind's eye. He had done this each day, so it was no longer a difficult process.

The walls of his sphere were at their peak point and he was about to push them out of focus when he felt someone enter the Tower. Neesa's eyes flew open, and Perian's sphere wobbled and wavered in his loss of concentration. He found himself back in the physical world at a nauseating speed and gasped for breath.

Lili stood near the mat, unrepentant despite the look on Neesa's face. A conversation took place between the two women and soon Lili left with a quick bow. This was not the first time that Lili had interrupted a session, and Perian wondered if she chose her time carefully to interfere with his training. Ishra swept in soon after, so perhaps not.

Neesa waved her hand to usher him into the small waiting area beyond the curtain, but not outside the Tower. He found Lili also waiting, red-faced and anxious. She turned away from him and clutched her small hands together. Heat and irritation radiated from her, and Perian sat on the stone bench as far from her as possible and listened to the soft mumbling coming from the main room. Something had happened, but he wasn't going to ask Lili about it.

11

The interview went on for a long time, and Perian was on the verge of falling asleep when Ishra left at speed, barely missing his feet on her way out. Lili followed without looking at him.

Neesa was still on her mat, looking thoughtful, when he returned. She smiled at him as he entered. *We'll have a break and then try again, hopefully without interruption, although it was a useful experience. Our next lesson will be to keep awareness of the physical while retaining control of your Oracle space.*

He held out his arm to pull her up, even though she hadn't asked.

Ishra goes to the battlefield within the next week, she said. *She will take Lili with her.*

Perian wondered if the battle was going badly for Wellorn, absently taking a few dates from a platter on the table and placing them in line like a row of charging soldiers. He blinked and ate them quickly. If Saphrax broke through, he would probably head for Carios and miss Bresh altogether, leaving Perian and Valamer still incarcerated. His thoughts raced with various possible scenarios until he felt quite exhausted and turned his attention back to Neesa, who had been watching him. She shrugged as though she were privy to his tangled thoughts; it would be what it would be.

He released himself into the peaceful ambience of the Tower and they sat in a contented silence where no worries, no thoughts or words, were needed.

Lili came again the next day to seek Neesa's counsel. Again, she chose her time to coincide with Perian's sphere training. He did not doubt this time that she had planned her visit carefully, unaware that she was the instrument of that training. Although her entry was sudden and unannounced, he was able to keep his sphere stable, noting her presence yet undisturbed by it. His success earnt him a smile of approval from Neesa before they returned to their mat.

He removed himself to his mattress to give Neesa and Lili a sense of privacy. He tried not to watch, but his eyes continually drifted toward Lili. He felt her need and her disappointment, and he hoped that at some point it would be possible for them to become friends without rivalry.

All that remains is for you to continue strengthening your sphere and begin to see your visions play out upon its walls, as you saw mine do, Neesa said as they sat at the table, awaiting the arrival of a servant with their meal beneath the light of the third window. Ever since his training had begun in earnest, a temple servant had seen to their needs, while Lili acted as Ishra's seer. *Always remember, you form your protection with your mind and hold it in place through the power in your chest, in your heart. When not in your chamber, you can form a semblance of it around you to keep out those who would harm you or interfere in any way.*

Perian vaguely wondered why he needed such a reminder, but the smell of roasted meat and turnips that preceded the servant prevented him from asking. He thought he would faint with the waiting.

'Forgive me,' said the servant as he rushed through the curtain. 'The queen has an unexpected guest and I could not force the cook to speed.'

Neesa gazed at him blankly for a moment. 'What guest? Do you know who he is? I assume it is a man?'

'I believe so, but I cannot say. Such gossip hadn't reached the kitchen when I left, although it's probably there by now.'

'Thank you, Joshua.'

Perian took no more notice and attacked his meal with considerable enthusiasm. Neesa nibbled at a turnip while staring at the table. A worried frown began to crinkle her forehead. She caught Perian's gaze as he wrenched the last piece of meat from the antelope bone.

The look in her eye startled him. 'What's wrong?' he asked, his mouth still full.

You must control your fear, Tanais. Fear is the true enemy and will destabilise your protection, leaving you vulnerable to its source.

Another reminder.

She pushed her plate away, her food still untouched. *Ishra approaches with her guest. He has come sooner than I had expected and hoped.*

Perian wiped his mouth on his tunic and pushed the plates aside. The tension in Neesa's small frame was palpable, and a knot began to form within his belly, although he knew nothing of this guest. He began to wish he had not eaten so fast and quite so much.

Who is it that comes, Neesa?

She smiled at him; a sad smile, yet it illuminated the Tower. He had used her name unintentionally, but it seemed right. Neesa herself did not contest this, so, despite his trepidation at the arrival of Ishra's guest, he felt a certain elation that he had passed to the status of friend and peer.

Lili came through the curtain before Neesa could answer. She bowed low before Neesa and gave Perian a sharp nod. She began to speak, but stopped quite suddenly, and by the way she stood staring at Neesa, he assumed Neesa was speaking into her mind. What she was saying, Perian couldn't say, but the look on Lili's face forewarned him of trouble. Whatever it was clearly shocked her; she stood immobile, her small hands clutching at one another. Neesa urged her into motion with a wave of her hand and Lili ran from the Tower.

Neesa, Perian said as calmly as he could. *What is going on? Are we in danger?*

She smiled at him again. *Be calm, Tanais.* She eased herself up with the aid of one hand upon the tabletop. *Come, we will meet them on the path. I will not have my sacred space violated.*

He took a deep breath to slow his heart and settled within his protective shield. A terrible foreboding filled his heart, and he reached out and took Neesa's arm as he did when walking in the gardens.

They were greeted by a watery light and an icy breeze that swept around their ankles and tousled their hair as they stepped through the doorway. The gravel path had turned to gold with a heavy fall of bronze and yellow leaves. The courtyard around the Tower was unusually empty. The clear air held its breath, and as they walked slowly toward the temple, their feet making soft sounds on the tiny stones, Perian felt a sense of awe, as though that moment were a gift from a benevolent god; a small space of peace and transcendence. Neesa squeezed his arm with her left hand as though she felt it too, pulling him closer in a blissful bonding of mentor and disciple.

The moment was soon broken by the sound of Ishra's laughter and the rumble of a male voice, muffled and chill. Neesa stopped and squeezed his arm again more tightly.

Timary was the first to appear where the path rounded a large topiary fashioned to the likeness of the Eye of Ortus. Her frosty visage transformed to one of surprise at seeing them. She was followed closely by Ishra and a Faran Perian recognised.

All his calm vanished along with his shield. His mind turned to liquid and animal panic threatened to overwhelm him.

There you are, my little puppet.

Ishra came to a sudden halt and raised her arm to prevent her guest from progressing without her. The smile that had lit her face faded, and she took a step toward Neesa.

'Forgive me, Neesa. I told Lili to forewarn you that I was bringing a guest to the Tower. I had not intended for you to come out in this inclement weather.' She stepped aside as though to introduce her guest. 'Lord Armin here has expressed a desire to speak with you.'

'He can speak with me here.' Neesa looked away from Ishra to face Armin directly. 'What is it you want?'

Her curt response caught Ishra's attention, and Timary looked a little more alert.

Armin gave Neesa a syrupy smile and let his eyes drift toward Perian. 'I am overjoyed to find the prince here,' he said, ignoring her question. 'We are old acquaintances. A walk in the temple's excellent gardens would be most gratifying, my Zameel. I know you are anxious for my state of health.' He bent forward into a small bow and flicked a modicum of magic at Perian, making his muscles tighten even more and leaving him unable to speak.

Timary lurched very slightly, her eyes flickering between the two men, evidently unsure of what she had felt.

'You cannot have him,' said Neesa. 'I forbid his walking anywhere or with anyone other than me.'

A wrinkle of concern formed across the queen's forehead, and her eyes searched her Oracle for the meaning behind her words and tone. Armin glanced past Ishra at Neesa and stared at her for a moment. His eyes slid from Neesa to Perian again; laughing eyes of triumph. As addled as Perian's mind was, he could see that Armin saw no threat in those around him, not even the powerful Timary, who appeared as confused as Ishra by this turn of events.

No one moved. A haze of escalating tension began to gather around them, flowing from Neesa's words of defiance. Perian watched the shifting emotions of the group as at a distance, his shoulders still hunched and his body limp. His mind refused to focus. His entire being was dominated by the thunderous throbbing of his blood.

Tanais, Neesa called into his mind. A soft, musical sound that reminded him of a distant bell.

Her call, neither sharp nor fearful, pierced his confusion and struck at his core, opening the way for all his training to reassert itself instinctively. Her warnings and teachings ran through his mind rapidly and his fear began to release its hold. There was no room for fear in this moment; he would tremble later. Fear would be his downfall, he reminded himself.

He pushed the fright from his muscles and his cloak of turbulence dissipated. Without changing from his submissive posture, he formed a shield about himself while imperceptibly increasing its strength to a point that he hoped would keep Armin at bay. Even so, Armin's eyes widened, and Ishra flicked him a look of disapproval, although Perian doubted she knew what had happened.

She returned her attention to Neesa. 'Perhaps we should all return to the Tower, Neesa.'

'I will not have this daemon of the dark arts sally Ortus's sacred Tower. He will conduct his business here or leave and bother us no more.'

'It is of no importance, my queen,' Armin interjected before Ishra could respond. He tipped his head to one side and stepped back as though to withdraw, flicking another small streak of magic at Perian to test his protection. It pinged back at him and sent a shiver through Perian.

Timary was fully alert now and moved quickly to be close to her queen so the two stood together, just ahead and to the left of Neesa. Perian thought the mage had misjudged, but a smirk teased the corners of his mouth, leaving Perian in no doubt that Timary's move was part of his intention.

A slither of anger and hatred wormed its way through Perian's gut, stirring the furnace in his belly. His small store of magic pulsed at his fingertips, yet not enough to spark and crackle. He held tight the words of anger that nearly choked him with their need for release. *If only I were a powerful sorcerer like Jolint, or Elian.*

A noise from beyond the garden caught his attention, but it was probably just the wind. They were alone, and this was the moment he had dreaded – the moment that would determine the fate of all.

Ishra looked about her, but Timary's eyes were on her guest. The air was electrified. Perian wondered who would move first to break the apparent spell that held them.

Armin's eyes flickered to the left as the distant sound became more distinct. Perian listened more carefully, and hope surged through him: footsteps, many of them. Lili's rushed departure from the Tower now made sense. Neesa had sent her for help.

Perian's mind raced to think of some way to keep the mage occupied until assistance reached them, even though the approach of others was now apparent to all. But Timary hadn't understood the danger they were in and took her eyes off Armin to glance in the same direction.

In that moment, Armin struck out with a sweep of magic. It lifted both Ishra and her priestess into the air and thrust them back onto the pathway with such force that neither rose from where they lay.

Armin's eyes rolled in their sockets with a madness that was terrifying. In a swift and continuous movement that spoke of a sudden need for speed, he turned his attention to Perian and raised his hand to strike. But Neesa had already stepped away from Perian's side and moved in front of him.

Something inside Perian released with her movement to protect him. Desperate to keep her safe, he rushed past Neesa and projected his store of magic. It wasn't lethal, but enough to knock the mage off his feet.

Engulfed in fury he could no longer control, Perian launched himself at Armin, heedless of the streak of magic the mage released as he fell backward onto the pathway. It burned a line across Perian's forehead and singed his hair. Yet Perian felt nothing except a terrible, primaeval need to squeeze the life from this monster with his bare hands.

He reached Armin before the mage had time to gather himself and pinned him to the ground with his body. He hit Armin hard on the side of the head with his fist. Stunned by the blow, Armin was slow to respond. Perian had already raised his fist to strike again, but his aim flew wide as Armin jabbed his fingers into Perian's shield.

A shiver rippled through the shield's fabric and left him temporarily disoriented. A claw of icy words scratched at his defences, threatening to freeze his muscles. 'Don't think you will slip from my clutches a second time,' Armin hissed, puffing putrid breath into Perian's face. Perian gagged, but managed to hang on. 'You don't have the power to defeat me. Your abduction and rebirth was my idea. You are mine, and you will beg to do my will.'

Perian thought he would be sick.

Armin released another stream of magic even stronger than before. It leaked through Perian's protection. He screamed out his frustration as his shield quivered and creaked. But it held. And amidst the violence, anger and pain, a small part of him rejoiced at his achievement: he could at least protect himself against the worst that Armin might fling at him. There would be no begging to do this dark mage's will.

His hands still encircled his enemy's neck, but not with enough strength to squeeze the life from him. He willed magic to ooze from his fingers. Nothing emerged. How long could he hold out against this mad sorcerer and keep him pinned to the ground?

Blood dripped from the wound on his forehead into his left eye and over Armin's face, which swam beneath him as he fought to remain conscious.

The sound of pounding feet was close and distinct now. Armin heard it too. For the first time, Perian felt the mage falter, and the pulse that thrummed against his palm told him that Armin was beginning to panic.

Armin tried to push Perian off his body and wriggle from beneath him. But Perian wasn't going to let him go. This all had to end here. For once in this lifetime, he was glad he had inherited the Darna physique, larger and heavier than that of the Faran.

Armin made another desperate attempt to dislodge Perian by sending out another surge of magic. Perian jerked and shouted with its impact on his weakening shield, but retained his grip. Armin was right: Perian did not have the sorcery to defeat him. But he could delay him for as long as possible. It was going to be up to Ishra's people to finish this off.

He knew the priestesses were almost near enough to strike, and judged that the front line at least would be within range any second. Mustering all his energy, Perian rolled to one side, leaving Armin exposed and a clear target. The mage shot to his feet with his release, twisting at the same time. He made a grab for Perian, who rolled again out of reach and onto his knees. Armin shifted to make another grab, but swivelled back as the first of the priestesses appeared upon the path.

A sneer formed on Armin's face. Perian had seen this before, in Valamer's Council Room: Armin still saw no threat here, and soon he would drop an impenetrable shield about himself and spray his lethal magic into the oncoming group of priestesses.

Perian shouted in a desperate attempt to warn the oncoming sorcerers, but no one heard. He pushed himself to his feet and thrust his hand forward with the intention of waving them back. Instead, a silver spear of powerful magic shot from his palm, catching Armin in the chest.

The mage fell to his knees, gasping for breath.

Still clutching at his heart, he lurched forward onto his face, dead before he hit the ground.

Perian rocked on his feet and dropped to the ground again, shocked. He looked over at Neesa, also on her knees, and her face transformed into a wondrous smile. He threw his head back, laughing out loud in his joy; filled with the glow of his achievement, albeit accidental and unexpected, and intoxicated with a sense of liberation.

The priestesses surged forward. The ensuing blast of combined magic tore the air apart and sent ripples through the fabric of the temple garden in a great plume that stretched outward and then snapped back. It incinerated Mage Armin and lifted Perian into the air, slamming him hard against the leafy Eye of Ortus, where he lay stunned and unable to move his limbs.

The mage's ashes settled into a thick blanket over his body. They filled his open mouth and stung his eyes. He turned his head, spitting and dribbling out Armin's remains, his burning eyes watering in an attempt to clear themselves of the hated debris.

An eerie silence settled along the pathway. No one spoke or moved; any animal life, bird or other, had fled.

Within the strangeness of it all, Perian was pulled into a semi-trance; a sense of looking up, of being half in and half out, so that he stared into the nothingness between the worlds from his physical body. Suddenly, an explosion of blinding light burst before him in the void. Screams of pain and joy emanated from the glow as vast numbers of trapped ethereal beings fled from its epicentre.

They rushed around Perian at such speed he could barely register their passing. But the kiss upon his cheek would linger for a lifetime.

'We are free,' said Cerister. 'Have a good life, my love.'

And she was gone before he could respond.

The priestesses finally woke from their shock and flew into frenzied activity. Everyone was shouting, and the pounding of their feet vibrated through the ground beneath Perian. There was no time to think about what had just happened.

His body ached from the force of the blast. Panic gripped his chest as Neesa's smiling face came into his mind. He couldn't see her with so many people in the way, so he called to her. But she did not respond.

He called again, searching, and the emptiness into which his mental voice echoed told him that she had not survived the blast that had cast him into the bush. It was Ishra's priestess warriors, sworn to protect their Oracle as well as their queen, who had delivered the fatal and unnecessary blow, one that her failing body could not withstand.

A great vacuum spread rapidly within him to replace his joy, and beneath the vast darkness of his grief sat a realisation.

He was now the Oracle of Ortus.

PART II

12

A reedy voice penetrated Perian's mind. He turned onto his side to close it out. His body ached, and he wished he had remained on his back. The voice tried again with the additional stimulus of a prod in his shoulder, forcing him into awareness and opening the way for a flood of memories. A fist of sadness clenched in his chest.

He sat up slowly, the throbbing wound on his forehead preventing him from moving with any speed, before looking sideways, into the reddened eyes of Lili, who knelt beside him.

'Neesa?' he croaked.

'She's dead.' Her breath caught as she fought back tears that escaped onto her cheeks anyway.

He knew this, but Lili's confirmation brought with it a new wave of grief. While he was taking a moment for mourning, Lili gathered herself with a loud intake of breath. Her features hardened as she brushed at the wetness of her face.

'I am the Oracle now,' she bellowed at him. She held her chin high and pursed her lips. 'It is my right. You have no place here. The queen expects you to take the Mistress's place as Oracle, but I won't have it. This is what I have worked for my whole life, and you will not take it from me.'

She blinked at him, red-faced and panting with the effort of asserting herself, defying the wishes of her Mistress and her queen.

Perian put up his hand to stop her from continuing. 'It is yours, Lili. I don't want it and never have. Perhaps you have forgotten, or did not know: I was abducted. I did not walk through that door willingly. I am a prisoner here in the Oracle Tower.'

She stared at him, the blush fading rapidly. She hadn't known.

'Is this t-true?' she stammered.

Perian nodded. 'There is nothing here for me now that Neesa has gone, only hope of escape.' He had probably said too much, but he was too miserable to choose his words more carefully.

Her eyes moved rapidly as she absorbed what he had said, and a half-smile eventually softened her features. 'I will show you a way. I had intended to try persuading you to leave, but perhaps force is not needed.' She took his left hand and tied a string of seven rough amethysts about his wrist. He knew without asking that these had come from Neesa's string of beads. 'It is the symbol of our lineage. No one will notice that these are missing from the original string.'

Perian suspected that Neesa would have passed the full set of beads to him, but he was more than happy to share.

'Hurry,' Lili said. A rush of excitement had replaced her bullying tone. 'Most of the guards are searching the town and the surrounding hills due to the escape of a prisoner. There will be only a few left to search for you once I report your disappearance.'

Valamer – it had to be. Elian had taken his chance while everyone was occupied on the temple grounds; Perian was free to leave.

'I'll be picked up in no time if they're out searching,' he said.

'No. I'll show you a way that few will bother to go. It is a difficult route, I understand, but the Mistress went there often, so you should be safe.' Lili studied him for a while before continuing. 'I am not sending you into a trap. I want you gone forever and forgotten, not lingering on my conscience. Now hurry. The queen will be here shortly to pay her last respects to the Mistress before we all leave for the western border.'

She pulled on his arm to emphasise the need for speed, then disappeared down the hole that contained the hot spring. Perian grabbed his cloak and followed, taking a quick peek behind Neesa's curtain as he went. She lay white and tranquil upon her bed, flowers and herbs sprinkled upon her body. He nodded a quick goodbye and slipped down the ladder in Lili's wake.

She stood on the other side of the bubbling pool by a natural column, pointing to the mouth of a tunnel that had been completely obscured by nature's magnificent formation.

Lili thrust one of the oil lamps into his hand. 'I followed her once or twice in the early days. Not lately, of course – she hasn't been able to negotiate the ladder. It is a short walk through to the other end. I never went into the forest, but my Mistress would spend hours in there. I cannot tell you what is beyond the trees; that is for you to find out. At least you will be free and far away.'

She stepped back to let him through and turned toward the ladder.

'Ortus be with you, Prince Tanais. Don't come back.'

The tunnel was just large enough for Perian to walk upright if he bent his head, and virtually clear of obstacles, apart from sharp stones that littered the dry floor and forced the occasional high-pitched squeak from his clenched jaw and tight lips. He strode through the dark tube in a lumbering dance with a nagging fear that Lili had set a trap and priestesses would surge down the tunnel behind him. But she hadn't, and she had spoken the truth when she said that it was a short walk to the forest; he had been walking for less than half an hour when he lurched through the opening into the angled brightness of late afternoon.

Large boulders, fallen from above long ago, had prevented the forest from encroaching on the mouth of the tunnel. Propping himself up on the nearest one, he absently rubbed each foot along his trouser legs to remove obstinate stones from his soles, then lifted his face toward the forest. Basking in its exuberance of tangled green woodiness, he took a moment to inhale the exotic perfumes of tropical blooms with a dizzying sense of freedom before setting off.

As the mountain's pale pink aura began to fade and a dark shadow settled over the forest below, he stopped for the night within the protective buttress roots of a tree so tall and ancient that he could not discern its leafy umbrella. He thought of Neesa walking through the trees, the cuff of her Oracle trousers dusty with pollen from the ferns, which were impossible to avoid, and the pain of her loss struck him again. It left a lonely hole within him. He carried on her lineage through her teaching, something that was important to her, but he wished with all his heart that she were here to share the beauty of her forest.

As Neesa had said, the air was warm and windless. After removing the odd twig in difficult places, Perian fell into a deep slumber, stirring only occasionally at the call of night birds or a disturbing rustle in the nearby undergrowth.

He woke at dawn with the excited chirruping of birds and itchy bites over his face and hands that he had scratched to scabs in his sleep. His stomach growled; he had eaten nothing since late morning the previous day, and he felt hollow with hunger. He thought there was little prospect of his finding anything to eat without a weapon, and anything he could catch with his bare hands was probably almost dead already and unfit to eat. If he hurried, he might break free of the forest and find a village or friendly farmhouse before he starved to death.

The sun rose and set several times, and still the dense forest did not yield to farm or village. His bare feet were sore and the handful of berries he had found was scarcely enough to satiate his hunger. Rain was frequent and intensely heavy. It fell without warning and, although brief, left him sodden. Gradually, the novelty of being free began to wear off. His heart would skip a joyful beat whenever he thought about it, but that intense happiness with all things had faded. He had called to Elian once, only to be told that he was 'busy'. The clash of swords Perian sensed around Elian had left him worried.

When he came to a stream that flowed in the general direction he was taking, Perian followed along its bank, the sun rising directly behind him. Midday approached and Elian had still not returned his call, so he sat on a shaded log to attack a quantity of berries he had collected, and tried once more.

After the second attempt, he received a groggy response.

Elian, what has happened? Are you all right?

Yesh, I'm fine, Elian replied. Even though speaking into Perian's mind, he sounded slow and slurred his words. *I took a sword in my side. It's clean and miraculously missed anything vital, but Jolint was a little heavy with her administration of my pain potion.*

Perian laughed aloud; at the joy of speaking to his brother and with the relief of knowing he was safe. Jolint had never made a good healer.

Are you well, Perian? Where are you? Elian asked after a moment, clearer now in his concern.

Amazingly, I am well, though getting thin on a diet of berries and the odd nut. I'm in a forest and heading west toward Rashinder, I hope.

Ah, I thought it was you who caused the ruckus at the temple. We are in north Rashinder and riding as fast as we can toward Jasperen with two to a horse and my wound. Elian hesitated for a moment. *I had intended to stay behind and find you, but once I was injured, Jolint and Valamer insisted I go with them. But I will fly back for you, Perian, as soon as I can.*

No, you won't. I can make my own way to Jasperen. Promise me you won't try to fly with such an injury.

Elian grunted.

Is everyone well? How does Valamer fare?

All well. Mine is the only injury, with the exception of Jolint, who has a black eye. Valamer was a mess when we got to him. Unfortunately, he's recovered quite well and is his usual grumpy, bullying self.

Speak to me again when you are rested and recovered from Jolint's ministrations, Elian. I am no longer restricted, and lonely, to be honest.

There was no response, so Perian assumed Elian had been drawn back into the delirium of his potion. Brief though their contact had been, he was filled with a greater urgency to be with them.

He popped the last of his berries into his mouth and walked on with more speed until he came upon a cave. His skin prickled on entry, but further in, he found the chamber to have a peaceful and welcoming ambience. A cursory exploration of the cave's interior by the light of a few pathetic light bubbles showed many signs of old habitation: wooden bowls, a rusty knife, and on a little shelf he discovered neatly folded material, rotted by age and eaten by insects. He could see that it had once been a fine garment of bright yellow silk, even though it disintegrated between his fingers.

Flopping to the earthen floor and crossing his legs, he expanded his awareness to gather in the presence of the cave's previous occupant, whom he felt sure had been a mystic; possibly two or three. In the stillness he could hear their soft chanting echoing about the walls in a distant way, and he soaked in their sense of peace as one starved of such things.

Night-loving insects and frogs began their song beyond the cave entrance as though in harmony with the echoing, and the tinkle of the stream faintly penetrated his awareness. He absorbed it all as a sick man draws on the power of the healer. Until now, he had not realised just how desperate he was for such healing. He would stay here for a day or so, he thought, to recuperate from his journey and, if he felt safe, visit his sphere to allow his pressing visions to show themselves.

With the cessation of movement and a roof over his head, Perian finally allowed himself to look at the events of the temple garden. Until now he had managed to keep the memory at bay, not wanting to fully acknowledge Neesa's death. But he could put it off no longer. He touched the long burn line across his forehead that still had not scabbed over properly in the moist heat. Tears welled in his eyes as he saw again how Neesa had tried to protect him, and his teeth clenched briefly, reflecting the anger he had felt during his fight with Armin and the blast that blew him away from his Mistress and took her life.

Then, suddenly, he remembered the screaming in the silence, and the kiss …

He sat forward and put his hand to his cheek. Cerister! Amidst the triumph and sadness, another momentous event had taken place: Cerister was free, and so were all the Farans caught in the bubble of souls. The power that held them bound had disintegrated with Armin's death.

With his remembering, he felt again Cerister's ethereal breath upon his cheek as she wished him a good life. His tears of sadness turned to tears of joy and his heart ached with love. 'Have a good life,' he whispered back into the void of the cave.

Armin was dead. Perian could hardly believe it. That he had produced the rod of light that killed the mage amazed him. Where had that come from? Would he be able to do it again? He hoped he would never need to.

His new sense of freedom left him feeling lightheaded. He no longer had to fear Armin, nor worry about rescuing those in the bubble of souls. He could look ahead and concentrate on helping Valamer run the empires; perhaps even have some fun.

Just as he curled into a tight ball to sleep, Elian's voice filled his mind. *Are you awake?*

Perian yawned and sat up again. *Just. You feeling better?*

Clearer, certainly. Although 'better', I'm not sure. I have been verbally assaulted and physically threatened since I told the others that you were alive and well and crawling about some forest. Jolint was furious that she didn't know we could talk to one another, and Valamer suggested that it was treasonous to keep such secrets. Ben, thankfully, didn't have an opinion on the matter, except to say that it would have been useful to know. Jolint has threatened to withhold my pain elixir until I pass on her messages and report word for word what you say.

Of course Jolint didn't know — they had been parted by the time Elian discovered he could talk directly into Perian's mind, and Perian's only response once Neesa had removed his resistance to replying was to tell Elian not to contact him. No wonder poor Elian felt he was being punished unfairly.

Tell me how you rescued Valamer and then I'll answer Jolint's questions. And if it's death on the stones that Valamer has in mind, I'll answer his questions too.

Perian could feel Elian laugh. He could not have described the sensation to anyone; it was more a subtle wave than a voice.

Elian told him that after his abduction, they had waited before entering the town. He told Perian of the curfew, guards patrolling the streets and searching dark corners, excessively present during the day. They stayed out of sight for the first few days and then spent the next few ascertaining that Valamer was being held in one of the outer buildings of the temple. They had hidden in various shelters opposite to observe the routine around Valamer's captivity and work out a plan.

We just happened to be really close to the gate when a young woman ran into the building. You could tell there was something wrong by the look on her face. She very nearly fell over Jolint, who had decided to take a closer look inside. The next minute, Jolint was nearly trampled by the priestesses and guards that swarmed through the gate and toward the temple gardens.

Moments later, chaos broke out in the gardens. We couldn't believe our luck. We shot in through the door and down the stairs to the cells. Jolint nearly brought the building down in her rush to get the cell door off. Ben pulled a cloak off a peg to wrap Valamer in, and we sped back through the gate and out through deserted streets. Well, not exactly deserted, but free of guards. Whatever was happening in the temple drew them all toward it like a magnet. We grabbed a couple of horses from a stable and rode off into the hills.

How did you get your wound?

A troop of guards caught up with us. Valamer wasn't in any state to parry with an armed mouse, let alone one of Ishra's guards, so Ben and I did the honours. That was when you called. Jolint stood next to Valamer, tapping her foot at our labours as she does, until she yelled some foul expletive and swept all five Wellorns into the bushes with a strike of purple light. 'We haven't got all day,' she shouted, and then pointed at another troop closing in. This lot had a priestess with them, which kept Jolint busy, but Ben and I were already tired. Valamer staggered up and managed to incapacitate a couple of the guards.

Elian paused briefly.

Valamer was unrecognisable when we pulled him from the cell. They hadn't replaced that shirt they left on the side of the road, his hair stood out, and he was nearly buried in his beard, which he'd been unable to trim. Ben has tidied him up and scraped off his beard so that he looks more like a peasant. He's thin but not wasted and, as I said, recovering by the day.

Once Elian had finished, Perian told him what had happened to him, truncating his time in trance with Neesa. He had to stop in his narration occasionally for Elian to tell the others what he had said. When he had completed his tale, they had a thousand questions, but Perian was too tired, and asked that they wait for another day.

The next day, after he had finished a late breakfast of fish he had caught in the stream, he sought the sanctuary of his sphere. The relief he felt was breathtaking, even more so due to the knowledge that he no longer need fear an intrusion by Armin. Others would no doubt try in the future, but not yet.

No sounds, unusual or otherwise, penetrated his concentration; he was alone with himself. Shadows moved frenetically around him, but he ignored them for the moment. This was the first time he had ventured here without Neesa and the first time he would see his visions displayed across his walls. He felt her absence as though part of him were missing; her quiet, amused presence, their conversations, the camaraderie of two seers. He had talked to her often while walking through her forest. He didn't expect her to answer, but even a one-sided conversation was better than nothing. It helped him to answer his own questions. He put his hand on the amethyst beads and found it was enough.

He again saw Risenor in the distance, but this time Risenor stopped to look in his direction before moving on. Perian wondered whether Risenor had seen his sphere, and perhaps him on the inside, but had chosen not to communicate, for which he was thankful. He didn't want unexpected visitors in the one place he needed to be alone. He was sure Risenor was fairly harmless, but if he were to engage with his once-brother, these meetings would need to be properly organised for his own sanity.

After a while he could ignore the shadows no more, and turned his attention to giving them clarity. Saphrax appeared instantly, his sword pointing to the sky, his warriors in an uproar behind him as they prepared for battle. Perian averted his eyes from the carnage to look at their surroundings. The outcome would be what it would be; he didn't need to watch. Just beyond the clash of men and women, he could see the Silver River, indicating that the Wellorn troops were in retreat.

The scene of battle shimmered, the figures distorting long and wide, whirling as a wave withdrawing from a rock pool. Lord Vorten, his father's cousin, emerged in the settling disturbance. He appeared calm as he gazed through the window of his chamber, but the armed presence of Sky God soldiers told Perian that all was not well in Jasperen, and that the Voice had taken control of the palace.

His heart bounced and he struggled to stay calm so as not to interrupt what may follow, but his involuntary rise of emotion had already disturbed the flow, and a rapid succession of events burst upon his vision. Cells full of Darna warriors, his father's frightened wives huddled in one room, men and women laid out upon the sacrificial stones – then suddenly back to Elian and his companions, arriving at the palace gates.

All looked normal on the outside, along the grand fern path, and Perian waited for what he knew would come next. Soldiers of the Sky God swarmed about them as they approached the entrance. The four fought back, but were subdued quickly, although not before Jolint had swung out a lightning streak of searing magic that took the tops off the tree ferns and set the trunks alight. Perian's pulse thundered as the four struggled to break free, but their captors hung on doggedly and dragged them into the building.

The following vision was overwhelmed by Perian's distress and need to warn his friends. He left his sphere with sickening speed and immediately shouted into Elian's mind.

Where are you?

What's wrong?

Where are you? Perian repeated, more urgently.

Just approaching Crothmore. Not far now – we'll be in Jasperen by nightfall.

It's a trap, Perian gasped. *Don't go to Jasperen. Not yet.*

Give me a minute and we'll get off the road.

It seemed to take forever for Elian to speak again.

Sorry. I thought it best to find somewhere out of sight, since you sounded so worked up. What have you seen?

Perian recited as much of the vision as he could remember. No response came.

Speak to me, Elian.

Give me a minute. I think I'm still in shock.

Perhaps you should pass the information on to the others and get back to me. There are bound to be questions. I will remain here for another day, although where 'here' is exactly, I'm not certain.

He was dozing at the mouth of his cave when Elian finally broke into his silence.

We've stopped at a roadside inn. Valamer nearly exploded when I told him. Then he turned quite pale and silent. Ben, rather too obviously in my opinion, suggested we go for a walk to let Valamer come to terms with your prediction, which I thought a very good idea. Jolint elected to stay behind. Ben and I heard a lot of shouting as we walked away to nowhere in particular. I don't know what Jolint did, but Valamer was calm and quite the Zamir again by the time we returned.

The thought of Jolint as a calming influence made Perian smile. She had been better at that kind of thing than Cerister, but it was usually Elian who had fulfilled the role of pacifier in their early days, in his previous life, when they were confined to their constantly moving wagon.

We need more information. We should have reached the palace this evening, so the Voice has been in power for at least a day, probably more. Was Vorten injured in any way? And just how many guards were there? Who lay upon the stones? Did you recognise any in the cells? I suppose we, or Valamer, want to know the extent of the Voice's control and whether there is anyone left to enlist in a battle to take back power. If there is, where are they? Did you see Grison at all?

Perian quietly gasped at the volley of questions. It was obvious even to him that he didn't have enough information to help them move forward.

I cannot tell you when the Voice made his move. At a guess, as soon as Saphrax left for the battlefront. Vorten was unharmed, as far as I could see. As to the stones and cells, I didn't recognise those laid out, nor those imprisoned, who wore warrior uniforms. There were four Soldiers of the Sky God in the room with Vorten, who knows how many outside. As to

Grison, I did not see him. Perhaps he went with Saphrax. I'll return to trance after I have eaten and look again. You should all rest tonight. I will contact you tomorrow.

We'll amuse ourselves by making tentative plans while you drift about in our future. I would feel happier if you were here with us, but I doubt that Valamer will want to wait until you find us. Jolint sends her love, as I do. Good luck, Perian.

Perian made up a fire and cooked his fish, but ate without appetite. The question of Grison ran through his head. Perian wondered if he were dead. Saphrax, he felt, would have left Grison to assist Vorten. But Grison was a powerful sorcerer, and he wouldn't linger long in a cell.

Anxious to return to his sphere, he finished up his meal quickly, then settled himself to see what more he could glean that would be useful. The path would already have changed now that he'd stopped his friends from entering the palace unaware, but by how much?

He turned his mind to Grison. The shadows moved about, coalescing into a sleeping figure huddled on a bed typical of most inns. The figure moved, and a long lock of pale red hair slipped from the hood of his grubby cloak. As far as Perian could tell, the inn was within Rashinder, and he was sure he could hear the roll of the ocean in the background. It was a start.

He slept fitfully until released from the effort by the coming of dawn. Scattering the embers of his fire, he stamped on them to make sure they did not revive and went down to the stream to drink, splash his face and smooth down his hair as best he could, hoping he didn't look too wild. Gazing along the curve of the stream, he could see that the forest was beginning to thin. He expected the domination of trees to soon give way to scrubland and hopefully farms.

The forest came to a sudden end, and his thankful eyes stretched their vision unhindered over grassland to distant hedgerows. A rough road rutted with deep wheel tracks and pitted by both boot and hoof appeared soon after. It took him in a north-westerly direction and away from the glare of the descending sun. The track meandered a little and ran through a corridor of wooden fences and blackberry bushes. Sadly, the season for blackberries had passed, but Perian could see what looked like an apple orchard in the distance, and he sped along with renewed alacrity.

There were three people picking the ripe fruit – two brothers, by their likeness, and a woman. As Perian approached, the older of the two men stopped what he was doing to scrutinise him. He clicked his tongue, slid his old hat back on his head and threw an apple at Perian.

'Name's Alard, and this 'ere's me brother Hervy and his wife Rosie. We could do with some help here, and there'd be a meal at the end of it.'

Hervy looked surprised, but Rosie smiled. They didn't need help; this offer was charity. He must look in need of a good meal. The prospect of something to eat other than berries or fish made him feel faint, but he managed to thank Alard without sounding too desperate and set to work as soon as he had consumed his apple.

Agnes, the men's mother, was very welcoming and generous in his portion of the family meal. Despite Perian's strange clothing, bare feet and skeletal condition, they asked few questions, and it occurred to him that they probably thought he was an escaped slave. He thought of Hector and hoped that Grison had seen to his freedom, as Perian had asked.

He chose to go to the stables for the night, even though Agnes had offered him the floor in front of the fire. He needed to be alone and undisturbed to seek out what lay ahead, for himself and for the others. Images had pulled at him once he had filled his belly and it was a great relief to sit quietly upon the blanket she had given him, surrounded by the rich smell of fresh straw and apples, listening to the gentle movement and snuffles of their pony.

As soon as he entered his sphere, images danced about him, and he had to calm himself to bring them into focus. A cart containing three sheep emerged. Up ahead he could see a small group of Rashinder peasants hovering about the roadside. There was something odd about the scene, but it was replaced too quickly by Grison, and he had no time to study the image in detail.

Grison paced the room Perian had seen before, then turned suddenly to speak with someone Perian couldn't see, before leaving. Once out on the street, in full daylight, Perian caught a glimpse of a weathered sign he recognised: *The Oyster Shell*, in the coastal village of Rockby. As he recalled, the inn was run by a grizzled old sailor who ran a brothel out the back. An unpleasant man, but the rooms were cheap and he asked no questions. From what Alard had said, Perian was a day's walk from Rockby, less if he was lucky enough to come across the cart going the same way.

It was enough to know where he was going at last, and he turned his attention to Elian. He saw the group moving in the night, searching for an entrance into the palace. The scene moved rapidly to the secret passages, where Elian lit their way with his light bubbles. Then the bubbles went out and they began to run back, badly hindered by the confined space. Moonlight outlined their bodies as they emerged through a doorway into what Perian thought was the garden.

He lost the images and slid back into awareness of his body.

His heart pattered loudly in his chest with the consistency of the path. He called to Elian, who was awake, but thankfully still at the inn. Perian told him of what he had seen and said he would keep him informed of any other developments, then slept for a while until the rising moon lit up the yard. He placed the blanket on the floor, neatly folded, and left the stable to find the track again.

By dawn he had come upon the Coast Road and hitched a ride on the cart from his vision. The farmer and his wife rode on the board, so Perian slipped into the back with the sheep, watching for the group of peasants on foot to appear.

He had begun to doze when the cart jolted in a rut and his eyes flew open to see the group ahead. They were closer than he would have liked, but fortunately looking in the other direction. Instinct told him to hide, so he leapt from the cart and squeezed through the tangled branches of the hedgerow, peering back from between the foliage.

The group had turned about at the sound of the cart, and the shock of who they were left him feeling weak: Timary and a group of five Wellorn guards, who wore their disguise badly. Of course it was.

Lili had been trained to tell the truth; she would have seen this. Had she seen his escape, or had he changed her vision by having already seen this himself? Perian's mind boggled with the idea of conflicting visions, each a step ahead of the other, never knowing whether the other saw their counteraction. Neesa had said Lili had a limited ability, but she didn't have to be highly skilled for this, especially when her memory of him was still so fresh. She probably still had his old clothes to ruffle her fingers through.

He couldn't get his head around it at the moment. He needed to act quickly and think later.

13

The streets and houses of Rockby ran down from the rise to the waterfront with a clear view of the ocean and little fishing boats moored on the sand. Perian tugged his cloak tighter about him, holding his hood close to his face against a sudden gust of wind, walking as casually as he could manage along the shadowed side of the street. He doubted that any of the residents would recognise him or care if they did, but Timary would have realised by now that she had missed him and would be heading in this direction, if she wasn't here already.

He turned left along the bay, keeping close to the shopfronts, and slipped quickly past taverns that might conceal those on the lookout for a Darna prince dressed as a Wellorn Oracle. From memory, the Oyster Shell was in a side street, back from the shore and near the other end of town.

Rockby was a poor town – a place where sailors stayed and the homeless littered the dunes and back alleys alongside the town's detritus. Street gangs ruthlessly ruled their patch and robbers and pickpockets wandered the busy streets at night, going as far as Whitebay on market days.

Down amongst the dunes and spinifex, a group of drunks were stirring in their sandy nooks, already angry and argumentative with their neighbours and the day in general. Perian hurried past and crossed the busy street to where the angled mid-afternoon shadows grew outward from the buildings. He walked quickly to the corner of a side street and into the covered shopfront of a money lender to see if his pursuers were close by, or worse, following him.

He noticed an unusual number of sailors and let his eyes drift beyond the movement on the waterfront to a ship anchored offshore in the deeper waters. He was trying to work out the insignia when shouting erupted within the shop behind him, and Timary burst through the door, knocking him sideways and into the street as she strode, a ball of fury, toward two men who had suddenly materialised on the far corner.

The indignant shouts of the establishment owner followed her out. 'You can keep your Wellorn witchery trinkets! I'll have you arrested if you come in here again.' He slammed the shop door shut and Perian heard muffled shouting as he continued his tirade from within.

For a brief moment, he stared at Timary's back in a state of shock. Scarcely able to breathe, he began walking as casually as he could toward the stream of traffic along the thoroughfare. He chanced a glance back at the Wellorn group huddled on the corner as he approached the stream of pedestrians – and collided with a Wellorn guard coming in the other direction as the guard tried to cross the traffic toward his companions.

The guard shoved Perian aside with a large, meaty arm and a curse on his curled lips. Instead of lowering his head and pulling it further within its hood, mumbling apologies and sliding away, Perian automatically looked up in horrified surprise. Their eyes locked, and recognition flared on the guard's face.

Perian was the first to recover. He slid around the man and pushed his way through the crowd, leaving a trail of cursing walkers. A few pushed and punched him in response, others stepping aside, but his pursuers were clearly having a more difficult time by the increasing number of curses behind him.

When he found a break in the flow, he ran toward the buildings, where a group of sailors were being evicted from a waterfront tavern and physically projected into the traffic. He scooted around them just as two riders swerved to avoid three of the sailors face down in the dirt, and nearly trampled a small boy with his mother. Perian used the confusion to slip down a side alley, darkened by high walls. His bare feet pounded either side of a stinking yellowish stream that ran down the centre of the alley, occasionally skidding on reeking patches of slime.

When the alley divided, he turned left without taking the time to consider which way to go, but soon realised his mistake. The ghastly stream ran along one wall, following the slant of the landscape. He slowed his pace to a quick walk and tried hard to subdue his heaving lungs and not gulp the air, which became more fetid with every step.

Holding his cloak up to his face against the stench, he stopped and looked about, listening for the sound of pursuit. Due to the angle of the alley and the declination of the sun, it was very dark, but he could see enough to know that he had strayed into a dangerous part of town. The back entries to hovels that should have been condemned long ago ran opposite each other in even rows, and most doorways were either broken or gone. He'd already seen enough to know that most housed more than one family, and groups of disparate men and women stared at him as he passed, even though he had been silent and managed not to gag.

He looked ahead in the hope of seeing the end, but it seemed even darker than where he was, and when he looked back at the light at the end where he had turned off, it slowly filled with the silhouettes of raggedy clothes and roughly cut hair. Perian turned to run in the direction he had been going, despite its lack of light, only to find that it had moved, reshaping itself into more ragged figures.

Hope drained from him faster than the effluent from the tenements, leaving him empty and shaking, awaiting the inevitable outcome and vaguely hoping he would survive.

They came on now in a rush of shuffling feet and harsh whispers, knocking him to the ground and pounding his body with their fists. A knife glittered in his face while rough, expert hands ran the length of his body, along his arms and legs.

'Where's ya purse?' said someone close to his face.

Perian shook his head despite it being pressed into the ground. 'I have nothing,' he coughed, his mouth dry.

The man cursed and spat near his face. Perian struggled when someone pulled on his amethyst bracelet, breaking the cord so that most of the beads rolled away and into the liquid filth. He stretched out his hand to grab at what beads were within reach, but someone stomped on it and prised the two purple stars he had managed to grasp from his hand, then kicked him in the stomach. The knife twitched across his earlobe for good measure, and then they were gone, leaving the alleyway strangely empty.

Perian didn't move; he wasn't sure that he could. The individual blows, too many to count, flowed together to throb in unison. He thought the fight and fear in him depleted until he felt another presence silently appear at the turn-off, prickling its way along the alley.

'Damn,' whispered Timary. She threw a light along the confined space, nearly blinding him, but he was huddled too close to the wall for her to distinguish him from the shadows and garbage. After a short space of time, she left, and Perian released his held breath.

A voice filled his head. *Wait there, Perian, I'm coming.*

He knew he was hallucinating. Elian was in Jasperen.

Not surprisingly, no one emerged from their back gate to investigate. He pulled his knees into his chest and tentatively put out a hand to help him stand, but withdrew it and turned his head at a slight sound not far away.

It was just a raggedy dog, its dark eyes glinting in the feeble light. It was probably hungry, so best not to be lying down if it chose to investigate. To Perian's horror, it came on at a rush with his movement and stood over him, wrinkling its nose with distaste. He groaned and put more effort into rising, but by the time he had rolled onto his knees, he found himself staring at a pair boots.

'What is it about you, Perian, that makes everyone want to beat you to a pulp?'

Elian.

Perian dropped his head between his arms and mistakenly took a deep breath, causing him to gag and choke. Elian's warm hand rested between his shoulders, loosening Perian's tears of relief. Another set of feet rushed down the alley as Elian pulled him to his feet.

'Can you stand?' he asked.

Perian nodded, leaning heavily on Elian's arm while the newcomer threw a clean cloak about him, careful to keep his nose and mouth covered within the folds of his own garment.

'We'll have to take him through the stables,' he said. 'They won't let us in the front door with him stinking like a cesspit.'

Grison. Perian stretched out a shaky hand toward him, but Grison stepped back, muttering something from beneath his cloak. Perian pulled back his hand as they urged him forward. 'They're still looking for me,' he said.

'Who is?' Elian asked. 'Who were you running from? We were out walking when chaos erupted in the crowd. I just knew it was you, and we thought to catch you as you ran out the other end of the alley. But you didn't, of course.'

'Timary, Queen Ishra's head priestess, and a few guards. I came down here to get away from them.'

Elian whistled through his teeth. 'We'll chance the back lanes, then.' They moved off at a shuffle.

When they arrived at the inn, the girls and fancy boys not occupied in the back building were sitting about the stables and small courtyard. They squealed when Elian dragged Perian in and proceeded to put on a mock performance of horror, worthy of the most renowned travelling players.

Grison paid double for the bathhouse and impatient guests were kept outside until Perian had been scrubbed clean, dried and wrapped in Elian's cloak. Grison dropped Perian's clothes into the furnace; even clean, he couldn't wear them, and Timary would torture anyone found in them. His exit from the bathhouse caused a chorus of laughter and lewd comments, and one very pretty boy squeezed Perian's left buttock through Elian's cloak.

To Perian's tremendous delight, Hector waited for them in the inn room. He was dressed like a merchantman and looked so different with his stubbled beard and roughly cut hair, and without his slave's attire, that Perian scarcely recognised him at first.

'Hector, what a wonderful surprise, but why are you here? Grison was supposed to give you your freedom.' He turned about, looking for Grison.

Grison shrugged. 'I did.'

Hector stared at Perian for a moment, shocked at the state he was in. 'What happened?' he asked. 'Who did this to you, my Zameel?'

'Tanais. Call me Tanais.' He threw himself on the bed in his desperate need to lie down, which was a terrible mistake. He groaned and swore, then grunted pathetically until the pain subsided with his lack of movement. 'Why are you still here, Hector? I thought you would have gone off to enjoy the rest of your life.'

'I might well have done if events hadn't moved so quickly, and I had to flee with Grison before I could get back to where I had stored the money you gave me. I was halfway up the stairs when I saw Soldiers of the Sky God crashing into your chambers.'

'How dare they!' Perian exclaimed. The thought of the soldiers rifling through his meagre possessions made him feel ill. 'It'll be gone now, Hector.'

Hector shook his head. 'Even though I have already lost the money, Tanais, I thank you for the thought.'

Perian closed his eyes and smiled, pleased that Hector hadn't thanked him for something that no one had the right to take away in the first place – his freedom.

Perian lay naked beneath a sheet on one of three beds, contented now that he was clean and smelling of cheap soap. Elian sat on the bed beside him, holding his thin hand, while they waited for Hector and Grison to return from the markets, where they had gone to buy him something to wear. Grison had put a stitch in his earlobe, and everyone had stared at the scar Mage Armin had left across his forehead. Strangely, it would always remind him of Neesa's premature death rather than Armin's defeat.

'How is it that you are here, Elian?' Perian asked at last.

'We were discovered in one of those secret passages on our way to Vorten's room. After your warning that we would encounter soldiers in the passageway, Valamer thought to try a different route to the one he had intended in the hope that this change would throw up a different result, but it didn't. Our appearance surprised the soldiers and we only escaped because Jolint threw a "cloak of confusion", as she called it, around us, so the untrained eye couldn't focus on us as we passed. Valamer was so impressed he gave her a great hug when we got back, which, surprisingly, she seemed to enjoy.'

Elian rolled his eyes with something he wasn't going to share.

'From what you said, we knew you were close, and more or less where you were going, so we decided to wait for you. I flew here to find Grison in the hope that you wouldn't take too long to find him yourself.'

'And you found me instead.'

Elian screwed up his face. 'Yes, and you look worse than Valamer did.'

'Don't worry. Food and a night's rest, and I will be quite fit to travel.' At least he hoped he would. 'Do you know what happened at the palace after we left? Why Grison left?'

'According to Grison, Saphrax flew into a rage at the news that Wellorn had overrun the border patrol, and left the next day with most of the warriors without consulting him. Saphrax had scarcely passed through the gates when the soldiers swarmed about Vorten like bees to honey, and the Voice rarely left his side.'

'How is it that Saphrax took notice of my prediction? He thought I was a charlatan.'

Elian shook his head. 'Who knows what the Voice said to persuade him? Grison thinks he was only too pleased to flee the difficulties of being Zamir. Anyway, the next day, most of the remaining warriors were sent off to guard a couple of carts, which were to collect food and supplies from the various lords as part of the supply chain to the outer regions of Rashinder and on to barges going to Darna. Grison said he could see it was a sham – too many warriors, too few carts. He was blocked from speaking to Vorten, but did eventually get to see him – but in the company of the Voice, who took the opportunity to suggest he might leave. That night Grison fled here to Rockby, where he knew the Voice wouldn't go. Of course, the Voice knows now that Valamer is back. His soldiers will be searching everywhere, but quietly, so as not to alert Vorten or any loyal warriors that may be left.'

Perian wondered how many of those there would be, since many would be sorely conflicted. Every Darna warrior was tattooed on the inside of his wrist with the sygrilien wings, the symbol for Tarse, and the Voice was supposed to be his representative.

Perian shook his head to clear it of the complicated web that had formed in his mind. He was no scholar or philosopher; let someone else sort it out. 'What is your plan once we are reunited?' he asked, as much to find out as to help turn his thoughts to something more practical.

'There isn't one at the moment. Or at least there wasn't when I left. I only hope that Valamer can contain himself until we get there.'

Probably not, Perian thought, but said nothing.

He closed his eyes and drifted happily into a light sleep until Grison and Hector crashed through the door. They threw an assortment of clothing on the bed next to Perian and sat on its end, looking expectant.

'Dress quickly, Tanais,' Grison urged. 'We must leave, now. That Wellorn witch is everywhere, asking questions and handing out coin. The people don't like her. One of the stallholders said she was asking for someone with an amethyst bracelet. Was that you? We saw no bracelet when we found you.'

Perian nodded. 'The thieves have what is left of it after they wrenched it from my wrist. It will be only a matter of time before they come forward for their handout with this information, and I wonder just how many silent eyes watched my rescue and know where I am. You are right, Grison. We need to leave.'

The closer they got to their destination, the more frequently they encountered Soldiers of the Sky God, so they turned off the main thoroughfare, passing through small hamlets yet untouched by the events in Jasperen – though in the taverns they talked of nothing else. In some, a little closer, the villagers had hidden their shrines, and expelled priests lurked in back rooms. They found it deeply depressing; only Hector remained buoyant, which was no doubt due his change of status, Perian thought.

Despite his beating, days in the saddle and the less-than-nourishing food they had been served, Perian put on weight and regained his health, his bruises largely diminished and the pain less. They passed through the city gates easily enough, largely due to an argument between one of the priest's soldiers and a wine merchant. Elian led the way with Perian behind, then Hector and Grison. Hector guarded him so closely they were in danger of bumping into each other.

They turned off toward the markets, passing in the shadow of the Windy Path Inn, where he and Elian had stayed when they returned to Jasperen from Silaven, then Elian led them past the fish markets, arcing widely around the palace to the Common Tavern.

They settled around a table near the hearth. It occurred to Perian that even if he couldn't see a familiar face, most of the tavern's occupants would probably recognise him. He sank further into his hood.

Elian ordered beer, then sat patiently fingering his mug once it had arrived.

What are we doing? Perian asked into his head.

Waiting.

I know that, but for what?

A sign.

Muttering to himself, Perian scanned the occupants over the lip of his mug. He was hot and anxious within the confines of his hood and wanted desperately to fling it back to breathe in the comparatively fresh air. His hands left little deposits of sweat upon his mug and he wiped them on his shirt, wondering how long they would have to wait for a sign he probably wouldn't recognise. Most of the patrons were busy talking, and one or two slumped over their table as though in deep thought, or more likely, dozing.

Perian's eyes strayed toward a lone figure seated by the stairs. He wore a wide-rimmed merchant hat, battered with age and drooping in places, and a patch over his left eye. Something about the man kept Perian's attention, although he was sure he didn't know him. While he watched, the man tossed a coin and slapped it onto the back of his left hand as if it might help him make a decision, then abruptly got up and strode through the door, leaving the coin on the table.

After five, maybe ten minutes, Elian told them to drink up. Perian gasped and blinked as they stepped into the street. Clean, fresh air swept in from the forest beyond the common grounds and billowed within his hood. He put a sweaty hand on Hector's arm to steady himself as he savoured his release from the noise and tangled emotions within the tavern.

He had always loved taverns – the fuggy air and the intensity of people's intoxicated release from their hard lives – but the opening of his seer's eye and his time with Neesa had deprived him of this simple pleasure; he felt doomed to the isolated existence of an Oracle. He wondered how Lili was managing, so close to the battleground, the sounds of anguish and the smell of blood. She was probably in a little white tent somewhere, and perhaps her 'limited ability', as Neesa put it, protected her from the worst. He hoped so.

Elian broke into Perian's miserable contemplations by pulling on his arm, and he was thankful for the distraction of looking where he was going and consciously following the others. Despite the salt-laden air, he was surprised to see they were down by the harbour, and he let his eyes travel lazily over the water at the array of boats moored along the frontage and others sailing further out. He also saw the merchant from the tavern talking to a vendor of shellfish, where you could buy winkles, cockles, oysters, crab or shrimp served in little terracotta pots if you'd forgotten to take your own.

The merchant turned as they approached, and Elian asked him where he was going and if they could help him unload his goods at the warehouse in exchange for a ride.

'You're in luck – my goods are already stowed away, but I would welcome some company.'

The merchant trailed the smell of seafood as he guided them to his horse and cart, left outside one of the harbour warehouses. There were several warehouses along this part of the harbour, but this was one of the few old ones left: a double-storey building of pale stone, painted window frames and an entry of deep blue, with a red tiled roof that curved upward at each corner. Such buildings usually stored a variety of goods for different merchants who rented space from the owner, and Perian wondered what this merchant was storing.

Even though the man was in no rush and let his horse plod slowly from the town, Perian felt as though he had scarcely had time to get comfortable when they stopped and the merchant ordered them out of the cart. As soon as Perian stood upon the grass verge, the merchant removed his hat and raised his fist to his chest, a mischievous smile spreading rapidly across his face.

'Welcome back, Tanais. I really thought we had lost you to the enemy.'

Ben.

Perian grasped him in a brief hug. 'I confess I thought the same at one point. But it is good to see you. What's happening? Are you taking us to Valamer?'

Ben put his hand up to stop the questions. 'Elian knows the way. I must go on to the next village and stable my horse. It would look a little too obvious if I left it here.' He nodded at Grison and Hector, then got back onto the driver's seat and set off along the road at a much faster pace.

They slipped into a field and hid behind the hedge, waiting to see if anyone followed, but no one came along the road. After about half an hour, Elian took them across the roadway and down a goat track toward the sand, turning off into the bushes and tall sand grass just above the beach and around the headland, where he disappeared into the low entrance of a cave and unfurled a few light bubbles.

'This is an old smuggler's tunnel and leads directly to the old warehouse where Ben left his goods, and where we'll find Jolint and Valamer.'

'How long does it take?' asked Grison.

'About fifteen minutes. It's more or less straight but for a few kinks that are useful if you're worried about the enemy coming in the other direction. It's an emergency escape route. We thought to bring you this way so that you knew where it came out, Perian, and so we could be sure that we weren't being followed.'

Perian thought this a good plan, especially in light of someone like Timary possibly still being on their tail. It wouldn't be long before she assumed he had gone on to Jasperen.

'Has Ben been waiting in that tavern every day for us?' he asked.

'I told him to give me a week before he took over the deliveries. I imagine he was more than pleased to see us!' Elian turned and smiled at Perian. The angle of light sharpened his features and caught the laughter in his eyes. He was enjoying himself, and adventure clearly appealed to him. Elian had always been braver than Perian, and calmer in difficult situations, but Perian had never thought of him as the adventurous sort before; perhaps being trapped in spirit form for so many years had given him an appetite for such things.

The fifteen minutes went quickly, but Perian was grateful for the sight of the door when it appeared. He was anxious to see Jolint and Valamer, and the tunnel had been made for shorter people who didn't have to stoop or suffer the occasional surprise bang on the head.

When they entered the brightly lit room, Perian couldn't at first comprehend what he was looking at. Jolint sat at a loom near the centre of the room, a look of cross frustration creasing her face. Standing over her shoulder was Valamer, pointing to something in the weave. *Jolint at a loom! This is a surprise!*

Their expressions changed instantly when they looked up and saw the newcomers. Jolint stood so quickly that she would have caught Valamer under the chin had he not stepped back.

Perian rushed forward to meet her and swept her into his arms. 'Thank the gods you've arrived,' she said into his ear. 'I was thinking seriously of incinerating the thing.'

'Well, it's good to know that you are pleased to see me, even if it isn't due to concern for my safety.'

She clapped him on the shoulder and kissed his cheek before pushing him away to allow Valamer to embrace his brother.

'I thought you were lost when they told me they couldn't get to you.' Valamer held Perian at arm's length to study him. 'You look better than I expected from what Elian told us. You are a lucky pair; what I would give for such communication.'

Valamer stepped around Perian to greet Grison, revealing a startled face Perian knew. Balon, the palace servant who had betrayed him to his father.

Sudden anger replaced his joy. He curled his hand into a fist and stared at the servant-turned-spy until all the colour had drained from Balon's face.

'What's he doing here?' Perian said to Valamer without taking his eyes from his victim.

Valamer swung about to see who Perian was talking about. 'Why, that's Balon.' A smile crept across his face as he began to make the connection. 'He's mine. A good man. Managed to ferret you out of the Common, if I remember correctly.'

Perian turned to look at Valamer, old suspicions surfacing without provocation. His thoughts must have shown on his face, as Valamer made an impatient guttural noise.

'He told me, then I told Father.'

Of course he did, Perian thought, not a little disgusted with himself.

Valamer beckoned to Balon. 'This is my brother, Zameel Tanais. Bend a knee, as is appropriate, and he may forgive the past.'

Balon continued to stare at Perian as though frozen in position, but moved rapidly as though touched by flame when Valamer clicked his fingers. Perian glanced at his half-brother, then slowly sighed away his excessive emotions as best he could and told Balon to get up. That he took longer than necessary to release Balon he thought enough punishment for doing what his new position required.

'Leave us, all of you. I wish to speak with Tanais alone,' Valamer said loudly, startling everyone. He smiled at Jolint, who was raising her eyebrows at Perian. 'And someone bring wine,' he added.

Valamer threw himself onto a bench near the far wall and spread his hands on the plain wooden table, stained and gouged, and dotted with blobs of wax at one end. After Hector had rushed in with the required refreshment, Valamer poured wine for them both and sat back, smiling at Perian, his mug clasped between his hands.

'Think of what an adventure you would have missed, Tanais, if Balon hadn't flushed you out.'

Perian gazed absently at his brother, still disoriented by Balon's presence. He reminded himself that Balon was a tool of fate like everyone else and that he was more than glad to have met his father and Valamer. He conceded the rightness of Valamer's statement with a tilt of his head.

'Were you badly hurt?' Perian asked at last. 'Elian said your blood was all over the bed.'

Valamer's expression turned to one of pain in his remembering. He shook his head as though to wipe his memory clean of the event that took the life of his lover and a close friend. 'A stab wound to the arm. It has healed nicely.'

They sat in silence for a while, each within his own memories.

'Thank you, Tanais. I hadn't expected you to rush out to rescue me. I thought I was lost and would die slowly in that wretched cell.'

Perian thought of what Neesa had said. 'The Oracle told me that you had not been harmed and that you were cared for, which I took to mean they hadn't tortured you to the point of death and that they fed you, but that your spirits were low. She also said that you were strong-willed and resilient and would survive. Fortunately, she was right. They said that as long as I cooperated you would live, but I confess that I had begun to think that you would spend all your days in that cell, and I imprisoned in the Oracle room. I could never have guessed that Mage Armin would be the instrument of our release.'

Valamer let out a short laugh that held no joy and raised his mug. 'To Mage Armin.'

Perian hesitated, then raised his mug and swallowed the contents. 'To Mage Armin.'

14

Later, when they had eaten, Valamer left with the others for a meeting, leaving Jolint 'to keep Tanais company', he said. In answer to a questioning look from Perian, he added that it was best she stayed, as he didn't want her to distract and disrupt the meeting, and in any case, the two of them would probably appreciate some time to catch up. It occurred to Perian that Darna warriors weren't used to female warriors, and Jolint had always been very vocal about her opinions. In fact, Perian thought that she had become even more assertive without Cerister, as though she had grown into a place that Cerister had once filled.

When they were alone and all was silent beyond the door, Perian walked over to the loom, which had been moved to one corner out of the way. He lifted the sheet placed over it to keep the dust off. He could see from the frame that the piece would be approximately three feet by five feet on completion; Jolint had woven less than a quarter so far. The end feathers of a white wing, with tips brushed by gold and pink hues as though catching the rising or setting sun, rested on the rich blue of a cloudless sky. Perian found it stirringly beautiful.

'Jolint, this is the work of a master. When did you learn to weave?' He twisted his head to look at her seated cross-legged on some sacking on the floor.

She screwed her nose up. 'Valamer is the master weaver. He was trying to teach me. He said I would find it useful and it would help me relax. He lied.'

'But I saw you working on it,' Perian persisted, unable to believe that his tough, bad-tempered brother could create something so delicate.

'He unpicks the bits that I do: too loose, too tight. He's very fussy. I'd like to get my hands on the person who thought to store that wretched loom down here.' She laughed and patted the sacking for Perian to sit beside her. 'Don't look so shocked, Perian. He said it helps him to clear his mind and find a space without thought. I can't imagine such a thing, but there you are.'

Perian compared her description to being in his sphere – peaceful, quiet, where only he existed – and found it similar enough. Valamer had found his own way of seeking separation from the cares and troubles around him, a place where he could think clearly and revive his spirit.

Jolint's voice caught his attention again. 'Evidently his father, your father, sent him to learn to fight amongst the mountain tribes; to toughen him up and make a man of him. He said he enjoyed their unconventional way of fighting, rough and physical, but what his father hadn't told him, or perhaps didn't know, was that these same tough fighting men were renowned as master weavers. Valamer said that for once in his life, he excelled in both tasks. His father was delighted and horrified in equal portion.'

Perian burst into laughter. He took Jolint's hand and they sat in silence, content to be in each other's company.

The sound of rushing feet made them sit up. Elian burst through the door with a look of relief when he saw them.

'Soldiers searching the warehouse,' he wheezed as the dust began to settle. 'We must go to the tunnel. Hurry.'

He scattered dust over the loom sheet and across the tables and benches, and toppled the mugs with a quick wave of magic, the spilt contents drying instantly and staining the tabletop. Perian coughed in the flying dust storm as he ran toward the door with Jolint, Elian at their heels. He glanced back into the room as he turned into the tunnel seconds before Elian extinguished the lamps; no one would know that it had been in use moments before, or even within the last ten years, but he hoped the owner would have a ready explanation for the slight lingering smell of recently used lamps.

Voices, both rough and pleading, drifted down from the floor above. Valamer waited for them anxiously at the door to the tunnel and flattened his back to the wall to allow them past. Jolint stopped and pushed back past Elian, asking if everyone was accounted for over her shoulder. At that moment, someone above screamed, and men began shouting. Smoke drifted down the hallway with the opening of a door and footsteps pounded down the stairs, people cursing as they fell upon each other in their rush.

Valamer pulled on Jolint's shoulder. 'Quickly, Jolint, what are you doing?'

'I was going to disguise the doorway, but there's little point now.' She turned and ran.

Perian and Elian were last, with the exception of those flowing down from the warehouse. They were following mostly by sound and the faint glow of Grison's light bubbles at the front of the group. An ephemeral black snake of choking fumes insinuated itself along the tunnel from the warehouse, parts of it separating to enclose the retreating individuals as it searched for an opening at the other end.

'What's in that warehouse?' Elian rasped between coughing fits. He covered his face with his arm.

'Everything, I imagine,' Perian answered. Tears ran down his face, and the insides of his nose and throat stung.

The noxious fumes wound their way past the escapees at a remarkable speed, hit the wall of fresh air at the end and doubled back. Those ahead surged through the poisonous plug, helping to dissipate it, and staggered into the bushes and sand grass around the opening, gasping for air. Elian tripped and fell; Perian fell over him just as darkness enclosed them with the loss of Grison's light bubbles. But he didn't have time to panic.

Hands grabbed them both by their shirts and pulled them out into the fresh air, where bent figures gasped amidst the tall grass. Perian lay on his side and coughed till he thought his throat would fall apart. He rubbed his eyes and watched as a group of warehouse workers poured from the exit, none of whom he knew. His eyes drifted to the red glow that already stained the sky. He stood carefully to avoid another bout of coughing and hobbled to where Valamer stood, watching the tips of flames rise into the air.

He inclined his head toward Perian when he felt his presence. 'Their personal hoard must be very great if they so freely waste what was in that warehouse.'

Perian continued to stare at the flames mixed with dark tendrils of smoke; a ferocious fire, even for an old warehouse, where the floorboards would be steeped in old seepage of oil, lanolin and wine. Then the full meaning of Valamer's words came to him: he was using the warehouse to collect food to feed the people.

No one had yet told him what was going on. He had thought to ask Jolint or the others once they returned from their meeting. Could things be so dire already that northern Rashinder and Jasperen were short of food? He saw the landscape of his vision and it made him feel weak. Whether Valamer's intention was altruistic or tactical, Perian knew that when the time came for Valamer's attempt, he would have the people with him.

Perian turned at Grison's approach. 'Did Saphrax not check the temple cellars for hoarding?' he asked.

'No. That was one of the things he chose to ignore, then run away from. Whether Vorten was told, I'm not sure.'

Valamer's head spun about. 'What did you say?'

Grison repeated what he had said. Valamer stared at him, his features hardening, but his eyes showed sadness and disbelief, and the depth of his feelings made Perian want to enclose him in his arms and tell him that Saphrax had probably misunderstood.

Valamer's eyes moistened, but did not grow to tears. 'Father was so proud of Saphrax – such a brave warrior, he would say, who would one day stand at Soas's side to rule together.' He looked directly at Perian. 'A brave warrior he is without doubt, and a marvellous tactician in the field and in the defence of our empire, but unless bullied by the strong voice of authority, he is less capable of ruling than an ignorant farmhand.' He shook his head and walked between Perian and Grison to begin calling everyone together. 'We go to the palace.'

Valamer didn't shout, yet everyone heard what he said. Perian counted ten warriors, plus five workers from the warehouse.

Ben separated from the group and strode toward Valamer. 'This wasn't the plan, Valamer. Surely it is too soon.'

Perian didn't need to see Valamer's face to know that it was flushed with anger. 'Everything has changed. We cannot wait. We go to the palace.'

Ben looked at Perian and Grison, his eyes wide as he walked around Valamer toward them. 'What did you say?'

Grison shrugged. 'I'm not sure. Perhaps it is the fire.'

Perian thought it more likely to be something to do with Saphrax, but exactly what, he couldn't say. Going to the palace didn't sound good, and from the faces around him, no one else thought so either. 'What is he going to do, rush the palace with just ten warriors, two sorcerers and a few unarmed warehouse staff?'

Ben shook his head distractedly. 'No. We have a hideout beneath the cells, but this was meant to be the last stage of our assault. We all agreed this was the best way.'

The Zamir would have his way despite attempts to change his mind, so Perian followed as they made their way along the coast while most of the population was occupied trying to save the remaining warehouses, and no doubt the city itself.

The hideout was easily accessed by yet another hidden tunnel and escape route, one that the Shanahan and his people had had no time to get to when the Darna warriors swarmed the palace. It was a very large room that spanned an entire floor, as far as Perian could make out. There was no furniture. Hessian sacks had been placed on the ground for people to sit or lie on. Perian noticed a vat of water and a pile of small boxes in one corner, suggesting that someone had been preparing the room for occupation. Even so, the place smelt damp and unused, and dust puffed into the air with every footfall and crunched beneath his feet. He looked for Elian, whom he hadn't managed to catch up with on their journey, and spotted him amongst the warriors.

Perian pulled him aside. 'What's going on?'

'Who knows? We must await new instructions from the Zamir.' A wave of anger pulsed through his words. 'You should ask Jolint. She may know more.' He pointed to where Jolint was waving her arms about and Valamer was growing very red in the face. 'If he hits her, I'll be on him,' said Elian.

'No, you won't. I will.'

As they watched, Jolint suddenly stopped her frenzied movement and put her hand up to rest it on Valamer's chest. Perian bristled in preparation to rush to her aid, but Valamer bent his head and shook it. The scene had changed so quickly that Perian couldn't get his head around it.

'What have I just seen, Elian?'

Elian laughed and clapped him on the back, all his anger gone. 'She's probably put a curse on him. You work it out, Perian.'

But he couldn't. He felt confused and claustrophobic, and looked about for Hector, who had been purloined by Valamer and just about everyone else, with the exception of the warehouse staff, even though they knew he was now a free man. 'I want my servant back,' he said distractedly, to no one in particular. He wasn't sure why he had said 'servant', except that he had been contemplating asking Hector to work for him at double pay until he was ready to branch out alone.

'Are you all right, Perian?' Elian asked, facing Perian and searching his eyes.

'No. I need to sit down somewhere. There is too much going on and everything is beginning to spin.'

Elian grasped Perian's arm and pushed through the small crowd to some sacking stacked in a corner, where Perian plonked himself down. The hessian gave no protection from the hardness of the floor, but at least he was sitting. He crossed his legs and leant against the wall, closing his eyes to relieve them of the stinging dust. He wanted to sleep. He wanted his sphere. He could hear concerned voices suddenly all about him: Grison, Hector, Jolint, then Valamer. He wished they would all go away.

Their words had begun to fade to a buzz when suddenly he was shocked into awareness, in a space that was neither sleep nor his sphere, by Risenor barking at him, 'Where have you been?'

He opened his eyes wide. A barely formed shape smiled toothily in front of him. No, this was all wrong; he was in the wrong place.

He stilled his panic and closed his eyes again, concentrating on the sounds within the room. He shouted to Elian to get him out. At first he didn't think he had actually made a sound.

Risenor snarled and laughed all at once, and moved closer.

Elian grasped Perian's hand, a hand that felt like someone else's, and rubbed it vigorously. His eyes opened of their own volition and he found himself staring at Elian. Jolint bent down and brushed his hair from his face. He struggled to breathe, every part of him shaking. Sweat ran down his face and covered his body. He could hear himself babbling uncontrollably to Elian about Risenor, but managed to stop as Valamer moved away from the small group.

'Let me know if he says anything useful,' he said over his shoulder as he left.

When only Elian remained, Perian described his experience more coherently, and how he could not account for the fear this encounter had engendered in him. 'Have you ever wondered, Elian, why it was that Risenor and I did not foresee such a major event as our abduction and Risenor's mutilation, even if such a prediction were couched as something happening to the other? I have found it strange for some time that the Magi appeared to have had no notion of this event, and it is now my belief that they must have known. And if so, why did they not stop it? Why did they not warn Aronaye?'

Elian stared at him as though he were talking gibberish again. 'What are you saying, Perian?'

'I'm saying that I am beginning to suspect that they just let it happen, and that the best way to avoid anyone forcing them to intervene was for them all to leave and watch events from a distance.'

'No, that cannot be. I thought they were on our side, helping as they did when they warned Grison of Armin's approach and sent a message for me to join the Almonos Guard and come to your rescue.'

'Perhaps they are, and perhaps I am wrong. I hope so. But if I am right, why? What was their motive?'

'Perian, this is not the time to worry about such things. We are in the middle of a crisis. Turn your mind to the present. We can worry about the past once we are back in our chamber.'

Elian suddenly looked anxious, and Perian wished he had kept his thoughts to himself. But he had a bad feeling the 'why's were about to become more pressing than he liked.

Suddenly, everyone was moving at once. Valamer was issuing orders, and warriors asked the odd clarifying question.

'Are you coming with us, Elian?' Valamer called.

'Uh – yes! Of course.'

Perian rose with his brother, who hugged him close and breathed hot air into Perian's ear. 'I'll see you soon.'

Perian shivered as an awful feeling of dread ran through him. He stared wildly at Valamer as he walked toward him. 'Wait, Valamer,' he said as Valamer gripped him tightly. 'Let me have a quick look, see if anything significant emerges before you rush off.'

'No, Tanais. There is no stopping what will be now. If your prediction is correct, Saphrax will return any time as a hero, and my moment will have passed.'

Only then did Perian realise that it had been Grison's comment about Saphrax that had sparked the urgency. Valamer believed that a triumphant Saphrax would win the people for saving them from the Wellorn monsters, and once he was within the grip of the Voice again, Valamer would have little chance at regaining his position, would be hunted until dead.

'I will come too,' Perian said. But Valamer placed an open hand upon his chest and shook his head.

'No, Tanais. You fight well, I have watched you, but you are no warrior. It will be your job to deal with Saphrax should things go awry.'

'Well, I can see that's going to work!'

Valamer tapped him lightly on the face as one would a child, and Jolint kissed him on the forehead. Ben just waved. Then they were gone; even the warehouse staff, who were probably warriors in disguise. Perian didn't even know where they were going or what they intended to do.

He thought himself completely alone until Hector appeared in the doorway. 'I have been sent back to protect you.'

Perian stared at him, but said nothing. He was agitated and afraid. He screamed internally, silently. Valamer should have waited, given him time to look. He recalled his feeling when he hugged Elian and grew faint with the sensation. He had to sit down again.

Hector poured ale from one of the caskets into two cups and carried them on a wooden lid to where Perian sat. He placed the tray beside Perian before sitting himself and, with a mischievous smirk, raised one of the cups. 'To my changed status, and success for the Zamir.'

Hector's actions had a strangely calming effect on Perian. He raised his cup. 'To your change of status and the safety of our friends.'

They drank and laughed, then Hector produced three dice from his pocket and threw them casually onto the floorboards. 'Elian told me to make sure that you didn't go into trance. He said you should stay alert in case you need to leave in a hurry.'

Perian stared down at the dice – Ben's dice, made of ivory and won from a sailor who had bought them in Soluwi, he had said. He had intended to go to his sphere, for the comfort it gave him and to check on what was unfolding, but he could see that to remain alert was the best policy, and there was little he could do for those above ground should he see anything disturbing. Dice was a good idea, even though he rarely played such a game.

'In that case, we will need a few of those pebbles that bruised the soles of my feet on the way in, then you can explain to me what they are doing.'

They laughed, whispered loudly, and eventually, Perian lost all his pebbles. He flicked his last five at Hector and flung his arms into the air with an expansive and exasperated sigh. Hector said that Valamer's idea was to release the prisoners first, then go back into the passages and take the Voice by surprise when he was with Vorten, which Grison had said was all the time when he left. By Perian's calculation, if they managed to release the prisoners, they would begin to trickle down into this room very soon. Hector agreed.

Hector was just asking Perian if he would like to try winning his pebbles back when they heard the first signs of movement upon the steps beyond the doorway. They stood together. Perian squeezed a little magic into his fingertips and Hector placed his hand upon the sword he'd been given. They waited, tensed for whoever may enter, friend or enemy.

The door eased open and a shabby warrior slipped into the room, initially dazzled by the dull light of the lamps. Perian breathed a sigh of relief and Hector removed his hand from his weapon. The first man through, an officer Perian knew by sight, nodded at Perian, then stood by the door as the rest flowed through – around thirty thin and dishevelled men, amongst them other officers Perian knew by sight but had no names for.

In their midst, Perian noticed a small, frail woman, carefully aided by two warriors. *Erely.* He felt ashamed that he had not thought of Erely or wondered what had become of her. Now he knew. She would have been a great threat to the Voice, as would Grison; she was a truth-seer and could see the truth of who he was and what he intended. The Voice hated her, and it amazed Perian that she still lived, although not for much longer, by the look of her now.

He raced across the room, pushing his way between the men, and grasped Erely tightly in his arms, easing her from her carers. She was little but bone, and her hand shook upon his arm. 'What have they done to you?' he whispered, appalled at her condition.

'It's more what they haven't done,' she replied in her usual spirited way as Perian and another more or less carried her to the corner where he and Hector had played dice.

Hector and another man were already handing out water in the few cups available, and the men were gathering together to sit in a group while the first officer counted heads.

A warrior who had accompanied Valamer approached Perian and knelt by his side. 'The Zamir and the others have gone on through the tunnels. We are to wait until nightfall, and if they have not returned, we are to leave for another hiding place I know of where we can assess what has happened and what to do.'

Perian had no idea whether it was day or night and wondered how they would know when nightfall came, since there were no windows, but he'd leave the warrior to worry about that.

The men sat about in silence. Perian's breath came short and ragged with worry. The stench of neglect was now strong within the room even though it was so large, and he longed to be called to the surface by one of Valamer's group, preferably Elian or Jolint so that he knew they were safe.

'Surely the door to the stairs will be discovered, whether the Zamir is successful or not,' he said, wondering how it was that they had not already found it.

The warrior shook his head. 'You can't see the exit from the other side. Evidently it has a disguising charm around it, placed there by a previous sorcerer. There are no sorcerers amongst the priests and their men.'

Radia – it had to be. Grison must have noticed it and shown Valamer after the uprising. In fact, they had probably expected another attempted coup and planned for it. But how could you plan for the abduction and sale of your Zamir to the enemy?

Hector and another man opened the boxes and handed out dried meat and hardened bread in the form of crackers that were more suited for use as a lethal weapon – at least, the one given to Perian was. He soaked it in his ale and nibbled at its edge while watching the men. Some had wounds that had not been properly attended; many of them dozed after finishing their meagre rations. The officers, four of them, watched over the men like shepherds tending their sheep.

They drifted over to Perian to squat by his side once everyone had eaten and settled. They were telling him their names, but their voices were distant, his attention having drifted to a stirring within the stairwell. Erely put her hand on his arm, her fingers tense yet not gripping as she waited, as he did, for the sound of approach that would tell them the outcome of Valamer's daring scheme by the speed and force of their steps.

They didn't have to wait long. Fear and panic seeped through the door, preceding any audible sound; Perian and Erely shot to their feet together, her grip tightening as they waited to see who would burst through and who would not. Perian's heart beat faster and faster as the sound of rushing feet grew in volume. His breath stopped altogether as they approached the threshold, the great drum within his chest banging louder still.

15

Jolint burst through the door, her face white, her wide, frightened eyes searching for him. Everyone stood obscuring his view of those that followed, even though they stepped aside for Jolint to reach him. She threw herself at Perian and clutched him tightly, her heart pounding against his chest so that he couldn't tell which was hers and which was his. Perian searched the room over her shoulder. Ben, Grison, two officers, the last of which closed the door behind him.

'Where is Elian?' He could scarcely speak.

Jolint pushed herself away from him and held his shoulders, tears streaming down her cheeks. She bit her lower lip. 'We must go, Perian, go now, before they work out that there is a hidden door.'

'Where is Elian, and where is Valamer?' he shouted unintentionally.

Jolint blinked. 'The Voice has them. They were waiting for us. They knew.' Bitterness tightened her speech. The volume of his question had shocked her from her fright, and he could see the clear-headed warrior regaining control. 'We must leave now, for the sake of the men and so we can devise a plan to get them back.'

Grison was suddenly behind Jolint. 'She's right, Tanais. Give your officers their orders.'

He stared at Grison for a moment, wondering what he was talking about. He didn't have any officers, and who was he to order Valamer's men around?

One of the officers, who he vaguely remembered had introduced himself as Simeon, stepped forward to gain his attention. 'I agree with

Grison and Jolint. We should plan their rescue from a safe place. If you would give the command to evacuate, my Zameel, we will get the men and Mistress Erely to safety.'

'Of course, Simeon. Do what you must to keep them safe. Ben, I leave you and Simeon here in charge of our safe removal.'

Perian felt like two people: one who was scared to mental blankness for Elian and Valamer, the other slowly regaining clarity and adjusting to his new position as the highest-ranking person in the room, essentially in charge. Fleetingly, he was angry with Valamer for putting him in this position, for endangering those close to him. He just wanted them both back.

The prisoners were made up of mostly warriors, with a few townsmen and senior palace staff who had put up a fight. The groundsman, Beckworth, was amongst them. The lack of ordinary citizens suggested to Perian that this takeover was very much confined to the palace at present, although he knew from experience that there were two floors that contained cells, so any number of people could be on a different floor to the one Valamer emptied.

The people were on the move, flowing into the tunnel behind Ben. Grison had gone ahead with Ben to light the way with a few magical globes. Two warriors urged Perian forward, while another two tried to assist Erely, who, being much revived after some dried meat and ale, swatted them off. Jolint took his hand and they followed through at the rear, Hector behind them. Perian moved in a daze.

It wasn't long before a brighter light than Grison's appeared in the distance, and shortly after, Perian found himself in an underground cellar, which, although large, was considerably smaller than their previous hideout and rather a tight fit for so many people. His attending officers made a path through the crowd to where Ben was calling his name.

'This way,' said Ben.

'Where are we?' he asked. But Ben had already slipped into a corridor and a room opposite.

Two men Perian recognised appeared through the door and placed a table at the room's centre, then pulled chairs from along the walls. One was a stocky lad with thick, dry hair the colour of dirty straw and adolescent beard growth just showing upon his chin. Perian knew him as Teskin, the son of the tavern keeper at the Common Tavern, and the other was the waiter he had spoken to the day he was discovered by Balon: a tall stick of a man with a wide, bony jaw and short black hair.

'Ale for us first, and then the men,' said Ben. 'We have brought some supplies with us, so the men will sort themselves out, but something a little more substantial for the Zameel would be appreciated.' He gave Teskin a hefty bag of coins. 'I think this will cover our expenses, but you must tell me if or when it falls short. Provide only what you can spare.'

'My name is Mastray,' said the waiter. 'I have been instructed to see to your needs.' He bowed and, with a quick look at Perian, as though he was still trying to place where he had seen him before, he left.

Perian dropped into one of the chairs and leant his elbow on the table. 'I can't help but feel that the entirety of Jasperen is riddled with secret tunnels and underground rooms.'

Ben snorted and sat beside Perian, rubbing his face until it was red; his hand shook slightly as he held it over his mouth. Jolint stood behind him and put her hand on Ben's shoulder. Perian wanted to ask what had happened, but both looked as though they would burst into tears if he did, so he said nothing.

The officers came in with Grison and took their places at the table at the same time as Mastray arrived with ale and cheese, and bread that had been baked that morning – hard but unlikely to break any teeth. Perian drank down his ale and fed his body while watching those about the table. There was too much activity. He craved peace and quiet; he needed to trance and see what was unfolding. If only Valamer had given him space in which to look, this horror may have been avoided.

He thought of Neesa and Lili. This was the reason that Ortus's Oracle was protected and given her own building, travelled in her own carriage or on horseback, separated and surrounded by priestesses, and had her own tent – so that she could follow the paths and give warning should the outcome look grim. How could he seek which way to go amidst so much emotional turmoil?

'Tanais,' said Jolint. The talking had stopped, but he hadn't noticed. Jolint never called him by his Darna name. It was her way of telling him who he must be now.

He let his eyes come into focus and looked at her, then glanced at each of the expectant faces. He gestured to Hector for more ale and turned his attention to Grison. 'Who else knew about the escape route?'

Grison was a little taken aback by the question. 'Apart from me – Ben and Rolin, Saphrax, of course, and Valamer's closest officers.' He spread his arms to incorporate those at the table. 'It was a very tightly held secret.'

Perian looked at the faces again and wished that Erely had joined them rather going with the men into the room opposite. But he really didn't need her to tell him that these men had kept this secret. 'Would Saphrax have passed the information on to Vorten, do you think?'

'I'm sure he would have, since he was left in charge. What are you suggesting, Tanais?'

'Nothing. Just trying to get my facts in order.' He took a deep breath; now was the time to take charge. He glanced about the table. 'I am no strategist or warrior – that is your job. You will discuss the options and come up with a plan to save my two brothers from death and torture.' He felt Jolint tense at the word 'torture', but he imagined that was precisely what the Voice had in mind, and it made him feel sick. 'I am the Zamir's Oracle. My expertise is in tracing the pathways of the near and distant future, which assist you, the strategists, with your decisions. Whether your personal opinion is on the side of scepticism or trust, Valamer, if he were here, and Grison, I believe, would vouch for me when I say that I am amongst the most gifted of seers living. But I need privacy and space.'

He stood and pointed to a darkened corner of the room.

'I will retreat into that corner with Hector as my listener, and do what I do best to save my brothers and the Empire.' He couldn't help but notice the sense of relief about the table, even though some of them probably believed he was going to have a nap.

'Is Hector skilled as a listener?' Jolint asked. 'Would you prefer that I accompany you?'

'Hector has a good memory and is a patient listener. He has observed Elian and me, and will know what to do. This is where you should be, Jolint. This is what you're good at and trained to do.'

He bent and kissed her on the head, but in doing so, he saw what had happened in Vorten's room. He saw them waiting for Valamer at the hidden doorway, and as soon as Valamer entered, someone pulled on a rope attached to the keystone so that the entry collapsed behind him. Elian was in the doorway and Valamer had pulled him away from the falling stones and into the room with him.

Jolint put her hand out to steady him as he wavered above her, knowing what he had seen. He gathered himself quickly and strode across the room to his corner, trying to erase what was already the past from his mind. The loud exchange had already started about the table.

There was nothing to sit on, so they sat on the bare floorboards. Perian entered his sphere quickly and easily and immediately turned his attention to the shadows around him. A raw image of Risenor flared into life on his walls, angry and deranged as he floated about his own trance world. Perian was confused at first. This was a different man to the one he had expected. Then, with a shock, he remembered their brief and unnerving encounter when he had drifted between sleep and trance. He would have to revise his plans regarding Risenor. He pulled his eyes away from his once-brother and concentrated on what he needed to know.

He saw Saphrax leading his men home, his head high and his eyes wide with triumph. From the lay of the land, he guessed that Saphrax was still a good week away, assuming this was the present – longer if, as he hoped, this was a future event.

Finally, the images settled on a dark cell. Valamer was chained to a wall, as was Elian, but Elian was limp, as though dead or drugged. He thought the latter, as that was their only means of containing his magic, since they didn't have a sorcerer to control him. He was bruised, and dried remnants of a bloody streak ran down his cheek. Perian could see no other signs of violence. Valamer was similarly bruised, but no sign of torture yet, as Perian had expected. Perhaps they were letting him dwell on the possibility of such an event. The Voice was cruel enough.

Lili slid across his vision from nowhere, blocking the scene of misery with the whiteness of her Oracle tent. She sat upon a lilac mat and glowed in her joy and the fulfilment of her dreams; she had come into her own. A smile briefly touched Perian's lips with a surge of happiness for her.

Another scene burst upon his vision, hazy at first but clearing with his unblinking concentration. The Voice stood upon the platform erected near the sacrificial stones. He was blood-spattered, and he pointed a long stick, reddened from use, to indicate a bloody mound on the floor that had probably once been human as he explained something to a gathering that Perian couldn't see. The corpse moved and Perian felt his physical stomach lurch. Then, to his horror, he realised that it was Valamer, beaten almost beyond recognition.

So shocking was the sight that he felt numb, devoid of any emotion. When he saw himself upon the platform, he knew, almost without seeing it, what the next sequence of events would be. He knew what he must do.

He was already talking as he slid back into his body. 'Call for Mastray!' he shouted toward the table, where they were still sorting out the fine detail of a plan that no one was really happy about, if the looks on their faces were anything to go by. 'Hector, help me up.' His ankles were stiff and painful, but not as much as he had expected; he couldn't have been there for very long.

He hobbled to his seat at the table and sipped the ale he had left in his cup. A glance around the table immediately told him who believed in him and who thought him a charlatan by the looks of expectation or irritation on their faces, the latter being most of the officers.

'How long?' he said to Jolint.

'Quick – half an hour, maybe less.'

Ben and Grison confirmed her assessment with nods.

That was fortunate. 'They are going to make a spectacle of Valamer, and soon – before sunset, I believe. They will call the people to a sacrifice.'

Jolint stood suddenly. 'No!'

The terror in her voice stopped Perian's racing thoughts. For a moment, her wave of fear nearly overcame him, and the thread of what he needed to do wavered. He saw her wince as he shaped his shield about himself. 'I'm sorry, Jolint – I cannot afford to be distracted by my love until they are safe. We will all need clarity of thought and precise timing.'

Jolint's reaction told him that he had changed, that something new and unexpected was taking place.

Mastray came through the door and walked to the table. 'You called for me, my Zameel.'

'What time of day is it, and have you heard any rumours of a sacrifice?'

Mastray shook his head. 'No. All such events are held at dawn, and it is late afternoon outside.'

'Thank you, Mastray. Please don't mention my question to anyone, and inform us the minute a summons comes.'

One of the officers snorted. 'Perhaps now we can get on with our plans.'

Perian glanced at Grison and shrugged, then turned to stare at Jolint, whose eyes had never left his. He let them blur within his unfocused gaze. What was different? He felt different. How? He felt as though he were still in trance.

He grasped Jolint's hand and squeezed it. He could feel its warmth, feel her lifeblood pulsing through it and her responding squeeze, and at the same time he could see Teskin passing Mastray on the stairs as he raced toward their door. He was both within himself and still in trance, both places at once. How could that be? Neither Aronaye nor Neesa had mentioned this possibility – but then, Aronaye was no seer, and Neesa lived in isolation with no occasion to use such a skill. He thought now that perhaps he had been too anxious to get back to the room, afraid Valamer's life would be over even before he returned from trance. What had he missed by not staying?

'We should finalise our plans if we are to get to the Zamir tonight,' said an officer with buck teeth and a birthmark on his left ear. He was irritated; clearly Mastray's denial had confirmed his belief that Perian was wasting time. The rest murmured and shuffled, taking up the conversation where they had left off.

Jolint ignored them and leant closer to Perian. Grison did the same. 'What is it, Perian?' Jolint asked.

'Stay close to me for the moment, Jolint, and you, Grison. The future is still unfolding within my mind's eye, and we may need to change our plans in an instant.'

Grison asked him something, but it was lost as Teskin entered.

'My Zameel, the people have been called to a sacrifice. It is very unusual. A sunset sacrifice, they are calling it – representing the dying of an old order, the priest's callers say.'

Perian thanked him and indicated to Ben that he should give the boy a coin. The young man turned to leave, but Perian called him back. 'We are nine in this room. See if you can borrow hooded cloaks for us all and bring them down as soon as you can without drawing attention to yourself.'

Perian stared across the table at a general point in the centre.

'Valamer has been beaten very badly, and timing will be tight to get him off the platform alive. I believe the Voice will spout any number of lies, and most certainly blame Valamer for his own heinous crimes. I doubt that many will believe him; he has foolishly been too arrogant in his abuse of the people. But any grumblings of objection will be quelled by the force of their soldiers, and warriors whose faith and loyalty have been conflicted.'

'That'll change once we show ourselves,' said Simeon, with more faith than Perian had. 'Our warriors will come to our side.'

'I hope so, Simeon.' The sacrificial stones hovered uncertainly in his vision, but he couldn't bring them into any form of clarity. He looked over at the officers. 'I would like one of you to speak with your warriors – tell them what I believe will take place and disperse them amongst the crowd in positions that will enable them to come to our aid should we need it, even though they are without weapons. The rest of you will come close behind me to aid Valamer, and myself, if necessary. If the situation appears to be going awry, you must whisk Valamer from the platform and get him to safety as best you can. Grison, you will come with me.' He turned his attention back to Jolint. 'Jolint, you and Ben will go to the far side of the platform near the stones. There is something taking place around the stones, but I cannot yet see what that is.'

'You think someone will be strapped to the stones?' asked Ben.

'Yes. Jolint should be able to prevent any rash action from a distance.' He stared down at his open palms upon his lap and asked if there were any questions or anything they wanted to add, but there was nothing. He had caught them up in his certainty and a concrete plan, which was clearly better than the one they had been discussing.

'What will you do?' asked Jolint.

He looked into her eyes, at the concern and worry in them. 'I will confront the Voice on his own platform.'

'But that's suicide!' she exclaimed.

'Perhaps, but I must try. If we lose Valamer, all is lost.' He wanted to say that if Saphrax became Zamir it would be as titular head to the Voice, but he didn't dare cast doubt on a man the officers and warriors held in such high esteem. It would make them suspicious. But he didn't need to; he could see that Jolint and Grison understood, as did Ben.

Teskin and Mastray arrived beneath the weight of cloaks and placed them on the table. 'The tavern is empty. We must all go,' Teskin said. 'Father said to tell you that he has left the door from the kitchen unlocked, but he would be grateful if one of the sorcerers could lock it once you are out to stop any looting.'

'I'll make sure,' said Jolint.

Perian found the smell of the cloaks distracting. He could almost see their owners and had to look away to continue studying his palms. 'We should go now, so we can mingle with the crowd and not arrive late and risk being noticed. Simeon, see to your warriors — we will follow. Erely is to stay here with a man to guard her.' He spoke without lifting his eyes, allowing the scenes to unfold. Still, nothing emerged from the stones, and it worried him.

Simeon left, and they listened to the hushed movement of the warriors passing in the corridor. When the sound receded, Perian stood and said he was going to have a word with Erely.

She sat on a chair by a table that Mastray had placed there. He could tell by the look on her face that she was furious with him for leaving her behind. He ushered the remaining warrior to a distance and sat in the chair next to her.

'Don't look so cross, Erely. I will need you whole if we are successful, not trampled by the crowd. Grison believes the Voice knew about that tunnel. If we win the day, I would like you to stay close to me and inform me if anyone, and I mean anyone, is lying.'

Her demeanour changed to one of alarm. 'You suspect Valamer's officers? Saphrax, Vorten?'

'It could be anyone, but most certainly someone who knew what we might plan.'

'Then I will remain here until you come for me,' she said, trying to remain grumpy.

The others waited anxiously in the corridor for Perian. Jolint handed him a cloak. 'It's the biggest one I could find, but I doubt those boots will give you away.' He looked down automatically to where his toe had pushed through the leather to stare at him like a small white eye. He certainly looked the part.

They took the stairs two at a time, through another cellar and into the eerily empty tavern. Jolint locked the door as promised and they joined the thinning swarm of citizens around the palace wall toward the sacrificial site. As agreed, Jolint and Ben pushed through the people to stand at the far right of the platform while Perian and Grison swung to the left, followed by Hector and three officers. So closely packed were the voyeurs that they had to move to the edge of the throng to get through. More than once, Perian had to pull hard on his cloak to stop it being wrenched off.

When they were finally in position, he looked toward the stones to see what his visions would not allow. He was a good head taller than anyone else and had a clear view.

Elian lay upon a sacrificial stone, struggling to free himself.

The shock was so great that a high-pitched sound escaped Perian's tight lips and his legs weakened beneath him. He grasped Grison's arm to steady himself. When Grison asked what was wrong, he found he couldn't speak.

He rubbed at his eyes so he could see Elian clearly. Elian's naked chest heaved with his ragged breath and Perian was sure he could see his thumping heart in the movement of his skin. Whatever drug they had given him to dull his sorcery in the cell, and no doubt to get him on the stone, had worn off. But even with his hands tied, he should be able to free himself with his magic, or he could change into a bird or some other animal and slip his bonds. What held him there? The only reason Perian could think of – other than a threat to someone he cherished, which made no sense, since they would probably die anyway – was that he was too terrified to calm himself, thereby unable to change.

Elian, he called into his brother's mind. *Elian, I'm here. Calm yourself so you can fly away should my plans go awry. Don't look, but Grison and I are just beyond the platform.*

At first he didn't respond, although Perian could see by the slowing of his chest that he had heard.

Perian, you should have stayed away. The palace is swarming with the enemy. His voice rose rapidly to a falsetto and toward hysteria. *The Zamir's own warriors have turned on him. I don't know what has happened to Jolint.*

Stop, Perian commanded. *Elian, concentrate on your own survival. Breathe, calm and live, my brother. You are not destined for this death.* He wasn't sure if that was a lie or not, but if it gave Elian hope and helped him to compose himself, it didn't matter.

Perian could see by the slowing of Elian's breath that he was beginning to take control of himself again. Perian could now concentrate on what he had to do, knowing that Jolint would intervene should Elian not relax enough to escape.

Four soldiers stood side by side along the back edge of the platform nearest to the steps. About ten priests huddled on the edge nearest to the stones and the far steps. More stood watching from an area closer to the stones. All eyes were fixed on the Voice, at centre stage, and Valamer, who had been beaten so badly he couldn't stand. Blood dripped from his mouth as his face bent toward the floor, spreading across the planks from the hands that kept his head and chest from a position of complete defeat.

Perian pushed aside the fleeting vision of a young priest and turned around to the side of the dais, toward the stairs, where he was stopped by a Darna warrior. Perian stared at the man and lifted his arm to show his tattoo of heritage. The man's eyes bulged with indecision, showing clearly the conflict these warriors faced.

'It will be all right,' Perian said softly.

The man continued to stare, unsure of what to do. One of the soldiers near the steps turned toward them and the warrior looked about at the movement. Perian and Grison pushed him aside while he was distracted and advanced up the stairs to the platform where all the action was taking place.

They stepped onto the stage simultaneously as the Voice raised his stick to pound Valamer one more time. His scabrous flesh quivered with delight. Perian had to force down a surge of hatred that threatened to overwhelm and blind him.

'Stop,' he shouted. He flung his hood and cloak back and crossed his arms over his chest to display his markings. Grison did the same.

Shocked murmurs rose from the audience in a wave, punctuating the moment, and the Voice froze, his stick still in mid-air, fresh blood dripping down onto his hand. With his eyes fixed on the Voice, Perian turned his head a fraction so the people would hear him.

'You will step back from my brother, your Zamir, and place your weapon on the floor slowly and carefully, as will your soldiers.'

The Voice blinked and stared as though unable to comprehend who Perian was or what was happening, but with the speed of a viper strike, he swung his stick at Grison on Perian's right and knocked him from the platform into the crowd. A blast of magic that Grison had held ready in case of trouble shot wide of the Voice and felled one of the soldiers close by. Shouts of alarm came from those closest to the platform as they tried to move away from the fallen sorcerer. Shuffling and excitement spread outward like a wave amongst the gathering. Two of the soldiers grabbed Perian and pinned his arms back. The crowd shouted its disapproval, yet they were caught in the unexpected heightening of the evening's entertainment and gripped by the threat of violence.

Perian's heart pounded in his chest and his body throbbed with the sudden turn of events. He wavered on the brink of fear and failure, but the trance that still hovered about him pulled him back from disaster and held him fast in his vision. He glanced at Jolint and was relieved to see that she still had her eye on Elian. Ben watched the proceedings from just behind her.

The Voice held up his hand to silence the crowd. A thin, serpent-like smile split his face in two, displaying a strangely perfect set of white teeth. Valamer dropped to one elbow and twisted slightly to see what was happening.

Perian inclined his head toward Valamer. 'Is this the way you treat your Zamir? It's becoming a little repetitive, don't you think? Have you told the warriors you tricked into following you with threats of eternal damnation that you were one of the killers of Zamir Maltha – my father and the father of the people – who you ripped apart in a bloody frenzy and tore limb from limb while he yet lived?' Perian couldn't bring himself to say more about what they had done to his father; he felt faint every time he thought about it.

The people obviously didn't know, but the warriors hadn't known either. No announcement had been made about how the Zamir had died or who the culprits were. A collective intake of breath hissed through the charged atmosphere.

'You lie,' shouted the Voice. He swung his stick at Perian, hitting him on his left shoulder. The soldier holding the arm fell back to avoid the blow. He tripped and fell to the floor with a thump.

Perian's knees gave way with the shock and the pain, but he was prevented from collapsing by the remaining soldier. Numbness travelled across his shoulder and down to his fingers. His mind floated dizzily. A kaleidoscope of new possibilities opened up and danced about him, all showing a variety of potentially horrific outcomes. Many became more detailed and pushed for supremacy, as though the pathways themselves fought for dominance. He clung desperately to his original vision, which threatened to collapse under the pressure. Panic rose from his core, leaving him weak and confused within the maelstrom. All the while, the Voice continued to talk, snagging only a small part of his attention.

'I had no part in your father's death,' the Voice was saying. 'That was my predecessor.' He waved his hand as though the idea were preposterous, moving his stick slowly toward Perian again, unaware that he had effectively implicated the priesthood.

Neesa's warnings about fear travelled like a cooling stream through Perian's mind. He leant back on the remaining soldier to let her words and training seep through him, allowing his physical body to regain its strength, his breathing becoming less jagged. He felt the soldier's alarm and uncertainty through their close contact.

In his peripheral vision, Perian could see that Grison had reasserted himself and was making his way to the steps. The fallen soldier grasped Perian's arm again, but both men had eased their grip as their concentration wavered between the crowd and the Voice.

Perian's visions began to settle, and to his great relief, the original path overcame the others, closing the gap created by the Voice's unexpected attack. Perian straightened and focused his mind on the Voice with one eye on the stick. He forced his quivering body and vocal cords to calm.

'So, my good Voice, as the instrument of the Great Tarse, the Sky God to whom you send so many souls to wash the blessed one's feet – show the people your sorcerer's tattoo, the one that demonstrates your ability and qualification to be a true mediator of Tarse.' Perian yanked his arm free to display his own tattoo.

The Voice's eyes widened and his insipid smile wavered into a snarl. 'The Voice is chosen by the Great Tarse of the Sky. We need no pathetic symbols to show his approval.'

'To receive and transmit the wishes of your god, our god, you must be an Oracle, a foreteller. If you possessed this ability, you would surely have been marked as a baby, as I was, before any could possibly know that your destiny was to be the Voice.'

'We are chosen by the Great Tarse,' he repeated, 'and need no such baubles.' His gaze drifted to Perian's left forearm. The muscles on his face moved subtly and the beginnings of comprehension crept into the look in his eyes.

'Do you know why Ishra wanted me?' Perian said in a less volatile voice.

The Voice lowered his rod a little, forcing sympathy onto his face and into his voice. 'It would be better, Tanais, if we discussed this in private.'

'How dare you address me so familiarly?' Perian boomed, making everyone jump. He pulled his other arm free. The soldiers made no attempt to seize him again, although they remained close either side of him. 'I am Zameel Tanais to you. It is you who has chosen to humiliate the Zamir in public and demonstrate the brutality you mistake for power with the aid of your hirelings. We will play this out in public rather than in the privacy of the palace or the temple, which I'm sure you would prefer. Let the people see who is fit to rule over them. Who will protect them from domination by Ishra's Empty Eye, ensure that they and their country relatives are fed despite the horrors of drought that creep up from the south. Have you told them of the hoard of food and wine you have hidden beneath your temple?'

Loud muttering rose again from the crowd, reflecting Perian's own anger. Someone shouted from their midst. Perian lifted his hand to silence further disruption, unintentionally moving his cloak further aside.

A bright red glow fell on the Voice and fire reflected back at Perian from his startled eyes. Perian stared at the wash of colour upon the Voice's clothing, uncertain at first as to where it came from. He was as shocked as everyone else when he realised that the glow came from his chest; his semi-trance had allowed his ethereal light to become physical.

All his old fears around the wings filled him with horror, and his hand twitched with an instinctive need to cover himself. He again forced himself to calm. From somewhere in the depths of his mind, a voice laughed, *The light comes from your heart and your desire, Tanais. Wings of freedom. They will light your path wherever you go.*

The light showed his anger, and with understanding, its hue changed to pink, although its normal white was not yet achievable.

He grasped the material of his shirt at the neck and ripped it in two, exposing the glowing wings for all to see. The crowd gasped, as did the soldiers nearby and at his side. The Voice took a step back and staggered, nearly tripping on his robe. Perian felt rather than saw the warriors amongst the crowd stand alert.

He pulled himself up to his full height. It was now or never. *Get it over with,* he told himself. Sweat prickled his hairline and moistened his hands. His light wavered slightly, but no one appeared to notice. He felt faint, but pushed on. He had seen this. It would be all right.

'I am Zameel Tanais,' he boomed. 'Oracle to the Zamir, marked by the sygrilien wings of the Great Sky God and confirmed as his true mediator by the light that shines from them. By this sign I name you Pretender and, with the Zamir's permission, relieve you of your assumed duties as Head of the Priesthood.'

Perian glanced at Valamer, who feebly waved a bloodied hand of approval.

The Voice stared in disbelief. The multitude had become unnaturally quiet and the huddle of priests stopped shifting about nervously. Valamer pushed himself onto his knees and turned a bloody face toward Perian.

Elian's voice burst into his head. *What are you doing?*

Perian glanced over the Voice's shoulder at the stone in the distance and shouted into Elian's mind, *Get off that stone, Elian, before one of the priests spikes you with that fork anyway.*

The words had hardly left his mind when one of the younger priests grasped the sacred fork and rushed toward Elian. A hooded figure separated from a group of four nearest to the stone and flicked a streak of purple lightning at the young priest, sending him skidding across the grass and melting the sacred fork into a bent, misshapen rod of meaningless metal. At the same time, Elian released his bonds, sliding from the stone to the ground and into Jolint's arms.

The sudden action broke the frozen silence and the crowd erupted. Someone who knew about the hoarded goods loudly confirmed Perian's claims. Word began to spread noisily through the gathered populace, reminding Perian of an approaching swarm of bees.

The Voice roared and ran at Perian with his rod raised to strike him, but one of his own soldiers stepped between them and seized the Voice's wrist, forcing him to relinquish the weapon. He shouted at the soldier, ordering him to release him and arrest the charlatan, Tanais. The crowd became noisier, waving fists in anger, shouting and stamping their feet until the ground shook with their pounding.

While hysteria grew toward riot amongst the people, Grison had gone to Valamer's aid and was helping him to stand. Perian waited to see what his brother intended to do, the Pretender now in the firm grip of two soldiers. Valamer wavered on his feet and looked, for a moment, as though he would fall, but regained himself. He pushed Grison gently aside and raised his hand to quell the growing tension. The crowd was now roused to such a point that it was some time before they quietened to a shifting silence. Valamer looked ghastly, and Perian thought it possible that this alone was enough of a spectacle to shock the masses to silence.

Valamer waited patiently. His voice faltered at first, but gained strength with use. 'Take this man, the Pretender, to the palace cells.'

The soldiers didn't move, but looked to Perian for permission, which took him by surprise. He gave them a startled nod. He'd have to sort that out somehow.

Valamer waited until the soldiers had shuffled off the stage with their struggling and screaming charge. A roar went up from the crowd. Valamer raised his hand again to silence them. He beckoned to the warrior on the steps and whispered into his ear. When the man had run off, he addressed the crowd once more.

'My men and the Soldiers of the Sky God will punish those who have taken for themselves what should have gone to my people for their many treasonous acts. The hoarded supplies now discovered in their vaults will be distributed to those they were meant for.'

A roar of approval erupted, and the shifting became more intense. Valamer waited for an easing of their response before continuing.

'Be aware that any who take it upon themselves to snatch or raid this hoard will be punished severely. Many of you are hungry and desperate, as are your relatives and countrymen who live outside of town, but attempting to steal what you can will bring down my wrath and show you to be no better than this man who has just been removed from the platform. Now, return to your homes so that we may begin our task without interference and bloodshed.'

Exhausted, Valamer leant against Grison. The crowd was slow to move and individuals attempted to disrupt and shed disbelief amongst the masses. But the show was over, and eventually the crowd began to disperse until only a few lingered discontentedly.

'I need a bath and a healer,' Valamer said, his jaw tight against the pain. 'Sort your priests out, Tanais, then come straight to me.'

Perian looked about at the trodden and dishevelled space where the crowd had been, at the priests being herded like compliant sheep and Elian still huddled in Jolint's arms. Ben watched beside them for trouble. Perian was torn between running to them and doing as Valamer bid. He could see that a different sort of trouble brewed now within the town.

'Tanais,' Valamer called again. 'The warriors will take care of what will follow.'

'The warriors who stood by and watched the soldiers do this?' Perian pointed to Valamer's injuries.

'They have been given a lifeline between religion and state; no more division. They will do what is right and what they are told.'

16

The moon was overhead by the time Perian walked through the palace gates with Hector and one of the warriors Valamer had released from the cells. The warrior had been given a sword, although he didn't really look strong enough to wield it should there be a confrontation. But that was unlikely just yet; revolt and resistance would happen later, Perian thought. The priests were still too shocked by the events of the day to be difficult. But his semi-trance, which had not abated, told him who would resist and who would attempt to retrieve the Voice and crush the Zamir forever. Why, he wasn't sure. What had their faith taught them about the Zamir and his rule?

He walked over the foyer's double-headed kroyer in a daze and was met by one of Valamer's personal guard. 'They're in the Zamir's chambers, and I am to take you there as soon as you arrive.'

Perian was exhausted, but anxious to see both Valamer and Elian. He called to Elian as he took the stairs as fast as he could. *I'm on my way up – how is Valamer? Are you all right?*

I'm fine now, Elian said. *Valamer is a mess and in considerable pain, I imagine, but cheerful enough. A few broken ribs, gashes and bruises over his entire body, including the soles of his feet; he can hardly walk. That he grits his teeth with every step Grison says is a good thing as far as his feet go, although I doubt that Valamer would agree with him at the moment. Oh, and a broken nose that I don't think even the healers will be able to put back the way it was.*

He won't like that.

No, but he doesn't know yet. I wouldn't mention it if I were you.

I'm in the corridor. Come and meet me.

Elian was already standing in the doorway to Valamer's chambers. When he saw Perian he rushed down the corridor and he threw his arms about him, nearly knocking Perian off his feet. 'Thank you, Perian. I was so frightened, I couldn't think.'

'I know.' He extracted himself from Elian's grip and stood back a little to run his eyes over him, looking for any injuries. 'Did they hurt you?'

'No, apart from a terrible ache in my shoulders where I hung from those chains. Not that I remember that bit. I didn't see what they did to Valamer, and he hasn't said. By the time I came to on the stone he was being dragged onto the platform, already near crippled from his beating.'

They turned into the foyer as Jolint was bouncing through the far door. Pushing Elian aside, she took Perian's arm. 'Erely has gone to her rooms, to gorge herself until she's sick, she said, and then go to bed. She asked me to tell you that she'd see you in the morning.' She raised her eyebrows in mock surprise, or possibly a question.

He chose to ignore it and pulled her close so he could wrap his arms about her and inhaled the gentle perfume upon her skin. 'You smell fresh; bathed and fed,' he said into her ear.

She chuckled and bent her head back to face him. 'That was an amazingly brave and foolish thing you did today on that platform. I could scarcely believe what I was hearing; none of us could. You gave us no warning.'

'You don't warn people of your intended heroism. That reduces it to a plan!'

Jolint gave him a shove and he pulled her tighter.

'It was the only way I could see that would save Valamer and solve the problems of the priesthood, which of course aren't over yet. I must see Valamer, see with my own eyes that he will live.'

Hector came up beside them. 'I'm going for a bath. I'll order some food for us on the way.'

Perian turned to Hector with a wistful smile. A bath and food. He could think of nothing better. He was desperate to be clean again and for a change of clothes. 'I'll be up soon.'

'He's waiting for you,' said Jolint. 'He refused to go to bed until you had returned.'

Perian groaned. 'I suppose he's furious about the soldiers needing my permission.'

'I think he's too sick to be furious with anyone,' Elian added over his shoulder, 'and he's certainly in no condition to hit you.'

The dining room smelt of healing herbs. Valamer sat amidst thick cushions, his chair at a slight angle with the table, on which there were wine glasses and near-empty carafes. A flushed Grison smiled crookedly at Perian as he entered and a jovial Ben looked up, his left eyeball sinking toward its lower lid.

Valamer's mouth twitched into what was probably meant to be a smile, but a quick frown suggested that it hurt too much. His face was puffed and red, one eye barely open, but it was his nose, swollen and angled with a hint of blue beneath the bandage, that dominated his features and made him nearly unrecognisable. Perian could see what Elian meant about not mentioning it; he would have to make a special effort not to stare.

Valamer waved a bandaged arm toward the chair next to him, where a glass of wine waited on the table. Perian bowed very low before taking his seat. He would have embraced Valamer in his joy at seeing him alive and able to move, but Valamer's injuries prevented such a show of emotion, and it would have been unwise while his semi-trance continued, even though it was less than it had been. He hoped to be back to his normal self by morning. He sipped carefully and waited for the wine to calm his agitation and slow his mind a little.

'Have you settled your charges and put them to bed?' Valamer said suddenly.

Perian gazed at him to judge his intention and, deciding that Valamer found the situation amusing, rolled his eyes. Elian was right: what had he been thinking? 'I will sort out the line of command,' he said quickly. 'I have no wish to be in the way of your supreme leadership.'

'I didn't doubt that, but the line of command is the least of my worries at the moment. Was there any trouble with the priests or the soldiers?'

Perian sighed and gulped down another mouthful of wine. 'No, not at the moment. That it will come I have no doubt. Many of the priests are confused, many angry, and many plot already; they need time to adjust. They blame me for the Voice's humiliation in public, and their humiliation by association, but most, I hope, will remember that it was the Voice who chose the venue, not I. Tomorrow will be a different game, so we shall see.'

'Do you have an idea yet of who will try to reinstate the Voice?' asked Grison.

'Yes, a fair idea. But that may change depending on the internal politics.'

'Does anyone know what the Voice's name is?' Valamer asked. They all shook their heads. 'We must find out, since he's no longer "the Voice", Tanais having stripped him of that title.'

'Does that mean that Tanais is now the Voice?' Ben put in.

'No,' Perian blurted, louder than was necessary. 'The structure of the priesthood hierarchy needs to be changed, but I have had no time to think about it, not having expected to find myself as mediator for the Sky God.' He shook his head and rolled his eyes again. 'I don't even believe in such a thing.'

'Perhaps that is the best way,' Valamer said. 'Do what you must, Tanais, and I will send for you tomorrow to gain your insight and to discuss your concerns and any thoughts you may have on the future of the Empire's religious representatives.'

'Have you seen Vorten?' The atmosphere changed so abruptly at the question that Perian thought he might be dead. 'Did they harm him?'

'No, no,' said Grison, before anyone else could answer. 'He was badly disturbed by the whole event and retired early.'

Valamer glanced at Grison. 'He apologised so many times, I'd have thrown him out anyway.' He scratched his thigh, which was bulky with bandages beneath his robe. 'Now that I have seen you, Tanais, my bed awaits me, as does a sleeping potion. I am exhausted, as you all must be.'

He stood awkwardly and two slaves rushed from some hidden part of the room to ease him through the doorway. As soon as the ungainly group had turned into the hallway, Jolint jumped up, kissed Perian on the cheek and vanished after them. Perian watched her go, his mouth half open to say something that wouldn't come out.

Don't say anything, came Elian's urgent voice into his head. Perian's neck clicked loudly as he spun it about to look at Elian. *Don't – not here,* Elian said again.

What's going on? Have I missed something?

Obviously! Elian stood and nodded to Grison and Ben, who looked as though they may stay to finish off the dregs of wine. 'Let's go, Tanais. The food Hector has for you will be cold if we don't hurry.'

The thought of food took Perian's mind off Jolint for the moment. He was so hungry he didn't care what temperature it was. He bade Ben and Grison goodnight and followed Elian up to their chamber, and once through the door, the smell of food emptied his mind of all else. He followed it to the dining room.

Hector appeared at the doorway, looking clean and smug, but still wearing his merchant's clothes. 'I couldn't wait,' he said in answer to a look from Perian.

'Good. Did you find your money?'

Hector leant against the doorframe and shook his head.

'Go to bed, Hector. We'll talk about it in the morning.'

Thick slices of antelope leg lay on a plate of baked onions and carrots, with fried and shredded cabbage generously sprinkled with vinegar and black pepper; Perian thought he would faint before he could get his knife into a slice of meat. Elian watched him eat, happily swinging his leg and snatching up the odd morsel from Perian's plate.

When Perian had finished his repast, he pushed the plate aside with a contented sigh. 'I didn't think Valamer liked women in that way. Lono is hardly cold in his grave.'

'It would seem you were wrong. He's more of a free spirit than you give him credit for. Perhaps they're both a little lonely.'

Perian snorted. He felt quite put out and unreasonable. Valamer had no right to play with his sister. 'It's incest,' he burst out, unable to contain himself. 'He's my brother!'

'Don't be stupid, Perian. Jolint isn't your sister or Valamer's.'

'She *is* my sister, and yours, in a companionship way.' He was being childish, he knew, but he couldn't stop himself; he was shocked and possessive, as he had been when Jolint first showed an interest in Radia. 'We are siblings by adoption.'

'Gisela never adopted us! She abducted us. Even Jolint and Cerister, I imagine.'

'Yes, you're right. Jolint was old Frish's granddaughter and probably the leverage Gisela used to take the leadership.'

Elian stared at him, aghast. 'When did you find that out? Does Jolint know?'

'No, not yet. I haven't found the right moment, and I'm not sure it will help at all, but she should know. It was when we sat around the table discussing your rescue. She grabbed me, and I had one of those sudden side flashes that comes from who knows where. But I had far too much on my mind to relay my insight, and the timing was completely inappropriate, anyway.'

'What about Cerister?'

Perian shook his head. 'Perhaps I'll know one day, but too late for Cerister.' He smiled at Elian, then gulped down the remainder of his wine and headed to the bathroom for the unusual experience of having a bath alone in his own chambers.

By the time he had reached the temple gates the next morning, Perian was drenched from the light drizzle that had descended on the city. The muted hues of dawn touched the cobbled pathway through a blanket of cloud and their feet crunched slightly on the hard surface. He was accompanied by the two guards Valamer had assigned him: Heribrand, known as Heri, and Gunther.

He could see little of the entrance from beneath his hood, but when he pulled it back from his head within the dry warmth of the temple foyer, he found himself in a cavernous and ornate room with stone benches along the walls, where mock pillars had been carved into the stone. Reliefs of the sun and moon filled the spaces between the pillars, and from the ceiling hung a scrolled chandelier. Only the lower tier of candles had been lit, casting long shadows and leaving the corners in darkness.

The sounds of their shuffling entry filled the space, but as soon as they had stopped and shaken the excess moisture from their cloaks, Perian found himself enclosed by the sounds that came from the inner temple. The humming travelled softly down the passageway opposite, beating upon his chest, and he had to quell his instinct to run away. He felt his guards tense, but he pushed on, hoping they wouldn't make a fuss. The sound pricked every nerve in his body and he was certain he shuddered as he walked. Two startled soldiers stepped out from the shadows as he approached the main door, and although uncertain, they allowed him to slip through to stand along the back wall, but without his own guards.

The priests knelt in rows beneath a huge glass dome that was beginning to glow with the rising sun. The source of the humming came from an older priest who stood on a dais at the far end of the inner temple, dwarfed against an enormous silver sygrilien. The growing light caught on the statue, reflecting an aura of dusky pink into the temple and about the priest, who appeared to have wings by his position before it. Four others, two a side, added to his sonorous voice.

The mass of bent, kneeling forms began to sway, and it took all Perian's strength to stop himself from doing the same. The longer the noise went on, the less he was able to keep it at bay, and gradually his personal shield began to waver, his mind drifting from its anchor of self-will and his body easing to the left and then to the right, where his head encountered the sharp edge of a shelf and brought him back to his senses with startling speed.

His eyes flew open, his heart racing. He tightened his shield about him and pulled his cloak about his chest, where his tattoo had begun to glow again. He felt out of place, as though he had returned out of order, and searched within to see where the disjunction might be. Eventually he decided it was due to his shock rattling against a light trance that had descended of its own accord. Perian waited for it to settle, then turned his attention back to the priest.

He had begun swinging a thurible in the shape of sygrilien wings, spreading swirling clouds of frankincense back and forth till the air was thick with it. The humming stopped abruptly.

Perian slipped back through the door before he began to choke, followed by a swathe of clinging smoke that made one of the soldiers sneeze. 'Tell Priest Berig and the priest presiding over this dawn ceremony that I will meet with them in the old Voice's audience room later this morning.'

As he swept down the corridor, he heard the old priest telling the gathering to go about their daily chores as usual and dwell on the reading of the day in their meditations. He had obviously arrived late and missed perhaps the most telling part of the ceremony – did these people never sleep?

'What are you hoping to do, Hector?' Perian asked. They were in the study, staring out the window at the main entrance, and Perian had been nervously tapping his finger on the sill. He wanted Hector to stay with them in some capacity, but he hadn't really known how to start such a delicate conversation. He wasn't good at such things, nor did he know how to proceed now that he had initiated it.

Hector turned to Perian with a look that asked for more information.

'With your life,' Perian clarified. 'Where would you have gone if things had been different and no one had stolen your money?'

'I'll do it,' said Hector. He slid back from the window and propped himself up against the desk.

Perian followed Hector's movement with his head.

Hector laughed at his confusion. 'You called me your servant in that miserable cellar. I'll do it if you pay me well.'

Perian stared at him for a moment until he remembered. He hadn't thought it out properly then, but he had now. He walked over to the couch and sat facing Hector, feeling lighter now that the prospect of losing him had been put off, for a while at least.

'You will be, Hector. Find the tailor and get him to make you up new clothes, and I'll get someone to organise your pay. And while you're doing that, I need to see Valamer.' He slipped from the couch and made for the door. 'I'm still interested in your plans for the future. Another time, over a glass of wine.'

Valamer was seated in a large, cushioned chair, still wrapped in his silk dressing gown. He looked worse than he had the evening before, but that may have been due to the bright sunlight that filled a plain and delightful room Perian hadn't been in before. Chairs with brightly woven cushions stood loosely about a low table, paintings of mostly rural scenes hung upon the walls, and on a smaller wall space near the door hung a portrait of Lono smiling happily, his eyes looking directly at the observer, no matter where one stood in the room. Valamer's eyes followed Perian's as he stared at it, but he said nothing.

Perian moved one of the seats so that he sat facing Valamer. 'How do you feel?' he said. 'You look awful.'

Valamer snorted. 'I feel dreadful, but it could be worse; I could be dead. If Saphrax wasn't so cowed by the Voice, or ex-Voice, I should say, I'd let him loose in his cell. As it is, he can fester in the depths until I feel up to dealing with him myself.'

Perian hoped that wouldn't be too long. He needed the ex-Voice and his fellow conspirators out of the way, but that conversation could wait for another time.

'I haven't thanked you for your intervention, Tanais, and I do thank you; a very brave and foolhardy rescue. I thought I was going to die. I would have made an angry and difficult ghost.'

'I can imagine.'

Valamer's mouth twitched into the semblance of a smile. 'I would have made his life miserable, if a ghost has any power to do so.' He poked at something soft and unappetising in a bowl on a table by his side. 'That was a remarkable performance you put on. I didn't know that those wings of yours lit up, or did you do it with magic?'

Perian shook his head. 'No, I don't have such power. They lit up of their own and surprised me as much as everyone else. It must have been because I was in a semi-trance, since they light up in the sphere I go to when in full trance. Wings of freedom, the Wellorn Oracle called them.'

'How did you find it, shut away with Ishra's Oracle?' Valamer must have caught the uncertain look in Perian's eye. 'I am not trying to catch you out, Tanais. You should know that I trust you implicitly, and while I don't always understand your methods,

I have no doubts about you. Remember that when I am feeling better and shout at you.'

'Well, if you want the truth, I found it very pleasing, although tiring. Neesa taught me about things that I had no idea existed, encounters that I will no doubt have in the future but may not have survived without her lessons. I am a far more skilled Oracle now than I was before I met her.

'Ishra rules by fear and cleanses the cities she chooses to abide in, expelling the homeless and malformed, and probably the dissidents more permanently. I believe this is how the Voice would have ruled had he been successful in his attempt to overthrow you, but not for the reasons of religious fanaticism that drive Ishra. Her cleansing began with the ousting of all other forms of worship.' He crossed his legs and tapped his index finger rhythmically upon his thigh. 'I went to the priest's dawn service this morning. Have you ever been into their temple?'

Valamer shook his head carefully.

'I could be wrong, but I believe it was built by the followers of the Empty Eye, although the Voice has added buildings around its perimeter.'

'What makes you say that?'

'The inner temple has a vast and magnificent glass dome, and although not obvious at first, it is the shape of an eye.'

Perian watched Valamer's mind tick over, but he said nothing.

'The service was taken by an older priest who spoke with the accent of the high nobility from the north of Darna. I only recognised it because that is where my foster mother came from. He used the same mesmerising hum they use at the sacrifices, sending his audience into a trance-like state, which I believe opens them to suggestion.'

Valamer's facial expressions were quite limited, what with the swelling and bandage, but somehow the puffiness shifted into a look of astonishment. 'Do you think the Voice used this to control and direct them?'

'Perhaps. I don't know enough to be sure, and much would depend on what is written in their texts, but it would certainly be useful for shaping their attitudes and beliefs. The power of this tool should not be underestimated. It nearly sent me into a trance. I was only saved by banging my head on a shelf unreachable by most. Before the humming, the priest gives them a passage from their texts to contemplate during the day's meditations, providing those with an agenda the perfect platform from which to bend minds if they choose. Unfortunately, I arrived too late for this morning's.'

'Did you sleep at all last night?'

Perian smiled. 'Not a lot.'

'How do you want to play this, Tanais?'

Perian gazed through the window at the tight puffy clouds that had replaced the grey blanket that had drizzled over him earlier that morning. They moved slowly but steadily, like bloated migratory birds toward an unknown destination – as he did, he thought.

'I'm not sure at the moment,' he said, turning his attention back to Valamer, who clasped his bandaged hands together, forming an arch from the elbows that rested on pillows. 'I'll have a better idea when I have spoken to Priest Berig, the one I selected to see his fellow priests safely to their rooms last night, and the older priest who took the service this morning. Perhaps I will meet with other elders of the priesthood if they haven't all gone to the cells. I want to have a look around, especially in the Voice's rooms. But one thing that must be done as soon as possible is to get rid of their mercenaries before they have time to think about their next move.'

Valamer dropped his arms to his lap and sat forward with a wheezy groan. 'What mercenaries? Are you sure?'

'Fairly sure. We all knew there were too many soldiers and wondered where they came from. They didn't bring them from Darna, and I can't imagine too many Rashinders were rushing to enlist. How many guards do they need around a temple when their main protection is the same as everyone else's – the Darna warriors? You are a better judge of this, but I would think no more than fifty. There is currently more than twice that number that I can see, the vast number disappearing after the attempted coup that took our father. It is my belief that they have gathered them slowly and house them in those new buildings they put up, and possibly beneath the temple, along with the hoarded supplies. Your men will be able to confirm this when they begin moving all the goods into the city warehouses. I intend to get the mercenaries paid off from the temple funds and sent home; if you approve, that is.'

'Of course I approve.' Valamer's temper was rising, but not with Perian. 'Meet with me later when you have a better grip on things and have made some decisions as to how to proceed.'

'I meet with Captain Alaric of the Soldiers of the Sky God later this afternoon. I intend to take Erely with me, and wondered if you could spare Simeon. I know nothing of the warriors' way of life and I would find his expertise invaluable.'

'No, take Ben. Ben isn't arrogant in the way that Simeon is, and his deformity makes him appear less of a threat. I'll tell him to wait for your summons.'

'Ben will be perfect, but one thing before I go,' Perian said. 'A favour.'

Valamer raised his eyebrows, which did little to widen his swollen eyes.

'I need a place in which to retreat that is not my living chambers – an Oracle room, where I will be safe and can trance without disturbance – and a place that is not the temple grounds nor within the palace building, where I can meet with the priest's chosen leader.'

'You want me to build you a house?'

'No. There is an old visitor's cottage by the lake. If you have no use for it, I would like to take it as my own for my sole use. It has been neglected and is a little rundown, but with the help of the palace carpenters, it could be made quite comfortable.'

'It's yours, Tanais, as long as I don't have to go all the way down there to make use of my Oracle.'

Perian stood. 'You are safe. You won't be required to take a stroll to the lake. I'm pleased to see you are recovering. I should go – my charges will be waiting and wondering why they haven't been able to get into the Voice's rooms, which I put a ward on before leaving last night.'

17

Priest Berig was taller than Perian remembered, thin with a near-porcelain complexion, stark against his black hair. Like all the priests, his hair was cut straight at shoulder-length and he was clean-shaven, having taken the trouble to scrape off the previous day's beard growth. And he vibrated with anger.

Hector had organised seats away from the desk where the Voice presumably intimidated just about everyone, and Perian motioned Berig to one opposite his own. He ignored the animosity displayed upon his face and pulsing from his body.

'Did you encounter any trouble after I left?' he asked casually. The tension emanating from Berig was disturbing, but Perian was determined to keep their meeting as relaxed and open as possible.

Berig glared at him. His jaw quivered as he struggled to contain his emotions. 'You are mistaken, my Zameel, if you think by choosing me to do your dirty work I am come to your side.'

Perian felt Hector's hand move toward his knife. He removed it again at a signal from Perian.

He pushed down his irritation and kept his facial expression neutral, his disapproval evident only in his curt response. 'I wasn't aware that being asked to calm your fellow priests as best you could – ensuring they were fed and your nightly routine kept as a way of making them feel safe and making sure they went to their individual rooms, where they could be protected from the rightly angry citizens of this city – was "dirty work", as you put it. My concern was that one of their own provide leadership, since those who profess to be your leaders have been imprisoned for the very act of endangering their wards and the very existence of your Order. How is this "dirty work"?'

Berig flushed bright red as he lost ground. He opened his mouth slightly as though to say something, but Perian pushed on.

'To talk of sides is not helpful, nor sensible. There can only be one side, and that is the Zamir's. The other is treason and punishable by death. So, Priest Berig, which do you choose?'

The flush vanished rapidly and Berig looked as though he was going to be sick. Perian had no sign for 'he's going to throw up', so spoke directly to Hector. 'Take Priest Berig to the Voice's pumproom, Hector, so that he may splash his face and recover.'

Perian tried not to listen to the ghastly sounds of retching and Hector's soft voice of sympathy, concentrating instead on the sounds beyond the door. The older priest had arrived, but Perian wanted a few more words with Berig before calling him in.

Berig looked even paler than he had at first, but held himself well considering his performance in the pumproom. Perian continued, warming to his task.

'Have you forgotten so soon that it is I who bears the mark of Tarse's Oracle and the symbol of his mediator, the Great Sygrilien, upon my chest? I am the true Head of the Order of the Sky God. I do not seek power; I have power, and it comes from within. If you are unhappy with your role, Priest Berig, I can choose another to assist me in understanding the workings of your Order, but I would prefer it to be you. There will be enquiries and each of you will be interviewed, and I know now that there are those amongst you who are guilty of being complicit in the actions against their Zamir. But it is what is in their hearts that I seek – whether they see right from wrong, whether their involvement was forced or due to the influence of those in power. I will seek out those who desire dominion over others. So, Priest Berig, which way do you turn? Are you to assist me willingly, or must I find another?'

Berig threw himself upon his knees and dribbled words and saliva into the floorboards. 'Forgive me, my Zameel. I have been verbally battered and accused of being your willing instrument and a traitor to the Order by those who are confused and do not like what has occurred. But they quickly forget what took place on the dais, as I had, it all being so alarming, and I have no doubt that you are the intended head of our Order. I am very happy to assist you.'

Perian relaxed a little, even though the atmosphere in the room was still volatile. Berig's refusal would have been a dramatic diversion from the pathway he was expecting, and he wasn't sure he was quite prepared for that yet. 'Get up, Berig, please. I'm merely seeking to allay the fear and uncertainty of your fellow priests.' He waited while Berig regained his seat and began to look more composed and alert. 'Who is the priest who took the dawn meditation?'

'Priest Theo. He has been with our Order since a young man and is well respected by all.'

Perian called for Theo and moved a chair next to Berig. Theo was a man of slim build with a slight stoop. His thick hair, entirely white, capped a long face. Perian knew he had never met the priest before, yet there was something very familiar about him that he could not quite place. Once he was seated, Theo patted Berig's knee, drawing a tentative smile from the younger priest.

'Priest Theo,' Perian began. 'What was your message to the gathering this morning? I arrived a little late.'

Amusement tugged at the corners of Theo's eyes and mouth, and he placed both hands on his lap to give Perian his full attention. 'I was surprised to see you there, my Zameel, but honoured, of course. I read them a passage from the Book of Morgansen to contemplate during the day. The passage dealt with looking into their own hearts to find their own truth within, and their connection to the Great Tarse, who sees the vast picture of men's lives and whose ways we cannot at first fathom. It seemed the most appropriate in the circumstances.'

Perian allowed a smile to break the sternness of his features. 'Thank you. It does indeed seem appropriate.'

Theo had brought a calm amusement into the room, yet it didn't stop Perian from feeling cramped in his seat under the concentrated attention of these two men. He wasn't used to interviewing people, and never in such a position of power. It made him feel awkward.

He crossed his legs and shifted in his chair to ease his discomfort, his eyes drawn to the paperless desk and the near-empty bookshelves behind it. Where were the Voice's books of learning?

Theo answered him as though he had spoken out loud. 'The Voice was not a great reader; he left that task to others.'

Perian studied the priest for a moment, trying to read his body language and the subtle message in his words that suggested more than just laziness. Perian was impatient to know what was going on within the priesthood, but the pieces would unfold of their own, he felt, and there was always Erely, should it take too long.

He inclined his head toward Theo, who was studying his hands, and asked him to provide a register of all the priests' names, including those in custody, their positions within the Order and for how long they had served, as well as an account of their daily routine. That

Perian wanted this information that afternoon caused Theo to raise his eyebrows, but otherwise he showed no sign of complaint.

'First, though, I would like you to gather your fellow senior priests together and meet me in your usual meeting room,' Perian continued. 'And while you are doing that, Priest Berig here can give me a tour of the temple and grounds so I may acquaint myself with the layout of the temple compound.'

As the priests were about to leave, Perian called to the older man.

'What is the ex-Voice's name?'

'Goar.'

Perian passed the information to Elian for him to tell Valamer.

The senior priests sat around a large oval table, its high polish accentuating the dark, regular lines of walnut and the carved feathers that whirled around each leg and ended in a clawed foot. The chairs they sat in were no less ornate, with clawed feet and feathers carved into the arms and backs. The four men stood and bowed very low as Perian entered, remaining on their feet until he had taken the seat Theo pulled out for him. Hector stood by his side: his protector and witness. Indignation and aggression heated the thick, tense air of the room, and Perian wished he could have left the door ajar or opened one of the windows that looked down into the inner temple.

This was going to be a very different meeting to the one he had had with Berig and Theo earlier, which he hadn't found pleasant. But he would make it brief. He only wanted to see who was left in positions of influence within the Order here in Jasperen.

'Priest Theo, please introduce me to your fellow priests,' Perian said.

Theo's face was hard to read, blank and unsmiling, relaxed, yet Perian couldn't dislodge the feeling that he was enjoying himself. Theo motioned first toward a portly man nearest to Perian. His white robe contoured his belly, which folded over his knees, smothering his blue cord belt. He was round-faced with a red complexion, his eyes small but not unpleasant. 'This is Priest Heidren.' Theo introduced the other two as Monteth and Carolin.

'What can we do for you?' asked Monteth in a surprisingly deep voice. He had greying hair, a thin chin and unusual blue eyes, which suggested mixed race.

'At this stage, I merely wanted to meet you. Your seniority in the Order means that you will move up to the position of elder since your predecessors are no longer available. Please consider yourselves as temporary elders and use the title until there is time to confirm your new status. Initially I would like you to keep the Order running smoothly and as normally as possible. I will meet with you again as soon as I am able. In the meantime, Elder Theo will be your spokesman. He will report to me each day and any requests, or proposals for the future, will be relayed through him. Do you have any questions?'

No one spoke until Carolin's dark eyes fixed Perian's with loathing. 'You know nothing of the running of our Order. You are not fit to claim to be the Voice.' His breath stank and his words froze the air, and it took all of Perian's willpower not to scream; the man had magic.

Perian stared back and reinforced the shield he had fortunately remembered to strengthen about him before entering, rejecting Carolin's burst of power with a vigorous pulse. Carolin's eyes bulged, then he coughed as though choking until Perian thought the priest would pass out, smothered in his own projection. The atmosphere suddenly rose to a new height of unease and bewildered tension. Perian could scarcely hold his fury at bay.

'That I know nothing of running a religious order of any description is the reason you have been promoted to elder, so that you can ensure the comfort and progression of those whose job it is to pray and study for the betterment of themselves and all sentient beings. As to being the Voice, I make no such claim; that particular position no longer exists. At the moment I am the Head of the Order of the Sky God, and my job is to foretell and translate what Tarse deems fit to tell his subjects.' Perian wasn't sure about translating for Tarse, but he couldn't think of anything else to say.

He stood suddenly, taking the priests by surprise. They belatedly stood with a loud scraping of chairs, although Carolin was a little slow. Perian glared at him.

'In future, Elder Carolin, remember who you are addressing. I will not tolerate such acerbic accusations. Perhaps you should contemplate using your skills for something more useful and humble.' He turned to the others. 'The priests will be interviewed this afternoon. I want all of you to be there.' He inclined his head toward the men and strode from the room.

Perian threw himself into his favourite chair by the hearth and called to Elian to tell him he was back in his chambers. He closed his eyes and wiped the grime of his meeting from his face with a damp towel Hector had given him.

I'm with Valamer, and he wants to see you, said Elian. *They haven't found the mercenaries and the stashed food stores aren't as big as they should be.* He sounded put out; Valamer was in a bad mood.

Give me a minute, I've had a difficult meeting. Does he have any food down there?

I think there'll be enough left if you hurry.

'Get yourself something to eat, Hector, then wait for me in the Zamir's foyer.' As Perian left, he glanced at his dining room table, still strewn with the Voice's papers that he hadn't yet had time to look at, then dashed down the stairs, followed by his guards.

Valamer's meeting room was just as tense as the one Perian had just left, but not so hostile. Jolint, Elian and Ben looked miserable, Simeon had wiped his face clear to blankness, and Valamer was near bursting from his bandages with frustration. Vorten sat on the far side, staring out through the window, and didn't bother to turn. Perian launched himself at some bread and cheese left abandoned on the table before flopping into a seat a little too close to Valamer's aura of anger and heat.

'I've just come from a very unpleasant meeting with the new elders, so please be nice to me,' Perian said before filling his mouth with hard cheese that stuck to his teeth and sent ripples of pleasure down his gut.

Valamer waited a moment for Perian to stop chewing. 'They're not beneath the temple, nor in the extra buildings. Some of them are, but not in the numbers we expected. Where are they?'

Perian hoped it was a rhetorical question; he certainly didn't know. 'They must be somewhere. We've seen them with our own eyes on the streets of Jasperen; they were there yesterday. The former Voice's name is Goar, by the way.'

He leant toward another piece of cheese, but Elian got there first and swept it toward himself.

'What are you holding back?' he asked, holding the cheese between two fingers and waving it about.

Perian glared at him. 'I'm not holding anything back. I've only just got here.'

'Stop playing about, both of you,' said Jolint. 'Tell us quickly, Tanais, and then Elian will give you your cheese.'

Tanais again! He would ask her about it when they were alone together.

'I found some of their hoard, ale and wine, in a storeroom in the building to the right of the temple. Not all, I'm sure – that's probably somewhere else.' The building also held an old and unused scriptorium and a once-magnificent library filled with books in a language neither he nor Berig understood. Both Perian and Hector had been shocked to discover that the priests had not set up their own library.

He crossed his legs and stared through the window at a spider spinning its web across a glass pane, reminding him of Valamer's weaving. He automatically glanced at Valamer's hands to see if they were damaged and caught Vorten's profile as he faced the window. His presence made Perian uncomfortable, but even though he couldn't account for his feelings, he was careful to give only a brief account of his morning's activities, and even less of his thoughts and discoveries. He wanted to question Vorten with Erely present. He would have to leave that to Valamer, but how he was going to approach such a request, he wasn't sure.

When Perian had finished his report, Vorten turned slowly from his study of the sky beyond the room, his face pale and defiant. 'The Voice brought only fifty of his priests. You can hardly expect such a number to fill all the rooms of a monastery that was obviously built to hold a larger number of the devoted, whatever it was that they were devoted to. That five or six went the way of the previous Voice leaves even less. Did you really expect them to bring the entire library from Loren?'

Perian shrugged. He wasn't going to be drawn into an argument about books. His concern wasn't that they hadn't brought the whole

Loren library with them, but more that there didn't appear to be enough to set up even a fledgling Order in Jasperen. Even if there had been few books elsewhere, he would have expected the Voice to bring most of his own, for his personal contemplation and for the instruction of those who came with him. How could they expect the Sky God to gain purchase in Rashinder without their books of knowledge to sustain them?

He suddenly felt completely out of his depth. He would ask Valamer in private if he had anything in his own library that would inform him on the ways of this group of miscreants he now found himself leading.

Vorten turned back to the window and Perian turned his attention to Valamer. 'I intend to speak with the priests this afternoon. Can you spare Erely?'

Vorten glanced back at him with a look of derision. *Well, I don't like you either,* Perian thought.

'Of course,' said Valamer. He sounded tired. 'I'll speak to you later.'

Are you coming? Perian asked Elian silently.

No, not yet. I have a feeling I need to be here. It could get interesting any minute; at least I hope it will. See you later.

Hector waited for him in the foyer. 'Would you get me something to eat please, Hector;' Elian lied, there was nothing left. 'And when you've done that, get someone to tell Erely that I'll need her services in an hour.'

Not until later in the afternoon was Perian able to wander through the palace gardens toward the small structure that was to be his Oracle house. His head throbbed with the effort of the afternoon and lack of sleep. He dropped onto the grass beside the path that ran from the cottage to the water's edge and stared across the lake into the thick spinney just beyond. The tops of the trees had bitten into the descending sun, leaving a jagged edge and casting dark versions of themselves across the rippling water. Frogs had emerged from their daytime quiet to test their singing voices along the lake's edge, and tiny insects began their twirling dance above the water's surface. Hector was contentedly standing on the lake's edge and Heri and Gunther were sitting beneath a nearby tree. Slowly, Perian lay back upon the grass and drifted into a deep sleep.

Jolint's head blocked out the remainder of the sun as he woke with a start to the happy sight of her smiling down at him, her face pink, perspiration sparkling along her hairline.

'Jolint,' he exclaimed. 'Please tell me that you are on your own.'

'I am alone,' she said. Her smile broadened and she flopped down at his side so they lay together, watching clumping clouds drift by overhead. 'I've been honing my sword skills with Ben, which is quite an exercise in concentration. He cheats by swinging that eye of his around so it becomes distracting.'

Perian chuckled and, after a moment, propped himself up on one elbow to face her and feel the warmth of her exertion. He plucked a daisy and offered it to her.

She accepted the gift and twirled it about in her fingers. 'Flowers, Tanais! What do you want?'

'To know why you have suddenly taken to calling me "Tanais". Have I offended you? If so, it was completely unintentional.'

She shook her head and sat up, encircling her knees with her arms. 'How could you possibly have offended me? I just find it confusing with two names, the old and the new. You may not want to hear this, but you are Tanais now. Your old name, Perian, belongs in that dreadful wagon we lived in; it belongs to a past I never want to repeat and would prefer to forget, although that is impossible, of course.'

There was anger in her voice and in the way she twirled the daisy about again. She held it to her nose.

'It is time that you accepted who you are now. You are no longer that shy, bumbling seer cowed by Gisela, as we all were, and afraid to let Elian out of your sight. You have become strong in your power, and every bit a prince in your independence and your dealings with others.' She glanced at him to see how he took her praise. 'The Empire needs people like you in positions of influence: strong, balanced and compassionate, with a deep desire to make life better for all.'

He smiled at her. 'That's too much praise. You know me better than that.'

'Is it? I know that you worry and wonder whether you do the right thing. But that is good. No one should be overconfident about their own view on life. You are becoming what you were meant to be, Tanais. Not the puppet that Gisela wanted to control, but the prince that fate had in mind. Accept it.'

She moved as though to get up, but Perian held her back. 'There is something I have needed a chance to tell you, then we can put the past aside for the moment. I know where you came from, who your parents were.'

She stared at him, pink gathering about her cheeks. 'And?'

'You were old Frish's granddaughter. I saw it when we were in the bowels of the Common, but have not had the opportunity to tell you.'

Her deep emotions fluttered about her, but the shock was too great to produce tears. He could see that she understood the enormity of his statement.

'So that is how Gisela managed to coerce so many tribes into servitude. I often wondered. What about Cerister?'

Perian shook his head. 'I do not know. She is beyond my touch and ability to find out.'

'Thank you,' Jolint said, and bent forward to kiss his head. 'I must go and clean up for dinner. Valamer is watching for you at his window – you should go to him before he falls over.'

He laughed, following her with his eyes. 'What about me? I might fall over!' he shouted after her.

'No, you won't.'

He found himself staring at his cottage. Perhaps she was right: he was Tanais now, and to cling to his old name only proved he was afraid to let go of the past – afraid of losing his intimate connection to Elian and Jolint; the memory of Cerister. But they were all together still, with the exception of Cerister, and he felt their bond just as strongly as he always had, so why was he so reluctant to move on as Jolint and Elian clearly had?

He looked closer at the intense feelings that stirred with his prodding, and slowly the strands bobbed to the surface as waterweeds beneath a disturbed pond. Cerister's death and the torment of so many kept that past alive, as well as his rage at Gisela – his humiliation, even – for her abuse of them that he had buried deep within; and, if he were honest, his need for some retribution. All this still linked him to what he should be putting behind him and had nothing to do with his name. He would discuss this with Elian.

He sighed and rubbed his face to separate his thoughts from the intense feelings that dwelt within him until he had time to sort through them again. As he stood and dusted grass from his clothing, he caught sight of his cottage reflected in the lake.

It burst into flames.

He swivelled his head about to look at the real structure, which was unscathed. He turned back to the reflection, calm now and rippling with the true image. He would have to revise the plans he had sketched out over breakfast for the renovation of his Oracle cottage.

He turned about abruptly and made his way to the palace.

18

Valamer was alone, lying on a couch in a nest of cushions, when Perian was ushered into his living room. Perian took a chair opposite and stretched out his legs. 'What I didn't mention earlier was that it is my belief that about two-thirds of the priests the Voice brought with him are barely literate.'

'What! How is that possible? How do you know?' Valamer's head jutted forward, chin first, as it did when he was surprised or shocked. The movement dislodged several of his smaller cushions, which slipped to the floor.

Perian picked them up and patted them back into place while answering his questions. 'It was a leading comment by Elder Theo that I could make no sense of until I saw the disused library and asked Berig why there was no collection of books for use by the priests. He told me that the Voice, both Leeman and Goar, considered books to be purveyors of nonsense, with the exception of the one book – and only those chosen, the Voice, could interpret its message.'

Perian threw himself carelessly back into his chair, knocking a small table on which his wine glass wavered precariously until he grabbed it.

'I always thought that the Order was a place of learning, debate and writing. These men, the Voice's radicals, learn mostly by rote, with little ability to check on what they are being taught, even if they had any books.'

Valamer put a wadded hand to his head. 'Grooming, I believe it's called. Training them to think and act as their masters. To become fanatics.' His eyes moved rapidly back and forth, accentuating the fire and despair in his voice. 'How is it that this was allowed to happen and Father didn't see it? What of those left in Darna?'

Valamer's explosive response sent ripples across the room and reverberated against Perian's own sense of hopelessness. He raised his eyebrows and shrugged by way of an answer. 'I don't know. I am meeting with Elder Theo and Priest Berig tomorrow in my rooms and hope to get more information from them away from the temple enclave. I have a list of the priests' names with a few notes from the interviews this afternoon. I also had Hector take notes, and he will combine his with mine for you to look at when you feel up to it, but I can tell you now that we will have problems with at least twelve out of a possible thirty-two. The rest are no doubt the ones who can read and write and have had no direct input into Goar's plans, as far as my preliminary enquiries can detect.'

'That's too many. I hope you have imprisoned them in the temple grounds?'

'Yes, but how we are going to fully enforce that, I am not sure. With your permission, I am going to insist that Theo keeps them busy with lessons on how to read and write, as I believe they have been misled about what is in the Order's texts. At least I hope they have. But this will take time – more time than I believe we have.'

'You have foreseen another attempt?'

'Speculation. I haven't had time to trance. At least one of the senior priests, and now new elder, is possibly with Goar, but until I can get hold of something he has touched, I cannot prove this to my satisfaction.'

Valamer's face softened as a little humour appeared in his eyes. 'I'll have a pile of hair for you to look at tomorrow.'

Of course you will, Perian thought. He felt suddenly weary. 'Where is Grison? I haven't seen him since last night.'

'Reinstating the city shrines in the hope of calming the population a little. There's still too much unrest out there. Most of the taverns were looted, including our friend in the Common. I'm hoping they'll all drink themselves to sleep rather than into rebellion.'

Valamer closed his eyes as though to sleep, and Perian took the opportunity to leave for his meeting with the Soldiers of the Sky God – in particular, one Captain Alaric and his lieutenant, Rodolph.

'The soldiers are an arm of the priesthood,' Ben told Perian, 'and have taken vows of obedience to the Voice, chastity and service to Tarse. They are devout, strict and do not question openly. I suggest you be straight with them; they will not appreciate nuance. They will think it an insult.'

When they arrived at the barracks, they were ushered into a large, sparsely furnished office. The two officers inside stood unnaturally stiff at their entry and placed their right arms on their chests, displaying the tattooed sygrilien wings at their wrists.

Captain Alaric, a man in his early forties, strong and fit with short dark hair, a thick beard and chiselled features, motioned for them to take the seats already placed opposite himself and his lieutenant. Erely pulled her chair close enough to Perian for her to discreetly tap his heel with her foot whenever someone lied. This little deceit had worked perfectly when they were interviewing the priests and avoided a lot of signals that made the interviewee nervous.

'I will come straight to the essence of this meeting, Captain Alaric,' said Perian. 'To whom do you and your men swear allegiance: me or Voice Goar, or perhaps another?'

'To you, my Zameel,' the two men said in chorus, and would have thrown themselves upon the floor had Perian not stopped them.

'We have seen with our own eyes that you are the true voice of Tarse,' added Captain Alaric. There was no tap from Erely, and Perian breathed a private sigh of relief. At least he had the soldiers on side and, at a push, could use them to control the priests without resorting to Valamer's warriors. He had his own army!

'How many soldiers do you have?'

'We came with fifty; we lost fifteen. That leaves thirty-five of us.'

'And the mercenaries – what can you tell me of them?'

'Very little. They came and they went, and when they were here we worked alongside them as best we could as instructed. Thirty or more lived with us in the barracks for some weeks until the second building was built. The numbers that materialised for the first attempted coup were a shock for us as well as the Zamir.'

'Did you or any of your men have anything to do with the mutilation of my father?'

The atmosphere shifted. Alaric showed his first signs of emotion in the hint of pink below his lower eyelids.

'No. We stood guard on the door and fought the warriors with intent to kill, as were our orders.'

No tap. He wasn't going to ask if they had participated in Valamer's abduction and the slaughter of his guards and close friends; he knew they were. 'Thank you, Captain Alaric. We can now leave that behind us, I believe.' Or at least he could; they probably already had. 'Initially I want to meet with you every day, so I can keep abreast of what is happening and we can become better acquainted. You will come to my chambers at the palace two hours after sunrise, until the renovations of my cottage near the lake have been completed, which should be in a day or two.'

Hector was in the study, just finishing his compilation of notes and about to start a second copy, when Perian got back to his rooms. Elian had been asleep on the couch, but stirred with the sound of Perian's voice. 'Where have you been?'

Perian walked into the dining room and brushed the Voice's papers to one side of the table, then poured wine from a carafe Hector had brought in while repeating the day's events and discoveries to Elian. But Elian had been speaking with Hector, so there was little, apart from his latest meeting, that Perian could tell him that he didn't already know, which he found irritating. With no news to give Elian, Perian asked him whether the midday meeting had perked up at all.

Elian's eyes lit up. 'Vorten,' he said, shaking his head as though still unable to believe what he'd seen. 'He'd come to the meeting a changed man, all arrogance and with a superior air, and tried to present himself as the older and wiser relative to whom Valamer should defer when making decisions. Valamer finally exploded after you had gone and verbally beat Vorten into the window case until he stormed out in a rage. He was later arrested for taking a knife to the cells, with which he said he was going to take his own revenge on the Voice. Valamer has confined him to his rooms.'

Perian was surprised, and yet not. 'Did he hide the knife or hold it in full view?'

Elian looked confused. 'I don't know – is it important?'

Perian shook his head. Elian then expounded on how he had spent a boring morning looking for the elusive mercenaries, then a lovely afternoon wandering about the city with Grison, organising for the shrines to be reinstated. Perian had stopped listening, the papers on the table having suddenly caught his attention.

'You're not listening,' said Elian. He drained what remained of his wine and stood. 'I'm going for a walk in the garden to watch the sunset. Do you want to come?'

'Uh, no,' Perian said, suddenly concentrating on his brother. 'I'm sorry, I'd love to, but there is something I need to do.'

Elian clucked his disapproval and waved goodbye as he left.

Perian reluctantly pulled the papers toward him. He found little of any relevance: a register of priest names; half-written letters in a horrible scrawl that said nothing of importance; a few messages from Darna, creased from being rolled up for the pigeon canisters. He stopped for a moment to rub his eyes and stared at the pile of loose papers still to go. He had expected to find a book of accounts, but he could see it wasn't amongst the papers. It was probably locked away somewhere and therefore something he definitely needed to see.

He was tired and wanted to go to bed, but continued anyway, knowing that he wouldn't rest until he'd checked everything. Then he found it: a single line in a messy note, a reference to the occupation of property not far from the city. He went through everything again, but he could find no formal notice of eviction of the previous occupant, which was probably in the same place as the accounts book.

He looked at the darkening sky beyond the window and wondered whether to wait until the morning, but it couldn't wait; he was too excited. He stood and called to Hector and then Elian. Accompanied by his two guards, they raced through the palace gates and on to the temple to search the Voice's rooms properly this time, even though by lamplight.

The soldiers at the temple gates initially mistook Perian and his entourage for a group of thugs come to make trouble, but quickly waved them through when they recognised Perian. The group also surprised the warriors on guard outside the Voice's door by waking them up, something that Heri went to some pains to try to disguise, since one of them was his cousin. Perian pretended not to notice.

Hector rushed in and lit the lamps about the walls.

'Take a room each and search every cupboard, every shelf, and keep your eyes open for a loose panel that might lead to a secret hideaway,' Perian instructed. 'We're specifically looking for a notice of eviction, the accounts and keys; he must have had keys.'

Perian took the study, but had hardly begun his search when Elian's voice burst into his head.

Got it.

What?

The keys.

Perian called to the others and met Elian in the bedroom, where he had moved a trunk to one side. On the floor where the trunk had been lay a set of three keys on a ring.

Elian changed into a wolf and vanished through the door with Gunther close behind. Perian continued searching the study for the other items, but eventually gave up. One of the keys did open a cupboard behind the desk, but it was suspiciously empty.

'How is it going in there?' he shouted at Elian and Gunther.

'Two boxes of incense and a cupboard full of different body perfumes so far,' Gunther shouted back.

Perian couldn't imagine what the body perfumes would smell like to a wolf – his human nose found them disgusting enough. Elian sneezed several times as though in answer to his thought.

Finally, Elian entered the study and began a cursory exploration of the room before settling into a more detailed search as he had in the other rooms. He came to a halt at the drawn curtains. *Got it,* he said into Perian's head.

Perian strode to Elian's side and pulled the curtains apart. The window gave way to a view of the inner temple and his eyes were immediately drawn to the large statue of the silver sygrilien he had seen that morning. A lantern shone above it, its light reflecting off the bird's wings to fill nearly the entire temple with a soft silvery glow. Elian caught his attention with a wet nose on his palm and Perian automatically ran his fingers through the wolf's fur and scratched its ear rhythmically. He pulled his eyes from the beauty beyond to study the edge of the window frame for signs of an opening and ran his fingers along the wooden frame. *Where?*

'Are you sure, Elian?'

'Yes,' said the man now at his side. 'Beneath the ledge.' Elian crouched down to look under the shelf.

Perian followed the decorative beading along the edge of the shelf, which had the double purpose of keeping the window in place and forming a neat transition from wood to glass. Studying the way the window was set back from the interior wall, he bent to look at the wall beneath the ledge where Elian was running his hands; it protruded. Grasping the ledge with both hands, he pulled firmly but gently, and it slipped away from the window to reveal a cavity that contained a box and the faint but distinctive smell of ulla.

Perian put the box on the desk and opened it with one of the keys. Inside he found two purses filled with coins, a quantity of what looked like promissory notes bound together with string, some loose papers and an accounts book bound in red leather. He flicked through the ledger to make sure it was what he thought it was. Then he scooped out the loose papers and scanned through each, but none was the notice of eviction.

When Hector woke Perian the next morning, he felt as though he had hardly slept at all. The heaviness of sleep hung about him and he was near screaming with a need to enter his bubble of silence and solitude.

By the time Jolint came to announce that the Zamir was ready for an audience with his Oracle, Perian was struggling to keep ahead of a semi-trance state akin to that of the day before yesterday, but less controlled. He stood at Jolint's entry and she threw her arms about him and squeezed him tightly. Her happiness was overwhelming and swept away the darkness that threatened to enclose him. Perian glowed within her merriment, laughing like a child. He looked down at her smiling face, which swirled and distorted in his tears of joy.

She gave him a gentle shove. 'Hurry up, he's in a bad mood.'

'What's he got to be in a bad mood about, apart from a bit of pain and suffering?'

'An interrogation to go to, and not enough pain relief.'

'Yes, that would do it. What are you two going to do?'

'Jolint and I are going for a walk into town with Grison, then lunch at the Common,' said Elian.

Perian stared at them. 'At what point did everyone else get to have fun and I got left behind?'

'The point at which you decided to return to being a Zameel, if I recall,' Elian answered. He took Jolint's arm and they swept out the door.

Perian followed close behind and passed them on the stairs. Turning into Valamer's doorway, he glanced at Hector just behind him, and for a fleeting moment he saw black smudges on Hector's face. Perian sighed and clicked his tongue; he had to go to his sphere soon before his visions overtook him.

He could hear Valamer shouting at Frin, Lono's replacement as his personal slave; a niriller slave a long way from home. They passed in the doorway and Perian had to step aside for the healers who followed.

'What do you want?' Valamer snapped without looking at him. He stood looking through his window. He still looked a mess, although not so padded out with bandages.

'The mercenaries,' said Perian. Valamer turned to look at him. 'I have found a reference to a legal document evicting a local tenant farmer from his land amongst the papers in the Voice's drawer. Unfortunately, I cannot find the official order, but this kind of event will be the talk of nearby villagers and a worry for landlords and tenant farmers alike. The people will know about it. I thought that perhaps a day out in the countryside for a few of your warriors might solve the mystery. The soldiers don't know.'

'Let's see if Goar gives the information freely first. Anything else?'

'There was something else, but it can wait. Leave that pile of hair with Hector when it's ready and I'll deal with it as soon as I can.' Perian hoped Valamer wouldn't wait too long before sending out a search for the farm. Any planned rescue of Goar was likely to happen soon, and they didn't want to find the mercenaries the hard way.

He raced back to his chambers, where a very agitated Ben waited in his rarely used audience room, ready for their meeting with Captain Alaric and his lieutenant.

'This will have to be quick,' said Ben. 'Valamer will send for me soon to go with him to the cells.'

Perian began to feel faint with the speed at which the day was progressing. He hadn't even had time for breakfast.

The two soldiers arrived exactly on time, giving Perian and Ben only a moment to compose themselves. They had nothing to report except that the night had been peaceful. Alaric had spoken to his men to reassure them of their continued service and that the Zameel was looking for the hired soldiers. He had asked if any of them knew where they were, but no one had come forward. That Erely wasn't in attendance seemed to please them. Ben's summons came as soon as the men had gone, and he left in a hurry, muttering under his breath.

Perian sent for Theo, who arrived accompanied by Elder Monteth. Perian ushered them into seats and asked them whether there had been any trouble during the night. Theo shook his head, saying that nothing out of the ordinary had taken place as far as he could tell.

'But there is a prickle in the air,' he added. 'I cannot tell you who or what; we just felt a certain excitement, or perhaps tension, we could not quite place. It may just be due to the recent events and uncertainty of what will follow, but I feel it is more than that.'

'Do you think some of the priests are hatching a plot to rescue Goar or try for another coup?' asked Perian.

Again, Theo shook his head. 'I don't know.'

'Have you spoken to Berig?'

'We haven't seen him. He didn't come to the dawn service, which is unusual.'

Perian stared at the men, wondering why this anomaly hadn't worried them. He had a bad feeling about Berig's absence. 'You must find him. Get the assistance of Captain Alaric if you must, but find him and send word the minute he is discovered. You should go now. I have grave fears for Berig's safety.' After a moment he added, 'Look to the stones.'

19

The sun was near its zenith by the time Perian got back to his chambers, having met with the carpenters at the cottage and given them his revised plans. Word had come that Berig had been found on one of the stones, badly beaten and nearly dead, with a flock of sygrilien gathering expectantly about him. Captain Alaric would take charge of the investigation personally. Perian cursed himself for not anticipating such an attack, since the signs of bullying had been evident yesterday. He felt confident that Alaric would find the culprits, no doubt the same ones who caused the air to 'prickle', as Theo had put it.

He sent Hector for a light meal before he was near-delirious with his simultaneous needs for sustenance and solitude. With his hunger satisfied, he rushed into his study and dropped onto his padded mat.

Movement immediately crowded about him on the wall of his sphere, blotting out its clarity as the scenes rolled over one another like a storm tide, ever new and changing as though the future itself were trying to force him to catch up. He closed his eyes on it all and sat for a long while in the nothingness of simply being. The creation of his sphere meant that his visions didn't dance on the backs of his eyelids or invade his mind as they had before, and as they did sometimes still when he was not sitting. His thoughts trickled through his mind like luminous snakes flashing for attention, but he urged them onto an imaginary notebook, where they rolled into words for future recall. There was no Hector or Elian to dictate to, so this notebook would quickly fill with small prompts once he began looking at the visions that surrounded him.

When he felt sane and peaceful within himself and could not put off the moment of seeing any longer, he opened his eyes. With a deep breath, he allowed his vision to slowly focus and began concentrating on the image before him. Initially confused and frenzied in its movement, it transformed into clarity with his attention to reveal Saphrax and his men riding at speed through countryside Perian recognised; his half-brother would be home within the next day or two.

A terrible darkness followed in Saphrax's wake, gathering and roiling into a powerful mass that obscured the mountains in the distance. Perian turned his focus to the darkness in order to see what it was that moved within. The mass split apart with such suddenness and such a clap of thunder that it nearly knocked him from his sphere.

A man on a white horse looked straight at him, threatening Perian with his spear, which bore the standard of Wellorn. He wore white trousers and a metal breastplate and helmet that caught the light in such a way as to make it hard to see whether it was silver or black. Upon his helmet was the image of the Empty Eye, filled with fire.

The image disappeared into the ocean and was replaced by a fleet of warships. Before Perian could determine the timeline, he found himself observing a farmhouse that overlooked the mountains south-west of Rashinder, peaceful in the early morning light. Unwashed mugs and plates and empty jugs littered a long table, and on the ground at one end lay a man dressed in the uniform of the Soldiers of the Sky God, too drunk to find his bed. Perian could hear women weeping, but could not see them.

The weeping turned to laughter. Jolint danced in a circle on bare feet, her slender body, willowy and supple as a tall shoot, bending and twisting to a rhythm he could not hear. She wore a silk gown the colour of blue lilac with small pearl buttons that ran from the hem to the lace collar about her throat, and when she stood still, the man who wound the garland of samarill flowers around both their waists and tied it so they were bound together was Valamer.

Their wedding day. Perian was suddenly overwhelmed with both happiness and sadness. But Valamer was whole with no blemish, except that nose, of course, so he would have time to sort out his emotions. He wondered if Jolint knew that Darna royalty usually took more than one wife.

Having lingered a little on Jolint, the visions moved on apace. He saw Vorten rush at someone in a rage, but who, he was not sure; Saphrax running down the stairs to the cells, his face black with anger; homeless and starving people on the streets of Loren; fat priests in a heated debate that looked near rebellion; a double guard on his half-sister Zameela Untha's rooms, and her son's nurse carrying a knife.

There was unrest in Darna. Perian watched, waiting for some clue as to when this image was taking place, and was rewarded with a view of the garden. The giant maple that grew at the centre of the palace gardens was leafless; it was winter, a month or two away.

The images finally began to slow down. He saw Aronaye sitting by a bed, but he stood when someone entered. Whoever it was shocked Aronaye, and he put a hand to his mouth. Perian couldn't decide whether he saw joy or fear on his Faran father's face. Aronaye bowed very low, which Perian found odd, since his father was the Leader of the Felfar Farans. The vision faded away before he could see who was in the bed, but his instincts told him that it was Risenor.

The crystal wall cleared and only translucent shadows moved about in place of the chaotic activity of a moment ago. Perian could see past them into forever.

He felt the pressure of company in his room, but stayed for a while anyway. Whatever news they brought, he didn't want to know it just yet.

It was late afternoon when his curiosity became greater than his need for peace. Ben and Elian sat on the couch, playing an uncharacteristically quiet game of cards, and Hector sat at his desk, tidying up his lists. Ben's right eye was swollen and turning a purplish blue and his unruly eyeball was floating about in rheumy redness. Elian's knuckles were grazed and his shirt torn, but otherwise he appeared unharmed.

'What injuries do you have, Hector?' Perian asked. They hadn't realised that he had returned, and Elian dropped his card face up, making Ben gasp and quickly reshuffle the cards he had laid upon the table.

Hector looked up from the blot he had just made on his list. 'None, my Zameel. I am your servant, and as such, thankfully miss out on the dangerous pursuits of the warrior.'

'What rubbish, Hector,' said Elian. 'You looked quite jealous when you saw the new arrangement of Ben's eye!'

Hector let out a deep bellowing laugh and turned his attention back to Perian. 'I have taken a few notes, but you said little other than a list of memory prompts.'

Perian quickly checked Hector's list to ensure he hadn't missed anything, then asked what had happened.

'The hired soldiers made a brazen daylight attempt to rescue the prisoners,' said Ben. Perian hadn't expected such an answer; he had been thinking along the lines of a tavern brawl.

Elian gave up studying his cards and put them down. 'We were on our way back from the Common when we saw about twenty soldiers disappearing through Prisoner's Gate, so we followed. The warriors on the gate said they had shown them an order for the removal of the prisoners signed by the Zamir. Ben sent one of them to fetch reinforcements and we hurried after the group, who had already gained entry into the cell block and engaged with the warriors on guard. Grison and Jolint pushed past Ben and I – you know how tight that stairwell is – and blasted the lot with a surge of magic we could feel halfway up the stairs. When we got there, bodies lay on top of one another, including the guards, and the only ones standing were the prisoners, with looks of frustration and anger on their faces.'

'By the time the reinforcements arrived,' added Ben, 'we had pulled out the two guards and revived them, and relieved all the others of their weapons. Someone fetched Captain Alaric to identify the soldiers, who he said were unknown to him and probably part of the mercenary group. But the disturbing part of it was that they had keys to open the main door, which the guards had refused to open, and the cells.'

Perian's mind raced. *How could they have keys? And who signed the order?* If they hadn't been seen, it was possible their plan could have worked. 'Who gave them the keys and order, and how did you receive your injuries?'

'Some of them woke up too soon and we had to wrestle them into the cell,' said Ben. 'As to the keys and order, someone is interrogating them as we speak. We have the keys, but not the document, as far as I know.'

'Where are the keys?' Perian asked, his sense of peace evaporating at speed.

Hector jingled a bag on his desk.

Perian sighed and wished he had stayed in his sphere. 'Water, please, Hector. My mouth has gone dry.'

He waited until he had composed himself, eased his beating heart and drunk a full glass of water before taking the bag from Hector and peering in: three keys on a large ring.

'Do we know which key opens what?'

'No, but one is obviously the door to the cells and another presumably the cell door,' Ben said. 'The third we don't know; we didn't check. Grison whisked them from the floor with the aid of his tunic and dropped them in the bag before anyone else could touch them.'

At least that was one extra person Perian wouldn't have to filter through. He watched Hector prepare a clean sheet of paper, then closed his eyes to recapture some of his previous calm and centre his mind before emptying the keys into his left hand.

As usual, a feeling of the most recent user surged through his senses, and his fingers prickled with the anger and hate that filled this young, violent man. But he was merely the carrier, so Perian moved the sensation aside before it became too graphic.

All keys had passed through two more hands, or at least been touched by them, and both were unknown to him, before he came to one he did recognise: Vorten, radiating excitement and an insatiable desire for power. Frustration and disappointment permeated the threads of avarice, but more disturbingly, his hatred of Valamer, while mingling within was a deep, sad longing for his wife Untha and their son. Perian saw him sitting on the throne, sorting through Valamer's desk drawers and drinking with Goar. He saw him handing the keys to someone beyond Perian's view, his eyes large and manic. But none of this was proof that Vorten was implicated.

He searched deeper for who else had handled the keys, but the only one he could find of significance was Saphrax, who had probably passed the keys to Vorten when he left.

Perian dropped the keys on the floor, rubbed his hands together, then scrubbed one through his hair, slowly breathing himself back into the room and into the present. He opened his eyes on Ben and Elian, both staring as though he had said something obscene.

'What's wrong?' He looked over his shoulder to see if something was taking place that he wasn't aware of, but there was nothing there.

'Vorten!' said Ben. 'You must be mistaken. Vorten wouldn't have handed the keys over – not willingly, anyway.'

Of course no one would believe that Vorten, beloved by Zamir Maltha and married to his daughter, would act against Valamer. Perian needed to be careful not to make any accusations; he had enough enemies. But, if his instincts were correct, the truth would show itself eventually, and others could do the accusing. He acknowledged, though, that a little surreptitious guidance would speed things up a bit.

Elian was asking him who else had touched the keys when someone banged loudly on the door. Hector slid from his stool and rushed out. Frin's nervous voice echoed through the foyer and into their room, announcing that the Zamir wanted to know if his brother had finished cavorting with the clouds and returned yet, as Valamer required his presence as a matter of urgency – and if he hadn't, could someone please ring his astral bell and get him back?

Perian groaned. 'What happened to my peaceful evening and early bedtime?'

'If you hurry, you might still make the early bedtime bit,' said Elian. 'Let's see what the Zamir is about. We'll come with you.'

Hector put his head round the door.

'We heard,' said Perian. 'Bring that list of prompts in case I get a chance to tell anyone.'

Valamer was pacing the room with the aid of a stick; he was white with anger, or perhaps pain – Perian wasn't sure which. Both Jolint and Grison looked relieved to see him. Simeon just nodded.

'You've heard about the attempted rescue?' Valamer suddenly noticed Ben and Elian. 'Of course you have.'

Frin pulled out a chair for Perian and brought in more wine. Perian smiled at Frin and he nearly dropped his tray. He'd get Hector to have a word with Frin before he was sent back into the slave pool or sold again. It was no good for him to be afraid of Valamer.

Perian sipped gratefully on his wine and waited for Valamer to sit down. 'How did the interrogation go this morning?' he asked, looking at the faces around the table as a way of opening the question to them all.

'Nothing,' said Grison. 'Goar must have known about the rescue due to take place later in the day, and he is under the misapprehension that Valamer won't use torture to find out what he needs to know.'

Perian turned to Valamer and raised his eyebrows. 'Will you?'

'No. I won't have to.' Valamer smiled and pointed to a tray set on a table near the door, covered in tufts of hair with little labels attached to each piece.

Perian let out a groan. So much for an early night.

'If you are up to it, Tanais, perhaps you could look at Goar's now. I want to know more about him and what he's been up to before I bring out the weapons tomorrow. Saphrax is only a day away, and I want Goar dead before he gets here.'

'You must feed me first,' said Perian. 'I've had an exhausting afternoon.'

Valamer laughed. 'Bread and cheese for the Oracle, Frin.'

'Did you find anything useful on the keys?' Grison asked.

'I'm not sure. The carrier was a nasty young man in his twenties. There had been two others before that, but they hadn't handled the keys much, as their trace was recent but weak.' Perian took a sip of his wine before continuing. 'Vorten was the next significant handler, and before him, Saphrax.' No one said anything, not even Valamer. There was something they weren't telling him. 'What is it?'

'Goar tried to implicate Vorten after the failed rescue,' said Grison. He slid his hands together so they vanished within the long sleeves of his coat and looked toward a corner of the room, closing his eyes as if trying to block out the implications of Perian's statement.

There was a long silence. The room shimmered with Valamer's emotions and his struggle to contain them, and Jolint, who had been staring at Perian, turned to look at Valamer with a need to comfort him. Perian shook his head and she withdrew the feeling, seeing that it wouldn't help.

Frin arrived with Perian's cheese and bread, breaking the electric tension that held everyone mute. 'Send one of my warriors to fetch Lord Vorten,' Valamer burst out suddenly.

'Erely. Erely should be here,' said Perian when he could breathe again. He could hardly believe it was all unfolding so fast, even without his surreptitious guidance.

'Erely too. Ask the warriors to get her first.'

Erely was seated next to Perian, nervously fussing with her skirts, when Vorten swept through the door with an air of indignation.

'I see you need my assistance after all,' he said, completely unaware of the tension that held everyone upright in their seats. 'You could have sent a slave rather than having me marched through the corridors by your warriors like a common criminal.'

He sat heavily in a seat opposite Valamer, and only then did he notice the look on Valamer's face and those around him. Perian wondered if Vorten had thought Valamer needed his assistance to prevent further rescue attempts, and he did, in a way, but not in the way that Vorten probably had assumed.

'I need to ask you a few questions,' said Valamer with unexpected control. 'The Voice, Goar, has accused you of being the mastermind behind my abduction and this afternoon's rescue attempt. How do you plead?'

Vorten's jaw dropped slightly and his eyes took on the wide bulge of the accused. 'How can you ask such a thing?' He glared at Erely with a look that could have killed had he the power. 'What is Erely doing here?'

'I wouldn't have done so if Tanais hadn't found your hands upon the keys that opened the cell door.'

'Ah, the pretender.' He gave Perian an oily smile and sat back in his chair, satisfied that he was safe.

'The "pretender", as you call him, is my brother and the Empire's Oracle. Do you accuse him of lying?'

'He's a charlatan, Valamer. Can't you see that? He wants to sit in your place as Zamir.'

'I see nothing of the sort, and you will cease your insults, which in turn insult me, your Zamir. Now answer the question: were you involved or not?'

Vorten's eyes flickered about the room as though searching for an ally or a way out.

'Answer the question!' Valamer bellowed, clenching his fists as his tightly held patience began to fray.

'Why would I do such a thing? Of course not. The keys were stolen.' Perspiration glittered upon Vorten's forehead, his voice shrill with escalating fear. He automatically looked at Erely, as did all those present.

Erely looked directly at Valamer, calm, her hands still, and shook her head.

Vorten didn't wait for a response. He launched himself at Erely before anyone registered that he had stood. Perian, who was closest, pushed him aside, knocking Erely's chair backward in the process. Vorten quickly regained his footing and turned his attention to Perian, closing his hands around his throat while Perian was still trying to regain his balance. Elian jumped from his chair and shot a streak of magic down Vorten's back, leaving Perian's head dancing with colours from their close contact.

Valamer surged from his seat and hit Vorten hard across the face, then called for his warriors. 'Take this man to the cells before I kill him with my bare hands. The lower cells – and lock him up. I want at least three warriors on duty to watch him.'

Vorten was dragged away, shouting that Valamer would be sorry and that rebellion rumbled through his precious empire. His comments reminded Perian of what he had seen that afternoon, but he thought he'd wait until everyone was settled again before mentioning it.

Grison and Jolint had pulled Erely off the floor and sat her back in her seat. Elian was checking her for any injury. He nodded to Valamer to say she was all right. Valamer called for more wine and sat with his head in his hands for a while. Perian's bread and cheese remained untouched.

He stared at his hand, where Vorten's hair protruded through his fingers; an unintentional prize from his struggle to stop Vorten from strangling him. He tightened his fist around the dark fibres and closed his eyes.

What he saw and felt was hard to believe. He could hear his own voice begin to rumble as Vorten's existence unfolded within his vision.

Vorten and Goar were old friends from their days in Darna. He had conspired with Goar and Leeman over the mutilation of Maltha, and with Goar over the abduction of Valamer. He and Goar had planned to kill Saphrax soon after his return, and for Vorten to take the Zamirship for himself. He also planned to rid himself of Goar, despite their friendship. Vorten had been bullied by Maltha, despised by Soas and shunned by many unless they wanted something from Maltha. He hated all the royal family, with the exception of Untha, whom he appeared to love. Goar had been stirring up trouble amongst the priesthood in Darna, and Vorten was hiding the situation by having all communication given to him, by order of the Zamir.

Perian had already dropped the hair onto the floor. He brushed it aside with his foot as he emerged from his trance, blinking as he looked up. 'Did everyone get that?'

'Sadly, yes,' said Grison. He had slumped in his seat and looked older than he was. 'He's probably destroyed most of the communications, but maybe not. We should check.'

Valamer stirred. 'Simeon, take a few warriors and gather up the contents of Vorten's desk drawers and anything else you think may be of interest, and bring them here for us to go through.'

Simeon's features had finally changed from immovable to shocked. He shouted at the warriors on the door as he left by way of relieving his tension.

Trance and scrying made Perian extremely hungry, so, even though he felt it inappropriate, the atmosphere being so like a funeral, he grasped a piece of bread and a little cheese before his stomach embarrassed him by rumbling. It brought a slight smile to Erely's face; obviously she knew how depleting scrying could be, and he pushed the cheese board toward her.

Perian's mind rushed ahead as he chewed, this latest scrying of Vorten connecting seamlessly with his visions earlier.

'We have some time, I believe,' he said, washing his morsel down with wine. 'That Untha is afraid for her life and that of her child is certain, since the nurse carries a knife. The priesthood is in uproar with its elders in verbally violent discussion, but the giant maple tree at the centre of the courtyard has lost its leaves. I surmise that, since it has a late leaf drop, we have six weeks, maybe more, to sort the situation out.'

Valamer and Grison both stared at him with that startled, frightened look of a trapped fox or rabbit.

'I saw it this afternoon,' Perian said quickly in his defence. 'I haven't had time to share my visions yet.'

'Tanais,' said Grison, scarcely able to speak. 'That tree has been dead for the past fifteen years. Maltha was heartbroken when it died and wouldn't let anyone pull it down. He had played in it during his childhood, as had most of his dead sons. He said he could see them still, clambering over the branches.'

Perian hadn't seen any dead children, and he hadn't bothered to look further than the tree to get an idea of timing. He said he would go back in to check.

'Before you do that, Tanais, tell us what else you saw while we wait for Simeon and his men to bring Vorten's papers.'

Hector, who stood beside his chair, produced his notes, and Perian described his visions in detail, leaving out the bits about Jolint and Valamer and Aronaye, but adding the suffering of the Darna people to his previous description of unrest.

'South-west of Rashinder,' Ben mused, grasping Perian's description of where the mercenaries were housed. 'That would be near the village of Crothmore; they will know of any tenant farmer who has been evicted and will no doubt have been brutalised themselves by the hired men.'

'If you round them up,' Perian said, 'make sure the men check for a cage or slave posts. I could hear women crying and believe they have been given female slaves, and probably the odd male slave, to keep them amused while waiting for the action to start.'

Hector's head shot round. Jolint's face turned red, her eyes moistening with her inability to express her instant anger appropriately.

'I'll sit over there, out of the way.' Perian pointed to a corner couch where the light barely penetrated. 'Bring my wine and what's left of the bread and cheese, please, Hector.' He squeezed Jolint's shoulder as he passed and whispered in her ear, 'Ben will make sure they are found and a healer sees them.' There was little else they could do.

He sat cross-legged on the couch and leant wearily on its back, wondering if the turmoil would ever end. Drifting into a light trance and putting aside all the new possibilities that had already gathered, he sought Untha in Loren; a sister he had never met.

The vision again took him to her chambers. She sat with a shawl over her knees as she had before, the nurse bouncing a baby on her lap near the window, but the vision refused to show the view from the window other than the tree. In frustration, Perian looked more carefully at the room. It was daylight. There was no fire burning in the hearth, nor wood for lighting one; the nurse wore a light jacket, and the window was open. He estimated that this was only a few weeks away at the most. He turned his mind to the people on the streets, who wore coats, but not furs yet. The poor and homeless had not gathered about communal fires.

When he opened his eyes, Valamer and Jolint were reading the contents of Vorten's desk. Rolled messages formed a pile near Grison and Ben. Elian had come to his side and held his hand.

'The depth of betrayal is awful,' Elian said softly. 'He has kept Untha's letters and some from members of her council and the elders, but we believe many have been destroyed or are elsewhere. He has been intercepting the mail for a long time, even Untha's letters to Valamer and your father. Many of the letters describe frustration, unrest, a desperate need for supplies and guidance, and none can understand why there is no response from their Zamir and why he does not address the issues they have referred to.'

'Why didn't Untha send a delegation? And why is it that Valamer didn't notice a lack of correspondence?' asked Perian.

'That's what we can't understand, and may be the topic of conversation tomorrow when Valamer speaks to Vorten. He did receive messages, but we now believe that someone of great skill was rewriting them and cutting out the bits of concern.'

Valamer suddenly threw up his hands and turned to Perian. 'Anything?'

He told them what he'd seen, and they agreed: his vision could not be far off.

20

Perian was amazed at the speed with which Valamer moved once he had read Goar's hair sample. The ex-Voice was executed the following morning in front of all the prisoners, including Vorten, who viewed the proceedings without apparent emotion. When Perian mentioned this, Elian suggested that he was probably glad to have his co-conspirator out of the way so he could spin a lot of lies without contradiction. But even after the morning's execution, Vorten still refused to answer Valamer's questions.

'I'll send Saphrax down to sort him out,' Valamer said at last. He had been strangely patient, but had come to the end of it.

They had come straight to the Council Room, where they were joined by Valamer's most senior warriors. A sombre group, Perian thought. The taking of a life, even when clean and quick, was a shock and a disturbance to their equilibrium. He wondered briefly where such a nasty individual would go now that he had been released into the afterlife.

Valamer had sent off nearly the entire loft of pigeons with messages to Loren and dispatched a messenger with letters for various council members, and a package with letters from Perian, Theo and Monteth to the Loren elders, which the three had spent half the night composing. The spray of messages had sped off via the airways, roadways and riverways at dawn while they were busy with Goar's execution.

'Saphrax will be here later today,' Valamer continued. 'His rider came in late last night. I have given orders for a feast, although that is the last thing I want at the moment. Perhaps a small feast will do. He'll be expecting something, having given us warning, but hardly enough time for anything lavish.'

He rubbed his finger back and forth over the edge of the table, tapping it occasionally on the tabletop as though he were ticking off points.

'What do you make of the darkness you saw in your vision, Tanais? The one that followed our warriors and blotted out the mountains? And who do you think this Wellorn warrior is?'

Perian looked up, startled for a moment. 'I cannot be sure. I suspect the darkness means that their attempt to invade is not over and they will come again, but with a different purpose, a darker one. The actions of the Wellorn warrior confirm this in my mind, as does the fleet of ships. This man had fire in his Empty Eye; he is blinded by fury and no longer all-seeing. Ishra may be the counterbalance to any reckless push by her army, assuming she lives. I think she will wait before trying again. The ships may be a surprise for us in the future.'

'But not such a surprise now we know about them,' said Ben.

'The ships had no colours that I could see, and the scene was brief; I could not tell what coast they sailed by. They could be friend or foe – I do not know. If the path is strong, it may come again.'

'Let's hope that Saphrax doesn't bring that cloud in with him,' said Grison. 'We have enough dark spots here already.'

'I'm sending a contingent of warriors, to our sister, Lieva, and her husband, Lord Urfan, who live in the south of Rashinder,' Valamer said to Perian. 'I've asked them to go to Loren to assist Untha. When word gets back to Loren that Vorten has been arrested on charges of treason and murder, she will find it difficult to keep control of the situation there, one that is already unstable thanks to the machinations of her husband.' He took a moment to calm his breath, his eyes traversing the ceiling. 'Do you want to send one of your priests with my men to speak personally with the elders of Loren?'

It hadn't occurred to Perian to send a delegate in person. 'How much time do I have?'

'They leave in two hours.'

A bit tight, but it could be done. He'd send Monteth. 'Yes. Let me speak to my priests and I'll get word to you within the hour.'

The walls of Vorten's chambers had been painted in lilac and olive, deep reds and ochres, the furnishings twisted and curled by master carvers, with the sinuous bodies of a variety of animals. The only painting was one of Untha, which hung in his lounge. But it wasn't to check on Vorten's taste in furnishing that Perian was there. He was looking for the Order's money with which to pay the mercenaries.

He checked every cupboard in the study, releasing those locked with a trickle of magic, until he found it. As he thought, it was filled with bags of gold and silver coins. Someone needed to look more carefully through all the cupboards in these chambers, but Perian didn't have time for that at the moment; nobody did, he imagined, with Saphrax's return so imminent.

He loaded Hector, Heri and Gunther up with bags of coins and they dumped them on the table in Perian's study next to the red ledger. 'That's a little job for you, Hector, when we return from the cottage.'

He glanced out the window; not yet midday. He'd have time to try out his new Oracle room, the repairs and alterations having just finished.

He called to Elian. *Where are you?*

We're going to the Council Room. Where are you?

Just off to test out my Oracle house. Can you tell Valamer that he will find the money on my desk in the study, and that Berig is, or was, the genius copyist? See you later.

You'd better be back for when Saphrax comes. Valamer is already fretting about everyone being there.

I will, Perian laughed. He wondered why they were going to the Council Room, but he'd find out later.

Perian felt rather than heard the heavy thud upon the door and walls of his cottage. A woman in yellow silk robes that flowed lazily about her like a moving flame flashed upon the wall of his sphere, and he heard Hector scream the trigger word: *fire.*

He roused himself as quickly as possible and prepared to return, smoke already teasing his physical nose so he had the sense of a distant need to sneeze. But just as he began to slide back, he was stopped by the voice of Risenor, who laughed in that strange way he had.

'The game is over, Perian. This is the real thing now, and I will win.'

Risenor's appearance took Perian by surprise. His words and tone made no sense, but there was no time sort out his confusion; his life depended on a quick exit.

'Out of my way, Risenor,' Perian shouted. He could feel his lungs filling with noxious fumes and his breathing had become difficult. If he perished here, would he float in his own bubble for eternity? *No, no, that must not happen.* His rising panic gripped his throat so he was nearly asphyxiated by his own fear.

'I could keep you here,' Risenor boasted, 'but where would the fun be in that?'

He was too terrified to comprehend Risenor's words. His body already struggled with the worsening conditions in the cottage and a discordant vibration travelled between his inner awareness and the physical. The cottage would be a pyre within minutes. His sphere shook with his desperation to return to his body and leave via the tunnel that had been dug for this very moment.

Perian felt Hector's hands grab him, and the shock would have sent him mad had Risenor not suddenly vanished, trailed by his lunatic laugh.

He woke coughing, the smoke thick yet illuminated by the flames that surrounded them. Hector had cast the mat aside and was heaving the wooden door open. He grabbed Perian again, dragged him into the tunnel and closed the door. In pitch darkness they felt their way through the smell of freshly dug soil and smoke, covering their faces with their shirtsleeves as best they could. They banged knees and heads on the wooden supports. Perian thought he was going to expire from lack of oxygen and smoke-clogged lungs when the poisonous air began to thin and light shone in the distance. He could hear Elian's voice calling, both in his head and aloud, and he finally responded with *I'm alive* into Elian's head, his voice rendered useless by smoke and fear.

Hector burst through the exit ahead of Perian, turning to help Elian pull him out and onto the twiggy ground between the trees, where he and Hector coughed and wept smoke from their eyes. He could hear shouting from the lawn as slaves were organised into rows to throw buckets of water over the burning structure, and others shouting about a woman in the blaze. Nothing made any sense. He lay back on the prickly ground to look at the sky through the tree canopy waving gently with the breeze.

Elian knelt beside him. 'Are either of you hurt?'

'No, I don't think so,' Perian wheezed. He turned to Hector for confirmation.

'I'm fine, considering my near-death experience,' Hector squeezed out after a coughing fit.

'You left it a bit tight,' Elian complained. 'I thought we'd lost you. Didn't you have a trigger word to snap you back?'

Perian pushed himself up on one elbow. 'Yes, but I hit an obstacle on the way back in the form of a seriously insane Risenor.'

'Risenor! How can that be? Didn't you say you thought he was ill?'

'Precisely. But if he's unconscious, he will be floating about in the other planes – and, it would appear, looking to do mischief.' He grasped Elian's arm. 'He has turned against me, Elian.'

Before they could say more, Jolint burst through the trees and skidded on her knees to embrace him. 'Don't you ever do that again,' she said in his ear, too close for comfort. Grison bent over his knees to catch his breath, and a very pale Valamer, leaning heavily on his stick and Frin, came up behind him.

Grison sank onto a convenient stone, even though it was an awkward shape. 'Speak to us, Tanais. In future you must warn us of such occurrences. Not that we could have prevented the fire, since even you didn't know when this would occur, according to Elian, but it would help us be more prepared. At least I would find it so.'

'I'm sorry,' Perian said finally. It seemed the only thing he could say. He felt as though he had committed the crime. 'Did the men get them, the perpetrators?'

'There was only one,' said Valamer. He sat next to Grison on an equally uncomfortable-looking stone. 'And she is very dead.'

Perian remembered the woman in yellow. He wondered in what way he could have offended her, since he had never seen her before.

'Who was she?' asked Jolint.

'One of my father's wives, I believe. I didn't know her,' said Valamer.

'Siri,' said Erely, just arriving. 'She must have blamed you, Tanais, for the death of Goar. They had been lovers for years. She never bore Maltha a child; the only child she ever had looked so much like Goar that she smothered it – according to rumour, that is.'

Valamer snorted and looked down at the ground. 'Father would have killed her if he'd ever found out.'

'Yes, that's what everyone thought, which is why they kept quiet. But it doesn't matter now; let the festival of gossip begin.' Her eyes searched Perian from head to toe. 'Are you hurt, Tanais?'

He said that he had escaped unscathed, apart from several grazes to his head and knees and the odd splinter.

'You were lucky,' she said. 'There are a few benefits to the dreadful burden of foretelling after all, it seems.'

Perian quietly agreed with the 'dreadful burden' bit.

He was trying to relax in his bath when a warrior came to the door to announce that the Empire's heroes were ahead of time and would be entering the city gates sooner than expected. Perian groaned and sank beneath the water until his breath ran out.

He arrived at the main palace entrance just behind Valamer and Grison, a little flushed and out of breath. They stood on the top step, Simeon and Grison slightly behind Valamer and Perian. Elian and Ben watched from the doorway.

As they had the last time Saphrax returned triumphant, they heard the roar of the crowd before the troops turned slowly into the boulevard. Saphrax waved, nodded and bowed. Valamer shifted from one leg to the other, leaning ever more heavily on his stick.

Perian had to admit to himself that Saphrax looked magnificent, even wearing his dogskin waistcoat. His thick, shiny hair blew behind him in the wind; his helmet hung from his saddle and caught the light, blinding the onlooker. Perian would have felt the thrill of the occasion had it not been for the dark mass that surrounded two leather bags bouncing against the side of his horse. It gave him a terrible presentiment, and his nose twitched with a foul smell that wasn't quite a smell yet.

Saphrax glowed with pride as he came to a halt near the bottom step. His whole demeanour, not just the brightness of his eyes, demanded adoration, which Perian doubted Valamer would submit to.

'Welcome back, Saphrax. You return a hero, as always, it seems,' said Valamer.

'My Zamir,' Saphrax said, loud enough for all to hear, inclining his head. 'I bring back the tokens of our victory.' He pulled on the cords of the leather bags and, with a sense of drama, emptied the contents onto the paving below the steps.

Two putrefying heads bounced upon the stones and rolled forward. Even eyeless and with shrunken lips that displayed their teeth, Perian could see that they had belonged to Lili and Ishra.

For a moment he felt as though he were empty and weightless, and the physical world around him shimmered and grew pale. How had he not seen this? How had he not felt Lili's death, the death of a sister Oracle?

Lili's head crashed against the step and a fragment of clotted blood hit Perian on the cheek. It felt like a burning coal eating its way through his flesh, but it concentrated his mind away from paralysing shock. He swiped at his cheek to remove the offending spot. It smeared across his fingers and released the horrifying details of her dreadful abuse and execution.

Nearly blinded by her terror, Perian fell to his knees. He found himself staring into Lili's face, distorted and bloated by decay. The smell seared his nostrils, and a scream threatened to escape him. He vomited down the side of the steps.

Grison, who was closest, ran to his aid, and the sorcerer's touch thankfully cleared the visions from his mind. He was about to turn away from the gruesome spectacle when a single amethyst bead rolled from the head's open mouth and shone in the sunlight; innocent, yet tainted by something that shouldn't have been there, something that he recognised.

'The beads, Grison,' Perian coughed. 'He's stuffed them in her mouth. You must get them for me before the head is displayed on a spike.'

Grison stared at the bead and then back at Perian. 'Of course, but you must stand and greet your brother so we can get this over with.'

Leaning heavily on Grison, Perian did as he was bid and stood, prepared to finish the ceremony. Saphrax had dismounted and was sneering at him in disgust. His personal guards, faces Perian now recognised from his vision of Lili's last moments, smirked.

Perian's anger surged through him unchallenged. He was rigid with rage. A power he had known only once before – when he had killed Mage Armin – burst from his hands and crackled across the steps. Grison flinched and Elian shouted into his head.

With a great deal of self-will, he withdrew the magic and held it tight.

Saphrax knelt before his Zamir and was ushered rapidly into the palace. As soon as he disappeared through the doorway, Elian and Ben rushed out.

'Take him to his rooms,' said Grison. 'I'll be up as soon as I can.'

'The beads,' said Perian as Elian took him by the arm and dragged him away.

21

'What was all that about?' Elian paced the carpet by Perian's chair, in which Perian sweated and wept.

'She was an innocent, an Oracle. They had no right to do the things they did to her, or to anyone, come to that.'

'It's war,' said Elian, not unkindly. 'But I agree —'

'That's no excuse!' Perian shouted, cutting him off. 'These men are Saphrax's elite warriors, his personal guard, who should have better control of themselves; show decency and clemency toward prisoners, even if only to set a good example for the common warrior. I wonder how they live with their memories.'

Perian looked down at his hands, which shook uncontrollably until Elian knelt before him and took them in his own. Warm, healing hands that filled Perian and calmed him so he could think. Even so, he saw Lili's smiling face glowing with the pride of her new position, saw her scowl as she stood on his foot, saw her face covered in tears when she spoke of Neesa's passing.

He shook the images free to concentrate on Elian, who was asking him about the beads.

'They were our inheritance, passed from one Oracle at death to their apprentice. Lili split them in two, half for me and half for her. I lost mine in Rockby. Someone has stuffed hers into her mouth.'

'Do you want to wear these beads?'

'No! By the gods, no!' He leant toward Elian. 'There was something odd about them. Something that shouldn't have been there; a sense of

Risenor, I think, although I cannot be sure, and how that could be, I do not know.'

Elian stared at him. 'Risenor! Surely you don't suggest that he has been visiting Lili in her trances?'

'I do not know. Perhaps.'

'No, Perian, you think it is worse. I can tell.'

Perian nodded. 'The way he threatened me … He was so sure of himself.' Elian was about to say something else, but Perian stopped him. 'Let me look at the beads. It is pointless to speculate and frighten ourselves with all the ghastly possibilities, which may have no foundation.'

'I hope you're right.'

Hector announced the arrival of Grison, who came in close at his heels. He grabbed a chair and sat next to Perian, grasping the hands that Elian had just released.

'How is he?' Grison asked Elian, as though Perian were an invalid incapable of speech.

'I'm fine now, thank you, Grison.'

A frown crossed Grison's forehead. 'I can guess what you must have seen, Tanais, what you must have experienced, even though this is thankfully a gift I do not possess. But this is war, and men on both sides do terrible things to each other.'

'To each other, yes, but the innocent should be preserved, surely. There is no excuse for what they did. I keep seeing her smiling with the joy of finally achieving her lifelong dream. She wore her white belt with such pride.' Perian's eyes heated with a fresh burst of moisture. 'She was a child, just a child.' He brushed the stray tears from his cheeks. 'Forgive me, Grison, I will be myself shortly. It is hard to shake free of her fear as she faced the horrors to come.'

Grison raised his eyebrows at Elian and patted Perian's hands. 'Valamer will be here soon. Hopefully his mood will have changed.'

'Where is he now?' asked Elian.

'Arguing with Saphrax when I left. Saphrax has accused Tanais of being a traitor.'

'What! Why?'

'It seems she called out Tanais's name, several times.'

'Do you have the beads?' asked Perian. He chose to ignore Saphrax's accusation.

'Valamer has them.'

'Why? And why is he coming here? He never comes here.'

Grison called to his slave, who had been standing unnoticed by the door with Hector. He was a dark-skinned man, long-limbed and graceful, with shiny black hair that hung in ringlets to his waist. Perian stared at him. He'd never seen Grison with a slave before; he had never thought about it. But it wasn't for this reason, nor the exotic nature of this man, that he stared, but for the fact that he was a sorcerer.

Grison laughed at the look on Perian's face. 'Don't look so surprised. Shinwi has been with me for many years now. I spotted him at a slave market on the outskirts of Loren and thought I should buy him before anyone else noticed that he was a sorcerer and took it into their heads to cut off his hands or head.'

Shinwi smiled, showing small white teeth with a wide gap between the front two.

'You're not the only one who has a servant, not a slave. Shinwi is a free man like Hector,' Grison added. He returned his attention to Shinwi. 'Perhaps you and Hector could raid the Zameel's excellent wine cupboard to sustain us now and be ready for his guest, who will be in need of something calming. With the Zameel's permission, that is.'

'Of course, Grison.'

Perian stood and went to the bathroom to wash his face and cool his head. What a horrible day it had been. He had lurched from nearly burning to death to reliving Lili's last moments, and it was still only mid-afternoon. *It can't possibly get any worse!*

He was rubbing his head dry with a towel as he walked back into his bedroom and private living room, when Valamer burst through the door unannounced; a powerful ball of human energy that was ready to explode. The force of him made Perian drop his towel. Grison and Elian stood.

'Tell me what's going on, Tanais,' he shouted. Rage blotched his face and his eyebrows creased so closely as to form one continuous line. He lumbered precariously across the room, attempting to pierce the floor with his stick.

Grison forgot himself and pulled an easy chair forward with a loop of magic, into which Valamer flopped heavily, closing his eyes at the pain. Perian forced himself to remain calm and slowly bent to pick up his towel, threw it over the back of a chair and ran his fingers through his hair to bring it into some sort of order. He sat opposite Valamer and looked him in the eye.

'What is it you wish to know? I understand I have been denounced as a traitor by my brother because an innocent child called my name while she was being abused by just about every one of Saphrax's personal warriors. When they had finished torturing her, they hacked off her head.' Perian's hand began to shake again as he lifted it to his lips to stop himself from saying more.

Valamer looked stricken. 'You saw this?' He looked over at Grison. 'He saw this?'

Grison answered with the arching of his eyebrows. 'A clot of blood flicked up onto his cheek and he mistakenly wiped it off with his hand.'

Valamer took on the sucked-in, hollow appearance of shocked disappointment and stared at the rug beneath his feet – perhaps recalling things he himself had seen and wished he hadn't, Perian thought. Even though he said nothing, Perian knew that it was Saphrax, even more than Lili's suffering, that had caused this reaction; the wild brother who, by any law of conduct, whether it be wartime or humanitarian, common decency even, should have controlled his men. Saphrax had failed his Zamir, his family and the Empire of Darna, as their father had before him.

Hector and Shinwi arrived with jugs of wine. The men fell upon their glasses and Grison poured them another.

'Saphrax, or one of his men, stuffed the amethyst bracelet into her mouth.' Perian looked down at the floor as he spoke. 'Her beads of lineage passed down from our Mistress.'

'She put them there herself!' Saphrax bellowed, bursting in and striding across the room as Valamer had, his uncontrolled anger flickering about as though he were the god of lightning. '*Tell Tanais*, she said. So, what hidden message is in the beads that you are so keen to get your hands on them? You ruined my triumphal march and that of my men. They deserve more. More respect for saving the Empire from the Empty Eye, and you, my brother the pretender, vomited on it.'

Perian stood, which he knew probably wasn't the best thing to do, and suddenly felt small beside Saphrax's bulk, even though he was a good head taller. Saphrax shoved Perian with his left hand and hit him across the face with the right. Perian fell backward, taking the chair with him so that his limbs became entangled with the wooden legs.

Saphrax launched himself on Perian, grabbing him by the shirt and heaving him aside to deliver another blow, but Perian had freed an arm and plunged his fist into Saphrax's head, putting his brother off balance and wondering if he had broken his hand. Finally, he managed to free one of his legs and kick Saphrax in the side, but it was like kicking an immovable rock. Saphrax struck Perian across the face again before Grison and Elian managed to pull him off and force him into a chair. Valamer was shouting at Saphrax, who wasn't listening, but trying to murder Perian with a look.

Perian scrambled up, wiping blood from his mouth where his lip had split. Elian had righted his chair and replaced the cushion, and Hector rushed in with a damp cloth to ease the swelling. He also gave one to Saphrax for the redness upon his cheekbone, but Saphrax threw it back at him.

Strangely, Perian felt better. He'd not been in a brawl for ages, and it lifted his spirits a little to release his congested anger and frustration. Someone had sent for Erely, and she arrived while the two brothers were still glaring at each other. She made a clucking noise at the sight of them. Elian quickly found her a seat and a glass, into which he poured a healthy quantity of wine.

'What's she doing here?' Saphrax spat, still eyeing Perian.

'You accused Tanais of being a traitor,' said Valamer. 'She is here as a truth-seer.'

Saphrax snorted. Perian gave Erely a tentative smile, making his lip bleed again. He didn't wait for Valamer or Grison or Saphrax to ask the questions; he had an urgent list of his own. He tried to order his aching features into a neutral expression before addressing Saphrax.

'You said that Lili – that was her name, by the way – that Lili put the beads in her mouth herself and spoke my name. What exactly did she say?'

Saphrax frowned, continuing to stare.

'Please,' said Perian. 'This is important.'

Saphrax turned to look at Valamer, who said, 'This is not a leading question, Saphrax. Answer it as truthfully as you remember it.'

Saphrax's features softened a little with his attempt to remember. 'She stood as soon as we rushed the tent. You could see she was terrified, but she stood strong.'

'Get on with it, Saphrax,' Valamer growled.

'She said, *tell Tanais to look to the man with fire in his eye. Tell Tanais that I'm sorry.* Then she ripped her bracelet from her wrist. *These are for Tanais,* she said. *Make sure he gets them.* She dropped them in her mouth and clamped her jaw tight – except when she screamed, that is.'

'Saphrax!'

Erely calmly indicated that Saphrax had told the truth. He glared at her and made a deep guttural noise.

Perian knew that the last part of Saphrax's statement was to goad him, but his mind had already moved along, his need to know greater than the satisfaction of punching his brother in the face.

'Would that be the man you saw on a white horse, wearing a breastplate and helmet with the Empty Eye on fire?' asked Elian. The pieces were coming together, and he sat forward with greater interest.

Saphrax turned his attention to Elian, his complexion a little paler now, his eyes wide. 'How do you know about him?'

'You've seen him?' asked Perian. 'He wore white in my vision and waved the Wellorn banner.'

'Aye, white. We all noticed the trousers because they were clean, no blood or mud. He rounded up the remainder of Ishra's retreating troops and led them deep into Wellorn. We followed for a while, but we had already taken a substantial swathe of Wellorn territory. My men were tired, and we needed to rest and celebrate.' Saphrax looked from Valamer to Grison, then back to Perian, the strutting indignation gone, leaving a man confused and out of his depth. 'You saw this man?' he asked again, as though he couldn't believe it. When Perian affirmed that he had, Saphrax looked to Erely, who nodded.

'Why was Lili brutalised and beheaded?' Perian asked suddenly. 'She was just a child, an Oracle. No threat.'

'No threat!' blurted Saphrax. 'She gave us such a runaround. Every move we made, they waited for us, even with plans I made up on the spot. Not until I devised multiple plans in my head did we begin to progress.'

'Well done, Saphrax,' said Grison. 'It's quite a thing to outwit a powerful seer.'

Perian agreed; it took quite a skill – but Lili wasn't a skilled seer. He had seen this even without Neesa telling him. How was it that she could run rings around a strategist like Saphrax?

He turned to look at Elian and Grison. 'But she wasn't a powerful seer. Her skills were limited, which is why Neesa chose me to succeed her.'

'If, Tanais, you are better than this Lili, then you will accompany me next time we go to war,' said Saphrax.

'No, you don't understand. Her actions sound like those of a skilled seer – I could not do better. But when we parted company, she was a mediocre seer with no experience.'

Grison shifted in his chair and leant forward. 'What are you saying, Tanais?'

'I am saying that something else is going on, and the answer is hidden in the beads. She was trying to warn me of something.'

'Why would she do that?' said Valamer. 'We're the enemy.'

'Because to her, I'm not the enemy. We both trained with Neesa. Whatever it was that she was trying to warn me about was a threat against me, not the Empire directly.'

Valamer took a deep breath that was more of a sigh and pulled a small leather pouch from his pocket, which he bounced briefly on his palm. 'Read your beads now, Tanais, but you will have to do it with me present. I don't have the strength to move from this seat yet.' He tossed the pouch to Perian, who felt their essence stir even through the leather.

'I'm staying too,' said Saphrax. He sat defiantly, as though ready to fight off any who tried to evict him.

Perian shrugged. He wouldn't need to go very deep to find the truth in these beads, and their presence wouldn't bother him once he'd started. He took his chair to a corner of the room.

Elian followed. 'Are you sure of this?'

'I don't find it comfortable, but it is better they witness what I see rather than think I hold secrets.'

Perian emptied the beads onto his hand. The power of Risenor's trace made him gasp and turned his muscles rigid. Although prewarned of Risenor's presence, he was unprepared by the extent of it; Lili had been almost obliterated.

His mind spun within the white light of shock, separating him from his body and leaving him anchored only by Elian's hand upon his knee. Although almost lost within the haze, he heard Elian call his name, and he grasped the sound like a drowning man grasps the hand of his rescuer until the dazzling light faded and he felt secure once more in the physical present, his mind beginning to work normally again.

He tried to think of how this could be, weighing possibilities with what his senses told him, but there were none, only that Risenor had overtaken Lili completely. Even Mage Armin had not intended such an abomination. His mind raced, juxtaposing this revelation with his recent encounter with Risenor. Where would Risenor go now that his host was dead?

His lungs refused to fill, and his stomach knotted as though preparing for an assault. Speculation would not reveal the answers he needed. He closed his eyes, trying to isolate what there was of Lili and follow the sequence of events that ended with her death. He saw Risenor approach her while she was in trance and offer his help. Perian could see that she was desperate for assistance, to prove herself and to please Ishra. Knowing that her own skills were weak, she accepted Risenor's offer gladly.

With the lowering of her guard, Risenor took her by surprise and pushed her aside with a power and ambition that she was unable to expel. His thoughts and intentions burst over her, and himself by proxy, revealing the insanity that Perian had seen during his encounter earlier that day.

He remembered his feelings of compassion for Risenor, and that he too had considered lowering his guard – not to use his skills, but to include him and make his life less lonely. It made him dizzy and a little disoriented. He broke into a sweat when it occurred to him just how close he had come to rendering himself vulnerable. But perhaps not. No matter how sympathetic he was to Risenor's plight, he was always wary of his once-brother.

Calmer now, he moved the beads about a little to help release more information. Risenor knew of Lili's fate and showed her in graphic detail, but this display of sadism and petty boasting also revealed something else: there was another with the latent skills of a seer. That Risenor looked elsewhere and not at Perian as a host he could use was a huge relief. At least he wouldn't have that particular problem to worry about. This person also harboured the power of a sorcerer, although untrained. This man had loved Ishra and hated Rashinder and Darna with a blinding passion.

The burning eye flared around Perian, and he dropped the beads.

'He's insane,' he said to Elian. More questions rose in his mind about Risenor and his intentions, and he wondered again whether the Magi had known of Risenor's fate. Had they hoped for his death? Had Risenor been mad all along, in the same way that Armin had been? Or worse? He voiced his questions to Elian.

'How can we know unless we ask the Magi?' said Elian. 'Do you think Risenor intended to take you over when he visited you in that tomb?'

'I'm sure of it. But I think I was more powerful than he realised. Neesa left Lili vulnerable by allowing her to go with Ishra. It is hard to think that Neesa didn't see what would befall her apprentice. But how can I judge? The game is not fully on the board yet.'

Elian whistled through his teeth. 'This is all beyond me.'

'And me at the moment,' Perian replied.

Saphrax shifted noisily in his seat, with the purpose, Perian thought, of letting him know that his patience was thin.

Perian left the beads where they were and returned to his guests. 'You heard?'

'Who is Risenor?' Saphrax asked by way of an answer.

'My once-brother,' said Perian.

Grison told Saphrax of Perian's previous life as a Faran, of Perian and Elian's abduction and the mutilation of their brother, Risenor, amidst snorts of disbelief.

'What does this mean, for you and for the Empire?' Valamer asked Perian.

'I cannot be sure, but I believe it means that with the aid of Risenor, this man in white will rally what is left of the Wellorn army and prove a much more devious and dangerous enemy than Ishra ever was. As for me, I don't know. Possibly, I will have my own battle within the realms of the seer.'

Grison immediately grasped the implications of Perian's statement. 'Can you hold against him?'

'Risenor is very powerful and has always been the stronger, I believe. But I now have Neesa's training, and perhaps this is the battle she was preparing me for. Should I be overwhelmed, you have Elian to tell the difference. But it is through me that Risenor would have found Lili, so who knows what Neesa was about?'

'What I want to know is why you submitted to training.' Saphrax prodded his finger into the air as though it were against Perian's chest.

'Stop trying to blame Tanais!' shouted Valamer. 'I told you, he was saving my life.'

Saphrax stood in a rage. 'I'm going back to my men, who talk about things that are rational and that I understand.' He elbowed Shinwi on the way out and slammed the door so hard the walls shook.

Valamer pushed himself to standing and fumbled for his stick. 'You must attend the feast at my side tonight, Tanais, so that all can see you are not the traitor Saphrax has claimed.' Frin appeared from nowhere to assist his master across the room. Valamer looked over his shoulder as he approached the doorway, a slight smile loosening his tightly pursed lips. 'Try to get through the evening without incinerating anyone.'

22

'I do not see why I have to attend. I've already heard your talk fifty times; I know it by heart,' said Perian without looking up from the plan for his new Oracle cottage.

'Precisely,' Elian spluttered. 'You can prompt me if I miss anything or become confused.'

'You won't become confused, Elian. In any case, Ben will be there. You and Ben have been practising the Wellorn moves with those little wooden men they keep in a drawer in the War Room.'

'How do you know that?'

'Ben told me.'

Elian's nervous disappointment rolled across the table like the thick fog that sometimes comes from the sea, and Perian looked up for the first time, not realising until then how deeply Elian felt about this issue. Elian had gone quite pale, leaving his neck and cheeks blotched pink. Shocked, Perian stood quickly and skirted about the table.

'Forgive me, Elian. I wasn't concentrating and was too caught in playing my own game; of course I'll be there.'

Elian sighed and, having stood to leave the room, sat down again and allowed himself to be hugged and cajoled back from his near tantrum. 'I'm sorry too. I need a holiday – time away from all this rush and tension. I love the excitement, but at the same time, I miss the carefree life where each minute was our own, even though my experience of it was brief, at least in physical form. I miss Perian the carefree minstrel, as I miss my old self before I became obsessed with battle tactics.'

Perian pulled up a chair, and together they stared through the study window, where a cloudless sky called them to step out from the confines of the palace.

'I believe Valamer will announce his intention to visit the villages and local lords in the next day or two,' said Perian. 'I see no reason why we couldn't make a small diversion for a few days. What do you think, Elian? We won't be able to take Jolint, though. I believe Valamer has other plans for her.'

Elian's talk was that afternoon in the Council Room. Saphrax spoke first, informing his audience of the things he had learnt of Wellorn battle tactics during his two encounters with Ishra's army. He spoke eloquently and with considerable humour, and Perian found it very informative. Elian followed with a talk on battle tactics used in the past and juxtaposed them with Saphrax's experience on the field.

'From what Saphrax has said of his experience,' Elian summed up, 'it is clear to me that, compared to the past, our fight with Ishra has been a clean and honourable one – no doubt like Ishra herself and her devotion to her clear and all-seeing eye: black or white with no fuzzy edges. But, from what Tanais has seen, our next encounter will be quite different, and we will need every devious tactic we can devise.'

Perian glanced about at the stunned faces, the frown of worry that had formed on Valamer's face with the mention of another encounter, then at Saphrax, who sat forward in his seat, his eyes shining with interest.

Confused by the initial lack of response from his audience, Elian began to gather his papers, but Saphrax burst into a round of applause, and Elian nearly dropped the papers on the floor. Released from their stupor, everyone joined in and began to shuffle in their chairs by way of reinvigorating their circulation. Saphrax's appreciation reignited Elian's pleasure, and when Saphrax began to ask questions, he glowed with enthusiasm. Saphrax had found a new friend.

At first, this alarmed Perian and sent him into a spin, but as the thought of the pair becoming friends settled, he understood their mutual interest: strategy. Question and answer time became a conversation between them, so Valamer interrupted and suggested that the two adjourn to the War Room and report back to him on their conclusions. Perian looked at Jolint as the two disappeared through the door, their discussion barely halted by Valamer's intervention, and she raised her eyebrows.

The room was crowded, mostly with people Perian didn't know, and Valamer dismissed them by thanking them for their attendance and saying that he would keep them informed of further developments.

'Who are these people?' Perian asked Jolint as the gathering began leaving the room. He followed her and Valamer to a table that had been pushed aside to make room for the visitors.

'People with influence and troops that came with Maltha, as I understand it.' Jolint returned a smile from Valamer. 'You should ask your brother,' she added.

'Darna and Rashinder lords, advisers, and a few of Father's old councillors who won't have liked what Elian had to say,' said Valamer absently, before Perian could ask. But his attention was on Ben and Simeon, who had taken seats on the other side of the table. He left Jolint and Perian to join them.

'What's this about you and Elian going on holiday without me?' asked Jolint.

'Did Elian tell you that? Of course he did.' Perian was quite taken aback. He felt as though he had been caught out at some misdemeanour. 'It's hardly a holiday, and in any case, it was just a suggestion and may not happen at all.'

'Well, Elian sounded fairly sure of it, and he will be very upset if it falls through. But I won't, because I wasn't invited.'

Perian looked nervously at Valamer, who looked up suddenly to stare at him. Perian stood with the intention of leaving; he'd have to hide until Valamer had announced his plan to tour. Elian shouldn't have mentioned it, but then he knew that Jolint could wheedle a confession from a corpse.

Suddenly, Jolint burst into peals of laughter, and Valamer told him to sit down. 'She's playing with you, Tanais. I can scarcely believe you subjected me to such torture by letting her rescue me from that cosy cell!'

Jolint flicked a little magic playfully across the table, making Valamer's hair stand on end, and Ben's, who happened to be too close to Valamer. Perian threw a thick shield over himself and Jolint to cut out the noise of those around them, not unlike that of his sphere, and he swayed slightly in his seat with the exquisite sensation of an absence of sound and the agitated feelings of others. He opened his eyes, although he didn't remember closing them, and watched Jolint, who was clearly surprised by the sudden depravation of all external sensation.

'What have you done, Tanais? This is amazing.' Her voice sounded flat and strange, and she tested it with a few nonsense sounds of *ooh* and *ahh*. Then she turned to Valamer, whose expression was one of uncertainty. He knew something had happened, but he didn't know what, and she wasn't responding to whatever it was that he was saying. Jolint made faces at him, then stretched out her hand to touch the invisible wall Perian had created. 'Is this what your sphere is like?' she asked.

'Similar, yes, but fortunately I see no images floating about the substance of these walls.' He made himself comfortable and waved at

Valamer, who turned back to his business with Ben and Simeon. 'Tell me,' he said.

'How can I tell you what you already know?'

'Indulge me, Jolint. If you believe I already know, then you have already told Elian. Has Valamer asked you to marry him?'

Her joy and laughter filled his bubble and reverberated through his being until he was laughing with her. 'Yes,' she said at last, 'and I have agreed.'

Perian took her hands and looked into her face. 'Are you sure, Jolint? Have you thought hard about such a step and all that will be asked of you as Zamira? He'll want you to have babies.'

'I have never been more sure of anything in my life. Together we will be a strong central unit and help bring peace and unity to both empires; with a little help from you and others, of course!'

He instinctively tightened his grip on her hands, kissed them, then held them against his heart. 'You know they take more than one wife, don't you?'

'He won't. I've already told him that I'll slit their throats myself.'

Perian chuckled quietly to himself and dissolved his shield. Even Jolint screwed up her face at the blast of voices and background noise. The men looked up at the loss of whatever it was they couldn't see.

'Ah, you're back,' Valamer said, turning his attention to Jolint, who walked around the table to sit beside him. Perian suddenly found himself alone at one end of the table, and was about move a little closer to the huddle when Valamer stopped him with a question. 'Tanais, I need you to tell me what you've seen, apart from my long and happy life with Jolint and your holiday with Elian.'

The holiday! Well, it wasn't going to be a holiday, exactly, but he'd tell Elian that later. He relaxed back into his seat and threw one leg over the other to swing about, closing his eyes. 'You have sent, or will send, spies to watch the oceans for a fleet of ships, and others to Wellorn to ascertain what is happening there and who has taken Ishra's place. All probably organised by that snake, Balon.'

Valamer mumbled something that Perian ignored.

'In a few days, you will set out on a tour to meet with the landowners via the villages so the people can see their new Zamir. You will first go east to spend a night with a minor dignitary at his estate near Pinsen Forest, then south to Lord Pettifield and his wife, our sister Intha. There you will discover that he has been visited by Bardol, the Shanahan's youngest son, who met with a shocking accident soon after arriving.' He opened one eye to see their reaction, then closed it again, satisfied with their looks of astonishment. 'Elian and I will travel with you to the village of Athelim, then make a detour for our short holiday and rejoin you a few days later, either at Lord Essent's castle or on your way to Lord Dyanthanon.'

Valamer threw up his hands. 'Perhaps I should just relax; eat dates, drink wine, practise the odd bout of swordplay with Jolint and Ben, and come to you, Tanais, for my itinerary.'

'Oh, I don't think that would work.'

Having made his decision to set out on what he called his 'meet the people' tour, Valamer was in a rush to get going, and announced that they would set off within four days. Messengers were sent out to the receiving lords, giving all but the last on their circuit adequate time to prepare for such a visit, and the palace staff set an alarming pace preparing for their departure.

For once, Elian was up before Perian, who found him already in the breakfast room, a plate piled high with ham, cheese and a pyramid of boiled quail eggs before him. Perian yawned and shuffled toward the table, tightening his night coat about him. 'Have you left me anything?' He yawned again and rubbed his eyes to stimulate a little life into them.

'Yes, but you should hurry, because I'm aiming at seconds in view of the long journey we have ahead of us.'

Perian clutched a small roll and nibbled one end while eyeing off the quail eggs, speckled and glistening in a bowl. He loved quail eggs. 'It'll take all day to prise those eggs from their shells. How is it that they aren't naked and ready to pop into my mouth as usual?'

'According to Hector, the cook said she didn't have time and he would have to do it for you. Hector said he's far too busy cleaning your boots, so there you are! And no, I'm not doing it.' Elian took an egg and crushed it between his palms so the shell fell away with a crunch. 'See, easy,' he said triumphantly, throwing it into his mouth.

Perian ate a slice of ham instead in the hope that it would revive him enough to stop his eyelids from closing on their own.

Elian crushed a few more eggs and dropped them onto Perian's plate. 'This doesn't look good, considering the gruelling day we have ahead of us. Didn't you sleep last night?'

Perian grunted and shook his head. 'It had been such a fraught day, I thought I'd spend a little time in the peace of my sphere, but it was an informative mistake, as it turned out. Hector looked exhausted, so I sent him to bed early, knowing just how busy today was going to be. I had only been in my sphere for a short while, not even long enough to look at the surrounding images, when fire rose up all around me. The soldier in white glared at me from amidst the flames with a smile that was not his own. There is little doubt in my mind that Risenor now inhabits and controls this soldier, as he did Lili.

'When the soldier faded, Risenor's voice boomed out at me. The flames brightened and faded with the volume and cadence of his words: "Do you think you can trance without my knowing, my once-brother? Never! I will block your every view; I will send you insane." Elian, I cannot describe how shocking the whole thing was. Risenor's laughter resounded about my sphere, pounding me like a hammer. I think I must have passed out then, as the next thing I knew, I was lying on the floor of my study with my legs twisted beneath me and the moon past its zenith.'

Elian had stopped eating. 'How is it that he could penetrate your sphere, Perian?'

Perian shook his head again, slowly. 'He hasn't penetrated my sphere as such. More like imposed himself on it, blocking my visions. I have been awake all night trying to understand how he has done this and work out what I can do about it.'

'You mustn't trance alone again. Who knows how long you lay upon that floor?' Elian crushed a few more eggs and put them on Perian's plate. 'Eat up. The Zamir will expect his Oracle to look fresh and alert, and you will have hours upon horseback to work out what you're going to do.'

Over the next two weeks, they passed through hamlets, villages and small towns, most of which Perian had never visited. The people cheered their new Zamir, who waved and mingled with them when the royal party stopped at unsuspecting inns for refreshment. The enthusiasm with which they were greeted made Perian feel like a returning hero, but without the preceding death and bloodshed.

When they stopped for the night in a field a few miles from the small town of Athelim, Perian felt it was time to speak with Valamer before they separated the next day. Valamer's officers had gone to join their men, so an appropriately intimate group of Valamer, Jolint and Elian were left sitting within the welcome warmth of the fire.

The moment had come.

He began by telling them of his encounter with Risenor. 'I have thought hard about this along the way, twisting the various possibilities this way and that. While he fills my view and bombards me with his piercing voice, I now realise that the future still plays out along my peripheral vision. This is awkward, but enough to give us an advantage that Risenor doesn't know about. If I block him completely, which seems to me the only other possibility at present, I will lose sight of him, and that would be disastrous. Risenor must be destroyed, but that is not so easy to accomplish when he essentially lives within the realms of the visionary.'

'What is it you go east for, Tanais?' Jolint asked.

Perian smiled at her. 'A cave; the one I stayed in on my escape from Bresh that had once been inhabited by spiritual men who left their chanting imprinted on the walls and in the air.'

Valamer clicked his tongue. 'Are you sure you're one of Father's?'

Jolint gave him a shove and Perian laughed. 'I have the green eyes to prove it. The same extraordinary green that you have and Father had.'

Perian's small group split off from the royal caravan in Athelim, where Hector bought food for a lavish lunch to share with those at the orchard where Perian had worked for his dinner after his escape from Wellorn. It was an opportunity to repay their kindness to him and to warn them of the coming war. He was certain that the Wellorn troops would pass by the orchard when they made their next attempt, and he wanted to be sure the family had planned an escape.

He sent Heri on ahead to alert the household of his visit. He didn't want to spoil the occasion by his sudden and unexpected appearance. Elian went with him to minimise initial awkwardness, ease any concerns the family may have at hosting a member of the royal household in their cottage, and remind them that Perian had been there before and it was only his clothes that had changed.

Everyone threw themselves wholeheartedly into the party; laughter filled the easy, relaxed air of the small cottage's main room. As welcoming and friendly as the family was, Perian found himself a little out of step with the happy group, unable to relax as the others did, and he had to acknowledge that more than his clothes had changed over the intervening weeks.

When Alard's grandfather, Will, brought out his 'special' cider, Perian asked Alard and his brother Hervy if they would walk with him awhile. The cheerful voices from the cottage were slowly replaced by the heavy burden of what he had to tell the brothers.

'What is it?' Alard asked, while Perian was still wondering how to tell them what he needed to without ruining their day.

'Am I that obvious?'

Alard tilted his head to the side and gave him an encouraging smile.

'Wellorn prepares to march on Rashinder again, and it is my belief that this time, their route will take them down the road alongside this orchard.' He ignored the looks of shock on their faces and pushed on. 'I wanted to warn you so that you are prepared and have an escape plan in place. They are cruel and do not take prisoners, so don't wait for them to reach your orchard before leaving. Pack in preparation.'

Hector's raucous laughter boomed across the orchard. They all looked back toward the cottage, and a knowing smile spread across Hervy's face.

'It is time for us to leave,' said Perian, also smiling. 'I will leave our pack horse to help you evacuate with greater speed.'

The brothers thanked him and said they would tell the others when he had gone.

Due to the befuddled condition of Perian's companions, they had to stop earlier than he had hoped. They at least managed to set up camp before falling upon their blankets and beginning a cacophony of sounds that would likely challenge even the heartiest of frogs. It occurred to Perian that they had all taken the idea of a holiday far too seriously.

Irritated, he rummaged about in the panniers for something to eat. He wrapped a few morsels in a cloth and wandered down to the roadside.

Away from the snoring men, he could hear the sound of the Silver River on the bitter wind that blew over the snow-topped mountain from the east. Twilight was approaching, and Sun Mountain's icy peak began to sparkle like rosen stone; shadows grew long and the first stars shone faintly overhead. He sat very still within the cover of a large bush and long grass that made him hard to see.

He heard them before their shadow appeared along the roadway: a single individual walking their horse openly, apparently oblivious to the possibility of being observed. Perian put his hand on his knife and waited. Although the light was behind them, he knew instantly who it was as they came into view.

He removed his hand from the knife with a groan of defeat: Timary. He was defenceless against such a powerful priestess. No weapon would be of any use, and it was too late to retreat; she would know he was there.

He stood and stepped onto the road. 'What is it you want with me, Timary? Why can't you leave me alone?'

'I should have been with her instead of chasing about Rashinder after a pseudo-oracle,' she shouted.

He was surprised at her outburst, the first sign of emotion he had seen in her. That he was still alive suggested she hadn't come to kill him, which he found encouraging. He remained still and calm, externally at least. 'Why, so you could die with her?'

Timary's eyes grew large and wild. 'Yes, if necessary. I should have been at her side when she died.'

Perian turned his back on her. 'Come, Timary. Let's go into this field and you can tell me what is on your mind.'

He found a spot where the grass thinned beneath a tree and threw down his cloak. When Timary was seated, he emptied his satchel and spread between them what food he had brought with him. At first she ignored his offer to share his sparse meal, but he could see that she was hungry, the roundness of her face having been replaced by more angular features. Sooner than he thought, she had consumed her share.

'So, why do you still pursue me? I can be of no use to Ishra now, and the one who has taken her place does not need me.'

'Who has taken her place?' she snapped. 'How do you know?'

'You may believe I am a pseudo-oracle, but Ishra knew differently, as did Neesa. I do not know who he is, but I have seen him. He is powerful both as a sorcerer and a seer, and has gathered Ishra's retreating troops about him. But he has no right to this position and will bring devastation to both Wellorn and Rashinder. He has fire in his Empty Eye.'

Timary stared at him, pale beneath the light of the moon. 'What do you mean, "fire in his Empty Eye"?'

'He wears Ishra's band about his head with the Eye of Ortus upon it. But the eye this man wears is filled with fire – hatred, vengeance and violence – not the clear, all-seeing Eye of Ortus. He is the antithesis of all that Ishra stood for. Your people are vulnerable. Every family in every castle, town, village and hamlet has lost loved ones to defeat, and he will stir up vengeance rather than gather what is left and renew. Only famine and disease will come from such actions.'

Timary's eyes moved about in thought, her hand clenched in front of her mouth as though she wished to eat it. Perian doubted that she believed him, but he continued anyway.

'This man, whose name I do not know, has no great ability of his own. He has been taken over by a powerful sorcerer who is exceptional in both magic and foresight, but quite insane. He inhabited Lili first, then transferred to the other when she was killed.'

'Lili is dead?'

Perian gave his head a little shake to stop the images that threatened his equilibrium. 'Yes. Perhaps a blessed release, with Risenor in her head.'

Timary pulled a crumpled piece of paper from the pocket of her short tunic and ran her finger over the surface with deep affection to flatten the crinkles, suggesting that the message came from Ishra. She passed it to Perian to read.

My darling Timary,

All is lost, and I write this in the few moments I have before they come for us with the dawn. You must find Tanais, seek his wisdom and ask him what you must do. Neesa passed her knowledge to Tanais, and he is the continuation of her line. He will not lie to you or trick you in any way.

I have great fears for our country, although I cannot tell you what form this may take, since I do not believe the Darna lords intend to overwhelm Wellorn. Ortus has turned away from us, though I know not why. Alarmingly, Lili's abilities, limited as we both know they are, have taken a sudden turn toward an accuracy I think even Neesa would have found difficult. There is something wrong. The purity of Ortus no longer inhabits his Oracle.

Live a long and happy life, my beloved.

Ishra

Perian read through the short note again before handing it back to Timary. 'Come back to our camp and eat something more substantial than a few pieces of dried meat, then rest while I think on what Ishra has asked of me.'

Timary's hostility toward him had not abated, but she agreed that she was very hungry and badly needed to rest, so followed him back to the campfire. She sat against a tree on the outer rim of the fire's heat and ate the food Perian provided while staring at the flames. Perian sat a little closer, between Hector and Elian, who stirred only briefly, and also stared into the flames.

When Timary finally lay down on her blanket to sleep, Perian put another log on the fire and began devising a plan for her. He knew precisely what she should do. The game had changed; it was no longer about Wellorn, Rashinder or Darna and their ideas of expansion. It was about one thing and one thing only: Risenor, and how to stop his growing powers and his quest for domination – which, as it happened, began with Perian.

When Timary woke with the first bird calls the next morning, Perian still sat by what remained of the fire. He turned his head slightly at her stirring. 'Do you know who Ishra's rightful heir is? Does she have children, or siblings?'

Timary stood, rubbing her eyes, and came to sit beside him, dragging her blanket with her. 'Yes. She has a younger brother about your age who lives on one of the family estates in northern Wellorn, not far from Bresh. But he is blind. Ishra said that he lost his sight in a riding accident when he was nineteen.'

'No one else that you can think of? A distant cousin? Did she not name her heir?'

'I told you, no.' She looked about. 'Is there any more food?'

Perian gave Hector a shove with his foot, and when Hector's eyes focused, Perian asked him to get breakfast for the two of them and some for himself. Hector stared stupidly at Timary until Perian poked him again and he scrambled off to do as Perian had asked.

'I need to stretch my legs, Timary. Perhaps you would walk with me while we wait for Hector to provide us with something to eat.'

They walked through the trees until they came to the field again. Perian leant against the trunk of a tree and stretched his gaze over the distant hills, where a solitary sygrilien circled. He hoped it was a sign that his plan was the right one.

'Blindness is no barrier to becoming king, especially if he has had sight for most of his life. A king has many about him to advise and stand in his stead if needed. He merely needs someone he can trust who will be his eyes for him. That apart, the usurper will not see him as a threat, and will assume no challenge will come from that quarter. He will rightly expect there to be fighting amongst the nobility for supremacy, leaving a power vacuum, which he will fill – and by the time anyone notices, it will be too late.'

He turned away from the horizon to look at the woman by his side, who had been intently gazing at his silhouette. She surprised him by blushing, but didn't look away.

'Did Ishra like this brother? Have you met him? Do you like him?'

'Yes, yes and yes. Why such questions?'

'Good. I want you to go straight to him. You will lead him to victory over the squabbling nobles, and you will lead him through his kingship; you will be his eyes. But that depends on overpowering the usurper.'

'That's ridiculous. I am a warrior. I should be out hunting this person you talk of, not leading a blind man around like a seeing stick!'

'You will need to be more subtle than that for him to accept you. You are the only person I know who could do this. You are strong and powerful, and, as Ishra's brother, I doubt that this man is a fool. But he needs your sight and strength to succeed. Already, there will be factions within his circle trying to force his hand. He must not move until the usurper is dead. If he does, he will be crushed before he can begin, and he needs to be there to fill the gap when the usurper has been vanquished. Ishra held her country together with a firm hand. Without her, the nobles believe they have been set free, and they will destroy Wellorn in their quests for individual power. You proved your loyalty and love for Ishra by not killing me, for which I am grateful. I now ask you to honour her last request and do as I say.'

Timary said nothing, so he continued.

'You will go straight to the brother and tell him what you plan, then find the usurper and insert yourself within his inner circle, where you have access to him. He will recognise you as Ishra's most trusted priestess and will accept your desire for retribution, and in particular your chance to kill me, the one who separated you from your queen in her moment of need. When you see your chance, destroy him and slip away, back to the brother, so you are at his side to make his challenge. Unfortunately, the death of the usurper will not stop the spirit who inhabits him, and he will seek another to use – one who has the power of a seer. But it will leave him exposed, and make it easier for me to finish the job from within the world of the visionary.'

She raised her eyebrows. 'Can you do that?'

'Let us hope so,' he said. 'Now come. Mull my words over while eating breakfast.'

They returned to the camp, where Hector had made tea over a fire. He had woken the others, who sat about looking miserable until they saw Timary. She curled her lip at them as she sat to eat the food Hector had placed on a wooden plate. No one said anything, and Perian didn't bother with introductions.

When Timary had finished and drunk her tea, she stood to leave, and Perian walked with her as far as the road. She mounted her horse and turned a sombre face toward him. 'I will do as you say.'

'The man, whose name I'm sure we will all know soon enough, is merely the host to a malevolent spirit who will be busy elsewhere if he feels safe and unopposed. You will know when to take him.'

'Good luck between the worlds,' she said, kicking her horse forward.

23

They spent four blissful days at the cave. The others wandered about the forest, fishing and sleeping, while Perian learnt the priests' protective chant and all its variations. He listened and sang, the songs changing with his mastery of each as though the Sun Priests themselves were teaching him. Only once, toward the end of their stay, did his song go dramatically wrong. In a joyous moment of confidence and experimentation, he opened his lungs and sang from deep within, creating a near-visible sound of rumbling bass that snaked about the walls and resonated through the cave. The ground shook and a large piece of rock dropped from the roof, missing him by only an inch or two.

When Elian had first entered the cave, he'd touched the yellow silk still lying on the shelf. '"They went north over Sun Mountain. They wore robes the colour of the setting sun and shone as pale flames as they walked along the road",' Elian quoted. He turned to look at Perian. 'That's what an old miller we met on our way into Bresh said. The priests were expelled by Ishra's father, who dedicated their temple to Ortus.'

Perian laughed, not at the expulsion of the priests but at the solving of a mystery: sun worshipers. He fixed the image of them in his mind, holy men surrounded by the warm flame of wisdom and peace. He thought of the temple in Jasperen, and of Tarse, whose realm encompassed the sun, and the pieces of a giant puzzle began to move closer together.

Jasperen was more or less just as they had left it: no one had been assassinated or abducted, no one had been sacrificed or lost their heads, and the cells were empty, with the exception of Vorten in the lower depths. Saphrax had organised a magnificent feast to celebrate their return, one worthy of returning heroes.

The builders had finished Perian's Oracle cottage and he rushed down to inspect the work the morning after their return. There were a few things that could be improved, but these could wait; otherwise, it was perfect. He lost no time in filling it with the heady fragrance of frankincense and sandalwood, planting rosemary bushes near the front door and furnishing the interior with the essentials: pallets for himself, Hector and Elian, in case all three were there together, a small table, lamps, and a padded mat the colour of the rising and setting sun – a soft golden yellow.

Over the next week, he spent several hours a day sitting and chanting, filling his magnificent building with his essence and the gift of the Sun Priests. Whenever he entered his sphere, with the exception of a few occasions, Risenor would quickly blast his view with fire, and through the flames his host would emerge, taunting him as he had during Perian's occasional visits to his sphere during their travels. That Risenor knew whenever Perian sought his visions was no idle boast. But these visits had enabled Perian to subtly test out his defences with the gradual strengthening of his walls and the soft, near-inaudible chanting he had learnt in the cave.

During the following week, Balon's spies sent news from the coast and the Kingdom of Wellorn. Perian was called to the Council Room to hear his report, and was careful to make eye contact with Balon; it was time he got over his grudge.

'As we thought,' said Balon, 'the nobles are fighting amongst themselves for supremacy. As instructed, my men have watched for this other man who wears the crown of Ortus. Whether it belonged to the queen, they do not know, although he claims it did. The eye is the colour of fire and indicates a drastic change in the thread of Wellorn society and thinking. He goes by the name of Lord Adair, although some say they knew him as something different before he showed his powers.'

'Lord of Fire,' Perian interrupted. He looked up at Elian and Valamer before turning to Balon. 'Forgive me, Balon. Please continue.'

'Yes, no doubt. My source says that the nobles haven't noticed him yet, nor the way he is sweeping up the mess they leave in their wake. But that can't be far off, since already his army is larger than any one army within the mix. He will be unstoppable before they can get over their differences and think of joining against him.'

Perian stirred from peering through the window. The spy's report was old news now if Risenor was moving at the pace suggested by his visions.

'That information is about two weeks old?' he asked.

All eyes turned to Perian, then back to Balon, who replied, 'Yes, my Zameel, that's about right. I expect another in a day or two, since events are moving quickly.'

'And the seafront?' asked Valamer.

'Nothing yet, my Zamir.'

'Thank you, Balon. Good work.'

Balon bowed very low and left.

'How long before they come again?' Valamer turned to his

brothers. 'Saphrax? Tanais?'

Saphrax blew his cheeks out. 'Within twelve months is too soon, but I think he intends to come sooner.'

'Tanais?'

'A matter of weeks, I believe, unless we can stop him before he enters Rashinder.'

Saphrax sneered at Perian. 'And how do we do that?'

'Kill him before he gets to the border.' Again, all eyes focused on Perian. 'I have planted an assassin within his ranks.'

'Timary,' blurted Elian.

'Timary!' said Jolint and Valamer together.

Perian looked down at his hands, clenched upon his lap. 'She caught up with me while we travelled in disguise. Fortunately, Ishra still believed I was the answer, and Timary has accepted my request. She will know when to make her move, but I cannot guarantee she will get her chance before they cross the border – and she may fail, so we should be ready. They will enter along the northern road. I felt them pass by the stream.'

Grison chuckled to himself. 'What a gem you are, Tanais.'

He told them about Ishra's brother and how Timary would be his eyes in the future if all went well.

'Then it will start all over again with this Timary in charge!' Saphrax shouted.

'No. Wellorn will be in turmoil, famine hovering over the empty fields. He will strive for peace amongst his people, as will Timary. We can then, if the Zamir wishes, extend the hand of friendship. But that is in the future. We first have to obliterate Risenor, and that will be my task in all this.'

He turned to look out of the window, away from Jolint and the questions that were forming on her lips. The sky beyond was near cloudless but for a few wispy strands stretched long by the wind like an old man's beard. Perian rested his eyes on what appeared at first to be a white line, a little denser than the other clouds. Gradually, the line formed a V, and his heart jumped with recognition.

He turned back to the room. 'We have visitors.'

Conversation faded as they followed his gaze. Elian stood and pressed his nose to the glass, then turned to Perian beside him, his face reflecting Perian's own concern. He opened the window as though to wave, but instead, hoisted himself onto the sill and sprang into the air as he shifted into a large almonos. With a clatter and screech of quickly vacated chairs, those inside gathered at the window to watch.

Perian pushed through the sudden crowd to stand by a different window and followed Elian's flight toward his fellow almonos. Elian circled about them and their formation broke up, then rearranged itself, no doubt with Elian at their head, although Perian was unable to pick him out from the rest.

For no reason he could think of, he suddenly remembered the day that Elian first learnt to fly. He had stood next to their wagon, a look of deep concentration upon his face, and suddenly he shuddered into a huge eagle and fluttered precariously about the campsite until he eventually became airborne and vanished over the treetops. Garin, their keeper, had rushed about after him, terrified he would try to fly and fail. Perian hadn't understood at the time why Gisela had been so angry and had sent them all to their wagon without supper.

Elian didn't return to the campsite for several hours, and when he did, he wasn't allowed back to their wagon for two or three days. Perian now knew that Gisela had hoped Elian would forget whatever he had seen, and no doubt attempted to erase whatever she could from his mind. But Elian didn't forget. His tales of fighting elsewhere in the camp and of the friendly folk in a nearby village – as well as his brief game with the village children, which involved a ball made of rags – had puzzled them all for some time.

Now, Perian went up to his chambers to watch the Almonos Guard land from his study; he assumed they would come via the front courtyard, that being the official entry for visitors. Valamer and Jolint were already on the steps, waiting to greet them. He didn't need to be there too.

The grace of their landing and their shift into human form, rippling from the very first to land toward the last, left him breathless with its sheer beauty and perfection. Even the cynical Saphrax would have to admire these warriors. As he thought, they had made way for Elian at the head, although he doubted that Elian had expected this when he flew out to meet them.

Did you enjoy that? Perian asked him when he had shifted fully.

Elian looked up at the study window and waved. *Enormously.*

I'm in our chamber when you want me.

There would be all the usual welcome and refreshments, then, depending on how long they intended to stay, they would get down to the reason for their visit; until then, Perian wouldn't be needed, and he thought he'd have a short nap before he was summoned.

He was just drifting off when a great noise at his door informed him that there would be no summons. They were coming to him. He stayed where he was; he'd let Elian and Hector settle them all down before he wandered out. They were Elian's guests, after all.

Get up, Perian. Father wants me to go home.

Perian sat bolt upright and bounced from the bed.

Why? he asked as he raced down the corridor, nearly colliding with Hector and Frin as they walked quickly back and forth with refreshments for Elian's guests.

The sight of the Almonos Guards relaxing in the easy chairs of their living room brought a smile to Perian's face. They rose and bowed very low as Perian entered and sat next to Elian on one of the couches.

'Is our father well?' he asked the captain of this mission, whom Elian introduced as Guy.

'Yes, very well, as are the Lady Lipheneli and their daughters, although Risenor has slept for many weeks now and will not wake up.'

'I'm sorry.' And he was. While Risenor slept, he was busy elsewhere, ruining everyone's lives.

'The Guards have agreed to stay overnight and eat with us this evening,' said Elian. 'I have invited your brothers and Jolint, and Grison, of course.'

The volume of conversation during and after the evening meal was so loud that Perian had to go to another part of his chambers for brief periods of recovery. This was the first time Jolint had met Aronaye's Almonos Guards and been surrounded by so many Farans at one time, and Perian watched her with interest. At first she had stared at them with what he thought was indecision, but when Valamer took her hand, she lit up, and it seemed to Perian that she knew, in that moment, that she had made the right choice.

The evening went too quickly, and sooner than Perian had expected, Valamer and Jolint left, followed by Saphrax and Grison. Shortly after, Guy ushered his Guards off to their rooms, but by the squealing and noise that came from Elian's room, he had left one behind.

Perian woke early the next day, knowing that the Guards would leave with the sunrise. As Elian came into his room to rouse him for breakfast, Perian spotted a female figure dashing across the foyer and into the corridor.

'Isn't your friend staying for breakfast?'

Elian gave one of his most wicked smiles. 'No, she is expected to eat with the Guards. Come on, Perian, let's eat. I need your counsel before I go.'

'Do you have any idea why Aronaye wants you back?' Perian asked.

Elian shook his head. 'Guy wasn't told, just given instructions to bring me home and told to hurry. Since everyone is well, Father isn't about to take another wife, and no one is getting married; it must be to do with Risenor. Oh, and Guy said that someone had seen Rolwen, the Felfar's mage who left with the High Magi. He was the one who introduced me to the others when I was summoned by them.'

Perian stared at Elian, his hand suddenly stiff around his spoon. His thoughts immediately went to the vision he had had of Aronaye hesitantly greeting someone; this had to be Rolwen. 'The Magi are making their move. But why? Has something not gone to plan?' He felt on the verge of panic. 'You must find out why he is there, Elian. Was it part of their plan, or has something gone wrong? I need to know.'

Elian stretched across the table and grasped Perian's hand as it waved the spoon up and down. 'Please calm down, Perian, you are frightening me. I will do as you ask; you can ask whatever you like through me and I will pass on the answers as they come.'

Perian closed his eyes. Of course he could. Why was he getting into such a state?

'I'm sorry, Elian. Soon I will have to face Risenor, and it's wearing my nerves thin. So much depends on everything coming together at once. Many of the parts I do not see, and if I fail, what will become of you, of Jolint and Valamer, of Silaven and all that I love, not to mention the people of our two empires? I don't want to die, Elian, especially at Risenor's hand.'

His voice had risen, causing Hector to poke his head through the door and pull it back very quickly. Perian wasn't just in a state; he was falling apart.

Elian stood quickly and darted around the table. 'I'm not sure I fully understand, Perian. If the Magi are on the move, it will be to assist you. You won't be alone in this. Let me see what Rolwen wants and then we can plan together.'

Perian's heart began to slow a little, although he hadn't noticed it speeding up. 'You are right. I cannot think why I have given myself such a fright, especially when I cannot afford to lose any of the pieces. You are my anchor, Elian. How can I come through without your guiding hand in mine? Come home as soon as you can.'

Perian met with Theo, who thankfully had nothing alarming to report, then with Valamer in his chambers.

'Warships have been seen moving away from the northern coast of Wellorn,' said Valamer. 'We are outnumbered on the seas. Even so, I have given orders that our ships prepare and move to block the Wellorn fleet as best they can. Reports have begun to fly in from within Wellorn, and Adair's army is on the move in the direction you indicated. Saphrax is gathering his men as we speak and birds have been sent to call in the other armies.'

'Is there any good news?'

'None, except that Lieva and Urfan have relieved Untha of her duties and quelled the threat of revolt with the help of your man Monteth and the Loren elders. Evidently the rains have begun in southern Darna, which will mean flooding and disease, no doubt. Between man and nature, I begin to feel overwhelmed.'

Perian knew how he felt. Events were moving too fast on all fronts, and it was hard to keep up. 'I am going to the cottage with Hector and will send him to report on anything I see that will be useful.'

When he entered his sphere, Risenor was there almost immediately. His attack on Perian intensified; he banged on the sphere walls, shouting that the game was over and that he would destroy Perian and shred his spirit, so it would never return again. The overt violence of his attack shocked Perian, who had become used to the comparative calm of his previous visits, but he managed to still his instinct to display his full protection, knowing that this was just the beginning of something more violent and dangerous. Risenor's reaction indicated that he felt some threat, but what that was, he could not say – unless Timary's intent had been discovered, and even that he did not think would have posed much of a threat to Risenor.

He met with Valamer again the next day. Saphrax had left with his army of warriors toward the town of Athelim, where he would be met by Lord Pettifield and his men. Perian felt sorry for Saphrax; it seemed that he had hardly had time to rest before dashing off again to quell the Wellorn threat. New reports said that Adair's army approached the Silver River, leading Perian to believe they must be travelling both day and night to cover the distance at such speed.

Valamer looked exhausted, and Jolint and Grison, who were also present, sat stiffly in their chairs. Valamer snapped at Perian as though he were the cause of the invasion. 'What have you got, Tanais?'

'Not a lot,' he confessed. 'I was too busy fending Risenor off. He has intensified his attack, and I begin to think that something is taking place that he finds threatening. I doubt that it is the approach of our warriors.'

The atmosphere in the room changed: Valamer softened, and Jolint and Grison appeared more worried, if that were possible.

'Even so, I managed to catch a snippet that will be useful. As you surmised, Valamer, flooding and disease will overtake southern Darna. Nor will use this to make a push on our south-western border, to which the Darna armies will naturally respond, as they should. But it would be wise for you to urge your Darna lords to hold back, as the disease and decimation that affects southern Darna will also quickly overtake the Nor army and they will withdraw, their men dying on the field before they can fire their arrows or wield their swords.'

At that moment, Elian's voice entered Perian's head. *I have met with Father and Rolwen. They called me back to report on Risenor's activities. The Magi have seen what Risenor is doing, but wanted me to confirm his actions – for Aronaye's sake, I think.* Elian paused for a moment, but continued before Perian could ask any questions. *They intend to kill Risenor.*

Perian stood instinctively; a hot rod of fear shot up his spine and enclosed his lungs so it was hard to breathe. 'No!' he shouted into Elian's head and aloud at the same time. He dropped back into his seat with a thump, only vaguely aware of the startled reaction of those in the room. *You must stop them, Elian,* he said, silently this time. *If they kill Risenor's body, he will transfer completely to Adair. He will be fully embodied, but this time in a healthy being, and if Timary misses her chance, he will be unstoppable. Are you with them?*

No, but I'm running down the corridor to Risenor's chambers, where I left them. I'll let you know when I've spoken to them.

Now Perian knew what had caused Risenor's reaction. He told the others what Elian had said and waited. No one spoke. Tension crackled through the increasingly claustrophobic atmosphere. Perian felt hot and thought he would die from lack of oxygen, when Elian finally spoke again.

I am too late. Risenor stirred from his sleep, and Rolwen and Aronaye together smothered him with his pillow.

Perian ran for the door. 'They've killed him. I must see what he will do now.'

He raced down the corridor, pushing aside all in his way in his desperation to get to his cottage. Hector and Jolint followed as best they could.

I have told them what you said. I will be with you by evening. Perian scarcely heard what Elian said, blind and deafened by his rush. It was up to Timary now, and he needed to distract Risenor so that she had her chance.

Birds resting on the lawn scattered, ducks fled from the banks to the lake and the geese strutted about in honking protest. Perian burst through the door of his cottage. Without bothering to close it, he fell upon his mat and sat to catch his breath. The lingering smell of incense calmed his roiling thoughts, but his hands shook upon his folded legs.

Jolint, the first to catch up, threw her arms about him and pulled his head to her chest, her face in his hair, her breath hot on his scalp, her heart pounding in his ear. Slowly, within her grasp, the worst of his panic began to subside.

'He said he would tear my spirit apart. What happens to such a spirit, Jolint?'

The heaving of her lungs stopped for a moment, then she pushed him away from her and held his face between her hands as Elian often did, forcing him to look into her eyes.

'Nothing,' she said with conviction. 'He cannot do this. He is trying to frighten you and make you weak. They are words, Tanais, just words. The spirit is a different substance and cannot be pulled apart as a physical body can.'

'He is more powerful than I am. If you are right, then such words are for his pleasure alone.'

'No doubt he gets pleasure from trying to frighten you, but it seems to me that he has spent a lot of time convincing you that he is the stronger and more powerful, a lot of time taunting you with what he will do and what you can't do; these are not the actions of a confident sorcerer, who would neither need nor bother to tell you how much better they are. He has been spending his time jabbing at what he perceives is your weakness – your confidence – and laying the foundations of an insidious belief. Don't let him, Tanais. You must remove that arrow of doubt before you face him.'

She was right, of course; Jolint was invariably right, and he should have sought her counsel before instead of running ahead of everyone as he had been. Perian found that he was focusing fully for the first time in what seemed like ages, battered as he had been by Risenor's constant presence whenever he sought peace in his sphere. Risenor had been tactically nibbling at his confidence since their meeting in his tomb, and he wondered if he had actually set up this path himself by using his memory of Risenor as a foil. But then he remembered the way Risenor had stared at him during evening meals or family gatherings when he and Elian stayed in Silaven, and he was convinced that Risenor had been plotting his ascent even then, that his appearance in the tomb had nothing to do with Perian's memory of him. Risenor wouldn't have wasted so much energy verbally attacking him if he didn't at least consider him a formidable opponent.

Perian drifted away from his thoughts and focused on Jolint once more. She smiled happily at him. 'You see? I was right, wasn't I? Now, what are you going to do, so we may play our part?'

She had let go of his face and held his hands. He felt, without looking, that Valamer stood in the doorway. 'I will distract Risenor from within my sphere and give Timary her chance to kill the host. With no living body to anchor him to the physical, he will die and begin his journey to the next life.'

'And then?' asked Valamer.

'I will return. Hector has a trigger word to call me in case I am exhausted and drift into a deeper trance. If I am still engaged, I will ignore it.'

Valamer moved closer to stand beside Jolint. 'I don't like it.'

'There is no other option. The Magi have made a misstep and fate has put Risenor where he was always going to be: at the head of Wellorn to wreak havoc on all. As a seer, he will know in advance every move Saphrax makes, as he did before, only with greater accuracy. We must destroy him before he has a chance to find a back-up host, while he is still reeling from the death of his body and angry enough to make a mistake. I just hope that fate has marked me as the victor.'

'I will stay with you, Tanais,' said Jolint. 'Hector and I will be here.'

Perian smiled at her and twirled a lock of her red hair around his finger before settling himself into position. He nodded at Valamer. 'I'll drop by when it's over.'

24

He found himself alone in his sphere. All was as it had been, and he nearly cried with the sheer relief of it. At first he thought Risenor might not appear, so he ran through his chants and settled his mind so as not to dwell too much on what might yet unfold. Then, without him realizing it at first, the face of Adair slowly formed before him, his mouth twisted into a distorted smile that showed his teeth, and there was no doubt in Perian's mind that if Adair still existed at all, he had lost even the most meagre control of his own body and thoughts. It was Risenor who laughed aloud, his eyes wide with his successful transference and the fulfilment of his plan. Fire began to build around his image, rising in intensity with Risenor's own emotions.

'I am king,' he shouted. 'I am King of Wellorn.'

'And who has given you this title, Risenor? Not Ishra's heirs, nor the nobility. They will call you the Pretender who wears a false crown.'

'I have the people. I will make them bend. I have the power. They are all my slaves, as will be your brothers. I will ravage your Jolint and enslave my brother Elian to my side; I will kill my father – slowly. And you, my once-brother, will be my first triumph. I will pick your spirit from my teeth and vomit it out into the dark hole of visionaries from which nothing ever emerges. I will crush the Empires of Rashinder and Darna and Silaven. I will make them my own to play with.'

Perian had thought he would need to keep Risenor distracted, but Risenor was doing quite well without any assistance from him. His boasting was too elaborate, confirming to some extent Jolint's theory of inherent insecurity – and insanity, of course. But Risenor wasn't weak. He needed someone to brag to, and Perian knew the bragging had a purpose: to hit at his emotions and force a reaction.

Risenor banged his fist on the sphere wall in his frustration. It made Perian jump and the walls ripple with his fright. Risenor laughed without realizing that he had made a mistake. His action warned Perian of how fragile his sphere was, despite the sturdiness of its walls. Its integrity relied wholly on Perian's ability to keep his mind clear and firm.

All of a sudden, everything changed. The fire flared so Perian thought it should incinerate his sphere and him inside it. Risenor turned and lashed out with a scream that near burst his eardrums. Adair's body twisted and turned. It faded and reinstated itself by turns, the flames flaring in shades of deep red and blue.

The shape that had been Adair fragmented. Its strands flew free as Risenor howled. Perian watched the image disintegrate and the flames begin to fade, waiting for the last traces of Risenor to vanish.

Timary had found her moment. It was over.

He chanted, then chanted louder with the joyful beating of his heart, until he thought he could see the strands of sound take form in colours of gold and sunlight about him.

He was free. The threat over. Everyone safe.

But the frenzy beyond ceased abruptly, and the unimaginable unfolded before him.

Risenor did not fade into the darkness as he should. He held firm, glowing in the light from Perian's sphere. He stared at Perian with a hatred that seared Perian's vision as his hope and joy dissolved. Perian's stomach knotted with a cold chill that spread throughout his body.

He chanted more vigorously.

'You think I am finished?' Risenor growled, revealing his teeth. 'I do not choose to go. I will kill you first, then take another, you fool.'

Risenor howled like no animal Perian had ever heard. He thrust his hand through the walls of the sphere before Perian could gather his wits and touched Perian's cocoon of sound. It burned his fingers. He screamed.

Risenor stared at his charred digits for a moment, then looked up at Perian and laughed. 'You won't stop me with that old magic.'

He thrust his hand through again, bending the sphere inward, and pulled on the strands of music with his long nails, dragging Perian toward him. Perian chanted louder, strengthening his protection that yet kept Risenor at bay. He now realised that this alone would not save him; *he was going to die.*

The thought struck at his heart and formed cracks in his resolve. His mind and body began to petrify under the terrible weight of fear and despair as he struggled to maintain his defences. His walls wavered. His chant faltered.

Risenor threw his head back and roared his laughter into the abyss. The malevolent sound struck the strands of Perian's chant and set off an intense ringing, their vibrations clashing and reverberating to create different sounds.

Perian began to shake violently within the jarring tangle of musical chords. With the shaking, his mind cleared and a pressure began to build within him, as it had when Saphrax had dropped Lili's head from his bag.

In that moment he knew that his sorcerer's tattoo was not a mistake. He was as powerful as Risenor, and even if he failed, he would make sure Risenor did not survive their encounter unscathed.

Perian released the pressure with a roar of triumph. Magic flared from his fingertips as hope rose within his heart. The wings on his chest shone red through his tunic, taking Risenor by surprise and making him hesitate. Perian swept an arc of silver lightning about his sphere and projected Risenor back beyond his walls.

Risenor recovered quickly and rushed in again. His outstretched hand pierced the walls and sucked the sound of chanting from Perian's mouth. Perian shot to his feet, faltering under Risenor's barrage of lethal lights that scratched and scraped over his limbs and torso. The very structure of his sphere began to shudder and distort until he again managed to force Risenor back beyond the wall with a streak of silver lightning.

He shook with exhaustion. He felt blood dripping from his body, but all he could see were lines of burnt and open flesh left by Risenor's attack. He thought he felt Elian take his hand; so far away. The contact eased his pain, but left him more alone than ever, and he began to think again that he would not survive this fight.

His chant reasserted itself naturally and he sang his barrier into place, setting his mind to the strength of his sphere. Risenor laughed and roared, distorting the sound again so it reverberated discordantly about Perian's walls. This time Perian could see the brightly coloured strands of sound jittering around him.

Remembering the cave and the change of rhythm that had dislodged parts of the roof, he deepened his chant, singing from the depth of his diaphragm. The colours merged to form a delicate white cord, and with their merging they exuded a power that startled him. He glanced at Risenor, whose lips curled in laughter, shouting in preparation for another attack, his eyes bright with madness and the anticipation of victory.

Perian turned his attention back to the cord, which he had formed into a taut coil, ready to strike. He smiled to himself; perhaps he *would* win this battle. He released the cord, directing it with his intention. It shot through the sphere wall and whipped about Risenor, forming a tight spring around his chest.

Risenor shrieked and screamed like a dying monster from the depths as the cord shrank and began to squeeze the air from his chest, restricting his ability to replace it. His legs jiggled frantically, and he grabbed at the light strand.

Perian sang all his anger and loathing through the cord and watched without pity as Risenor began to disintegrate. Still Risenor screamed and thrashed.

The sight began to sicken Perian. He thought he would go mad. His abhorrence began to give way to pity and horror. He felt empty and weak and wanted it all to be over.

His anger spent, breathless from his efforts, Perian ceased his chant and the cord vanished, leaving Risenor near-lifeless and barely visible.

He gathered what strength he had left and blasted the shadowy form deep into the darkness. With breathtaking speed, what remained of Risenor was sucked into the black abyss until all was dark, leaving only empty space and a silence so profound it almost hurt.

Perian fell to his knees and wept. He was numb with exhaustion and the depletion that comes with the cessation of action. He stared at his damaged hands and arms. It was over. He was alive.

The wall of his sphere returned to its clear perfection, with only a few rippling waves across its surface to indicate his weakness. Images began to play upon the sphere's surface, but he ignored them; he was too tired and would look again in a day or two. For now, it was time to return.

'Perian, wake up.'

It was Elian's voice, shrill and urgent. In the process of returning to his physical body, Perian had given in to his fatigue and fallen into a deep sleep. He stirred just enough to tell Elian to go away.

'We can see it's over, Perian. You must wake up.'

They wanted to know if he had been taken over. He made an effort. 'It's me,' he slurred.

'Help me, Hector,' Elian bellowed above the terrible noise of men shouting and the clash of metal.

Perian couldn't make sense of what was going on. So much noise, and his hands felt sticky around Elian's as Elian pulled him sideways and dragged him from his mat. With an effort that seemed beyond him, Perian opened his eyes a sliver, just as the door shattered and Hector's great weight near crushed him. Magic flew about his cottage, eliciting desperate screams and fizzing as it ricocheted off the walls with a flash of blinding light that exploded through his eyelids.

Suddenly he was more alert, but in a distant way, as though his eyeballs stood separate from his head, watching what was happening yet unable to relay the information correctly. He could see men fighting just beyond the broken door; and there was Jolint, her sword flashing in the light. Perian couldn't breathe. The nauseating tang of burnt flesh filled his nostrils and Hector's weight crushed the air from his lungs. Elian's raspy voice called to him again.

Perian pushed on Hector, complaining about the pain in his arms, telling Elian to stop squeezing him and help him up. He stopped when Hector slid away from him in an unnatural way.

With Elian's help, he got as far as his knees and quickly scanned the room with a little more comprehension. Three of his priests lay dead and scorched upon the floor; Jolint and his guards fought with more priests just beyond the doorway; and Hector lay very still with a short sword protruding from his left thigh. After all he had endured during his battle with Risenor, Perian was drained of emotion, unable to feel anything but emptiness and disappointment.

'Come,' said Elian. He put his arm about Perian's waist and pulled him to his feet. 'Let's get you down that passage and out into the open air. It will be easier for Jolint and your guards if they know you are safe.'

Perian allowed Elian to lift him up and guide him down the stairs that led from his floor into one of the tunnels his builders had created for him. He had already fought one battle; he didn't have the strength or the will for another. His legs shook and he leant heavily upon Elian as they shuffled slowly toward the exit, navigating by Elian's mage lights.

Soon, Elian was lifting the hidden door, and the golden light of early evening lit the ascending stairs. Perian crawled up, one step at a time, into a small clearing, shaded by a grove of chestnut trees. Elian dropped the door back into place and propped him against a smooth boulder beside the exit.

Perian looked down at his hands and arms; his shredded clothing and deep gashes. His body was covered in blood. It surprised him that the injuries to his ethereal body had affected his physical body, and he vaguely wondered how that was.

Elian followed Perian's eyes and began to remove his shirt and study his wounds. 'We were shocked when your skin burst open and you began to bleed, and we could do nothing to help you,' he said close to Perian's ear. 'Are you all right? Apart from these injuries I can see?'

Perian clutched Elian's arm, his voice rising in pitch. 'Timary got her chance, Elian, but he would not die.'

Elian opened his mouth to reply, but turned and stood instead at the sound of feet crashing through the trees.

'Is he all right?' called Valamer, beyond Perian's view.

'Yes and no,' Elian replied. He returned to studying Perian's injuries as the clearing filled with people: Valamer, Grison and Ben.

Grison forced something that tasted like rotting seaweed down Perian's throat, and he knew no more.

He woke up in his own bed, swathed in bandages and sore all over. Early morning sunlight squeezed through chinks in his curtains, forming starlight spots about his room. He watched their slight movement for a while before attempting to change position and groaning happily with the pain. He was alive, Risener was dead, he was safe. The memory of fighting in his cottage spoilt the moment, but he chose not to think about it, attempting to return to his previous reverie. He could hear Frin's voice soft beyond the closed door and wondered what Frin was doing in his chambers, until he remembered Hector sliding to the floor with a sword in his thigh.

The rustle of clothing drew his attention away from thoughts of Hector, and he turned his head to see Jolint smiling at him. She brushed his hair back with her cool fingers and kissed him on the forehead before going to the door to call for Elian.

'Hector?' he croaked when she returned.

Jolint laughed. 'Lying in his bed and complaining about the service.'

Seconds later, Elian burst through the door and rushed to his side, placing a hand gently on Perian's bandages. 'Welcome back.'

'He's dead,' Perian said before they could ask. He was sure he had told them before he fell asleep, but he could see by the look on Elian's face that they needed confirmation. 'The threat is over.'

Later, when he had risen and sat at the hearth, picking at a few nuts with the fingers that poked out beyond his bandages, he told them of his ordeal. No one said anything when he had finished; there wasn't much to say, really, so he asked about the revolt of the remaining disaffected priests.

'Quelled by your Sky God guards, who followed them to the cottage after a hysterical Theo burst into their office,' said Valamer, sitting on Perian's left. 'A couple of them broke through Heri and Gunther's defences, only to be incinerated by Jolint. I don't think they realised she was there.'

'Their timing was nearly disastrous,' Jolint added, still flushed with the shock of it.

'Heidren was the initiator, evidently,' said Grison.

Heidren. He was difficult, but Perian hadn't thought he would lead another uprising.

Valamer scratched at his beard, looking happier than he'd looked for a long time. 'That's the last of them, I believe; all those on your list of suspected dissidents. They're locked up in the cells at the moment, awaiting questioning. You may want to do it when you're feeling better, Tanais, but take Erely. Then it's for you to decide what you want done with them: execution or the slave market.'

He'd wait a week or two before doing as Valamer had suggested. Everything was too raw, and he didn't want to decide the fate of anyone just yet. He was too angry and disappointed.

He found he was suddenly tired and wanted to sleep, so they all left, with the exception of Elian, who sat beside his bed as Perian slid happily beneath the sheets. The bed felt softer than he remembered, the light brighter, the birdsong beyond his room filling the air with music. He was free. No more battles, no more fear. Everyone was safe and his enemies had been defeated. He felt strong despite his injuries, and the way ahead was clear; no obstacles, no difficult priests – they had determined their own fate without his interference. He was happier than he had ever been.

Elian shifted into a more comfortable position. 'I'll sit with you a while, Perian – until you start to snore, that is.'

'Tanais,' Perian said automatically. His battle with Risenor had forced him beyond his uncertainty and into the capable and powerful man he really was. Perian had died along with Risenor, and at the same time severed the ties to his past; that chain of lies and responsibility that Gisela had clamped to his heart when she killed him, and that he had carried throughout this life. He was a different man now.

'Tanais it is,' Elian laughed. 'About time, too.'

Acknowledgements

My particular thanks to Peter Crocker, for your support through the highs and the lows, and for the cover design.

Claire Bradshaw, my marvellous editor, who pulled the whole thing into shape.

And a big thank you to Jennifer O'Donnell, Jennifer McGregor, Kathleen Wiggins and Gaby Klika, always there with words of encouragement.